A
DENIABLE
CONSPIRACY

By

Ade Clewlow

MentonBlackbush
ISBN: 978-1-8381564-3-5

I AM SOMALI

To those of you who say you care
whilst threatening me with chains,
you're like a vessel full of holes,
your two-faced treachery leaking away.
Attempts to betray me will never hold sway.
I AM SOMALI

Abdulqadir Hersi Siyaad, Yam Yam
(1946–2005)

Translated by:
Abyan Cusmaan, Jawaahir Daahir, Karin Koller, Idil Osman and
Marilyn Ricci.
The Somali-English Poetry Collective, Leicester.

Also by Ade Clewlow:

Under A Feathered Sky:
The untold story of NATO's role in newly independent Kosovo

To Seb and Tilly

PREFACE

Somalia, Autumn 2012

Mogadishu, the city immortalised in the film Black Hawk Down, where warlords reigned and clan-based disputes escalated into deadly combat on the city's streets, has been ravaged by civil war since the early nineties. By 2006, the fragile country faces another threat in the form of al Shabaab, an Islamist terrorist group intent on opposing western influence and international attempts to prop up the United Nations (UN)-backed government in Somalia's capital. Controlling much of the southern half of the country including the capital, Mogadishu, al Shabaab's influence is absolute.

The UN, together with its regional allies, responds by approving the deployment of African Union (AU) troops under the operational name AMISOM. Military forces drawn from Uganda and Burundi establish a ring of steel around Vila Somalia, the seat of power in the capital city, to protect the government and its institutions from al Shabaab attacks.

With its headquarters next to the city's only airport, the AU force, alongside poorly trained Somali National Army troops, deploys across the capital to fight the insurgents. Daily clashes between AMISOM forces and al Shabaab bring trench warfare to the streets of Somalia's capital, once a popular and thriving secular city known as 'The Pearl of the Indian Ocean'.

By 2012, the AU has managed to push al Shabaab outside the city's perimeter, from where its tactics change, conducting bomb attacks and close quarter assassinations. Meanwhile, to complicate this already grave situation, several countries from the international community attempt to shore up AMISOM's gains and invest in building military capacity in Somalia, a country low on security but rich in untapped mineral resources.

Among them is Turkey, a NATO country and key western ally, with strategic ambitions to significantly increase its influence in the Horn of Africa. With piracy rife in the Indian Ocean attracting global headlines and absorbing precious international military resources, the rising threat of terrorism from al Shabaab, now aligned with al Qaeda, slips under the radar.

PART ONE

1

Airport Camp, Mogadishu

Even when he was standing still, Christian could feel the beads of sweat running down his back. Leaning against an acacia tree at the side of a windswept, sand-covered track, his daysack and body armour propped against each other on the floor by his desert boots, he waited in silence.

Rubbing his hand over the back of his neck, he looked across the track to where a small guard hut, manned by a bored looking Ugandan soldier, stood alone, surrounded by blast walls. Christian had waved at the soldier after being dropped off by Fred, his Kenyan fixer, but the guard wasn't interested in what he was doing. He nodded back, but that was it. The soldier looked like he wanted to be anywhere but Mogadishu.

Next to the guard hut was a rusty metal security barrier, faded red and white, lying horizontal across the track that led out of the camp, motionless bar a row of loose chains hanging down to ground level, swinging haphazardly in the breeze. Attached to the chains in the middle was a round, battered metal sign, warning drivers to 'Stop'. Compared to what Christian had been used to in the British military, the security in Airport Camp was poor, but at least the lax arrangements at the back gate made it easier for him to get in and out.

Wearing olive-green trekking trousers, a white T-shirt and an untucked blue linen shirt, he was hardly dressed for an appointment in a government building, but this was Somalia and different rules applied. If he had been meeting a government minister inside Vila Somalia, the home of the Somali Government, he would have made an effort and taken a jacket with him.

Waiting in the shade of the morning sun, the heat and humidity slowly rising, Christian looked around and realised how peaceful it could be in the camp. The chirping of the birds on nearby branches and the gentle clinking of the chains induced a momentary sense of calm. He stared beyond the barrier, out across the open ground towards a residential area of the city a couple of hundred metres away. The sound of children laughing drifted across to him in the wind, triggering thoughts about what could have been. Unexpectedly, emotions swelled inside him and memories of the funeral flashed into his mind. Instinctively, Christian took out his phone and typed a quick message to his parents to share his thoughts. As he pressed "send", his attention was brought back to the present when he first heard, then saw, his security team approaching, moving cautiously over the uneven ground towards him.

'They're here for me!' he shouted to the guard. The soldier barely acknowledged him, as if even that level of effort was too much in the heat. Christian looked at his watch. As usual, his security team was bang on time. He slung his pack over his left shoulder, picked up his body armour and walked out of the camp under an azure sky towards a white 4x4 parked 30m away, its engine running.

The second vehicle, a white pick-up with eight Somali armed guards sitting in the back, each carrying a Kalashnikov, waited alongside. As he approached the vehicles, watched by the Somalis, Miko got out of the front passenger door and stepped towards him. He held out his big hand to Christian, who shook it warmly.

'Hello, my friend, how it is hanging? All set? Come on, we're late.'

Miko was Ukrainian, ex special forces, working for Horn Security who had responsibility for keeping Christian and his team safe when travelling around the city.

'Hey, Miko, all good,' Christian replied.

Miko didn't like to hang around in open spaces. 'Do you want to put your body armour in the back or by your side?'

'I'll keep it with me this time.'

Miko, who had opened the boot of the vehicle, quickly closed it and moved round the car to the rear door, opening it for Christian.

'Everything OK with you, Miko?'

'Yes, yes, you know me, happy every day.'

Miko's accent was strong, but his cheerfulness was evident whenever he spoke his imperfect English. After he closed the door, Christian put his pack on the seat next to him and placed his body armour between him and the car door to provide a degree of protection. Driving around Mogadishu in an unarmoured vehicle was considered extremely dangerous by some, but with so many clan chiefs and other Somali businessmen using a similar method of getting around, hiding in plain sight seemed to be a good approach. It was one of the main reasons he had chosen Horn Security, rather than getting lifts in one of the AU's Casspir armoured vehicles that lumbered around the city in convoys every day, attracting way too much attention for Christian's liking.

'Once again, I travel with a Christian into the city of Muslims, ha!' Miko had started to tell the same joke every time they drove to Vila Somalia, or VS as they called it, making Christian smile every time. 'OK, sir, are we going directly to VS? Or do you want to stop for coffee at B&B first?'

Miko had his man bag on his lap, containing a pistol and spare magazines, and was holding the walkie talkie in the air, looking ahead, ready to give the other vehicle instructions.

'Let's go straight there, please. I can go for coffee at the B&B on the way back if there's time. I think it will be a short meeting.'

The journey was not going to be long; without too much traffic, they could navigate the main roads and arrive at the outer checkpoint within 25 minutes if they were lucky. On instruction, the second vehicle moved in front and they accelerated away in convoy, emerging from the residential area onto a road that took them past the main entrance to Mogadishu International Airport, known to everyone as MIA.

Navigating six-foot-high concrete blast walls sent Christian back to other hotspots he had been deployed to around the world during his career as an officer in the British Army, their presence both reassuring yet depressingly familiar at the same time.

A small queue of taxis and private cars had backed up in the opposite direction, waiting to enter the check point and drive through to the relatively secure area in front of the airport building where they would drop off their passengers for the daily flight to Kenya. As Christian's 4x4 slowly navigated a set of road humps, he noticed a young Somali woman staring blankly out of one of the cars, wrapped in a brightly coloured *garbasaar*, her pale blue headscarf rippling in the breeze, her chin resting on her arms folded on the frame of the open window. As they slowly passed the vehicle, she appeared to look directly at him, no doubt catching her own reflection in the darkened window of his vehicle.

Accelerating away, Christian watched the hustle and bustle of life in Mogadishu outside as they headed towards the city centre, passing bombed-out buildings, occasional shops and other landmarks, all showing signs of having lived through years of civil war. Once they had safely negotiated the K4 roundabout, a major intersection that caused endless hold ups and was a regular target for al Shabaab bombers, he breathed more easily.

He turned to look inside the car. He hadn't seen the Somali driver before but he knew he would have been vetted and was trustworthy. Horn Security was good at what they did. Miko was sitting bolt upright in the passenger seat, a tall, powerfully built man who looked like a giant next to the wiry Somali driver. Sunglasses on, blond hair cropped short, wearing a white T-shirt and sandy-coloured trekking trousers, Miko was scanning the road ahead of him, his head calmly moving from side to side, assessing threats. He had been operating in Mogadishu for over a year and could intuitively read the mood on the streets.

'Is there any intel today, Miko?' Christian always asked whether there was a specific threat that might be relevant to their journey. Horn Security had a policy of remaining on base if there was specific intelligence that could cause their people trouble.

'Yes and no. Our contacts in the police have said that Shabaab are planning something in the coming days. There are no details, but it is likely to be a VBIED. We think it's OK to go.'

Car bombs – VBIEDs – were a constant hazard, but the lure of earning $1,000 a day often swayed Horn Security's decisions. Christian looked a little more carefully, his eyes scanning the changing scene for anything out of the ordinary.

Navigating their way through the busy streets, where market traders pushed barrows on the side of the road and cars pulled out unexpectedly, they started to gain height and leave behind the concentration of vehicles, people and shops. As they approached a more sparsely populated area of Mogadishu, close to the remains of the old parliament building, now roofless and with barely a wall standing, the journey was already almost over. Away from the narrow streets of Bakhara Market to their left and the area around the port to their right, they were on a wide tarmac road, travelling at about 25mph, passing parked cars and occasional minibuses, which often pulled over, with little notice, to drop passengers off.

Christian moved his daysack onto his lap and took out his notebook, the breeze coming through Miko's partially open window providing some light relief to the heat inside the car. He took out his water bottle and drank deeply to satisfy his growing thirst. Glancing up he noticed they were now only a few hundred metres away from a major junction, hidden from view by a bend in the road up ahead. Just beyond that was the outer cordon of Vila Somalia, his destination.

As Christian looked down at his notebook and briefly read some notes, the fierce crack and deep boom from an explosion out of sight up ahead made Christian and Miko instantly look up.

'Oh shit!' Miko exclaimed as they both stared ahead. Looking through the windscreen at the pick-up carrying the Somali guards, who were beginning to raise their heads above the cab, they saw a plume of dense black smoke drifting up into the air above the trees that lined their route. As they got closer, a dust cloud from the blast was beginning to reduce visibility on the road. Both vehicles had slowed right down and were now travelling at a snail's pace. As the drivers got their bearings, they moved forward cautiously. Rounding the final bend, they could see debris had fallen with deadly effect onto the pavement, vehicles and buildings in front of them.

'Jesus!' Christian said quietly to himself as he surveyed the scene, bodies motionless on the ground, his pulse racing as he shoved the notebook back into his pack. They had always managed to avoid incidents until now, but this was close. Everything started happening very quickly. Miko immediately took control of the convoy.

'Keep going, keep going,' he spoke calmly into the mike, the radio lighting up with chatter from the other vehicle which remained in front, providing a screen in case of secondary attack. 'We will turn to the right when we get to intersection, then head back. Go, go.' The convoy speeded up as the visibility improved. Miko gave his orders easily; he was a man used to taking control in a crisis.

Christian had already slipped his body armour on moments before Miko told him to. He could see through the windscreen that the blast had shattered windows in buildings along the roadside. Some people were helping those who were on their hands and knees on the pavement. As the vehicles approached the junction, driving over debris on the road, the scene of the blast was in full view. Just before they turned right, Christian spotted an AU armoured personnel carrier embedded in a line of parked cars, its back door swinging open and smoke pouring out of the engine. Christian grabbed Miko's shoulder.

'Miko, we have to stop to help.'

'No, sir, we have to leave now. This is as dangerous as it gets.'

'Miko, we have to stop. We owe it to the AU troops. Please, pull over, get the guys out, and let's see what we can do.'

Although the exchange lasted no more than a few seconds, it felt much longer. The driver had instinctively slowed down. Miko grabbed his radio and calmly gave orders to his colleagues in the other vehicle to pull over and form a protective cordon. At the same time, he tapped his driver on the arm, indicating that he wanted him to stop. The driver yanked the steering wheel to the right, the vehicle pulling into the side of the road beyond the intersection, braking sharply, forcing Christian to slide violently into the back of the driver's seat.

'Fuck!' Both Miko and Christian swore at the abruptness of the movement.

As soon as they had come to a halt, Miko stepped out of the vehicle. He checked the cordon was in place and only then opened the rear door to let Christian get out.

'You will get me fired for this.' Miko spoke quietly while looking away towards the seat of the blast, leaving Christian to wonder whether his words were in jest. The sudden silence, so soon after the explosion, enveloped them both. He knew that Miko was in his element.

'What's that over there?' Christian was looking towards a café on the other side of the street, just behind where the AU vehicle had ended up. He couldn't quite take the whole scene in. There was an eerie atmosphere, punctuated only by the sound of a car alarm going off somewhere in the distance and the coughing of victims further up the road. The dust in the air was affecting his eyes, but he could see a white woman wearing body armour just inside a café. An AU soldier was standing at the entrance. The woman seemed to be quite animated, talking on a mobile phone. The AU soldier was clearly in shock, staring blankly around him, his weapon pointing downwards rather than raised in an alert position. Christian was trying to figure out what had happened. It was clear to him that the woman was out of place and extremely vulnerable. He had to act.

'Miko, we have to help – she doesn't belong here.'

Miko could see for himself that the situation remained dangerous for everyone, but he had also noticed the woman. 'OK, but I make decision on what happens next.' It wasn't a question.

'OK.'

Christian waited for Miko to move, sticking close to him. One of the Somali guards in his security detail also joined them until he stopped to take up a fire position facing back up the street, covering their backs as they stepped carefully across the road, the crunch of broken glass under their boots accompanying every step. As they closed in on the café, the AU soldier noticed them and belatedly raised his weapon but soon lowered it when he saw Christian holding up his MIA security pass and gesturing to him in sign language: *Everything is fine, we are friendly.*

'Thank you, my friend.' Christian looked him in the eye and touched his arm as the young soldier, in a state of deep shock, let them pass.

Underneath the sign for *The Blue Café*, badly splintered and hanging on by a single nail, Miko slowly pushed the wooden door open, carefully stepping over the debris scattered on the floor. He stopped to let Christian slip past him. Inside the café, the blast damage was not as bad as he had expected. It must have been shielded by the armoured vehicle. The café was empty, the wooden tables and chairs still more or less in their place. Music was playing at the back near the kitchen and someone, perhaps the owner of the café, seemed to be having a one-way conversation, probably into a phone, behind a light blue wooden door with a sign hanging in the middle of it, the words *My Kitchen* written in English. Christian could hear his pulse pounding in his ears.

He could see her clearly now, standing between a couple of tables facing away towards the back of the café, speaking quietly into her phone. She was wearing flat shoes, dark blue linen trousers and a white shirt underneath blue body armour. Christian moved a little closer, not wanting to surprise her or interrupt the conversation.

'We have been hit by a bomb, Krish. I need to get out of here ... no, I'm fine ... no, we can't, the vehicle has been badly damaged ... listen, Krish, can you get onto Jonathan? He needs to send someone out to pick me up ... thanks, Krish... yes, I'm fine, honestly.'

Taking the phone from her ear, she turned back towards the entrance of the café and was startled to see Christian standing in front of her. She looked from his face to Miko's, who was just behind him.

'We have to go.' It was Miko who spoke first, as much for Christian's benefit as the woman. It had felt like a long time since they had got out of the car, but in reality, it had only been about two minutes.

'Who the hell are you?' Her voice was calm but there was an edge to her breathing that gave away the tension they all felt. Looking at Miko, the woman spoke with confidence and seemed to be in no mood to move or take orders from a total stranger. Christian half-turned to put his hand on Miko's arm who, by now, had drawn his pistol and was holding it by his side.

'It's OK,' he said, looking him in the eye, the message silently passed between them. He looked back at the woman.

'My name is Christian; I am ex British Army and now a contractor working in MIA. We were on our way to Vila Somalia when we saw the explosion. I have security with me; we need to get away from here as soon as we can.'

Before the woman had a chance to answer, her phone pinged in her hand. A message had come in which she looked down to read. 'Oh shit!' she said under her breath.

As she brought the phone up to dial a number, the rattle of an automatic weapon sounded outside on the street, the noise deafening them all.

'Get down!' instructed Miko, pushing Christian to the floor. The woman, who had also dropped to a crouch, turned back to face them. The rounds had come into the café along the far wall, splintering the wood and sending puffs of plaster into the air and onto their heads. 'They must have another team to follow up,' Miko said to nobody in particular. He immediately raised his radio and spoke calmly to his team. 'The front is a no-go. Find a PUP at the rear, move ... now.'

'OK.'

Miko had quickly realised that their pick-up point needed to be a more secure location than where his team had parked their vehicles.

Christian looked at the AU soldier by the entrance, who had slumped backwards across a table just inside the door. His rifle had dropped noisily to the ground, blood seeping out of a wound to his chest. He looked in a bad way. There was more automatic fire outside. Miko looked at Christian and pointed at the soldier's holster on his hip, saying quietly, 'I am going to get that weapon and you are going to use it if we need to, OK?'

Miko moved with extraordinary speed across the floor to the doorway, his boots covering the short distance almost silently despite the debris underfoot, keeping his head down throughout. When he got to the front of the café, he slowly began to stand up, scanning the street outside from around the edge of the open door. The gunman was somewhere to the left of the café. Christian turned to the woman and mouthed *Stay here* as he moved towards the front door. As Miko pulled the pistol out and threw it to Christian, another burst of gunfire sounded even closer, rounds flying into some of the café's furniture. The situation was becoming grave.

Christian caught the weapon, a Browning, one he had fired many times. He knelt down, removed the magazine, checked for rounds, reloaded and cocked it. He tried to control his breathing and turned to see that the woman, who was also keeping a low profile, had moved to be just behind him. In that split second, she looked him in the eye and spoke urgently in a low voice. 'My name is Megan Philips. I am the British Ambassador to Somalia.' She didn't need to say any more.

Miko was on his radio again, trying to contact his security detail. Christian, whose own radio was in the vehicle, hoped the AU soldiers had called in the incident. The area was now like a shooting range: anyone who moved would be targeted.

Miko said quietly, 'My guys think there is only one gunman, but they couldn't see him and now they've left,' he added quickly in a low voice. 'They are moving to a secure place to pick us up behind here,' he waved towards the kitchen door.

Christian passed the message on to Megan. His heart was thumping against his chest so loudly he was surprised she couldn't hear it.

In a split second, the gunman appeared just outside the café, turning his weapon inside. Miko instinctively dropped to his knee and took aim from point-blank range, squeezing one round off and hitting the man's shoulder, spinning him around.

Then a click. And silence.

Miko's weapon had jammed. Realising what had happened, Christian didn't need an invitation to act. He immediately stood up and raised his own pistol.

'Get down!' he shouted at Miko, who ducked his head.

Christian aimed his pistol directly at the gunman's chest. The man had recovered from being hit with the first bullet and was awkwardly lifting his AK47 into a firing position, facing them. Christian squeezed the trigger and hoped the weapon was well-oiled. The sound of the pistol firing twice, a double tap, boomed inside the café. The rounds found their target and the gunman fell backwards to the floor, his weapon clattering to the ground a few feet away from his lifeless body. Christian slipped the pistol onto safety, stuffed it into the rear waistband of his trousers and breathed deeply, his ears ringing from the shots.

'Good shooting.' Miko had a hint of a smile on his face as he turned to look at Christian, reflecting the irony of what had just happened.

'Now we go. We leave through the back. The team will meet us somewhere. We do not want to stay here. Come on!' Miko's order left no room for doubt. The sound of distant sirens indicated that the emergency services were approaching the area. They could hear from the AU soldier's radio that the quick reaction force, the QRF, had also been dispatched from MIA. Christian looked once more at the soldier in the entrance, deep red blood pooling beneath his uniform. He concluded that there was nothing anyone could do for him.

Miko immediately got up, snapping Christian out of his thoughts, and headed for the back of the café, keeping his head down, grabbing both Christian and Megan as he went past. The whole episode had taken no more than four or five minutes. They burst through the door marked *My Kitchen* and saw a man standing to one side, hiding behind a cabinet, looking terrified.

Heading towards the exit and leaving the safety of the café behind them, Miko led, followed by Megan, Christian at the back. Miko pushed open the rear door and they sprinted out along an alleyway, the bright sunshine almost blinding them, stumbling over rubbish bins as they went. Miko talked into his radio throughout. As they ran, they kept their heads down, Christian holding his hand against his back to secure his newly acquired weapon.

After less than a minute, they emerged onto a narrow, sandy path, flanked by head-height grey concrete walls, flaking and pock-marked, but providing some cover. The shadow from the trees lining the path gave them some respite from the intense sun. They all stopped to catch their breath, quickly looking from left to right, listening for anything out of the ordinary. Not far up the track, a small boy stood alone, holding an old bicycle wheel in his hands and staring at the foreigners. Beyond him, 50 metres away at the end of the path, they could see the waiting vehicles.

Miko spoke into the radio again, then gave them instructions. 'Yes, they are here, good, good, OK, let's go.' Christian could see the Somali guards jump down from the back of their pick-up and fan out.

They started walking quickly towards the vehicles, breathing deeply after their exertions, the sense of urgency diminished; they were nearly safe. As they approached the boy, who had backed away from them, Megan slowed down and carefully walked towards him, crouching down to his height. He was no more than five years old.

'*Sidee tahay,*' she spoke gently in Somali, tucking some loose hair behind her ear and smiling at him. The boy's eyes never left Megan's. Christian had turned and stopped, watching the brief exchange with a mixture of curiosity and admiration. Megan raised her hand to wave and headed back towards Christian. The boy lifted his hand and waved back.

As they arrived, Miko checked everyone was accounted for, then stood guard while Christian and Megan got into the back of their 4x4. Once inside, Christian wriggled out of his body armour and dropped it at his feet; Christian's pack, still on the back seat, was now between him and Megan. He removed the pistol from his waist and slipped it inside, making a mental note to return it to the armoury in camp. The vehicles pulled away quickly.

Miko gave instructions to drive north, then turn left towards Bakhara Market before looping back onto the airport road. Christian leaned his head back and looked at Megan, who was focused on her phone, sending a text. She sensed his eyes on her and looked up. The shock of what had just happened was finally beginning to wane, her face recovering some of its colour. They were both in a daze but their breathing was at last becoming more regular.

'How are you doing? Are you OK?' he asked.

'I think so. I need to let my guys know what's happening.' Her voice was calm and steady. As she replied, her phone pinged again.

Christian finally had a chance to take in the person sitting next to him. Megan's long dark hair was tied back, her skin tanned. Her dark blue trousers were smeared in mud and one of the sleeves on her white blouse was slightly ripped above the elbow. He noticed there was some blood on her body armour, which she was still wearing. It was only then that he noticed she had blood running down her cheek from a cut above her eye.

'Your face is bleeding.'

She lifted her left hand and touched her cheek, her fingers moving up to her temple, dabbing on the fresh blood. 'It's fine,' she replied, 'I've had worse.' She rubbed it with her hand and added, smiling, 'It'll blend in well with my other hockey scars!'

Christian reached into his pack for his medical kit and took out some antiseptic wipes, which he passed to her. He also grabbed his water bottle and offered it to her, which she gratefully accepted.

'Keep it,' he said, smiling.

He waited for her to stop drinking, her thirst apparent.

'What happened back there?'

He had a lot of questions. He was curious as to how she had managed to get away so lightly and why there was only one AMISOM vehicle. Anyone inside would normally have been suffering from serious injury from the blast.

'I honestly don't know. I was heading in to see the Economics Minister for a short-notice meeting, just me. I knew the daily replen trip was about to leave so I got a lift from the Embassy to the muster point, spoke to the MT Sergeant, and jumped in. The AU send a single Casspir across to VS every morning. Although I wouldn't normally take it, I did today. I was surrounded by cardboard boxes of food and supplies inside, and there were only a couple of guys with me in the vehicle.' She was talking more rapidly now, the shock of the incident coming out in the speed of her words.

'We were just slowing down for the checkpoint when this almighty bang sent us into the parked cars. The guy in the hatch doing top cover was hurt and fell down inside the vehicle, so one of the guys stayed with him while the other opened the rear door and took me into the nearest building, which happened to be a café.'

Her explanation made sense but he didn't understand why the British Ambassador would take that risk, travelling without a UK-provided security team.

'Why did you travel alone?' Christian asked.

'Well, it was an important meeting that I'd been waiting a long time for, so I took a risk. Obviously, as it turned out, it was the wrong call.' She half smiled, self-consciously.

'Do you know what happened to the AU soldiers in the vehicle?' Christian was keen to know as much as possible.

'No, I don't. I was told they'd called it in and the AU was going to send out the QRF to recover the vehicle and the soldiers. It all happened very quickly. The AU also have people inside Vila Somalia, which was why the replen trip was going in the first place, so I think they were also heading out to provide some support.' She paused for a moment, catching her breath. She turned to look out of the window as their vehicles navigated the K4 roundabout much faster than they had done earlier.

'Then you guys showed up,' she added.

They were making good time and the roads were pretty clear.

'Was the soldier in the café dead?' Megan closed her eyes as she asked Christian, as if to block out any bad news.

'Honestly, I don't know. There was nothing we could have done for him there, and the QRF was inbound. My medical pack was in the car and, anyway, we couldn't afford to get caught up in the aftermath. It would have caused a lot of problems if we had.'

Megan opened her eyes and said, 'Yeah, I understand, thank you.'

'I'm glad we were able to help.' They looked at each other again.

'How about we go back to B&B for cup of English tea?' It was Miko's attempt at humour by putting on an English accent, but he managed to break the mood and both Christian and Megan laughed quietly.

'My security team is based near MIA and they have a B&B which makes the most amazing cakes. Would you like to come along?' Christian added, hoping she would join him. The lightness of the invitation, so soon after the dramatic events in the city, made them both smile. 'I can drop you off in camp afterwards, wherever you need to be.'

Megan pulled out her phone and sent another text to her Embassy staff: *I am safe and will send more details shortly. MP*

'I've heard about the B&B although I've never been there, so yes, why not?'

2

Middle Shabelle, Somalia

The teenagers stared at each other, their faces still, eyes wide, waiting for the engine to start again. They were sitting on either side of the river, sheltered from the morning sun underneath the bridge that had been constructed the year before to give vehicles a more direct route to the capital, Mogadishu. Their heads were touching the horizontal wooden planks, laid evenly along the length of the bridge, sunlight piercing the small gaps between them as if to direct the driver's eyes towards the boys.

A minute before, the pick-up truck had turned the corner and started to make its way gingerly across the rickety bridge. As the vehicle reached the middle, three small explosions, in rapid succession, had brought it to a sudden halt. The sounds of the booms had echoed across the river valley and away towards the Indian Ocean. The boys had scurried back into their positions within seconds of the first explosion.

The driver had turned off the engine and got out. They felt him walking along the bridge, his sandals making little noise on the wood as he cautiously made his way back towards its southern end. They imagined the driver looking for signs of damage, or some other indication that a bomb had gone off. But there was nothing. All that was left to accompany his footsteps was the wind blowing through the reeds and the distant sounds of birds returning to their branches after taking flight. Despite the breeze, the faint smell of cordite lingered in the air, enough to make the driver sniff loudly as he looked around him. The boys, sitting on a 45-degree slope, slowly tilted their heads up to follow his progress above them.

They held their breath. They had set off the agricultural explosives a dozen times, but nobody had ever stopped to investigate. They looked at each other again across the river, the glance conspiratorial, their hearts beating so loudly in their chests they felt sure they would be caught.

But soon after they had hidden under the bridge, the footsteps turned back towards the vehicle and the driver's door slammed shut. The engine started with a rough sound and the grinding from the gearbox told them they could relax. As the vehicle started to move over the final few metres of the wooden bridge and accelerate away, the boys could hold their silence no longer.

'Arrgghh ...' They let out an excited shout, followed by raucous laughter.

'Ali, Ali, that was the closest yet ...' Mohammed scrambled down the river bank underneath the bridge and waded across the shallow river to his lifelong friend, Ali, crying with laughter on the southern side, lying on the verge close to where he had been hiding a moment before.

Mohammed scrambled up the river bank and embraced his best friend.

'We will never be caught!' Ali declared.

They hugged for a few seconds longer and started to half run from under the bridge to where they had stored their stash of explosives a little way upstream. Designed for farmers and imported into Somalia, the explosives were sold in very few markets. Not only did the boys know which markets they were sold in; they knew where they were stored and they had stolen a box the month before.

Naïvely, they had intended to use them to blow up an African Union vehicle if ever one came over the bridge, to avenge the death of their friend who had been killed in the crossfire during an AMISOM operation the year before. Except no AU armoured vehicle would ever be able to cross the wooden bridge. After waiting for weeks, they had decided to use them on unsuspecting Somali vehicles instead, just for fun.

Ali in the lead, they soon found the metal box that had been stored under an exposed, gnarly tree root. They were laughing and shouting so loudly they could only hear their own voices, and were so engrossed in counting how many explosive devices they had left, excitedly talking about their next victim, that they didn't hear the driver walking back across the bridge. He had suspected that someone was playing a game with him and had quietly pulled his vehicle over after rounding the first bend. With his truck out of sight, he'd decided to return to the bridge to see whether his hunch was right. He quickly saw the boys together on the other side of the river and crossed the bridge, carefully stepping off the wooden platform onto the verge, speeding up his stride as he walked parallel to the river, heading straight for the tree where the boys were kneeling together in the shade.

He approached them silently.

The first blow with the man's fist hit the back of Ali's head, knocking him off balance and onto his back, the slope taking his body away from the tree and down towards the river. The second blow, coming so quickly after the first, was with the back of his hand across Mohammed's startled face. Before he could escape, Mohammed was grabbed by his neck, his head lifted up, his T-shirt, caught in the man's grip underneath his chin, exposing his stomach above his shorts.

'Are you from the next village, boy?' The man, inches away, was spitting the words into Mohammed's face. Ali, lying dazed by the river bank, watched his friend, momentarily unable to move.

'Yes, sir, yes, sir, we are Ali and Mohammed, we are from Buulo Mareer, we are sorry, sir...' Mohammed was crying by now, but the man didn't let go and struck him with his hand again.

'Please, sir, we must go, please stop hitting me, sir.' Mohammed was half crying, half shouting, his arms useless against the strength of the driver who was still shouting obscenities at Mohammed and slapping his face. The bruising started to show almost immediately, his eyes closing as the blood from the cuts on his eyebrow started to run down his face. Mohammed thought he was going to die.

He couldn't see his best friend, Ali; all he could sense was this man's face close to his own, shouting at him, his rancid breath filling his nostrils, asking what he thought he had been doing, scaring travellers with their explosives.

'You show no respect for strangers! You are an embarrassment to your families! You are no better than Shabaab filth!' The man shook Mohammed more violently as he spat out the words.

Mohammed's brain quickly started to process the consequences of what he had said; would the man speak to his father? Did he know his father? What would he say to anyone? The questions soon began to fade with each blow. With what little awareness he had left, he heard moaning and a whimper, noises he knew *he* was making, but he suddenly dropped down on the grass, falling backwards, and coming to rest on his back, his head touching a tree root.

He was alive, he knew that much, but his shallow breaths came quickly, the numb feeling in his head, the dampness on his face making him feel as if he was floating away down the river. He could hear a dull cracking sound, over and over. He didn't know what it was. He couldn't place anything. He felt a darkness creep across his eyes and he passed out.

'Come on, Mohammed, we have to go, please wake up, we have to go now, come on!' Ali was kneeling over his friend, shouting into his swollen and bloody face, grabbing his shoulders, and shaking him as hard as he could.

After what felt like a long time, Mohammed finally moved his arm and wiped his face. He tried to open his eyes to help him see more clearly under the shade of the tree, using his T-shirt to mop up the blood.

'Come on, Mohammed, we have to go; the man is dead, we must go home.' Ali was holding Mohammed more carefully now he was waking up, helping him to his feet, putting his arm around his shoulders, ready for the walk back to their village half an hour away.

'What … what happened?' Mohammed whispered. He could barely speak as he began to sense the wind blowing gently onto his skin, ambient sounds returning, as if the last five minutes hadn't happened at all.

'He didn't see me creep round behind him. I hit him with the metal box until he let go of you, then I just hit his head again and again.' Ali was crying now. 'He fell to the ground and I don't know how many times I hit him but he is not moving.' He was talking quickly, the adrenaline coursing through his young veins.

Ali's now grubby T-shirt was splattered with blood. Mohammed was beginning to make out the shape of this friend through his swollen eyes. The boys hugged each other again and, as if a silent message had been passed between them, they immediately set off for their village, for the safety of their homes, leaning on each other as they staggered with slow steps along the dusty, narrow path. They never looked back.

'Nobody can ever know about this, Mohammed.' Ali was crying as he spoke. 'We had a fight, we hit each other, but we are friends again.' Ali rubbed his face with his free hand and carried on talking, the simplicity of the cover story laced with innocence.

'I will never let anyone hurt you, my friend. Never.'

Mohammed could barely hear Ali's words as they slowly stumbled along together.

*

The sun was beginning to set when the 4x4 pick-up, its bright blue livery shimmering in the fading light, swept around the bend and passed the battered old truck parked on the side of the road, the end of day shadows obscuring its outline. The driver turned to his left but paid little attention as he slowed down to navigate the final turn before he crossed the new wooden bridge, heading south. He had travelled this way many times in the course of his work as a courier for al Shabaab, conveying messages between volunteers and the leadership based outside the capital. He had a rendezvous that evening and was running late.

As his front wheels left the dirt road and he felt the solidity of the wooden planks beneath him, he instinctively looked out of his window, the sun almost blinding him as something caught his eye. The sun's reflection glinted on something metallic about 30 metres away from the bridge but he couldn't make it out. Once across the bridge, he pulled over and killed the engine. Moving quickly, the sudden silence putting him on edge, he reached for his pistol in the glove compartment. He left the track, holding the weapon with both hands in front of him, approaching the area cautiously where he thought the reflection had originated. As he got closer, he first heard the sound of buzzing, then noticed a body lying prone on the river bank, the head disfigured and dark with matted blood, close to a tree. Beyond the body there was a metal box on its side, lying open, tubular packets spilling out onto the dusty earth. He stopped and took in the scene. He could see the man was dead, the wounds on his head already the focus for hundreds of blowflies. Walking around the body, he approached the box, intrigued as to what it was doing there. The dried blood on its corner suggested it had been the murder weapon, but what had happened? He was not an educated man, but even he could see that this was not an accident. As his heart rate rose, he noticed the contents of the box and furrowed his brow.

'Explosives?' He said the words out loud to himself, puzzled by why they were there.

He needed to take the box, marked with writing and the word *Mogadishu*, back with him to show his boss, Rasuul, what he had discovered. He had been told not to turn on his phone, so he pushed the explosives carefully back into the box and closed the lid, the clasp locking it tight. Retracing his steps, he lifted the bloodied box and placed it carefully in the rear, using a bungee to secure it for the remainder of the trip. He would have to worry about it when he got back to the capital; he was running late and he needed to get going.

Still confused by what he had stumbled on, he started the vehicle and accelerated away fast, kicking up dust and stones that flew towards the dead body, wanting to leave the mysterious discovery behind him as quickly as possible.

3

Airport Camp, Mogadishu

Christian had hardly slept since the incident in Mogadishu two days earlier.

He ran his fingers through his slightly greying hair and covered his suntanned face with his hands, not for the first time since Thursday. Slowly rubbing his skin, scratching his stubble with his fingernails, he breathed out slowly. His eyes stung; he needed to rest but he would only be able to do that properly in his Kenyan apartment. His athletic frame was struggling, his shoulders hunched, and his trekking trousers still nursing the rips from where he'd tumbled over the rubbish bins during their sprint out of the back of the café. His adrenalin had kicked in from the moment he had heard the explosion, and the cuts and bruises on his legs had only made themselves known once he was back in his room.

And then he had to deal with the fall out.

Christian's private security contractor, Horn Security, didn't have any obligation to assist the AU's troops, but his insistence on doing something when they arrived on the scene had, in fact, gone down well with the authorities inside Airport Camp. He knew the AU commander, a jovial but fiercely determined Ugandan General, as well as his Chief of Staff, Joseph, a Ugandan major. When he got back to his room, Christian's first text message was to Joseph, to explain what had happened and to give him a brief run-through of the incident. He hoped the AU would understand that he had done all he could, even though they had left one soldier behind, clearly in a bad way. It was not what he had been trained to do, but under the circumstances, with a senior British diplomat relying on him and his security team to take her to a place of safety, he'd had to make a choice.

The detour via the B&B had been a moment to savour with Megan. Although he knew there were British diplomats in Mogadishu, and he had been meaning to introduce himself to the ambassador, for one reason or another, it had never happened. He knew of Megan from his contacts in the British High Commission in Nairobi but, as a first meeting, eating cakes and drinking tea so soon after a near-death experience had been surreal. It was certainly not what either of them had expected when they had woken up that morning.

Megan's phone had been pinging constantly while they were at the B&B, making conversation difficult. The embassy had agreed to send a vehicle as it was not far to venture from the camp, and they were in a fairly secure residential area close by. It was when they were standing in the garden, under the shade of a bright orange cotton canopy flapping in the breeze, waiting for her vehicle to arrive, that she explained what was going on.

Her regular driver and her security team were out of the country on R&R. Krishna, who he had overheard Megan talking to in the café, was in charge of logistics in the embassy but couldn't drive out of camp without security. At least, he wasn't meant to. The only other option was the UK special forces detachment, located in Airport Camp to support the UK's counter terrorist agenda. They normally didn't take their vehicles out during the day but, considering the circumstances, had decided to make an exception for Megan.

From what she'd said, Christian assumed that while her driver and security detail were away, she should have stayed inside the camp or used the time to fly to the High Commission in Nairobi, which acted as the regional diplomatic hub. Megan admitted she wasn't looking forward to writing her diplomatic telegram back to London, explaining what had happened.

The sound of birdsong brought Christian's mind back to the present. He had started to enjoy Saturday mornings in Mogadishu. It was a rest day inside the camp and across the city, so there was precious little going on.

His compound was in one of the better locations too, sitting on high ground, exposed to a breeze away from the humid bush area that surrounded the runway. Looking east, over the roof of his accommodation, he could see the runway's black strip of tarmac extend left to right 500m away, stark against its ochre-coloured surroundings. On the far side was a lagoon, filled with shimmering deep blue water, leading the eye out to the vast Indian Ocean beyond. He had already concluded there were worst places to be living. Although the compound was close to the perimeter of the camp, and to a public road, he felt pretty secure with an AU guard providing additional security at the compound's entrance.

He had grown to appreciate the absence of the normal hustle and bustle on Saturdays, save for distant shouts from Somali residents over the wall. He would normally do his washing, write up his diary, and speak to his parents in England via Skype. Basically, apart from the obligatory run around camp, he would generally do very little.

This Saturday morning felt completely different.

He was waiting for his transport to the airport, sitting on his pack outside the entrance to their compound under a make-shift faded cream awning that gave some cover to their fleet of old 4x4s, which they used to navigate the camp. The sun was baking already and the warm wind relentless; he could taste the sand in the air. Mogadishu's weather was giving him the once over before he escaped to the relative comfort of temperate Nairobi and his air-conditioned apartment.

For a change, he was early for his flight. He had something he needed to do before he left. As he was rubbing the dust from the sleeves of his shirt, a vehicle swung into the yard, pulling up close to Christian.

Fred shouted through the now open door: 'Hi Chris, sorry I am a little late, I was trying to confirm where he is being kept.'

Christian quickly got to his feet, picked up his rucksack and threw it onto the rear seat.

'It's fine, Fred, thanks for getting here early. Let's go, we don't have lots of time,' Christian replied as he swung his door closed behind him.

The news that the soldier from the café was alive and had been taken to the field hospital inside the camp had dominated Christian's thoughts since being told the evening before. He had decided the only decent thing to do was try to visit him before he left for Nairobi on the daily African Airways flight.

After he had texted Joseph once back in his room on Thursday, he had immediately received a call from him. Joseph asked what had happened and invited him to complete a post-incident report for the AU operations room. The following day, Joseph called Christian to explain that the explosives had detonated just after the vehicle had gone past the VBIED. The amount of explosive used by Shabaab was obviously smaller than normal, which explained why those inside had survived. He said that once the QRF and a detachment from inside Vila Somalia had turned up on the scene, there was no visible threat; the only insurgent they could find was dead outside the café, shot by Christian and Miko. Joseph had also shared the news that the soldier who had been providing top cover for the Casspir had been hit by shrapnel and didn't make it. Fortunately, the soldier, who had been inside the back with the ambassador, had survived. When the al Shabaab insurgent had started shooting in the street and at the rear of the Casspir, he had saved his own life by crawling underneath the mortally wounded body of his comrade.

The soldier had only suffered minor injuries and had already been flown back to Kampala for treatment. Which left the soldier from the café who, Joseph explained, was at the field hospital.

Fred turned the wheel and accelerated out of the vehicle car park, turning left onto a wide dusty track which led down to the main arterial route that dissected the camp. They soon turned right, driving quickly, their windows closed as the dust kicked up behind them, to the field hospital tucked away in the furthest corner of airport camp. During the ten-minute journey, they passed compound after compound, full of portacabins, vehicles and a few contractors, mostly suntanned white men wearing trekking trousers, polo shirts, and wrap-around sunglasses with baseball hats walking slowly through Mogadishu's heat. Christian hadn't been to this part of the camp since his initial induction, and he didn't recognise anything. As they navigated the final few turns, Fred slowed the vehicle, finally joining a metalled road before pulling up outside the single-storey building with two wings either side of the main entrance.

'You go; I'll stay in case the military police come sniffing around the vehicle,' said Fred.

'OK, thanks, I won't be long. I just need to see him,' replied Christian.

'Take your time, the flight is always late arriving.' Fred was chuckling, trying to lighten the mood after they had driven across camp in unusual silence.

Christian got out of the 4x4 and walked around the front of the vehicle before pausing to take in the dark green building in front of him. The main entrance was a plain-looking double door, a faded wooden sign fixed to the brick wall to one side with the words, 'AMISOM Field Hospital'. The building's windows were evenly spaced in each direction and, apart from a few antennas and a satellite dish on the roof, it was unremarkable. To the right and at the end of the building was a military ambulance parked up next to what must have been the emergency entrance. The whole scene was subdued and quiet, surrounded as it was by lush, green-leafed trees of all shapes and sizes, which gave the hospital a deep sense of calm.

Entering the building, he waited a moment to allow his eyes to adjust to the gloom, the slight smell of disinfectant infusing the air as he walked into the entrance. Through another swing door a long, dimly lit corridor ran left to right in front of him, the temperature noticeably cooler than outside. He made his way along the corridor to the right towards what was probably the emergency entrance as he thought he would find someone there.

'Hello, sir, can I help you?' Without warning, a female voice spoke from behind him. Slightly startled, he turned to see a nurse in a blue uniform wearing a patterned headscarf, standing close to him and smiling broadly. 'So, what is a good-looking man like you doing in my hospital?' Her remark, delivered so easily, momentarily left him tongue-tied, but he quickly regained his composure and smiled back at her.

'Hello, nurse, my name is Christian. I was involved in the incident in Mogadishu on Thursday, and I understand you have an AU soldier recovering in the hospital. I wondered whether I could see him.'

The nurse's expression changed, her smile quickly replaced with a look of scrutiny towards the man standing in front of her. Her eyes narrowed.

'Hi, Christian, my name is Mary. I'm a senior nurse here at the hospital.' She paused before adding, 'I take it you haven't been checked out yourself?' It was a question that he hadn't really thought about.

'No, but apart from cuts and bruises, I'm fine.'

Mary looked him up and down before adding, 'you might be fine physically, but what about your head?'

'What do you mean?' Christian's reply was short; he wasn't expecting so many questions.

'Have you spoken to anyone about what happened? I take it you are the contractor who saved the soldier's life by killing the Shabaab insurgent?'

He relaxed a little before replying.

'No, I haven't spoken to anyone about it, apart from the ops room, which is why I guess you know about what happened.' Christian tried to smile, but it felt forced. 'Honestly, I'm OK, I just need some rest. I'm flying to Nairobi today.' He brought his hands to his face, rubbing his forehead as if to emphasise his need for a change of scene.

'It's OK, darling, follow me,' Mary replied, chuckling to herself as she turned away, setting off down the corridor in the opposite direction. Talking over her shoulder, she added. 'But I think you need a new pair of trousers!' Christian looked down at the rips, sure that she was smiling as she led the way.

'He's in ICU. It's just up here. He is sedated, he has had a blood transfusion and we are keeping him here until we think he is OK to fly home to Uganda.' Mary walked past the main entrance and down the corridor to the other end where she turned right, pushed through two sets of swing doors, and entered a brightly lit ward. Inside, he could hear the quiet hum of machines and soft beeps monitoring what appeared to be about half a dozen patients. There were an equal number of empty beds, evenly spaced, stretching away down the ward. It was a complete contrast to the dimness of the corridor where they had spoken moments before.

Although they were standing inside the ICU, they were in a partitioned waiting area, separated from the patients by an internal wall that stopped short of the ceiling; large windows allowed visitors to see what was going on without having to enter the ward. A door to their left led into the ICU itself.

Mary pointed to the first bed on the right. A figure was lying on his back, eyes closed, connected to a multitude of machines, his black face and arms in sharp contrast with the pristine white sheets.

'That is Private Masika. And he is going to be OK, thanks to you.'

Christian turned to look once again at Mary. Her oval face, dark skin and her kindly brown eyes, which had a hint of a smile, looked back at him. She was a beautiful woman and he suddenly felt huge compassion for her, and for Private Masika. After a moment to take in what she had said, he turned to look at Private Masika again and added, 'Is there anything I can do?' Christian felt helpless but asked the question all the same.

'Ah well, now, as a matter of fact there is. What's your blood group? You must know, being an ex-soldier yourself.' Mary was not just hinting at a smile now; she was showing her perfectly white teeth and two dimples had appeared in each cheek.

'Boy, I haven't been asked that for a while. I'm O negative. Which I think is quite useful.'

Mary let out a whistle. 'Yes, it is. Look, we are always short of blood at the hospital. Would you consider donating some next time you are passing? Now I know you're O negative you're on my hit list!' Mary was laughing, filling the viewing area with the sound of her voice. Even the nurse at the far end of the ward looked up and smiled.

'OK, that's fine. I promise I will, just not today because I have to leave to catch my flight.'

'OK, but you know the flight is always late arriving.' She started to laugh again, and this time Christian joined in, remembering Fred's earlier comment.

He turned back to study Private Masika through the glass. He was a young man, his whole life ahead of him, but he was lying motionless, his face calm, his head slightly elevated. By his side, his arms were resting on the bedclothes, a drip connected via a canula to his left arm, a bag of liquid hanging on a stand beside him. On the bedside table, in a frame, was a photograph of what looked like his mum and dad. Mary was watching Christian's eyes and guessed what he was looking at.

'His friends called in yesterday. They brought the frame from his bunk as they wanted his parents' faces to be the first thing he sees when he wakes up.'

Without warning, Christian's knees began to give way, the emotion overwhelming him. He reached out to the wall in front of him to steady himself. Under Mary's gaze, he took a deep breath.

'What were his injuries?' He had been waiting for the right moment to ask but could barely get his words out.

Mary had been expecting the question. 'Well, he was shot through his chest and his abdomen. His body armour protected his vital organs, but two rounds still caught him and caused a lot of bleeding. Lucky for him, they didn't do much damage; both bullets passed straight through. The surgeon managed to stitch him up, but his days in Somalia are over.'

Christian looked at Private Masika one more time, then turned to Mary, indicating that he should leave. They both left the room in silence, making their way through the two sets of doors and back into the gloom of the main corridor. They were soon at the front door again.

'Thank you so much for letting me see him. I do feel better knowing he survived. I know he is in good hands,' Christian said.

'Thank you for coming over. I will make sure that he's told that the man who saved his life came to visit.' In the entrance area, a sliver of sunlight allowed Christian to see her face again as she smiled for a final time.

'Thanks, Mary, I appreciate what you have done for me this morning. And I will call in next time I'm in Mog, I promise!'

'Before you go, give me your number. I don't want you forgetting your promise now, do I?'

They exchanged numbers and shook hands. He figured knowing a nurse in the hospital was always going to be useful. As he stepped outside, the bright sunlight temporarily blinded him. It took him a few moments to readjust, put his sunglasses on again, and walk round to the side of the vehicle. Private Masika was going to live. He was elated. He got into his seat and immediately texted Megan to share the news. Then he sent a message to Miko.

'All good?' Fred waited for Christian to finish with his phone.

'Yep, all good, let's go.'

As Fred started up the vehicle, they both turned to each other, looking at their watches. The thunderous sound of a passenger jet touching down and reversing the thrust in its engines no more than 500 metres away signalled the arrival of his flight.

And it was on time.

4

Westlands, Nairobi

Christian took another sip of Guinness.

Perched on a stool in Paddy's, the nearest Irish pub to his apartment, he was watching international rugby on the TV behind the bar, holding his pint in one hand and his phone in the other.

In the four weeks since the bomb in Mogadishu, Christian had kept his head down and spent longer in Nairobi than normal. The excitement of living and working in East Africa had rapidly worn off following the incident. The consultancy in the UK that had recruited him, had recognised that he needed some time to process what had happened. They had been keen to give Christian time to recover by allowing him to work at their head office near the UN compound in Nairobi, reducing the frequency of his trips into Somalia. The last time he had been in Mogadishu was a brief visit two weeks before.

Drinking in the many bars that were always so welcoming to expats had filled his time at the weekends, but he knew he had to get on with his job. He wanted to be extended after his initial six-month contract and felt he had exhausted his usefulness working in Kenya's capital. There is only so much that you can do to influence the world's opinion-makers from a secluded villa in a smart Nairobi suburb. Being in Mogadishu, meeting key people, making things happen with his team of dedicated photo journalists, was where he wanted to be. And he felt ready to go back.

That morning, he had woken up to his phone buzzing with a message.

Hey Christian, how have you been? Are you in NBO? Can we meet later? M

NBO: the abbreviated term for Nairobi and its city code for international air travel. He rubbed his eyes and replied immediately.

Hi Megan, great to hear from you. Yes, fancy meeting for a drink? Paddy's? 5pm?

Great. See you then. I'll be bringing a friend. M

Although they had been in touch, Christian hadn't seen Megan since the day he had rescued her from the café. He knew she had experienced a torrid time in the incident's aftermath. She had been summoned back to London to explain to the Africa director why she had decided to take the single, relatively undefended AU armoured vehicle when she should have stayed in the camp and waited for the full convoy that travelled later. Although she was not threatened with any disciplinary action, he had told her that her enthusiasm to get a particular piece of legislation through the Somali Parliament, the hoped-for result from meeting the Economic Minster, had not, in the mind of the Africa director, been worth the risk she had taken. She had returned to Mogadishu via Nairobi a week later after taking some time off in the UK.

Receiving the text had put a spring in his step. He'd immediately got out of his king size bed and padded across the tiled floor to his en suite wet room, decked out with the usual fittings, two large, frosted glass windows giving the room a bright, fresh feel. He had turned on the shower, holding his hands under the spray, waiting for the heat to come through. Turning towards the full-length mirror, he'd looked at his naked body until the condensation had started to obscure his reflection. He was still fit and his regime of running whenever he could had kept his body in decent shape.

'You're doing OK, Chris.'

He said the words quietly to himself, but it felt as if the voice belonged to someone else. The lines around his eyes, the slightly drawn cheeks and the flecks of grey around his temple betrayed the trauma of losing his wife to cancer just over 12 months earlier. The events of the past 18 months – the shock of her diagnosis, her rapid decline, and her death in a local Macmillan hospice in England – had been life-changing. After the funeral, an event that he could barely remember, Christian had tried to carry on as before. He had been serving in the army, living in a married quarter on base and, in the initial period after Jessica had passed, he tried to keep his career on track. But it just didn't work out. He had struggled to find the same level of enjoyment day to day without Jessica by his side; everything had felt meaningless.

Christian realised he had to make a change. Walking back to his quarter one evening, late from finishing an important report and knowing he had an empty house waiting for him, he decided to put an end to his career. He resigned his commission the following day, which gave him six months to see out his notice period and find another job outside the military.

The army had been great from the moment Jessica had been diagnosed, and he could not have been better looked after by the regiment, but he knew deep down that he would never again be able to fully commit himself to the career he loved. Walking back to his quarter that evening also made him realise just how much Jessica had been the centre of his life. Now he felt untethered. He knew he needed some time to figure out what his future was going to look like. And with each passing week following her death, he felt more able to embrace the future. In tiny, incremental steps, he began to see some hope.

The decision to resign his commission had come as a shock to his parents, but they understood. At first, he had struggled with the implications of Jessica's death and deciding to leave was another unknown to manage. His parents had been by his side but it wasn't enough. Leaving the military was a decision he had taken far sooner than planned and, with a limited time to find another income, he started to consider becoming a contractor working overseas, a role that he knew attracted a decent salary. He had some good contacts; he could put some feelers out. The need to find somewhere affordable to live in the UK and a deep desire to find some space for himself had all contributed to his decision to take a job in East Africa.

But now was not the time for that level of introspection; he knew he had to get his life back on track.

With steam from the hot shower filling the room, he had leaned forward and wiped away some condensation. Christian had seen something in his expression that he hadn't seen in a long time. The text message from Megan had meant something to him. He felt excited about meeting her. OK, so she was bringing a friend, but he thought that was a good sign. He turned away from the mirror and stepped under the hot water, the pressure reinvigorating his skin, and his mind.

After what felt like a long time, he'd turned off the shower and, wrapped in a towel, walked into his living space. He opened the double doors to his small balcony, letting in the sounds and smells of Spring Valley, a leafy suburb close to the nightlife of Westlands and the Westgate Shopping Centre. The warmth of the morning burst into his apartment, the breeze making the sheer curtains billow into the room, instantly giving him a sense of home. Walking across to the open-plan kitchen, he switched on the kettle and touched his iPad, cueing up Elbow's latest album.

As he grabbed a mug from the drainer and a teabag from the cupboard, he flicked the kettle and lent back against the work surface, breathing in deeply. He loved being in this apartment. Living in Africa, a place he was reasonably familiar with from an earlier posting, gave him the space he needed. His parents knew he had always enjoyed being away overseas, but his father's final words to him, before he left the UK, were seared in his mind.

"Take as long as you need, Christian; your mother and I will always support you. But be careful not to forget who you are and why you joined the military in the first place. Life outside is going to be hard at first. But you are young, you have a bright future ahead, just make the right decisions. And don't stay away too long!"

He could recite those words in his sleep, but he knew his dad was right. Although some of his friends had questioned why he had left, in his heart he knew it was the right thing to do and, for Christian, that was his north star. He would be back soon enough. He just needed to deal with his emotions now, to trust that he had made the right call. The future could wait.

After Christian had finished his breakfast, he changed into a pair of jeans, put on a loose-fitting linen shirt, and slipped on his deck shoes. He needed to grab some provisions from the Nakumat supermarket in the Westgate Shopping Centre, then he would call a taxi and head across to Westlands, and the Irish pub. Although Westgate was close enough to walk to, he decided to drive, using the car from work that was available to him while he was in Nairobi. He grabbed the keys, turned to look around the apartment, deciding to leave the windows open. He walked out, locking the door behind him. He lived on the 3rd floor; it would be fine. As he skipped down the stairs and out into the warm Kenyan morning to find his old Land Rover, he realised for the first time in a while that he was happy.

When he had first arrived in Kenya, he had stayed for three weeks in a hotel, a period of induction and readjustment. It had also given him time to find some accommodation for the period of his contract. The first time he had driven in the city was two days after arriving. On that occasion, he'd got hopelessly lost, so much so that he was driving around downtown long after dark, something that was never recommended in the guidebooks. He had eventually found his hotel but only after driving in circles for about three hours. Since that experience he had spent a lot of time just getting to know the city, learning when to drive and when to take a taxi, knowing where to go and where to avoid.

Driving round to Westgate Shopping Centre was now routine.

The day had drifted away for Christian. He'd spent an hour or so drinking a coffee and reading a newspaper inside the Art Café on the ground floor. He had seen a couple of people on the international circuit, including a senior diplomat from the US Embassy. The Art Café was where many international staff and contractors went at the weekend, attracted by the artisan bread and decent coffee. It was a huge terrorist target as a result.

He had also bumped into an old military friend called Mac, who worked for the UN. They occasionally met up for a coffee and, on the spur of the moment, they decided to grab some lunch together. They chose a table at the far end of Art Café's long veranda, behind a large potted plant. It made catching the waiter's eye difficult but allowed them to have a reasonably discreet conversation. The morning rain shower had passed through and, although the ground was still damp, the sun was shining and they felt confident to be outside. Sitting just above the service road that led to the shopping centre car park, they caught up on each other's news. The sound of cars passing just below the veranda added to the background noise. Mac was older and taller than Christian, completely bald, looking as sharp and trim as ever. They shared a military background and a similar sense of humour. And they both understood the frustrations of working with the UN.

'Honestly, Chris, they're all bloody muppets.' Mac soon got down to it. 'They couldn't organise the proverbial piss-up if they were living next to the bloody vats.'

His Scottish roots always made an early appearance in their conversations. Mac worked for the security directorate in the UN, focusing on Somalia, trying to create some sort of international consensus towards supporting its beleaguered security forces. To Christian, Mac's job was as close to herding cats as he had ever encountered. Although Christian was leading the strategic communications effort in Mogadishu on behalf of the UN, he was well aware of the number of stakeholders who wanted a piece of the action when it came to security sector reform.

'I mean, there are some who are bloody good, but they are few and far between, and they all come from the same few bloody countries.' Mac's frustrations were well known, but he never openly passed on information that was confidential or sensitive. He had another way of doing that.

'However, I will say this to you, Chris, you need to keep your eyes and ears open when you go back to Mog. The apple cart is being royally upset by the actions of one particular nation which has a strong connection to Christmas.' Mac's habit of speaking in riddles to imply what he wanted to say without actually saying it was also something Christian was long used to.

Christian, with a smirk on his face, lowered his voice and turned away from the nearest table on the other side of the plant. 'In what way is Turkey upsetting things?'

Mac looked at Christian and winked. 'You're a smart cookie, Chris. Just watch your back. The Turks are desperate to be number one in Mog; they're using the old Muslim brotherhood card – small 'b' – and the Somalis are beginning to open their arms. It's playing havoc for the rest of us who are trying to do things the prescribed way; using meetings, collaboration and joint declarations. The bloody Turks have turned up, set up an embassy and opened their coffers.'

Christian knew they had opened a diplomatic mission close to the K4 roundabout because he had driven past it several times. He didn't realise they were starting to get into security sector reform, backed up by a lot of money. The security assistance space in Somalia was already full of nations competing with one another, not least the US, the EU, the Brits and even the Japanese. He made a mental note to see what else he could find out when he was next in Mogadishu.

By the time he had finished his lunch with Mac and returned from his weekly shop at the supermarket, it was already time to head out for his meeting with Megan. On his way to the pub in the back of a taxi driven by his regular driver, Henry, he felt another notification vibrate from his phone: *I'll be there in 15. M*

Just enough time to find a seat and order a pint, Christian thought. Henry stopped at the usual intersection and pulled into the small waiting area next to the security bollards.

'Have a good time, Boss.' Henry rarely spoke, so this was something of a surprise.

'Thanks, Henry, I'll call you later.'

The sun was low in the sky and there was already a buzz in the air as he walked across the pedestrianised street, which housed the international bars, all designed to cater for expats with nothing to do but spend their hard-earned money. Christian had tried them all at one time or another, but it was the Irish bar that he always gravitated to, mainly because they had booths towards the back of the pub offering a degree of privacy from the other guests. They also did table service if you were a regular.

Christian took a sip of his Guinness and caught his reflection in a mirrored door that had been opened behind the bar. He had a healthy tan, his beard was trimmed, his face was lean and his recent haircut had smartened up his appearance. It made him laugh that he was even thinking these thoughts. Since losing Jessica, he had not felt the slightest feeling for another woman.

In the last few days before she passed away, Jessica had said that she didn't want him to be alone. Until now, being alone was how it was. But something *did* feel different, for the first time in a while; he wanted to put himself back out there, both professionally and from a personal perspective.

Megan had managed to get under his skin following their life and death experience in Mogadishu. He had thought about her a lot since the attack and he knew it had to mean something.

The teams were warming up on the pitch at Twickenham when he heard Megan's voice behind him, talking to her friend at the front of the pub, which was open to the pavement. He slid off his stool, pocketed his phone, and walked over.

'Hey, Megan, great to see you again.'

'Hi Christian, it's been a while.' There was no awkwardness, no hesitancy, and they both reached for one another and kissed on each cheek. It was not how they had parted in Mog that day; time had perhaps given them both some perspective on their first meeting.

'Christian, this is Imi; she works in the High Commission. Imi, meet Christian!'

Christian and Imi shook hands. 'Hi, Imi, good to meet you,' he said.

Imi smiled and said, 'Hi Christian, I've heard a lot about you.'

Christian smiled. 'Look, we can sit at the bar, but I have reserved a booth at the back, which will give us a tad more privacy!'

They all chose the booth option and Christian ordered a white wine for Megan, a spritzer for Imi and another Guinness for himself, grabbing his nearly empty glass as they walked through to the back of the pub. They settled down in the booth, Megan and Imi on one side, Christian on the other.

'This feels like a job interview!'

Christian tried to break the ice and quietly laughed at his own joke. Finishing off his Guinness, he suddenly felt quite nervous, but he couldn't put his finger on it. As they waited for the drinks to arrive, he looked at Imi. She was shorter than Megan, her blond hair tied back in a ponytail, with a white cotton shirt tucked into faded, skinny jeans covering her slight frame. She had piercing green eyes and was oozing self-confidence. She held Christian's eye while he spoke, which made him feel on edge.

'Not on a Saturday, Chris, it's a day of rest, don't you know!' She had an accent, but he couldn't quite place it. North West? Yorkshire? He made a note to ask her when the time was right.

'Yeah, fair enough. So, what do you do in the High Commission?' Christian asked. 'I don't think we've met before.' He had visited the High Commission when he had first arrived in Kenya, ostensibly to meet a friend who worked in the defence section, but he had also been introduced to one or two other diplomats at a café inside the building.

'No, we haven't. I work in the political section, covering all the usual stuff including economics. At the moment I'm trying to figure out how to put UK-supplied boosters under the economy of the region, and Kenya in particular. Megan and I have been working on getting the law changed in Somalia to enable greater cross-border access for businesses here. It's all a bit boring if I'm honest, but I wanted to live and work in Africa and here I am!'

While Imi was explaining her role, the drinks arrived, Megan sliding their glasses across the polished table. 'So, I heard you saved our Megan a little while ago.'

'Ha, well, it really was quite a long time ago now,' Christian replied. He looked at Megan, who initially caught his eye, but then looked down at her drink which she was cradling in her hands.

'From what we have all heard, you were a bloody hero, Chris. It took some nerve to do what you did, under the circumstances.' After the incident, he had received a note from the British High Commissioner in Nairobi, thanking him for his quick thinking and for taking Megan to a safe place. After that, he hadn't heard anything else. Some people in British government circles knew what had happened, but it wasn't widely known within the expat community, which was a situation he was happy to maintain.

'Well, long forgotten training kicked in, I guess, and if Miko's pistol hadn't jammed, I would have been a passenger for the whole thing anyway.' He paused, turned from Imi to Megan, and asked her directly. 'How have you been?'

Megan smiled and looked back at Christian. 'Well, I wasn't sacked when I went back to London, and I managed to get the Economics Minister to propose the law change in the end, so it was all worthwhile.' She smiled but suddenly stopped talking, as if the memories of that day had filled her mind, completely blanking out whatever she was going to say next.

There was an awkward silence that followed until Imi stepped in.

'So, Chris, Megan tells me that you are pretty active in Mogadishu. What sort of things do you do when you're there?' Imi's question sounded natural, as if she was just keeping the conversation going.

'I'm working on a six-month strategic communications contract with the UN, leading a team of photo journalists and other media types to pull together positive news about what the AU is doing across Somalia then get it out to the masses, so the world thinks that it's doing a great job.' Christian's response was much rehearsed. Imi looked impressed.

'So, do you know lots of Somalis in government as well then?'

Christian was happy to be able to talk about what he was doing. Explaining the breadth of his network to Imi was making him long to be back in Mogadishu.

'Yes, I have weekly contact with various ministers, including the President's Chief of Staff and the Defence Minister who has a close relationship with the President, although that's as much because I am ex-forces, and he likes that connection.'

Imi nodded with interest. Megan was silently watching him from across the table, with a softness in her face that made Christian feel like he wanted to hug her. He was enjoying talking to Imi, but he wanted to be alone with Megan. Before he knew it, they had finished their drinks and Christian was calling to the barman to come to their table.

'I'll have a wine with Megan if that's alright.' Imi seemed to be enjoying herself. 'And I reckon it's your round, Megs!'

Megan had visibly relaxed since she had been at the table.

'Yes, it's my round Christian – let me pay for it.' As soon as she had ordered the drinks, she put some notes in the barman's hand and settled back into her seat. When Imi excused herself to go to the bathroom, Christian smiled at Megan.

'It's really good to see you. Thanks for getting back in touch.' He didn't want to say too much, and he was conscious that his glass of wine at lunchtime, together with his second pint of Guinness, could lead him to say something he might later regret.

'It's good to see you too. I'm sorry I haven't been around. The whole thing really hit me hard when I got back to London. I just needed some time to process everything.' Megan subconsciously moved a strand of dark hair from her face. 'But there was one missing part of the puzzle to put everything in its rightful place, so I texted you,' she added.

Christian's heart surged in his chest. He replied softly, 'Well, I have been called many things before, but that's a new one on me!'

They both laughed together, her face shaping into a most beautiful expression that he remembered, albeit fleetingly, from the back of the vehicle immediately after the incident. Imi returned to see them both taking a drink, clearly looking at each other over the rim of their glasses. Imi feigned to look at her watch.

'Is that the time? Oh my God, I'm late! I need to leave.'

After a moment's pause, they all cracked up and laughed, making so much noise that the barman looked across to see what had happened. They stayed chatting across the table for another hour until they had finished their drinks.

'Woh, OK, it really is time for me to leave.' Imi looked at her watch again and turned to Megan. 'Shall we get a cab together since we live reasonably close?'

Christian pulled his phone out of his pocket and sent a text to Henry.

Hey Henry, can you come to the PUP as soon as? Asante sana

They slid out from their booth and walked through the pub to the street. Day had turned to night while they had been inside. Standing together, Megan turned to Christian and asked, 'What are you doing tomorrow Chris?'

'No plans, although I need to get my gear together as I'm flying back up to Mog on Tuesday.'

'Would you like to come out to Lake Nakuru for a picnic? There's a few of us from the High Commission driving out for lunch. We should be back by late afternoon. It's pretty relaxed. No pressure if you would rather stay here.'

Christian didn't hesitate in replying, 'That would be great, thanks very much. I've never been.'

They stood together for a few minutes, talking about the plans for the following day. Suddenly Imi said, 'Here's our car.' Imi leaned forward and gave Christian a kiss on the left cheek. 'Thanks for the drinks, and the company; see you soon.'

Megan turned to Christian and this time she hugged him. He held her tightly, in an embrace that lasted for only a few precious seconds, but which meant so much to him, and he hoped to Megan as well. After they kissed on each cheek, Megan said quietly, 'We'll pick you up at 10.' And then she was away into the night, the sounds of their car doors slamming and the vehicle driving up the road into the dark streets. Christian noticed it wasn't a Kenyan taxi, and although he couldn't see the registration plate, he figured it must have been a High Commission car. His phone soon buzzed with a message from Henry to say he was waiting as arranged.

Christian walked back across the pedestrianised street with a spring in his step, listening to the sound of music, laughter and people talking loudly together, that hypnotic cocktail that accompanies nightlife the world over, evocative and enduring. He opened the back of the car and slipped in, smiling to himself.

'Where to, Boss?'

'Take me back to the apartment, Henry. Thanks.'

'Did you have a good time?'

'Thanks, Henry, I did ... I did.'

5

Spring Valley, Nairobi

The car pulled up outside the security gates and switched off its engine. Inside, Megan was sitting in the passenger seat. Richard, one of the High Commission's senior political officers, was in the driver's seat, and in the back was a colleague from the International Development Team. Megan turned to Josh, who was concentrating on eating some fruit from a Tupperware container on his lap.

'Hey Josh, do you fancy a ride in the front? Richard always gets me to do the map reading!'

'That's not true but fine, it's better to have a man in the front when it comes to maps!' As Richard spoke, he brought his hands to his head to protect himself. Josh looked up in time to see Megan punch Richard's left arm.

'Well, I'm not going to sit in the front if it's going to get violent.' Josh added.

'I take it all back. Come on, Josh, let's have a boys' outing and leave Megan to talk Somalia with our guest.'

Megan, wearing a stripy blue dress and sandals, her hair tied back, stepped out of the Land Rover Discovery and knocked on the solid metal gate, designed to prevent any sight of what was inside the compound. She heard the guard walking over to begin the process of lifting the spike out of the ground and removing the bolt.

'Morning. I'm here for one of your residents.' Megan spoke loudly to the metal gate while watching Josh shuffle out of the back seat and into the front, dropping his Tupperware container in the process, its contents spewing across the wet tarmac road. 'Bollocks.'

'Hey, Megan, I'm here,' Christian said.

As the gate opened, Christian was standing on the other side, having come down from his apartment after getting Megan's text.

'Thanks very much,' Christian said to the guard and patted his arm as he walked through the gap. He and Megan approached each other and briefly kissed on each cheek. Christian noticed the driver looking across at them. There were no hugs like the night before.

'How did you sleep?' Christian asked Megan. Josh, who had managed to save some pieces of Kiwi fruit, was just closing his door when they approached.

'Pretty good considering Imi and I stayed up on her veranda drinking whisky until midnight!'

Christian smiled, bent down slightly to look through the windows of the vehicle and opened the rear door for Megan. After they pulled away, Megan introduced Christian to both Josh and Richard.

'OK, so it's about a two-hour drive and the roads should be pretty clear on a Sunday morning.' Richard had taken charge and was enjoying his role. Josh was looking down at an old copy of *The Guardian*, holding his container of fruit tightly as he turned over a page. Megan and Christian briefly looked at each other as they settled into their seats, but the presence of colleagues from the High Commission kept any conversation between them centred on Somalia.

After about 30 minutes, Richard spoke again. 'So, Chris, Megan tells me you used to be in the army.'

Christian turned to look across at Megan, who was facing the other way, staring out of the window at the passing traffic.

'Yes, that's right. I served for 14 years all told. I left earlier this year. What do you do in the High Commission, Richard?'

Christian was uncomfortable talking about his military service and the subject change was noted by everyone in the car apart from Josh, who was on the phone talking to his wife back in Nairobi.

'What *do* I do?' Richard spoke almost theatrically, clearing his throat, posing the question as if he wanted Megan or Josh to answer it for him.

Megan turned back to look at Christian, mouthing to him to wait, using her hands to emphasise her observation. Christian winked at her, their conspiratorial exchange further cementing the bond between them.

'Well, I head up our political section, making sure the High Commissioner has all he needs when conducting his business out and about in the country. You know the kind of thing. It's all very boring, but it keeps me out here!' Richard immediately started humming some long lost tune known only to himself. 'Have you been to Kenya before?'

Christian assumed the question was aimed at him and answered, 'Yes, I've been out in uniform a few times for various reasons, so it's been great reacquainting myself with the country. So, you know Imi then?' Christian added.

'Imi? Yes, she works with me. Yes, that's right.' Richard answered the question without a pause. He looked across at Josh, who was still on the phone, and immediately launched into a commentary about the need to support micro farmers in western Kenya.

The small talk continued until they arrived at Lake Nakuru. They pulled into a small car park not far from the main road and found some shade. Everyone was stiff from the journey but pleased to have finally arrived. Throughout the drive, Richard had provided some insight on every aspect of the countryside they had been driving through, demonstrating his knowledge of the political climate, the strength of the economy in the region and even the plans for improving the infrastructure, a topic that drew groans from Josh who hated the Kenyan roads and was constantly telling Richard to slow down.

Christian watched Megan undo her seatbelt and smiled, as they had done throughout the journey while listening to Richard's monologue. Megan knew what was to come and gently patted his hand. 'Come on, you're going to enjoy this.' Once out of the vehicle, they all grabbed their day sacks and shared the burden of carrying the two huge cool boxes full of cold drinks and the ingredients for their BBQ.

'Here, Christian, can you carry this?' Richard handed over a long tube and what looked like a tennis racquet bag. 'We'll be needing those later.'

They picked up their things and, with Richard leading, they walked away from the dusty car park and followed a path towards a large old lodge with a veranda spanning the entire frontage of the property. As they approached, the building took on more shape; it was constructed of stone but had lots of wooden features, including an overhanging pitched roof, which gave it a homely, welcoming feel. A wooden balustrade across the front meant they had to walk around the side and up the steps to the front door. The lodge looked as if it had been there for decades.

'Well, this is Pennine Lodge and it's owned by a dear friend of the High Commission. Marjorie, whose husband was the High Commissioner back in the seventies and who sadly died last year, lets us descend on the place from time to time. She has lived here for as long as the house has existed.' Richard stopped on the veranda and put his bags down.

Josh, who had been very quiet throughout the journey, suddenly spoke with a great deal of enthusiasm. 'Right, give me those please, Christian. I'll get things set up while you guys fire up the BBQ.' Josh took the tube and bag from

Christian, who looked across at Megan. He put his own bag down and stretched his back.

'It's an amazing place,' Christian said as he leant on the balustrade and took in the view.

'Marjorie loves to get visitors so we do our best to get up here as often as possible. She'll be here in a minute.' Richard made himself busy pulling together the coals and the kindling for the BBQ, which were around the side of the lodge. The food was placed in the shade and everyone discussed timings.

'I think we have time for a quick walk through the reserve,' Josh said, grabbing his camera and sun hat.

'Christian, help yourself to a drink and I'll take you and Megan across to the zebra.' Josh added.

The lodge was on the edge of a private reserve that boasted a range of wildlife species but, unusually, there were no carnivores. The three of them walked away from the lodge and within 15 minutes they came across half a dozen zebra eating lush grass that had been refreshed by the recent rains. Josh wandered towards the zebra with his camera to his face, patiently waiting for the right shot. Christian and Megan held back and walked much more slowly, idly even, away from the house and towards a thicket of trees a couple of hundred metres away.

They had already crossed a low hill away from Josh and were now hidden from view in a secluded spot. 'So, are you sure there are no carnivores here?' Christian turned to ask Megan with a quizzical look, as if the idea was beyond him.

'Yup. The reserve is fenced in but you would never know because it is so vast. But I can confirm there are no lions ... apart from the one behind you!' Megan laughed as Christian caught himself turning his head. He instinctively reached out to hold her in his arms.

'Very drôle!' Christian could feel his heart rate rising. Megan didn't resist his embrace and they looked at each other for a moment before she gently touched his arm.

'What say we have a sit down?' Megan was in charge.

They walked a little further and found a broken tree stump to sit on.

'I've only come here a couple of times, but I love it.'

'I can see why. It's so peaceful.'

Megan smiled and turned to look at him again; this time they were even closer.

'I think the reason I like this place so much is because, in a way, it reminds me of my grandmother's farm, her *cascina*, in Italy. It's in the middle of nowhere, down a long driveway and then it suddenly comes into view, overlooking a lake. I would roam around the area for hours catching butterflies and giving them names. I spent lots of time there as a child before my parents divorced and, even now, it's the one constant in my life. And my grandmother, I call her *Nonna*, well, she just knows how to look after me!'

'It sounds idyllic.' Christian ventured to touch Megan's hand, a gesture she accepted.

Megan looked at their hands together and spoke again. 'When I was away, I realised that I needed to see you again, Christian ... I can't explain it, but what you did to save me that day was the most extraordinary thing. I spent days at home pacing around, trying to process what happened, knowing that I had to be with you. All I wanted to do was get on a flight. But I also realised that I knew nothing about you ... nothing at all ... I want to change that.'

Christian started to control his breathing, listening intently to Megan's words, but he didn't speak. Megan was looking at him, hoping for a response, but there was silence.

'Well, before I implode with embarrassment at having completely misread the situation, can you at least tell me how you feel?' She tilted her head to catch Christian's eyes which had dropped to the floor.

Christian shifted his position to face Megan, gently taking her other hand. They were looking at each other, inches apart.

'I felt the same, Megan.' Christian slowly moved his head forward, waiting for a reciprocal movement from Megan, until their lips met, a kiss so soft it felt like a dream. They soon embraced as they shared the moment they had both been waiting for.

After a few minutes, their passion was calmed, their heads side by side, their bodies held together as they quietly took everything in. They gently kissed one more time before moving apart to look at each other. A crack of a branch close by made them both look up, suddenly remembering where they were. An antelope had wandered into view, stopping to eat some grass before walking off again. It didn't have a care in the world; it was in paradise even if it didn't know it.

'There's a lot of things I have to tell you, Megan, nothing that's going to stop us ... *this*.' Christian held up Megan's hands to emphasise the point. 'But there are things I need to say. When we have some time.'

'It's OK, Christian, there's no rush, we can talk whenever you feel ready.' Megan lifted her hand and cupped his face in her palm, looking at him, smiling, but seeing the strain in his eyes. She knew instinctively that she wanted to be with him.

Christian held Megan close, both looking out across the plain and watching the antelope and zebra come and go in silence, both lost in their own thoughts.

Eventually Christian stole a glance at his watch. 'I guess we have to get back,' he said with little enthusiasm. 'Come on, Megs.'

Megan pulled away and ran her fingers through her hair, then linked her arm with Christian's as they started to walk back towards the top of the small hill that had served as the perfect shield from Josh and the lodge. 'You called me Megs!'

Christian turned to her and smiled guiltily. 'Sorry. Do you mind?'

'No, I love it. How about I call you Chris?'

'It's a deal.'

The sun was hot as they made their way back, walking side by side across the open plain, the occasional tree providing shade not only for humans, but also the wildlife. Christian was beginning to regret his choice of jeans and walking boots. As they approached Pennine Lodge, the ground shook with the vibration from a herd of zebra cantering close behind them.

'This place is amazing.' Christian briefly glanced over their shoulders to watch, bringing his arm up to Megan's back, touching her skin above the line of her dress. 'Today has already been amazing. Thank you for inviting me.'

They arrived with ten minutes to spare and were immediately given jobs. Marjorie was sitting on a bamboo rocking chair in the shade of a yellowwood tree, watching the commotion unfold. Josh had spent the entire time photographing animals and hadn't even noticed that Megan and Christian had wandered off together. He was busily explaining the rules for the badminton court that he had set up close to where they were going to eat, complete with a net and chalk lines. Christian listened to Josh and smiled.

'Playing badminton is a bit of a tradition here.' Marjorie's voice cut through Josh's instructions, which he was beginning to repeat. 'I can watch you play.' She was in her eighties, thin with white hair cut short, gently rocking on her chair in a pair of old jeans, a shirt and a sleeveless cardigan. Her gaze was impenetrable. Christian immediately turned and walked towards her to introduce himself.

'Hello, Marjorie, my name is Christian Travers. I work for the UN in Mogadishu.'

'Yes, I know who you are. Richard has explained everything to me.' She spoke with the self-confidence that comes with someone who fears nothing in the world. 'It's very good to meet you.'

'And you. This is a beautiful place you have here. Thank you for letting us visit.'

'Since Dominic passed away, you have all provided me with lots of company and entertainment.' Marjorie's attention drifted momentarily, her chair coming to a halt, lost in a memory from happier times.

'Do you still play?' Christian asked.

'Play? Ha! I wish.' Marjorie came to and smiled before once again closing her eyes.

A moment later, Richard quietly walked up to Christian's side as he looked at Marjorie in her chair. 'She has already been chatting with me for a while, so it's likely she will take a nap now; I would leave her to it.'

6

Bakhara Market, Mogadishu

The boys pressed their faces against the dirty windows of the bus as it slowed to a stop on the edge of Bakhara Market, located in the heart of Mogadishu. After two hours sitting on torn, plastic seats, Ali got up first, stretched involuntarily, followed by Mohammed, both boys standing in line behind a queue of adults carrying everything from cages of chickens to sacks of potatoes over their shoulders. They were behind an old woman who had got on the bus at the same stop as the boys in their village. Although they didn't know her, she knew them. Her voice was harsh, her language coarse as she turned her head and spoke to Ali in a low voice.

'I know why you are here, you tearaways; do you think we don't know what happened at the bridge? Do you think we are stupid in our village? You bring shame on all of us. You're no better than them.' The woman tilted her head to the side sharply, pointing outside the bus, but Ali knew who she was referring to; al Shabaab. She turned away, still mumbling under her breath as she shuffled forward, her words no longer audible.

'Brother, what did she say? I couldn't hear the old bag,' Mohammed said, tugging Ali's sleeve.

'Nothing, brother, relax, she wanted to know where to buy spices ...' The lie was easily delivered. 'Come on, let's get off this heap of junk.'

Mohammed had become a different person since their skirmish with the farmer weeks before. The impact of his injuries soon passed, and their story was believed by their families, but he knew what had really happened. Ali had also followed the news closely; everyone he asked said that the old man had been beaten by bandits who had then stolen his vehicle. Ali shared the story in the hope that it would become the accepted truth, but rumours soon spread and he had heard alternative versions of events, which he had decided not to share with Mohammed. When Ali had returned to the scene a week later, he carefully checked to see that nobody else was there before walking across to the tree where he thought he had left the box, but it was nowhere to be seen. It was as if nothing had happened at all. He was angry that he had lost all his explosives and vowed to steal some more. This was the reason for the trip to the capital and Mohammed had reluctantly agreed to go along.

The boys walked through the throng of people, women wearing bright *garbasaars*, their clothes blowing wildly in the breeze, shop keepers calling out, trying to entice passers-by to sample their goods. Market stalls were lined up in front of the buildings on both sides of the road, crammed side by side in places, leaving just enough room for vehicles and carts to pass in front. This was Bakhara Market, the commercial heart of Somalia's capital city.

Groups of men, idly sitting on the steps of buildings, many chewing khat, their yellowing teeth evidence of their long-term habit, watched the boys pass in front of them. Ali and Mohammed were on edge; this was not their patch and Mogadishu was a dangerous place for strangers. The sound of horns being blown as vehicles forced their way through the crowds made them watch their backs as they moved amongst the human traffic. The smells of spicy fried fish filled their nostrils and made them hungry. Ali grabbed a couple of samosas from a tray while the stall holder wasn't looking and passed one back to Mohammed. Somali music was playing loudly from traders selling cassettes and CDs; the sights and sounds of the market were overwhelming as the boys, dressed in shorts and T-shirts, wandered deeper into its heart. Ali navigated the narrow roads from his memory of their first visit, snaking their way between tall concrete buildings to where Ali knew they sold the explosives and, more importantly, where they were stored.

The boys rarely travelled this far from the village but, by offering to collect some provisions for their family, they had been allowed out with enough in their pockets to buy what was needed. Mohammed carried the bag they were going to use to hide the explosives after they had managed to steal another box.

'How far is it, Ali? We have to buy the vegetables for my mother and I think we need to get them first. If something goes wrong, we may need to run.'

Mohammed's logic was sound, but Ali was tired of how his friend seemed to have lost his appetite for revenge, and he didn't want to spend his time trawling market stalls buying vegetables before he had secured what he had travelled to Mogadishu to do.

'We are doing this for Assad! Our friend, remember? It's just round the corner here, we will buy the other things later,' Ali replied curtly, the finality in his voice frightening Mohammed.

The boys stepped off the main thoroughfare, dodging behind the line of stalls and stood, side by side, in a doorway next to a row of shops, watching the mass of people walking in both directions on the road in front of them, as if they were sitting on a river bank watching the current flowing by. Now that they had entered the heart of the commercial district, they were close to their target. Ali was scanning around him, looking to see if anyone was watching, but nobody paid them any attention.

'The boxes were stored in that building over there,' Ali said, jutting his chin across the road for Mohammed's sake. 'The brown door on the right should be open and they are inside on the left. At least, they were last time. Can you not remember?' Ali turned but Mohammed wasn't listening, his eyes darting up and down the road, the noise from the vehicles making it hard to hear his friend.

'Come on, Ali, let's get this over and done with. I'm scared,' Mohammed admitted.

As soon as there was a break in the flow of people and cars in front of them, Ali stepped off the curb and grabbed Mohammed's arm to pull him alongside.

'Come on,' Ali said and quickly crossed the road, stopping next to the brown door from where he could see the shop selling the explosive devices a little further up the road. 'That's the shop. Keep an eye on it and tell me if the shop keeper comes out, OK, brother?'

Mohammed looked hard in the direction Ali had indicated but couldn't see anyone.

'Ali, I can't see anyone, Ali ... Ali, don't go in ...' but his words were met with the click of the door as it closed behind Ali.

Mohammed's heart was pounding hard as he scoured the shop for the man. Minutes felt like hours. Suddenly the shop keeper appeared at the doorway and casually looked in Mohammed's direction. Mohammed instinctively looked down at his feet, immediately fearing the worst for their ill-conceived outing and forgetting Ali's instructions.

He was startled when the door behind him opened without warning.

'Mohammed, come on, I can see them, I need your bag,' Ali whispered, reaching out and grabbing Mohammed's arm, pulling him into the room and closing the door behind them.

The sunlight outside contrasted dramatically with the darkness of the large storage room, its depth momentarily visible from outside as the door was opened, but now its far wall disappeared into the gloom. With their eyes growing accustomed to the ambient light, surrounded by dozens of boxes and crates haphazardly piled up around them, Ali led them to the furthest corner. There, in front of them, were the metal boxes they both instantly recognised.

'Quickly, Mohammed, open your bag, let's fill it up!' Ali laughed while Mohammed, who was shaking with fear, told him to be quiet, their voices carrying easily throughout the space. They both struggled to put the first box into the bag, Mohammed's movements clumsy, his hands shaking.

'OK, let's put another one in, come on.' Ali was trying to fit two boxes into their bag but there was only room for one, and Mohammed knew it. Still, Ali tried, oblivious to Mohammed's pleas.

'Ali, let's go, we will get caught, come on!' He was trying to keep his voice low but the alarm he felt made him shout. 'Ali, let's go, *now!*' Ali grabbed the bag, the second box falling to the floor, the clattering sound echoing around them. They both turned and headed for the exit, their eyes now seeing the route to the door clearly.

Ali in front, they walked quickly. Ali reached out to turn the handle but before he could do so, the door suddenly opened towards them, sending them both staggering back in shock. Both boys gasped and regained their balance.

'Got you, you little shits!' The shop keeper stood in the doorway, the sunlight behind him sending his shadow deep into the room. He turned on the low-wattage ceiling light as the boys backed away, Ali holding the bag tightly across his chest. Without warning, Ali darted for the gap between the man and the doorframe, leaving Mohammed rooted to the spot, whimpering as the gravity of what was happening very quickly sunk in.

'No you don't, you little fucker!' The man's language was menacing as he grabbed Ali around the throat with one arm and closed the door with the other, dragging the boy into the middle of the room and dropping him and the bag on the floor next to the motionless Mohammed. The man was breathing hard but managed to pull out his phone and quickly dialled a number, while pushing his feet into Ali's stomach. Ali tried to fight back while Mohammed started to cry quietly, rooted to the spot.

'I have them ... yes, two of them ... OK.' The man spoke quickly into the phone. Still breathing hard, he hung up and grabbed the bag from the boys. 'You little bastards! Who do you think you are?' Neither boy spoke; Ali was struggling to breathe and Mohammed was frozen with terror.

A few minutes later, the door burst open for a second time and a tall, younger man walked in, dressed in high-street trainers and a designer T-shirt, sunglasses lodged on his head. He quickly surveyed the scene and turned to the shop keeper, who still had his foot on Ali's stomach, punching him hard in the face. The shopkeeper fell back and collapsed into a pile of crates, groaning with shock and pain.

'What are you doing, you mongrel? How can you treat these boys like dogs? I should beat you now for this.' The younger man drew back his fist ready to punch him again, but after a second, he dropped his arm and told the man to get out. A moment or two later, the door opened and closed as the shop keeper left the room, his hand holding his face, blood trickling from his nose. He looked back, evil in his eyes.

The silence was punctuated by Ali gasping for air, trying to get up, but Mohammed barely breathed. Both boys looked at the young man with pure fear.

'Come on, big man, get up, I'm sorry that happened.' He lifted Ali to his feet and told him to sit down on one of the many crates around them. Mohammed silently joined his friend, but neither boy spoke as they looked at the man in front of them, their hearts racing.

'So, you are the boys responsible for the theft, are you?' The man spoke with confidence, but his voice was soft, calming the boys who were beginning to get over the shock of what had happened. Ali started to shake his head but without much conviction. 'Boys, my name is Rasuul. What are your names?'

Ali and Mohammed mumbled a reply just loudly enough for Rasuul to hear them.

He pulled out a packet of Marlboro cigarettes from his jeans and offered them to the boys. Ali looked at the packet and realised who Rasuul was; only al Shabaab managed to get hold of Marlboro cigarettes, or so the rumours went. Ali took one, much to Mohammed's disgust. Rasuul pulled out a Zippo lighter and lit it for Ali, who put it in his mouth. He breathed in, then almost immediately started choking violently.

'Hahaha, my new friend has never smoked before, has he?' Rasuul laughed loudly, his voice resonating around the room. He leant back on the edge of a crate and lit his own cigarette, breathing deeply and blowing the smoke into the air above them. Mohammed, who was starting to calm down, looked at the box of explosives and then back at Rasuul, who held the cigarette between his fingers. Rasuul followed Mohammed's eyes. 'Ah, you think we should not be smoking in a room with explosives, yes?'

Mohammed slowly nodded.

'Then your friend here had better be careful, and nothing will happen!' He laughed once more. 'Boys, I will be honest, I didn't think we would find you, but we have been patient and guessed you would come back. One of our brothers drove over that bridge not long after you killed that farmer and found the explosives. It didn't take much to find out who sold them here and to discover that they had been stolen from this very room.' Rasuul was animated and pointed with both hands to the ground. 'I then told that stupid shop keeper to keep an eye out for anyone acting suspiciously and to call me when he did. It was only a matter of time. I guess, lucky for us, we have now found each other!' Rasuul laughed again, leaning forward as if to touch their shoulders, although the boys didn't join in.

'Come on, tell me what happened. Who killed him? Was it both of you? A joint venture?' The cigarette smoke, like the question, hung in the air, unmoving between Rasuul and the boys.

Finally, Mohammed found the courage to speak. 'Sir, we didn't mean to do any harm. Our friend was killed last year by AMISOM and we thought that we could blow up one of their vehicles on the bridge, but they never came, so we just let the explosives off to scare other drivers. Nobody had ever stopped there but the farmer crept up on us and beat me ...' Mohammed's voice tailed off, but Ali filled the silence.

'What will happen to us? The old boy was killing Mohammed so I hit him with the box. I didn't know I had killed him. Nobody knows what we did. But we wanted revenge and so we came here to get more explosives ... what will you do to us?' Ali had found courage from somewhere but still didn't understand why Rasuul was being kind to them both.

Rasuul listened to their story. The noise from the street outside suddenly increased as a car started using its horn to cut its way through the shoppers.

'Sir, we are s-s-s-sorry for what we have done. Please don't tell our parents. Please, let us go, we will not say anything ...' Mohammed started to stutter as he spoke, something he had never done before.

'Boys, you both want revenge for your friend, am I right?' Rasuul said. Ali had given up trying to smoke the cigarette but had been tapping the ash on the floor like he had seen in western movies, and now he dropped it, putting it out with the bottom of his sandal. 'And we want to help you achieve that revenge, so I am going to make a proposition to you both. I will arrange for you to be able to blow up an AMISOM vehicle, but in return you are not to say another word about what has happened today. And I will know if you have, trust me – we have people who work for us everywhere.'

Both Ali and Mohammed stole a glance at each other as Rasuul made this boast. Neither of them had any reason to doubt what he was saying; he seemed to have some sort of status judging by the way he dealt with the shop keeper.

'Would you like to do that, boys?'

Ali spoke first. 'Yes, we would like to do that, wouldn't we, Mohammed?'

'Yes, y-y-yes we would ...' Mohammed looked up from the floor into Rasuul's face smiling down at them.

'Ok, that's good. Ali and Mohammed, the dream team!' Rasuul laughed again as he got up, the boys following his lead, then unexpectedly he became very serious and looked directly into their faces.

'Boys, look at me ... this is what will happen.' Rasuul grabbed the outer arms of both the boys who were now standing side by side in front of him. 'You will come here in a month's time. You will come to this room and you will wait for me. You will speak to nobody apart from me, do you understand? If anyone asks, you tell them that you are waiting for Rasuul. Tell your parents you want to help them with getting provisions, which is probably what you have said today, yes?' Ali nodded. 'OK, you go now, get what you need and go home. Don't speak about this again, not even to each other. Be here in a month. I will see you then. Is that clear?'

Both Ali and Mohammed mumbled their agreement, removed the box of explosives, then quickly moved to the door, Mohammed holding the bag which was empty once more. A moment later and they were on the street. They briefly lifted their hands to shield their eyes from the sun and turned left into the flow of people, walking hurriedly away from the room that had changed their lives forever.

7

Airport Camp, Mogadishu

Christian jumped down from the 4x4 and dashed across the dusty car park towards the terminal, darting between the blast walls that acted as both the inner cordon for the airport and the entrance for those in the camp. He ran past the final barrier of overlapping cement walls towering over him, then slowed to a walk as he headed for the departure lounge. Walking around the front of the terminal building that faced the aircraft taxi area, he had to sidestep the Somali airport workers who were making a bad job of organising the luggage that had just been delivered from the inbound Nairobi flight. He slipped his sunglasses onto his head and moved as quickly as he could through the mass of bags, trolleys and people.

He finally reached the departure lounge entrance. Security was non-existent and he stepped into the deceptively large room, with its high ceiling and white-washed walls, the paint flaking in several places. Dozens of plastic chairs were randomly placed across the floor, many of them occupied by men in ill-fitting suits, women wearing hijabs and children in various states of excitement; it was a riot of noise and colour.

The departure lounge was full of passengers booked to fly to Nairobi on the aircraft waiting outside, about 50 metres away from the building, its engines idling, the pilots impatiently waiting to leave Mogadishu as quickly as possible. The heat inside was little different to that outside, the ceiling fans doing nothing more than moving the hot air around the cavernous space. Christian quickly searched the room for Megan. In the far corner he could see her silhouette through a window, standing in a VIP area, separated from economy class passengers. He walked across the room, manoeuvring between families and their bags, just as the first call was made for passengers to head to the gate. It was chaos.

'Megs!' Christian stood by a partially open door and half shouted above the noise to catch her attention. She looked round and smiled, picking up her bag and walking over to Christian who had stepped back into a corner of the main hall, away from the other passengers who were now grabbing mountains of hand luggage and making their way to the double doors that he had just walked through.

Megan put her bag down by their feet and hugged Christian. 'I didn't think you could come!' she kissed him on the cheek.

'My meeting with the Defence Minister was cancelled at the last minute so Miko managed to get us back in time. He's such a good bloke.'

Christian briefly placed his hand on her arm before dropping it to her waist. 'How long will you be in Nairobi?'

'I have to see a few people and we are going on another trip to Nakuru at the weekend. I'm due to fly back in a week's time.' She took his hand in hers, holding it gently, their faces inches apart, saying nothing for a moment.

'I have to go,' she said quietly. Her voice was soft and full of affection. He smiled at her and moved to pick up her bag.

'It's OK, I've got it, but thank you. I'll call you over the next couple of days, alright? Take care, Chris, please don't take any risks.'

'No, it's fine, I only have one more trip before the weekend, and we haven't heard any intelligence to suggest Shabaab are actively planning anything.' He put his hand in the small of her back as they both started to walk across the rapidly emptying departure hall.

'How did you end up in the business lounge, anyway?' Christian had a playful tone in his voice, but Megan could tell he was intrigued.

'Well, I do have contacts of my own in the Somali Government, you know!' she replied, pushing her elbow into his side.

As they were walking, he turned to look back at the room she had been waiting in and spotted the Defence Minister standing with another man. At least now he knew why their meeting had been cancelled.

'Is that the NSA?' Christian asked Megan, but he already knew the answer.

'Yes, we were just talking together with the Def Min.'

The NSA – the National Security Advisor – was Abdulkadir Aden, a well-known friend of the UK who had spent 20 years living in London before returning to Somalia to work in government. He had served as an elected councillor in Ealing, West London, responsible for keeping the streets safe from anti-social behaviour. A week after his arrival back in Mogadishu, reflecting his clan connections, he had quickly been elevated to the most important security role in the country. It was just how things were done in Somali politics.

'Ah, how is Councillor Aden?' Christian knew of him but he had not met him on any of his trips into Vila Somalia. Aden had kept a low profile since being back in Mogadishu.

Megan glanced at Christian and winked as they headed outside. They went through the door and paused on the sheltered walkway that surrounded this side of the 1920s terminal building. Most passengers were already queueing under the baking hot sun, waiting impatiently to enter the aircraft in a long line that snaked across the apron. Megan turned again and looked at Christian, moving her head close to his left ear so that she could be heard above the aircraft noise.

'See you in a week. I'll text you. Be safe.' Megan drew away from Christian, squeezing his arm as she did.

'Of course. Have a good flight.'

They held hands briefly, discreetly, and she turned away, stepped down onto the tarmac, and walked across to the aircraft. Christian watched her go for a moment, then scanned the onlookers, trying to see if anyone had been paying any attention to Megan, or to himself. Nobody trusted anyone in Mogadishu.

*

From her position on the back seat, Megan looked out of the Land Rover Discovery's window as it drew up at the main gates of the British High Commission in Nairobi, having already passed through one checkpoint to enter a service road completely empty of other vehicles. The strict security measures introduced following the 1998 bombings by Al Qaeda remained in force.

She had taken a detour to drop her bag at the house she used when she stayed in the city. She had also grabbed a coffee from their local café before jumping back into the vehicle that had collected her earlier from the airport following her three-hour flight from Mogadishu, via the customs check at Wajir Airport in the north of the country. It was always a long and tiring journey.

The security guard recognised the Kenyan driver and lifted the barrier to let the car in. After a brief pause to check for IEDs under the vehicle, the driver slowly pulled away, immediately turned right and looped around the modern High Commission building, descending via a ramp into the underground car park where it stopped on the first level close to a lift in the far corner of the garage.

'Thank you, David, it's always good to see you.'

'Thank you, Ma'am, and have a good day.'

Megan lifted her briefcase from her lap, opened the door and walked across to the elevator. She touched the call button. The doors opened and she stepped in, pressing the button for the 4th floor whilst simultaneously holding her security card next to the scanner. With a low beep, the lift started to rise.

As the doors opened a few seconds later, she entered a large room that looked no different to any other open-plan office in London or elsewhere. Except this was MI6's office which occupied the entire 4th floor, with access permitted for very few personnel within the High Commission. As Megan was the Ambassador in Somalia, a satellite diplomatic entity working to Nairobi, she was on the list. She stopped by the water cooler and looked around the room. There were several people sitting at their desks, typing on their laptops. At the far end was the 'box', the ultra-secure Tardis-like room impenetrable to even the most modern electronic surveillance equipment, which enabled the staff at '6' to have sensitive conversations in the knowledge that they were not being overheard.

She didn't know all the staff but soon recognised a friendly face. Megan dropped her coffee cup in the recycling and walked towards the first desk on the left where a blond-haired woman was sitting, head down, reading a document.

'Hi, Imi, how are you?'

'Oh, hey, Megan, great to see you! Good flight?' Imi stood up and gave Megan a quick hug.

'Yeah, same as ever, you know. The customs check at Wajir is such a pain. Anyway, what time is the meeting?'

'Matt's just having a chat with the boss so once he is back down from the 5th floor, we're on. Fancy a coffee?' Imi was already walking towards the kitchen.

'No thanks, I've just had one, but I'll have some herbal tea.' Imi raised her thumb in acknowledgement. Megan followed Imi, talking to her back, noting the fact that the head of MI6 was currently in conversation with the High Commissioner.

Fifteen minutes later, Matt Mackenzie stepped out of the lift and headed straight for his desk where he picked up a folder, marked 'TOP SECRET', and walked towards the 'box'. He looked across at Imi's empty desk and then waved at Megan, who was also making her way over, carrying her case and her tea. Imi was with her.

They all gathered outside, Matt punching in the code for access to the small, air conditioned three metre by three metre space. Inside there was a map board, a table and six chairs scattered around the room following the last meeting. The lighting was stark. Following Matt into the room, Megan grabbed a chair for herself and one for Imi, set them around the table, and sat down. Imi closed the heavy door.

When they had all settled, Matt opened his folder and took out a briefing document. He turned a page and looked up at Megan, who had taken out a notebook and was getting comfortable.

'Oh, notebooks away, I'm afraid, Megan. This is Op Trinket. What do you know about it?'

Megan had been invited down to Nairobi from Mogadishu to see the head of MI6 in Kenya, who ran the Secret Intelligence Service's operations across East Africa, including Somalia. It was an unusual request and one she was a bit puzzled by. Any important SIS related activity was normally passed to her via the Top Secret communications network that linked her newly built embassy in Mogadishu with Nairobi. Getting on a plane and flying to Kenya's capital city to receive a personal briefing from Matt was a first.

Megan remembered the background to the operation. Op Trinket had been dreamed up to gain a better understanding of who was pulling the strings at the highest levels of the Somali Government, especially in relation to the range of nation states who were vying for favour and influence over Somalia's politicians. The idea was simple: offer a credible individual to support the President and his Chief of Staff with security and other related advice, paid for by the British Government, to further cement the close cooperation they so often talked about in press conferences. The real purpose was to make sure that the individual shared what they were seeing and hearing with MI6. Megan's good working relationship with the NSA was going to be key. With Abdulkadir Aden introducing the idea to the President and his office, it was hoped that this would lead to the plan being welcomed with open arms. The blocker was finding the right person. Until Christian had put his head above the parapet by saving Megan a few weeks earlier, '6' had not managed to find anyone who was anywhere near suitable. Christian had dropped into their lap and the audacious plan suddenly seemed a possibility. They just needed to convince him to do it.

'Well, I know we are trying to place someone in the upper echelons of the Somali Government as an advisor, and you were looking for potential candidates.'

Matt, looking back down at his document, shifted uneasily on his chair. 'Well, we have actually found someone who is ideal for the role, but I wanted to discuss it with you first.' Megan looked confused and suddenly turned to Imi, who stared straight back at her, a dead-pan expression on her face.

'Imi, do you want to run through your thought process to give Megan the background?' Matt leaned back in his chair, responsibility shifted to his subordinate.

'Megs, as you know, trying to find someone we can place close to the President in Mog has been a bloody difficult thing to do. These opportunities do not happen very often, and we hardly ever find the right candidate for this kind of placement. But I think we have found someone.'

Megan was going to have to 'sell' the person to the NSA, so she needed to know the name. She had already sounded Abdulkadir Aden out and was maintaining a communications channel with him on the subject.

Megan didn't say anything. She continued to look intensely at Imi, who then delivered the punch line.

'We want to send in Christian when his contract ends in six weeks' time.'

When Imi stopped talking, there was a long pause. The sound of the air conditioning suddenly seemed much louder to the three of them sitting in such close proximity. The mention of Christian's name had been unexpected by Megan. She took a moment to consider what Imi had said.

'Well, his contract does run out in six weeks, but I know he is hoping to get it renewed. I think the UN want him to stay for another six months. But it's true that he is very well connected in Mogadishu. How do you propose getting him to buy into it?' Megan stopped herself saying any more. The implications for their burgeoning relationship, and for him as an individual working at the heart of the Somali Government, terrified her.

Matt leaned forward again. 'I've had a chat with Tom in London and he agrees we have to try it. Christian is bloody well connected, he is ex-military and, from what I have been told by various sources, he is a decent bloke who is still keen to do what he can for Queen and country.'

Megan quickly realised that one of those sources had been Imi, when she had asked Megan if she could go along to "meet the man who had saved your life" at Paddy's Bar earlier in the month. Megan felt faintly sick.

'So, let's cut to the chase, Megan. I know you and Christian have been seeing each other, which is absolutely fine, and none of my business, but the management of this cannot go through you. Imi will approach him, make him the offer and, if successful, she will run him. She will manage things from here in Nairobi and occasionally she may need to visit Mogadishu for meets. The special forces detachment commander in Mog will be briefed on the extraction plan should things go pear-shaped, and you will be copied into everything. But I cannot emphasise enough, you must be careful.'

Megan took a sip of her tea and processed what Matt had said. That's why she had been invited down. So that she could be personally told that Christian was going to be approached. And, in the politest way possible, she had been warned not to mix her knowledge of the operation and her relationship with him. Matt had also made the point of dropping Tom Burbridge's name into the conversation, the Africa Director back in London, to let her know this had been cleared at the highest level in the FCO. She knew Matt would never normally have brought her so close into the op, but he had had no choice.

Megan knew how to play the game and wanted to make that point. 'That's fine, Matt, I appreciate you letting me know. I will do as much or as little as you need to make the op a success.'

She turned to Imi, whom she had known for several years from their days working in London, and acknowledged what had just happened with a nod of her head.

'Great, that's what I was hoping you would say. Imi will take things from here. Any final questions?' Matt started getting his papers together, needlessly as he had barely touched them, and slipped them back into the folder.

Imi got up first and released the security door, waited for the rush of air to escape, and stepped back into the office. Matt followed Megan and touched her arm as Imi walked away back to her desk.

'Tom has told me what happened in Mogadishu. About the reason you were there and what Christian did to get you out. This is going to be a very important op so just be careful. Please, Megan, no more impulsive trips into the city, OK?'

Without waiting for an answer, Matt walked back to his desk, leaving Megan standing outside the 'box', somewhat numb at what had just happened. After a moment, she wandered back through the rows of desks heading for the lift that would take her to the ground floor and the High Commission's café. She suddenly felt very hungry, and needed to sit down, alone.

On the 4th floor, Imi picked up the phone and dialled a number. In the corner office of a non-descript building of the UN Headquarters in the Gigiri district of Nairobi, nestled amongst the 140 acres of landscaped gardens and managed woodland, a phone rang.

'Procurement Ops, Tina speaking. How may I help?'

'Hi, Tina, it's Imi. You OK?'

'Hi, Imi, yes, all good here. Just the usual. What can I do for you?'

As Tina was talking, Imi could hear her getting up and moving through an office, presumably to a quieter place.

'Can you talk?'

'Yes, go ahead.'

'Tina, we are on with the plan we discussed. Please make sure the contract is not, I repeat, *not* renewed. I will let you know when to send the email. Are you happy with that?'

'Yep. That's fine. I'll get on with it and await your text.'

'Great, thanks. I'll meet you at the usual place next week.'

Imi disconnected the call without waiting for a reply. She sat back in her chair and put her hands on her head. She had been planning Op Trinket for months and her window to place someone at the highest level of the Somali Government had been rapidly closing when Christian popped up on the radar. Since then, she had been looking forward to this moment. Everything was in place, but so much could go wrong. And her friendship with Megan was a concern.

She needed to tread carefully, with both of them.

8

Hodan District, Mogadishu

As Megan was entering the underground car park in Nairobi, two black SUVs with dark-tinted windows driving in formation headed along Industrial Road. Sweeping left at the Damanyo Army Barracks intersection, they pressed on towards the K4 roundabout along Jidka Tarabuunka under the baking Mogadishu sun. Their speed got them noticed. Two boys close to the road, standing proudly next to a line of bicycles waiting to be hired out, turned to stare at the cars. The dust kicked up by the vehicles lingered in the air, momentarily blurring the road in front of them, so much so they had to cover their faces with their hands.

As the vehicles approached the K4 roundabout, travelling barely ten metres apart, the security gate swung open to reveal a small parking area and, to the rear, two heavily armed men, dressed in black fatigues, black sunglasses, and black body armour, carrying automatic weapons. The vehicles finally slowed down to navigate the security bollards and turned into the compound. The two SUVs were soon off the street and the gates swung shut once more.

On the opposite side of the road, dressed in the clothes of a man used to living on the street, a turban scarf wrapped around his shoulders, his head covered with a *kofia*, a Somali man sipping tea and sitting on an upturned barrel reached for his phone. He tapped in a message before returning it to his pocket, picking up his glass of tea once more.

Inside the compound, a man stood on the steps at the entrance, the sun beating down on his balding head, the few strands of hair little defence against its powerful rays. He blinked and held his hand up to shield his eyes from the brightness. His skin was pale from spending too long inside, his frame slight, his shirt too big for him, his tie loose and his top button undone. He moved slightly back towards the shadow of the entrance when the security teams got out of their vehicles and began clearing their weapons in front of him.

The man Hassan had left his office to see was in the rear of the first vehicle. A diplomat like himself, Osman had a taste for danger and was as comfortable on the streets of Mogadishu as he was hosting an embassy cocktail party in Nairobi. The two men could not have been more different. Osman spotted his colleague immediately and walked across to the entrance, joining him on the step.

'Hello, Hassan, this is a first!' he joked, slapping his upper arm in a playful gesture.

'Come inside, Osman, we cannot talk here.' Hassan's reply was curt, emphasising his seniority and the seriousness of the moment.

They walked side by side into the old colonial mansion, observing its marble flooring and high alcove ceiling, then along the ground floor corridor. They passed several doors on either side before turning to their right. Hassan looked round at Osman, indicating that they were going to take the stairs down to the basement, where a secure meeting room had recently been built to host sensitive conversations. As they paused at ground level, they spotted their embassy attendant, Yusuf. Osman asked him to bring two teas as quickly as possible. Hassan led the way down the steps and took the seat with his back to the door, leaving Osman no choice but to sit opposite him, on the only other chair in the dimly lit subterranean room.

'So, tell me, what did they say?' Hassan was in no mood to waste time on pleasantries. He was under pressure to deliver and Osman's meeting was key to their entire strategy in Somalia.

'OK, OK, calm down, Hassan. I know you want to know the answers but let's not forget our civility now, shall we? We are Turkish after all, so we know how to do things properly.' Osman smiled but Hassan was irritated and about to reply when Yusuf knocked on the closed door.

'Come in!' Osman's voice boomed out.

Yusuf carried the tray into the small room and put it on the desk between them, carefully placing a glass in front of each man before quietly lifting the tray and walking out of the room, closing the door behind him.

Osman looked at Hassan closely. 'As planned, I met their regional commander; his nickname is al Dyihb – the wolf – and he said that he was able to make decisions relating to Mogadishu. So, I explained what you asked me to relay, about our offer to help them to be more effective militarily against the African Union. He wanted some evidence that we were serious so I handed over the explosives you supplied and told him that we would bring the detonators and a lot more hardware if they agree to us placing some advisors into their field units over the next few months.'

Osman paused to drink his tea. Hassan sat in silence, writing notes. Osman continued. 'He said that he would meet me again in a month's time to finalise numbers and locations, and that he would communicate with us via the usual means.'

Under the low-wattage single bulb in the meeting room, Osman's dark skin and black hair gave him a sinister look. The scar on his right cheek, received when he'd met the wrong kind of al Shabaab jihadist a month earlier, was beginning to heal, although the knife wound had been deep and had needed a number of stitches. He was the complete opposite in looks to the career diplomat in front of him. Hassan was pallid, used to living in buildings and never comfortable working outside the security of the embassy walls. Although Hassan was the senior of the two, Osman, with his military background and experience in field work, knew that he was central to their plan being a success.

'Did you get a guarantee that they would not use the explosives until we deploy our people?' Hassan looked up as he asked the question, his pen poised over his notebook.

'Yes, but he added that if we double-cross them, they will get hold of detonators and use the plastic on our embassy.' Osman laughed quietly to himself, knowing Hassan would not find it funny. Hassan sat back in his wooden chair. The desk between them was bare, other than the glasses holding the remnants of their tea. He crossed his arms and turned away from Osman, staring into the darkness beyond the glow of the light above the table.

'And do you think they will observe total secrecy?' Hassan turned back to face Osman again.

The Turkish plot was radical, and very few knew that it had even been conceived. The Turkish Government's strategy to increase its influence in Somalia was unwittingly being supported by a highly secretive plan to undermine the African Union's military effort in Mogadishu by supporting al Shabaab with weapons, explosives and military advisors. Then, when it looked as if the AU were on the brink of losing control of the city to al Shabaab, the Turkish military would withdraw its advisors, securing the weapons and explosives they had supplied. They would then use their knowledge of al Shabaab's tactics and locations to neutralise the jihadist threat once and for all by deploying a military force to defeat the terrorist group. Turkey's standing with the political leadership in Mogadishu would soar. Hassan, the head of Turkey's National Intelligence Organisation in Somalia, the *Milli Istihbarat Teşkilati*, or MIT, was responsible for making the arrangements in secret.

Osman also knew the stakes and had been working on securing the meeting with 'the Wolf' for four months. 'Yes, I do.'

'OK, you must make the arrangements as planned. I want you to be the one to work with them at first, to understand how many advisors we need to deploy and how they will be used. We will wait for a month, bring over half a dozen of them from home, and then initiate the plan. Are you comfortable with that?' It was a question that didn't need an answer.

Osman stood up from the table, pushed his chair back, and said, 'That is why I am here. We will be successful and we will prevail.' He walked past Hassan, slapping his hand onto the more senior diplomat's shoulder as he headed for the door.

Hassan waited until the sound of his footsteps had receded into the embassy building and took out his secure mobile phone. He started to type a message to his headquarters in Ankara: *The goods have been received and the invitation has been accepted. We start in 30 days.*

He pressed "send".

9

Airport Camp, Mogadishu

Christian rolled over in his bed away from the window. The blinds in his portacabin were broken at the top, so the sunlight always began to seep in around 5.45am. He could sense the change in light inside the room and tried to banish the thought from his wakening brain.

But it was no good.

He had already started to think about his early morning RV with the AU Commander at the vehicle park. He opened one eye and checked the time: 5.46am.

He rolled onto his back and began to take in the sensations of waking up in Mogadishu. He could hear the Somali workers arriving through the compound's main gate over the sound of his air conditioning. The screech of the hinges were a daily reminder that he needed to get someone to oil them.

He gently swung his feet around to the side of his bed while pushing back the duvet, taking a moment to fully wake before getting up slowly. He padded across the room to his desk chair where he had laid out his running kit the night before. Within minutes, he was out in the pale morning light. The sun was beginning to lighten the sky over the Indian Ocean, bringing with it a slight coolness to disguise what was to come later. He walked quickly along the pathways that connected each of the portacabins within the compound across the front of the shower block, its lights on, a plain white shower curtain half pulled across the only cubicle in view. He continued past the briefing room that had been converted to a store by Fred, where empty cardboard boxes of all shapes and sizes were strewn around the sides. By his office door a sand-filled blast wall doubled up as a nursery for the team's water melon crop. He arrived at the now open main gate within a minute.

'Morning!' Christian greeted the AU guard who was slumped on a plastic chair, his weapon resting on his lap, his hat at an angle on the back of his head. The recently arrived Somali workers had clearly only just woken him up.

'Morning, sir!' The guard was taken by surprise, as he always was, and started to sit up to look more official. Christian waved his arm and set off out of the gate and onto the dusty tracks for his morning run.

He found that running in the morning was a perfect way to set himself up for the day. The heat was tolerable and it appeared that the flies were late risers. His route took him to the far end of the camp, alongside the main thoroughfare, which then looped round via the runway and back towards his own compound further up the hill. The final climb was always a lung-buster if he had pushed himself too hard. He reached the ocean, where he often went swimming, and turned left next to the makeshift firing range, used by close-protection teams and special forces. The final stretch, via the private military company camp where they ate their meals, was always the harshest. The track was open to the elements, sandwiched between dense bush on the left and the runway to the right. He picked a path over the rutted tracks, found his way back onto the main drag, and was soon turning left for the final climb up to his compound and a shower. He reached the gate in 28 minutes, not his fastest, but good enough. He looked over to the guard and nodded, bending over and taking in the warm air with deep, heavy breaths.

'Good run, sir?' The guard was sitting more alertly now, his cup of tea steaming on the small table next to his chair, his helmet squarely on his head.

'Thank you, yes, not my fastest ... but not bad.' Christian was struggling to speak fluently. He paused by the side of a brick wall close to the soldier to briefly stretch his legs, then walked back towards his office. He punched in the security code on the key lock and took out the key. Once inside, he turned on the air conditioning and took out some water from the fridge. He gulped down a couple of mouthfuls and turned to look at the diary on the wall. His meeting with General Okello was at 8am. He had 90 minutes to shower, dress, grab some breakfast and either walk or get a lift with Fred to the AU's vehicle park. His trip today would not be with Horn Security; he was travelling with the AU Force Commander in his convoy. He quickly walked back to his room, closing the door behind him.

*

'Come on, Chris, we'll be late.' Fred was standing in the open doorway of the office, smiling at Christian who, now showered and changed, was finishing the last few spoonfuls of the cereal he kept in his office drawer.

'You can't rush cornflakes, Fred – has nobody ever told you that?' Christian was smiling as he got up to put the bowl next to the coffee machine.

'And has nobody ever told you it's rude to talk with your mouthful?' Fred said, laughing too.

'Touché!' Christian wiped his mouth with a cloth next to his desk and put his jacket on. He picked up his helmet and body armour, lifting his rucksack over one shoulder and headed for the door, jokingly pushing Fred out of the way before turning around to lock the office.

'I'll drop you at the vehicle park, Chris. You won't get there in time if you walk. I'll go and pick the other guys up from breakfast on my way back.' Fred took the office key from Christian and they walked together back down to where their 4x4 was parked under the awning. Christian put his sunglasses on as soon as he had dropped his gear on the back seat.

'What time do you think you'll be back, Chris? I have some chores to do this morning but I should be free by midday,' Fred manoeuvred the vehicle out of the car park and accelerated onto the track outside their compound, heading down and turning right onto the main road towards the headquarters of the African Union forces and their extensive vehicle park.

'We have a meeting with the Defence Minister to discuss the international journalist visit into Vila Somalia next month, so there is bound to be a lot of waiting around, but I am hoping it will be finished by then.'

Christian turned to look out of the window at the passing scenery. They had arrived in what felt like a matter of minutes, pulling in close to the main reception, where all vehicles, convoys and passengers needed to check in with the Chief of Logistics. It was a good system; convoys left the camp bound for Vila Somalia pretty much every day, but they also visited other locations around the city, including the stadium located in a north west suburb of Mogadishu, just off Industrial Road. At more irregular times, convoys also headed out to the city limits delivering resupplies for AU forces deployed on the front line. The Casspir armoured vehicle was the workhorse of the fleet and, although they were enormous bullet magnets for al Shabaab and were regularly targeted, there was still a lot more metal between the attacker and Christian's UK specification body armour, which gave him a degree of comfort. If push came to shove though, he would rather drive round the city with Miko any day.

Christian got out of the vehicle and grabbed his things from the backseat.

'See you later, Fred, and thanks again for the lift, my friend.' He closed the door and tapped the window with the palm of his hand. Fred put the vehicle in 'drive' and moved off, heading for the main exit as he manoeuvred around Christian, leaving him standing on the side of the vehicle park.

In front of Christian, the AU's armoured vehicles of choice were lined up in rows, reversed up against the acacia trees, which offered some shade to the crews gathered at the rear. The sun was already making its way up into the sky and the heat was rising. Many of the Casspirs had their rear doors open, some their engines running. While he was walking the 20 metres towards the reception building, four Casspirs slowly pulled out from their overnight parking places and chugged across the vehicle park towards him, the sound of their engines filling the morning air, pulling up in convoy across the front of the purpose-built reception building. This was his convoy; it was 7.55am, perfect military timing, five minutes before a parade.

'Hello, sir, how can I help you today?' Christian had walked into the building's reception area and approached a sergeant, who was standing close to the main office with a clipboard. He knew he was the dispatcher.

'Hi, Sergeant Mugisha, I'm travelling with the Commander into VS at 8am. My name is Christian Travers.' Christian pronounced his rank as 'Sar'nt'. He easily slipped back into a military environment, using language that he knew the soldiers would recognise.

The Burundian soldier immediately paid him more attention. He looked at him and for a moment Christian thought he was going to say something. Instead, he nodded imperceptibly and checked his list. 'Thank you, sir, that's fine. He hasn't arrived yet but if you could wait over by the front door, I will tell you when he is here.'

'Thank you.'

Christian had already left his stuff by the front door having taken AU transport into Mogadishu before. He grabbed some water from the cooler and stood quietly observing the scene. 'Sar'nt' Mugisha had walked back into the main office and Christian was watching him through the window. Mugisha was talking to another soldier and suddenly pointed at him through the glass. Christian raised his cup as the two soldiers inside smiled at him. He felt awkward and knew they recognised his name from the incident at Vila Somalia. He watched Mugisha lift the walkie-talkie to his mouth and speak into it. He then disappeared from view for a moment until he re-entered the reception and walked across the room to Christian.

'The Commander is just arriving outside; you need to go now. You are in the second vehicle.' He paused momentarily before adding. 'We were just saying that we are not sure whether having you in a convoy is a good or a bad omen, but on balance we think it is a good thing!'

He was smiling at Christian, who looked back reassuringly into his friendly face, gently patting the top of his arm in a companionable way.

'Thanks, Sar'nt Mugisha, I'm sure nothing will happen today.' He turned to pick up his things and went back outside into the growing heat.

Christian walked across to the rear of the second vehicle and handed his rucksack to the soldier who was already inside. He took his jacket off and put his body armour on at the bottom of the vehicle steps, fixing the Velcro tabs to keep it securely in place. He had forgotten how constricting it was. He indicated to the soldier inside that he would be a minute. He turned to walk round to the third vehicle where he hoped to see the Commander, General Okello.

'Good morning, sir, how are you today?' Christian approached the AU Force Commander as he was being given a folder by his Aide de Camp.

'Christian, good to see you. I'm well, very well. Are we all sorted for this meeting? Sorry we haven't had time to talk before now but things have been a little hot with our NGO friends.' General Okello took Christian by his elbow and led him a few yards away from the rear of his vehicle, even though the noise from the engines was enough to mask their conversation from the soldiers dashing around them. He didn't explain what he meant by "NGO friends" but Christian knew that the conduct of AU troops when deployed away from Airport Camp was always being scrutinised by local and international NGOs.

'This meeting is important, Christian, as you know. I want to make sure we get the international journalists sitting with the Defence Minister and, ideally, with the NSA. The impression of a joint effort is vital when this gets covered in the press, especially here in Africa. There are plenty of African Union members who don't see what we are doing as advancing peace and security. As long as we are all on the same page, and our Somali friends understand the context, I will be happy.' Christian had been nodding as General Okello spoke. He knew the General was not a great fan of the media, but he recognised they had a role to play in shaping international opinions, even if he didn't like the lack of editorial control. The General also knew that Christian's relationships with key people inside Vila Somalia were strong enough to make things happen.

'OK, that's it. You know I have another meeting straight after seeing Defence Minister Hassan, so one of my men will come and get you from the tea room when I am finished.'

'That's fine, General. I am sure it will go well. I'll see you when we get there.' Christian turned and walked quickly back to his vehicle and climbed up the steps, taking a seat on the left-hand side of the Casspir. Close to a tiny, reinforced window slit that gave passengers a passing view of life on the streets of Mogadishu, Christian felt like he was travelling in a large, metal coffin. The sudden burst of radio chatter between the driver and the other vehicles in the convoy indicated that they were moving off towards the city's streets. His heart rate rose. As the vehicle negotiated the ruts on the camp roads, he briefly reflected on the unwritten plan for the morning. With both General Okello and Christian meeting the Defence Minister, Abdulla Hassan, he also hoped to have an opportunity to introduce himself to the NSA, whom he still had not met and would likely be in the vicinity. Maybe he could even take him for a cup of tea. The more influential people he knew, the greater the chance of him extending his contract with the UN.

He briefly looked round his Casspir; the driver was fighting the steering wheel and talking to himself as he tried repeatedly to engage the right gear. Good luck charms hung everywhere, including across his field of view, but the Ugandan drivers were highly vulnerable and their faith in God was their shield. With him in the back was a soldier who had been assigned to accompany Christian during the journey. There was also the top cover, whose legs were planted firmly on the raised metal floor underneath the hatch, which rotated as he turned round to provide overwatch. The soldier manning the machine gun sticking out of the Casspir, partially protected by a series of metal plates welded on the roof, gripped the automatic weapon tightly as he swung round in the turret, taking aim on both sides of the vehicle as they drove. Christian settled back on his bench seat, holding his rucksack across his lap, his jacket draped over the top, his helmet involuntarily banging against the metal side of the vehicle as they negotiated the road humps at the entrance to the airport. He closed his eyes and breathed deeply, trying to find some inner calm despite the noise and movement inside the vehicle.

The journey was mercifully incident-free and he even managed to share a few jokes with Private James Adongo. The soldier initially seemed nervous to be accompanying Christian, but, as the journey progressed, he relaxed to the point that he was telling him about his family back in Entebbe. He enjoyed the banter with soldiers. Even though his military experience had been quite different to Private Adongo's, soldiers the world over always had something in common; it never took Christian long to find it.

After pulling up inside the Vila Somalia compound in the centre of the city, he patted Private Adongo's arm, jumped down from the steps, and walked across the tarmac parking area to the main government building and into the large entrance hall. Once inside, he slipped off his body armour and put his jacket on over his now drenched shirt. Perfect for sitting inside an air-conditioned office.

Christian looked around the entrance, seeking a familiar face. He recognised a few of the Somali staff who criss-crossed the entrance, carrying armfuls of papers or battered folders. He smiled at those he had met and acknowledged those he hadn't. Christian assumed General Okello had already gone to the conference room, so he took the stairs up two flights and calmly walked down the long corridor for the meeting with Abdulla Hassan. When he arrived at the room, General Okello was already seated with his ADC. One of the Defence Minister's officials was loitering by the door, waiting for Hassan to arrive.

'Morning,' Christian said.

'Morning, sir. Minister Hassan will be here shortly.' The official seemed nervous, but his English was perfect.

'Come and sit down, Christian. I'll lead but feel free to add some detail on the visit itself.' General Okello was in a hurry and wanted to manage the briefing efficiently so he could get on with his other appointments.

The meeting with the Defence Minister lasted 15 minutes. General Okello emphasised the importance of the visit and asked Christian to fill in the key activities. Christian had already given the Defence Minister a heads up on the day's details when they had been in the presidential office on his previous visit, so he didn't need to elaborate. What caught him off guard though, was Minister Hassan's praise of Christian's ability to offer sound advice whenever he was in Vila Somalia. Slightly embarrassed at Hassan's words in front of General Okello, after the meeting broke up, Christian quickly slipped away back down to the entrance area in the hope of bumping into the National Security Advisor.

He was about to give up and walk to the café for a cup of tea where he had arranged to wait for General Okello, when the Minister for the Diaspora walked into view. Her bright blue *garbasaar* and matching head scarf, contrasting with the faded white walls, chipped and peeling from years of neglect, seemed to float towards him. She locked onto his eyes as she closed the gap between them.

'Christian, hey! How are you? It's great to see you again. How long has it been?'

Muna Hussein's accent was unmistakably North American, another emigrant who had felt the calling to return to the country of her birth and make a difference. Except Muna was well educated, had worked in government at state level in the US, and had the potential to really help her country if only she had a more influential brief.

'Hello, Muna, great to see you too. You're looking well.' They shook hands and she grabbed Christian's arm, ushering him through the doorway into the café next door. They occupied a seat in the far corner away from the serving hatch and the general hubbub by the door. Muna raised her hand and indicated to the Somali attendant behind the counter that she wanted two teas brought over. She instinctively slid the sugar bowl closer to her as she spoke.

'I am well but Shabaab are making my life difficult. Bastards.'

Christian had got over the shock of hearing her swear in their conversations, something she had recently started to do more frequently. He had also stopped suggesting to her that it was a bad idea in the circumstances. Muna was discreet and saved her obscenities for him alone, or at least it felt that way. She had lived in the States a long time.

'We need so much expertise in this government and trying to entice the right Somalis to come back is getting increasingly difficult as Shabaab seem to set off bombs every week.' She paused while the tea arrived. 'People are getting fucking nervous.'

'It's normal, Muna. Why would people give up their comfortable lives in Europe, Scandinavia and the US for this?' Christian raised his hands as if to emphasise the lack of investment in the decoration of the tea room.

'All we seem to get are willing volunteers with little or no experience in a proper job. You can't run a fast-food restaurant in Minneapolis one week and then take on the responsibility for running a city's refuge collection the next.' Muna let the comment linger in the air and, as Christian turned to look her in the eye to query whether she was using a real-life example, she silently nodded, then looked down. 'It's quite disheartening.'

The teas arrived and she immediately took a sip after piling three sugars into it, as if the sweetness would cool it down enough to drink.

'That'll give you diabetes if you're not careful.' Christian winked at Muna as she raised her head at his standard comment, smiling again after her moment of melancholy. Her brown eyes sparkled with life and her charismatic personality gave Christian a lift.

'So, what are you doing here today, Christian? Who are you meeting and why?' Muna was an unashamed gossip, a consequence of growing up in the US, but also a handy trait in Vila Somalia's corridors of power.

'Well, I'm hoping to see Abdulkadir Aden; we have a visit coming up and I wanted to catch him for a few minutes to introduce myself,' Christian explained. 'I was told that he was likely to be heading this way at some stage.'

'Well, I think I might be able to help you there. I know for a fact he will be calling in for a tea before he attends the morning security brief which, as you know, takes place across the road in the presidential office.' Muna was enjoying her role as fixer. 'I'll call him over when he arrives.' She patted Christian's forearm as he cupped his warm glass with both hands.

After sending some messages on her phone, Muna soon got up and disappeared into the warren of corridors that criss-crossed the ground floor of the government building. Christian finished his tea and ordered a second cup from the attendant, borrowing Muna's approach of ordering from his seat. Within a few minutes, his second cup had been placed in front of him and Muna was back, once again sweeping into the café with a smile on her face.

'Christian, Abdulkadir Aden will be here in a couple of minutes. You will have a chance for a chat. I'll order him some tea to save time.' She turned on her heel and marched back out of the door, evidently pleased to be doing something more interesting than her mundane brief with the diaspora.

And, true to her word, she reappeared a couple of minutes later with the National Security Advisor just behind her.

'Abdulkadir, I don't think you've met Christian Travers – he's our resident Brit working in strat comms.' Muna's North American accent seemed to be even more pronounced when she said "strat comms".

Christian immediately got up and stepped away from the table where he had been sitting, extending his arm to shake Aden's hand. 'Very good to finally meet you, sir.'

'And you, Christian, but please call me Abdulkadir. I only have a few minutes before my next meeting. Shall we sit down?' No sooner had they both settled at the table than Abdulkadir's tea arrived with the attendant. 'Oh goodness, that's service for you!'

Aden's words were a curious mix of heavily accented Somali with a smattering of west London, with the "you" sounding closer to "ya". He was dressed in a grey suit that was slightly too big, a pair of sunglasses protruding from his breast pocket, his white shirt complemented by a subdued gunmetal and brown striped tie. His shoes had definitely seen better days. But people like Aden did not come back to Somalia to make money; he had returned to make Somalia more stable. He looked as if he was living an austere life. This was what fascinated Christian.

'I think Muna pre-ordered for you.' Christian felt as if he had to explain the tea's sudden appearance.

'Yes, and she seemed very keen for us to meet. What can I do for you?'

Christian wanted to make a good impression, conscious of his desire to extend his contract, so he launched into his prepared speech about the importance of hosting the international journalists during their upcoming visit to the city.

'I was hoping you may be able to spare a few minutes to address the media during their visit to Vila Somalia. We obviously hope to line up the Defence Minister, and a couple of other officials, but it would be great if you could spare the time.' Christian looked him in the eye throughout, just to make sure his message wasn't lost on his guest.

'Christian, I'll tell you what I will do, I'll give a short talk about the current state of security and the importance of international donors working together to help our army become a force that everyone will be proud of. And I will make a point about the need for good people from the international community to come here to help us. Will that be OK? It's vital for us to be able to get that message out too.'

'That would be great, Abdulkadir, thank you.' Christian immediately relaxed as they both took a moment to sip some tea. 'And how are you finding things now that you have been back in Mogadishu for several months? Do you miss London at all?'

On mentioning London, Abdulkadir burst out laughing, a raspy laugh that filled the café and made the attendant look across to them.

'Yes and no, Christian. I miss some of the processes that existed to allow us to do our jobs, and the general sense of collaboration. Those processes are missing here, along with many other things needed to deliver a country's administration, but I know that this is where I need to be now.' He took another sip of tea and lowered his voice. 'I understand you have been doing a good job in the UN, and that you helped out your – *our* compatriot – a few weeks ago. That has impressed me.' Christian was pleased that Abdulkadir had corrected himself, as he knew he had British citizenship as well as holding a Somali passport.

'I did what any ex-military man would do, Abdulkadir.'

'Well, even so, I have a huge respect for the UK Armed Forces and wish there were more involved here in Somalia. Alas, we have to work with what we have and make the best of it.' Abdulkadir glanced at his watch and took a final swig of his tea. 'I must head off now.'

'Of course.' Christian stood up, moving his chair underneath the table to give Abdulkadir an easier route to the exit.

'Thanks for your time today. I'm glad we finally met. Also, thanks for agreeing to help out with the visit.'

'Here is my card, look after it. If you have any issues you need me to address before the visit, text me.' Christian took the card and slipped it into his pocket, amazed and delighted he had been trusted enough to be given direct access to the country's National Security Advisor, any thought of him as a councillor in Ealing long forgotten.

'I will, and thanks again.'

'One last thing – when does your contract finish?'

Christian was taken aback by the question but kept his composure. 'I have about five weeks left. I'd like to stay for a further six months. I should know pretty soon whether they will renew my contract, but you know what the UN can be like.'

Abdulkadir smiled and patted him on the arm. 'I'm sure something will come up.'

They shook hands and looked each other in the eye one last time before Aden turned and walked out of the door, across the reception area and out of the building for his meeting in the presidential office. Christian sat back in his chair once again, taking a moment to absorb what just happened.

As if she had been listening at the keyhole, Muna reappeared and joined Christian at the table again.

'Honestly, Christian, the things I do for you!' She winked at him and then looked around, keen to know who had entered the café so she could work out who she would be talking to next. She was a social butterfly and Christian's allotted time was up. She sat there sullen and brooding for a minute or two without speaking. Finally, she roused herself and tapped Christian's hand which was resting on the table. 'OK, I have to go now; I hope your meeting was fruitful.'

She got up and turned to face Christian, who was now also standing. It felt like they were playing a strange version of musical chairs. She lowered her voice so they would not be overheard.

'Listen to me. There are some bad things going on in Mogadishu at the moment, Christian. We had that terrible bombing that destroyed the AMISOM vehicle down south last week, killing everyone on board. Take care of yourself and your team. I know what a great job you are all doing. And look me up soon!'

Without warning, she hugged Christian and left, her blue *garbasaar* flowing behind as she disappeared from view.

As Christian watched her leave, he couldn't help thinking about what she meant when she referred to "bad things". His mind returned to his conversation with Mac at Art Café a few weeks earlier. The situation was complicated enough without cryptic comments from people he knew were on the inside, and he made a mental note to follow up Mac's reference to Turkey. All he wanted to do was get back to his laptop and start digging into their activities in Somalia.

His trip back across the city to MIA couldn't come soon enough.

10

Spring Valley, Nairobi

Christian closed his laptop, got up from the kitchen table and walked to the open French windows, juice in hand. The warm air blowing gently through the sheer curtains enticed him onto the balcony.

He had got back to his Nairobi apartment the evening before, after spending two weeks in Mogadishu. Having seen the National Security Advisor in Vila Somalia and talking to Muna on the Monday, he had stayed in his office inside Airport Camp for a couple of days, taking care of routine matters with his team whilst also researching on the internet, trying to understand what the Turks were up to in Somalia. Now back in Kenya, with its more relaxed atmosphere and better climate, he had a little more time to digest what he had found out.

He stood looking out across the secure forecourt of his apartment block, over the security wall and the service road beyond, which was lined with huge cactus plants and a variety of impressively sized palm trees. To his right, out of sight, a moped started and began to head towards him, the thunder clap rasp of its two-stroke engine growing louder every second until it came into view, a result of poor tuning and makeshift parts. The engine filled the tranquil scene with an ugly, machine gun-like noise that startled the birds and assaulted the ears, the helmetless rider oblivious to the effect on his ever-changing environment. Christian waited until the sound had been muffled by the vegetation and sat down again.

The Turks had opened an embassy, which he knew from being in the city. According to *Al Jazeera*, they had also made a financial offer to support the training of the Somali National Army. The SNA, as they were known, had been supported by a mixture of international donors over the years, but the result was a disjointed, often poorly trained rabble. Turkey was promoting their version of soft power in Muslim-majority countries around the fringes of Africa. They had made a strategic decision to reel in the Somalis, at least that's what it looked like from the reports Christian had managed to find online. A recent senior Turkish politician had met Somali leaders in Vila Somalia. In response, senior Somali military leaders had been invited to a training facility outside Turkey's capital, Ankara. It all made sense but, on the face of it, it wasn't particularly threatening or unusual for there to be an unhealthy competition amongst international donors to help countries in need. He would at least be able to check some of his assumptions next time he met up with Mac and decided to drop him an email.

Subject: Christmas

Hi Mac, hope all's well with you. Did a bit of digging on the subject we talked about over lunch and nothing came up as out of the ordinary, just another player on the pitch! Looking forward to catching up soon. Christian

He pressed "send", looked at his watch and prised himself out of his deck chair. He had an appointment to make. Once out of the building, he turned left and was soon sitting in the Land Rover's battered leather seat. With his hands on the steering wheel, he took his phone out and looked again at the message he'd received the evening before from Imi. He had only been back in Nairobi a few hours when it had come in.

Hi Christian, it's Imi here, got your number from Megs. Fancy a coffee tomorrow morning? Shall we say 11am at Amaica Café? I

Christian hadn't seen Imi since their drinks at Paddy's Bar a few weeks before and was looking forward to a chat, although he was intrigued as to why she wanted to meet him without Megan being there. He had sent a text to her in Mogadishu, telling her about the meeting with Imi, but the message had bounced, which wasn't unusual for Somali mobile providers.

After driving for ten minutes, he turned right off the tarmac road that snaked through Spring Valley onto a bumpy track that led up to Amaica Café. The high canopy of dense trees forced the sun to cast deep shadows over the ground and he immediately hit a huge pothole. He hadn't visited the café before, although he had driven past it many times on his way to his office next to the UN compound in Gigiri. He drove into a large car park, the uneven surface overflowing with pools of water glistening in the sunlight, the early morning rain having left its calling card on the muddy ground.

It had just gone a quarter to eleven.

He eased the Land Rover into a parking slot close to the building, and opened his door, looking down to make sure he didn't step into a puddle. Amaica Café was hidden away from the main road, surrounded by dense bushes and trees encouraged to grow to gigantic proportions by the fertile soil and favourable climate, masking its presence from all but the most knowledgeable clients. The small sign on the main road was easily missed. Set back from the car park, a large decking area with a canopy of rectangular cream-coloured parasols providing shade for the dozens of empty tables neatly arranged below, the café was the epitome of discretion.

He slipped out of his seat and, swinging the driver's door shut behind him, headed towards the steps. There was no need to lock it: car thieves weren't going to bother stealing a 20-year-old ex-military Land Rover with 150,000 miles on the clock. He chose a table to one side of the decking area, facing the car park but out of earshot of two men, probably western diplomats, who were talking quietly on the far side. The waiting staff, dressed in white shirts buttoned to the collar and black trousers, were quietly attentive. He quickly caught the young waitress's eye and when she arrived at the table, he ordered a coffee.

Looking around, Christian wondered why Imi had arranged to meet at Amaica. It wasn't anywhere he had visited before as it was off the beaten track; perhaps she'd chosen it for that reason. He wondered whether it was to tell him something about Megan, or perhaps to ask more questions about his role in Mogadishu. Either way, he was certainly curious.

A few minutes later, he heard a vehicle approaching slowly up the track from Peponi Road. He didn't recognise the car when it turned into view, but he knew the driver. His coffee arrived as Imi drove across the car park.

'*Asante sana.*'

'You're welcome, sir.'

The sound of the vehicle slowly splashing its way through the puddles echoed between the tall trees on all sides. When the engine was switched off, the silence was so sudden it felt as if all living things in the vicinity were holding their collective breath. As quickly as the silence had enveloped the scene, normality returned. The low murmur of conversation from the two men sitting outside at the far end of the decking began to creep back into his consciousness and the constant tweeting of birds, chatting away with excitement in the branches above, made him involuntarily look up to the trees. He decided he would come here again.

As the door slammed shut, he heard a faint curse. 'Arrgghh, bloody hell!' Imi's voice carried to his table. As she came into view, she looked across at Christian and shrugged her shoulders, smiling self-consciously before heading towards the steps and his table.

Christian stood up and smiled; they kissed each other once on the cheek and sat down together. He turned round to look for the waitress but she was already walking across to their table. 'Hey Imi, what can I get you? Pair of dry socks?'

She was grumbling quietly to herself, questioning who on earth had come up with the idea to meet there. 'Hey, Christian. Very funny.' She turned to the waitress. 'I'll have a green tea, please.'

They both sat down in silence while Imi took off her wet shoe, wrung out her sock, and replaced it again. 'It's good to see you, Christian. How have you been these last few weeks? Have you heard anything about your contract yet?'

Christian stole a look at Imi. She was wearing skinny jeans, white pumps, a white T-shirt and a blue unzipped hoodie which was slipping off one of her shoulders. Her blond hair was loose, sitting on her shoulders, and she looked as stunning as the first time they had met.

'I'm fine thanks, everything is going well. We have a key visit coming up in a week's time and then I hope I'll get confirmation of an extension for six months. You know what the UN is like, though – with four weeks to go they still haven't made a decision, which I think is pretty much in my favour ... but it all rests on the "good offices of the UN".' Christian used his fingers to apply inverted commas to emphasise the final words. 'I am expecting confirmation from procurement any day now.'

'That's good. But you shouldn't put all your eggs in one basket. Have you got any other options in case it falls through?' Her northern accent seemed to underline the need to make sensible choices.

Christian sighed immediately. 'You're right. To be honest, I really haven't looked around for anything else. I definitely don't want to go back to England yet, I'm not ready. So, if this falls through, I guess I will be packing up my apartment at the end of my contract and taking the first flight out.'

He turned away and stared into the distance for a moment. She took the opportunity to look at Christian again. She could see tension in his face and he was biting his lip, no doubt unaware that he was doing so. She could tell that he was dreading the thought of having to leave. Although Imi knew about his professional background, and the recent trauma in his private life, she hadn't really got to know Christian beyond the basics. She needed to learn a little more about him.

'Do you have plans for Christmas? Will you be staying in Kenya or heading back to the UK?' Imi was making small talk while waiting for the tea to arrive.

'That's a great question. I would love to stay here for Christmas but I haven't seen my parents and friends for months, so I'm heading back regardless of the contract outcome.'

'Where do your parents live in England?' The question she really wanted to ask was left unsaid. *How are you coping after the loss of your wife last year?*

Before he could answer, the waitress arrived with Imi's tea, placing the cup in front of her and putting a bottle of water on the table. Imi poured some into each of their glasses and took a sip. The arrival of the drinks had broken the flow of conversation.

Christian reached for his coffee and drank some just as the sound of a dropped pan inside the café made them both exchange a knowing glance. Christian, feeling apprehensive, stayed silent, waiting for Imi to speak. *She* had invited *him* to have a coffee after all.

Imi leaned forward in her seat and then spoke quietly. 'Chris – do you mind if I call you Chris? OK, good, I'll come straight to the point; we would like you to do something for us.' Imi paused while she scrutinised Christian's face, which was showing signs of surprise. 'Basically, we have been looking for someone to help us steer the Somali Government in a more, how should I put it, western facing direction when it comes to national security. We have been in negotiations with Vila Somalia for months, through Megan and her team, to get them to agree to someone, a Brit, working alongside the Defence Minister and, by default, the Office of the President. I know you have contacts in the defence section in Nairobi, but this is outside their remit, so I would appreciate it if you could keep this to yourself for now.'

Imi paused again. This time she took a drink of her tea and waited a few moments before speaking again.

'They agreed a while ago to someone being embedded in Vila Somalia, but we've never managed to find the right person with the right background, credentials and local knowledge. You know how these things go.' Imi was looking directly into Christian's eyes, which never left her face. 'That is, until you popped up on the radar after saving Megs from al Shabaab.' Imi smiled and looked away at the two men sitting on the other side of the decking, inviting Christian to fill the silence. He didn't.

Imi continued. 'I know you are waiting for your contract renewal to come through but, if it doesn't happen, I would like you to consider working for the High Commission in an advisory role on an initial six-month contract. The role would be to provide strategic advice to the Defence Minister on the best approach to building up the SNA, acting as a confidential sounding board for him while he is dealing with so many donors within the security space. We will arrange for you to be able to reach back into the UK military for anything you may think is needed to support the work you do. I know it's a lot to take in, but how does that sound?'

This was not what Christian had been expecting. He shuffled uncomfortably in his chair and took a drink of coffee. 'Well, erm, I'm flattered that you think I could do that kind of role. It's obviously a very interesting offer, but I have my contract with the UN and I am sure they will be asking me to stay.'

Imi had been expecting Christian's response. She knew from his records that one of Christian's strengths was his loyalty and turning his back on his strat comms role at short notice was not in his make-up.

'That's fine Christian. I told my colleagues that I didn't think you would want to do it, but I was asked to put it to you all the same. And, if you're wondering, Megs knows I was going to find an opportunity to raise it with you.' Imi lifted a small bag onto her lap from her feet and took out a pen and paper.

'If this is supporting the Defence Minister, why isn't it going through the defence section? And I thought you said you worked on economic policy,' Christian said. Knowing how things worked in High Commissions, he was intrigued why someone like Imi had approached him.

'We debated this for quite a long time to be honest and we all agreed that it was primarily a political appointment, reflecting the company you will be keeping ...' she flashed him a smile. 'My role covers our political effort in support of Megan as well ... And the defence section is far too busy anyway; I'm sure you know that already,' Imi added, hoping that Christian would accept the explanation as a *fait accompli*.

She started scribbling some notes in a notepad and then handed a sheet of paper to him over the table.

'Chris, these are the terms, in abbreviated form. If you decide that you want to come and do this, call me and we will get the contract sorted out. You would have access to the B&B in Mog but you would be expected to be living in accommodation in Vila Somalia for four-week stints, hence the day rate. I did my best to make it attractive.'

Christian took the paper from her and looked down at what she had written:

£1000 day rate, 4 weeks in Mog, 2 weeks out, 6-month contract, support from the embassy in Mog if needed, security/med support while in Africa. Starting New Year.

He exhaled quietly, quickly calculating how much he would be able to earn over the course of the six months. Not that money was everything to him but being able to put something towards a house deposit was one of the reasons he had decided to head out to Africa in the first place. It was a dream come true. He would be able to afford a mortgage when he finally returned to the UK to get on with the rest of his life. And he would be able to see more of Megan, which until then had been proving to be quite a challenge. His mind was racing. He had almost forgotten that Imi was still there.

'Anyway, Christian, if you want to know more, give me a shout. I'm normally in Nairobi, but I do travel up to Mogadishu from time to time.' With that final comment, Imi got up, taking the bill with her, and walked inside the café, leaving Christian to finish the dregs of his coffee. He stood up and started to walk towards the steps. Imi joined him as they walked to their vehicles.

'You know, Chris, you are very well respected by the Somalis and they are in real need of advice from someone they feel they can trust. Have a think about it. Take care, see you soon.' Imi reached up and kissed him on the cheek and turned away, carefully navigating the path back to her car.

'Bye, Imi, and thanks for the coffee. Oh, and Oxford. My parents live in Oxford.' He shouted after her.

Imi didn't turn around. She raised her hand and waved before disappearing from view.

Once in the car, Imi checked that Christian wasn't watching from his seat and pulled out her mobile to send a text.

Hi Tina, it's Imi, send the email in the morning, please, first thing, as discussed.

She quickly sent another message to the Head of MI6 in Kenya;

Hi Matt, it went as planned. He has taken the bait. Delivery tomorrow. Imi

She threw her phone on the passenger seat of the MI6 vehicle and started the engine. There were some aspects of her professional life that she found difficult, but her engagement with Christian was not one of them. She had immediately taken to him when researching his background after his heroics in Mogadishu with Megan. Her boss had doubted the likelihood of her idea to get someone on the inside and then use his presence to give the UK strategically important insight within Somali decision-making, but that was until Imi had presented Christian as the solution. Not even she could have dreamed it would work out as well as this. The decision to go ahead had been taken in London at a senior level.

Placing Christian at the heart of the Somali Government was going to be a coup for her personally and professionally. It felt to Imi that her years of working in MI6 were beginning to pay off. Although nobody from MI6 had "tapped" her on the shoulder, a lecturer at university had once remarked during a tutorial that she had all the attributes of being a spy after she had been less than open about some of her sources for an essay she had written about the rise of Islamic fundamentalism. Having studied politics with French, he had concluded that with her northern background it was unlikely that she would be successful joining the Secret Intelligence Service and had told her as much. Instead, he suggested that she consider the UN, or journalism. His comment had stung. Joining MI6 had always been an ambition for Imi once she had learned more about the role. As soon as she had joined, she felt that she had something to prove. Finally, she was in touching distance of pulling off something that would get her noticed.

The intelligence product that she was hoping to secure through Christian's position in Vila Somalia would be vital if the UK was going to keep one step ahead of its rivals in the region. Megan had already tapped into the dual citizenship loyalties of Abdulkadir Aden, the National Security Advisor. Imi knew that a member of his extended family was living in West London illegally and, although she had no plans to use that piece of intelligence just yet, if she needed to she would bring that into play. It had been a long-term team effort. She just needed the last couple of pieces of the jigsaw to fall into place.

Most of all, she hoped that Christian was going to be willing to take the risk. The signs so far were good.

11

Spring Valley, Nairobi

The following day, sitting at his kitchen table preparing a presentation for the journalists' visit the following week, Christian saw an email notification on his laptop screen. It was from the UN. He minimised what he was doing and opened the message.

Subject: Renewal of Strategic Communications Contract

Dear Christian,

After a great deal of consideration, it has been decided that the role of strategic communications delivery in Somalia in support of AMISOM is going to be brought in-house, and therefore the remaining period of the contract will be managed from within UN resources. All relevant parties have been informed of this decision, which is final.

We would like to take this opportunity to thank you for your significant contribution to the mission and wish you well in your next role. Once you have handed over any in-flight projects, all existing commitments and activities will be assumed by the UN management team. You will of course have the opportunity to collect any personal effects remaining in Mogadishu and receive full compensation.

Yours sincerely,

Tina Worthington

Deputy Head of UN Procurement (People)

After the first three lines, Christian had hardly taken in the rest of the message. He was stunned.

'Shit!' He sighed. He had just booked a return ticket to London for Christmas, leave that had been planned for a long time. He was not going to make any changes to that trip, but it was a return ticket and the only reason for coming back had been snuffed out. He wasn't ready to go back to the UK, he needed more time; more time to save money and more time to get ready for whatever the future held for him.

'Shit!' he shouted at the top of his voice.

He sat back, his head resting on the chair. He needed to get something sorted, and quickly. He leaned forward and put his head in his hands, trying to take in the unexpected news.

'Shit!' He almost whispered the word. The visit that he had worked so hard to coordinate would now be taking place without him. He got up and walked towards the balcony, the morning warmth beginning to penetrate the apartment inch by inch along the floor as the sun rose quickly in the sky.

His thoughts immediately turned to Imi. The chance to work for the British Government as an advisor was a great opportunity and he hadn't been happy leaving the military prematurely, so this looked like a brilliant way to make a difference for his country again. He couldn't believe his luck; his meeting with Imi the day before was just the break he needed. He put his hand in his jeans pocket and pulled out the piece of paper that she had written on, flattening it out on the kitchen table. The timing could not have been better. He grabbed his phone. *Megs, call me as soon as you can, no emergency, just need to talk. C*

He hoped that the message would get through this time.

Christian paced around the room. He felt a strong sense of duty towards his team and, in particular, to Fred who had supported him in his mission with such dedication over the last six months. He knew he would see him again but it didn't alleviate the sense of loss he suddenly felt. There were too many loose ends for his role to be cut so abruptly. It felt as if he had been sacked, but he knew it was nothing personal, just UN bureaucracy.

He felt both disappointed about losing his role but elated at the same time. There was nothing for it but to get drunk.

The next message was to Imi: *Hi Imi, I'm going drinking tonight. Feel free to join me. Same place. It looks like I may well be taking you up on your offer after all. Chris*

By the time he finally received the call he had been waiting for all day, he was already on his second Guinness in Paddy's Bar.

His phone rang. 'Hey, Chris, where the hell are you? I can hardly hear you,' said Megan.

'Megs, it's so good to hear your voice. I'm out at Paddy's, drowning my sorrows. The UN have cut the contract and haven't renewed my position.

Some bullshit about taking the role in-house. Jesus, I did everything to deliver that contract ... Anyway, I'm here; where are you?'

'Oh, Chris, I'm so sorry. I haven't been able to call you because I've been travelling.'

A group of what sounded like French expats walked into the bar and stood behind Christian who was sitting on a bar stool. He watched the group in the mirror behind the bar. The volume went up, making conversation all but impossible.

'Sorry, Megs, a group has just walked in, what did you say, you've been travelling? Are you still in Mog?' Christian had his left hand pressed against his ear to try to cut out some of the noise. 'It's really hard to hear you, Megs – can you send me a text? I'll try to find somewhere quieter in a minute to call you back.'

Megan was speaking but Christian could barely hear what she was saying and ended the call. His phone buzzed almost immediately. *I was saying that I am in Nairobi. I'll be with you in an hour. M x*

Christian read the text over and over. Megan had never ended a message with a kiss. And she was unexpectedly back in Nairobi. And she was coming to see him. He smiled and held up his pint to the barman. 'One more, please, my friend.'

He replied to Megan: *Excellent! Can't wait to see you. Imi might be coming too. C x*

The French group moved away to one of the stalls at the rear, the sound of excited chatter going with them. Although it was only 5pm, the bar was filling up fast with westerners, both men and women, racing across town from their UN or other international charity jobs to enjoy a few drinks during happy hour on "the strip", as the street was colloquially known. Christian took another sip from his pint and picked up his phone to send another message to Imi, to tell her that Megan was in town, when a call came in from her.

'Hey, Imi, how are you?' Christian said.

'Hi, Christian, I've just got your message. Where are you?' Imi replied.

'I'm still drowning my sorrows in Paddy's Bar.' Christian added a laugh at the end to let her know that he was OK. 'You?' Throughout the afternoon, he had spent a lot of time pacing around his apartment, weighing up his options, which were extremely limited, and had come to the conclusion that he had no choice: he needed to take the advisor role in Mogadishu. He wanted to see Imi to confirm his interest face to face.

'Ah OK, no problem, I thought you might be. I'm on my way but I can't stay. I should be there soon. Bye.' Imi hung up almost immediately.

'Bye, Imi,' Christian replied but the line had already been cut.

He didn't have to wait long before he heard Imi's familiar northern twang cut across the bar to where he was sitting. He got up and kissed her once on the cheek before grabbing his drink and leading her to a booth he had reserved a few minutes before.

'What will you have, Imi?' Christian assumed she would be joining him.

'I'm OK thanks, Chris. I know Megs is back and that she is on her way over here so I won't stay long. I just need to clarify a few things about this role. Are you OK to talk about it briefly now?'

Christian was sitting facing Imi, his pint in front of him, when the barman came over to their table.

'Let's have one to celebrate my acceptance of the job, Imi; come on, it won't do you any harm ...'

'OK that's fine, I'll have a glass of white wine, please.' The barman nodded and walked off. The French group were a couple of booths away, their celebrations continuing.

'Chris, I am going to get the contract sent over in the morning. I need you to sign it and get it back to me asap. I know you are going on leave so that's fine, take your time, but we need you to be on the Mog flight on 10th Jan. You'll be able to keep your apartment here as we will cover all expenses when you are in and out of Somalia. You have the basics on that piece of paper but it will all be confirmed in the contract's T&Cs ...' Imi was so focused on getting this information across to him she didn't notice her wine arrive. Christian was all ears.

'Chris, I'll not be in touch with you until the new year, but from that moment forward I will be your point of contact for what you are going to be doing. We'll meet again before you fly up there, just to clarify things, but otherwise I am delighted to tell you that you will be our first strategic advisor to the Somali Government. Congratulations!'

They both held up their glasses, chinking them loudly together, simultaneously saying 'Cheers!'

They drank and sat back on opposite sides of the table, thinking their own thoughts, unaware of the din surrounding them.

After a few moments, Imi leant forward and said, 'Right, I have to get going. I don't want to play gooseberry *again* ...' Imi's emphasis on *again* made them both laugh, but she was soon shuffling out of the booth, making sure she had everything with her. Christian also slipped out and stood opposite her, trying to keep his voice steady and as low as he could get away with, despite the alcohol he had already consumed affecting his volume button.

'Imi, this is cleared at the highest levels in Vila Somalia, right? I don't want to be having to fight my way into conversations with senior ministers if they are not expecting me.' Christian's face was as determined as she had ever seen it, but his question had already been anticipated by Imi, who moved closer to reply.

'It's cleared with the Defence Minister, the National Security Advisor and the President's Chief of Staff. You'll be presented in this role to the President in due course. The government in Mog needs support on national security and they already pretty much know you, so I don't foresee any issues. The international community may feel a bit put out but we can live with that. The most important thing is that the Somalis trust you.'

Christian nodded and shook Imi's hand.

'If I'm going to be working for you, we should be a little more formal, don't you think?' Christian said. Imi responded in kind and gave him a wink as she turned to fight her way through the now very busy bar and out onto the street beyond. Christian lost sight of her and retreated to the booth to wait for Megan.

It wasn't long until she arrived, drink in hand, working her way through the crowd to Christian. He was lost in his own thoughts, cradling his drink, when she appeared at the table,

'Penny for them ...?'

He looked up and stood up in the same action, opening his arms as Megan moved towards him. They embraced and, without any hesitation, their lips met for a long passionate kiss.

'Well, now Chris, that was unexpected!' Megan had managed to keep the wine in the glass that was still in her hand, placing it on the table and pushing Christian down on one side of the booth. She slipped onto the bench seat next to him, their backs to the entrance.

'I think you may be getting drunk, Mr Travers,' Megan said, smiling as she took a long gulp of her wine, subconsciously making up for lost time. 'I can see I'm going to have to get another drink in to catch up!'

Christian kissed Megan again, holding her face gently in his hand as he did. Megan had rushed back on the morning flight as soon as she realised that Imi's plan was in play but delays at the normal immigration stopover at Wajir had meant her travelling time had been extended to five hours. She was exhausted and hungry. But she knew she had to be with Christian, if only to make sure he didn't change his mind about the job in Mogadishu. This was just the start of the conflict she had felt after being briefed on the plan by Matt all those weeks ago. It unnerved her.

'Chris, I'm hungry and I'm tired. Can we grab some food and head somewhere less crowded?' The suggestive way she phrased the question meant only one thing to Christian, who by now was losing his inhibitions.

'Well, I made a Bolognese sauce last night and there's enough for two, so if you are happy to come to my place, we can have dinner there ...' Christian let the sentence drift into silence, the exchange so close and intimate that the ambient noise failed to break the spell. 'I can text Henry and he'll run us to the apartment; it's only ten minutes from here.'

'Thanks, Chris, I'd like that,' Megan said.

They got up from the table a few minutes later when Henry texted to say that he was waiting at the usual place. Megan clutched a small bag and Christian put his arm around her as they bumped and bounced their way through the crowd of drinkers, both of them independently scanning the room for anyone they might know. Once out on the street, the darkness was punctuated by the flashing neon lights from the bars lined up along the strip, people walking in every direction, groups laughing and joking together, oblivious to what was happening around them. Christian spotted Henry's car and opened the door for Megan.

'Hi, Henry, thanks for coming at short notice. This is my friend, Megan,' Christian said.

'Hello, Ma'am, good to meet you.' Henry looked in his rear view mirror at his new passenger and smiled.

'You too, Henry, and thanks for the lift,' Megan replied.

The journey passed quickly, Megan holding Christian's hand tightly until they came to a stop outside the metal gates, which immediately started to open.

'Goodnight, Henry, be safe.' Christian tapped the car roof as he said it and thanked the guard as they both walked the short distance from the gate to the entrance of the apartment block. 'I'm on the third floor,' Christian added nervously.

Once inside the apartment, Christian switched on a couple of side lights and headed to the kitchen while Megan walked round the room slowly, taking it all in. Christian busied himself with preparing dinner and clearing the kitchen table of his laptop and papers that were spread across it. He had forgotten what a mess he had left the place in.

'Sorry, I wasn't expecting company!' Christian looked at Megan who was standing by the French windows, pulling the sheer curtains to one side to look down onto the darkened scene below.

'You have a great place here you know.'

Christian looked at her, her yellow cotton dress emphasising her figure in the half-light, her hair loose on her shoulders; he was struck again by how attracted he was to her.

'Thanks, it's been my sanctuary in more ways than one these last few months. It took a while to find it when I first came to Nairobi, but once I did, I knew I wanted to stay here. I feel at home. The only downside is the pool never gets the sun so it's brassic!' Megan laughed at his use of the word.

'That must be a military term. The only other person I've heard use that word is the Defence Advisor.' She laughed and accepted the glass of red wine Christian had offered her.

The pasta was nearly done, the sauce was bubbling away in the pan and the kitchen table had been transformed into an intimate table for two, together with a half-used candle and saucer he had found in a cupboard sitting on top of an old Le Carré novel.

'Yeah it's military slang. I'm afraid I often use words and phrases that leave people non-plussed!' Christian said as they sat down on the blue two-seater sofa. Megan sank backwards and only just managed to keep her glass upright. 'Sorry, Megs, should have warned you, it's very, how should I put it, welcoming!' They both lay back, the sofa all but consuming them, and felt the warmth of each other's bodies as their arms and legs touched.

'How long have you known Imi?' Christian said after a few moments, still thinking about his earlier meeting.

'We used to work together in London when I was a desk officer looking after the Balkans. We got to know each other through work, you know how things are in the FCO.' She was looking at Christian with a knowing look. 'But we don't want to be talking about Imi do we ...?'

'You're right, come on, let's eat, I'm hungry!'

Christian couldn't remember the last time he had anything close to a romantic meal and said so to Megan. 'I know we haven't talked so much about our lives, and living in the moment is a great thing, but I have strong feelings for you, Megs.' Christian had not planned to discuss how he felt, but the combination of the earlier beers and the red wine had given him the courage to finally tell her. 'I hope that's not going to make you run for the hills.'

'No Chris, it's not ... I feel the same way.' She paused to take a mouthful of pasta, trying desperately not to fling spaghetti onto her dress.

They ate quietly after that, both content in the mutual feelings they had for each other, occasionally talking about their previous jobs and how their lives had been so different. Imi's job offer came up again and he told her that he would be taking it in the new year. They were both happy about the potential of seeing more of each other. Music was playing on the iPad, the candle was crackling as it burned, and the wine flowed into both glasses.

'When do you fly back to the UK, Chris?'

'Well, my flight is in about nine days but I could bring it forward; I haven't decided. How long are you in Nairobi?' Christian said.

'I'm flying in a week's time then back to Mog for the New Year – it's all to do with giving everyone a chance to have some family time, so I get Christmas and my deputy gets New Year in Scotland!' Megan said.

'Why don't we try to get on the same flight? I'll speak to the airline in the morning. There's nothing keeping me here now the role has ceased, apart from a quick handover to the UN,' Christian said.

'That would be fun, Chris, let me know how you get on before I check in.' Megan smiled at the idea of spending eight hours alongside Christian rather than a total stranger.

They were both at ease, but they knew they needed to open up. A silence followed the discussion about flights, both working out in their own minds how much and what to say. Finally, Megan spoke.

'I was always the sporty one at school. I was pretty good academically too ... I went to private school as a boarder ... and when I got into Cambridge, my career seemed to be mapped out. I was always going to be a diplomat, it runs in the family: my father was an ambassador back in the day, too. Chile of all places. So, everything in my life was on track, then ... bang, it was all over ... I had a serious relationship a while ago, I can't even bring myself to say his name, we were going to get married, have kids, the normal routine, but things changed and for reasons I still don't really understand, we broke up. I was lost at sea. It wasn't part of the plan ... it really shifted the tectonic plates beneath my feet ... so, I've just been focusing on my career and getting appointed as Ambassador to Somalia is something I am very proud of, even if it is a junior post in the big scheme of things. And I've not been in a relationship since.' Megan took a gulp of wine. Her abbreviated life story was as unexpected as it was welcome, and it felt to Christian that she had unpeeled an important layer of her life away for him.

Christian sensed their relationship was heading into new territory. He knew he had to talk about his own story, something he had avoided doing for over 12 months.

'I'm sorry about that, Megs, it must have been so hard, especially if you never really worked out what went wrong.' Christian took her empty plate and exchanged a smile with her. She was now propping up her head with her hand. When he sat down again after placing the plates in the sink, she noticed that he looked preoccupied and didn't seem to know where to start.

'Just take it one sentence at a time. I'm not here to judge you and there's nothing you can say that will change how I feel about you.'

Christian slowly looked up into Megan's eyes. He took a deep breath.

'OK, well, I didn't go to Cambridge. It was Nottingham for me. I joined the army straight after graduating. And with me every step of the way was someone I had met at uni, who I knew I wanted to spend the rest of my life with ... I was married for ten years when my wife, Jessica, was diagnosed with an aggressive form of cancer and ... I can't explain how sudden it all was ... after undergoing all the tests under the sun, we realised there was nothing that could be done ... then she went into a hospice and died last year. We never had kids. I was an Army officer, as you know, but without Jessica I couldn't make sense of my career any more. She'd been such a big part of everything, it all seemed completely different after she passed.

'So, I left. I needed a complete change. And here I am, nearly six months away from the UK with potentially another six months working out here. I know I need to reconnect with friends and family soon, but for now I need to be away. My parents have been great and when I go back, I want to live close by, but for now ...' Christian turned away. He had never spoken about Jessica to anyone. He got up and walked to the sink to get some water. The emotion of the story, combined with the alcohol, had taken its toll. He was struggling to keep it together.

'It's OK, Chris, that must have been hard to explain.' Megan had got up and embraced him from behind, hugging him tightly against her body, her arms across his chest. The last track on the iPad ended at that moment, leaving the apartment in silence.

Looking down into the sink, Christian spoke quietly. 'Thanks, Megs, it's hard to take it in. You probably think I'm just running away from my troubles, but I need to find a new direction, and being here is helping me.' He wiped his face and turned to look at her again, their bodies never losing contact, now closer than ever.

Megan broke the silence, whispering in his ear. 'I don't think that, Chris. I understand. And I want to help if I can. Thank you for telling me about Jessica. And, by the way, dinner was bloody delicious.'

'So, now's the time to run!'

Megan held Christian tight before replying. 'I'm not running anywhere Chris, we both have baggage; I get that.'

Her words, spoken so meaningfully, immediately overwhelmed Christian. He buried his face in her shoulder and sobbed, uncontrollably, for what felt like minutes until eventually his breathing slowed and he regained control of his body, his emotions now raw and on edge. He pulled away from her, holding her shoulders.

'Sorry, Megs, that's probably not what you expected from someone like me. I really know how to woo a girl over dinner, don't I?' He looked up and laughed self-consciously, his eyes wet.

Megan laughed too, adding, 'Actually, I was going to ask what's for dessert.' She raised her eyebrows and he smiled as he saw the mischievous look in her eyes.

She held his face in her hands, gently stroking his cheek, and kissed him on the lips with such tenderness that he wanted the world to stop. 'Come on, let's go to bed.'

12

Fifteen Kilometres West of Mogadishu

'Turn right here.' The order was given after the co-driver had been scanning the road for the last 2km, one eye on his hand-held satnav, the other on the rapidly decreasing urban environment through his side window. 'I think it must be next to those buildings in front.' It was easy to pick out the rendezvous point, but in 20 minutes the area would be dark, the evening meeting the preferred option for the al Shabaab leadership.

Osman pulled out his side arm and cocked it, putting a round in the chamber before checking the safety catch and slipping it back into its holster on his waist, visible to anyone who cared to look. The driver brought the first of the two black SUVs to a halt. He switched off the engine and, after pulling up alongside Osman, the second vehicle did the same. They were bullet-proof cars so they waited, scanning the horizon, doors closed, unable to open their windows to listen for signs of their al Shabaab contacts approaching. Osman had taken no chances after confirming the meeting location the previous day through a dead letter drop near K4 roundabout. He had deployed with a full complement of Turkish Special Forces soldiers, three with Osman and four in the second SUV. If there was a last-minute change of mind, or a hint of a set-up, he was pretty confident they would be able to fight their way out.

Sitting in silence, radios on with an open channel to speak between the vehicles, they waited.

After a tense ten minutes, they saw through the gloom the dust trail heading towards them, rising into the darkening sky. As it got closer, Osman could make out three Hilux vehicles driving in convoy, carrying several armed gunmen wearing black headscarves perched precariously on the edge of the rear compartment, their heads down to avoid the clouds of dust being kicked up from the erratic driving. Approaching their position, Osman counted at least ten men with AK47s, excluding whoever was sitting inside the cabs of the three vehicles. After a further minute of waiting, fingers lightly touching their trigger guards in the SUVs, the al Shabaab convoy finally came to a dramatic halt, braking unnecessarily quickly and locking their wheels, sending a squall of dust into the growing gloom, enveloping the vehicles so that they momentarily disappeared from view.

'Fucking cowboys,' Osman said under his breath, a quiet chuckle coming over the radio in response.

After a minute to let the dust dissipate in front of the two SUVs, Osman opened his door, followed as planned by two men from each vehicle, weapons pointing down to the ground, unthreatening and passive. The al Shabaab vehicles opened at the same time, the sound of voices and the clatter of metal catching on the doorframes as they got out. Once everyone stopped moving, a strained silence followed.

Osman had his hands out, showing he was not holding a weapon, scanning the faces for al Dyihb – The Wolf. The tension of the moment was tangible, the Turkish special forces soldiers standing outside their vehicles staring resolutely into the faces of the al Shabaab gunmen arrayed 20m in front of them.

'Al Dyihb?' Osman shouted, as much to establish some control of the meeting as well as to draw out the leader of al Shabaab's militants in Mogadishu.

'I am here.' The man stepped out of the vehicle closest to Osman, dressed like the others in military fatigues together with a coloured headscarf to distinguish him from the guards in the vehicles. He approached Osman, holding his hand to his chest, speaking English with ease.

'Salaam Alaikum ...'

Osman remained fixed to the spot, holding his hand to his chest in response. 'Alaikum Salaam ...'

Al Dyihb spoke again. 'I like your vehicles; I think perhaps we should have them to protect us from drone strikes ...' He laughed, looking back in the fading light at his armed guards who dutifully laughed along with him. 'Have you brought the detonators you promised?'

'Yes, we have brought enough for the previous shipment of explosives, and we have a crate of weapons and ammunition, but first we need to confirm the details of where we will deploy with your teams and when the first attack will be.' Osman had delivered Hassan's instructions to the letter.

'OK, we can all relax. Come with me, Mr Osman, I want to speak to you alone ...' The Wolf calmly waved his arm, encouraging him to walk towards the nearest building, 30m away.

Osman's team started to follow but he turned and put his hand up, indicating they should remain where they were. 'It's OK, stay here.'

'Boss, it's getting dark and we will not be able to see you.' The voice came from one of Osman's men in the second vehicle through his earpiece. The Wolf walked ahead oblivious, expecting Osman to follow.

'It's OK,' Osman said quietly, then caught up with al Dyihb, who had stopped by the first building's entrance. Night had arrived quickly, the moonless sky already making it difficult to see more than a few metres in front of them.

The building loomed over both men as the Wolf spoke first. 'Mr Osman, we are planning an attack against the Army training camp south of the airport as soon as we can. You will come with us. We want you to help us coordinate the attack. We appreciate this support from our Muslim brothers in Turkey; there will be a reward for you when we defeat the western-backed government, *Insha'Allah*. Your commitment has been welcomed and recognised. Now we need to make it count. The enemy have their own advisors and we need parity.'

Al Dyihb spoke with the hint of an American accent. Osman knew his background in the Balkans twenty years before and wasn't surprised by his language skills. He had been flagged up as an irreconcilable Islamic extremist who would commit murder with little provocation or remorse. The intelligence team supporting the Turkish operation had warned Osman to be on his guard.

'Did you bring night vision?' al Dyihb asked.

Osman had anticipated the question and wanted to reassure him that the plans were on track before breaking the news to him. 'I have my kit and will come with you now to start planning. We will transfer over the equipment now and next week we will deploy another five advisors to the other teams as discussed last month.' The shipment of highly sought-after night-vision goggles hadn't made it onto the transport that arrived in Somalia the week before. Al Dyihb's group would have to go ahead without the capability. 'But we don't have night vision,' Osman continued. 'They will come in the next shipment in a month. You will need to delay the attack.'

Suddenly the mood changed.

'It is not your place to tell me when to attack the infidels! We have been waiting to strike them for many months and we will kill many with our Turkish bombs and guns,' Dyihb replied, his voice rising as he spoke, his finger pointing in the air, staring at Osman. But he knew he needed the night vision goggles.

The Wolf was becoming agitated before he was shocked into silence by Osman, who grabbed his right forearm out of the sky, pulling it down to waist level and gripping it tightly, at the same time bringing his face close to the Somali's.

'You will never speak of Turkish weapons again, do you understand?' He said the words quietly but with enough menace to get the message across. He didn't trust the militants and had begun to doubt the wisdom of the entire operation. He let go of Dyihb's arm as suddenly as he had grabbed it. Stepping back, al Dyihb quickly tried to pull his AK47 round from the back of his right shoulder into the firing position, but Osman already had his weapon out of its holster and aimed at al Dyihb's head from one foot away. Dyihb looked straight down the barrel of Osman's SIG Sauer pistol.

'Put the fucking weapon down, or you and your men will die right here,' Osman said quietly.

The dialogue was being monitored in the SUVs. Osman heard the doors opening and his men stepping out of the vehicles, all now wearing night-vision goggles. The militants also heard doors open in front of them, but they could barely see the SUVs and weren't completely sure what to do. They instinctively raised their weapons but couldn't see the Turkish soldiers. The lack of any moonlight made the darkness impenetrable to the naked eye. One false move by any of the Somali gunmen and it would have been a bloodbath. For a few moments nobody breathed.

'OK, OK, that's fine,' the Wolf said, then added, 'No mention, that's OK, now let's get moving. Tell your men to be here in a week's time when the others will join us.' Osman lowered his pistol and put it back into its holster with an exaggerated movement to show Dyihb that the moment had passed. Dyihb cleared his throat and spat on the floor. 'And don't ever touch me again, or I will kill you in your sleep, my friend.'

Al Dyihb walked away, catching Osman's shoulder as he approached his vehicles, barking orders for the rear doors to be lowered and to carry the crates from the SUVs. Osman walked back to his team more slowly, speaking into his radio. 'One box of detonators, the ones we have marked, one crate of AKs, along with two boxes of ammunition. We will leave the second load in the other SUV; these fuckers are not going to get everything at once.'

Osman had disagreed with Hassan during their final briefing in the embassy about how much hardware to give to the militants. Hassan seemed to think that by deploying advisors they would be able to keep tabs on where everything was being stored, so they could recover them at a later date when the time came. Osman had explained from the beginning that it didn't work like that in the field. Hassan, as usual, had pulled rank and told Osman to get on with it. Osman had disobeyed orders by retaining one vehicle's worth of weapons and detonators, but he would find a credible reason why he kept them. He walked back to the SUVs in deep thought. As the Somalis were manhandling the crates from the SUV to their own vehicles under the watchful eyes of the Turkish troops, Osman pulled the special forces team leader to one side, turning off his microphone so only he could hear his words.

'Captain, I am going with them now. I will get my kit and leave. Head back to the embassy immediately, do not stop for anyone; you are diplomatic and nobody has jurisdiction over you. Tell Hassan's assistant what has happened and tell him the al Shabaab team didn't have enough space for the full load of ammunition. OK?'

'OK, boss, leave it to me.'

'And remember to pass the details of the rucksack tracker to the operational team to monitor where I am. I'll use my phone for emergencies only. If I need to extract, I will trigger the beacon, OK? Otherwise, keep the boys on standby, four on four off until I say otherwise.'

A voice came onto the radio. 'That's it, Boss; they are all loaded up.'

Osman pulled his earpiece out and removed the radio from his belt, handing it to the Captain. He then picked up his rucksack and stepped towards the al Shabaab vehicles, the gunmen shouting amongst themselves as they jumped on board.

'You will travel with me, my friend.' Al Dyihb's voice cut through the darkness, making Osman veer towards the first Hilux vehicle. Once inside, the three Shabaab drivers simultaneously started their engines and revved them unnecessarily as they aggressively accelerated away, spitting dust and stones towards the SUVs which were still in darkness. The special forces team watched them drive away through the green ambient light of their night-vision goggles.

'Total amateurs,' came the voice over the radio.

The Captain cut in, 'Those *total amateurs* have got Osman's life in their hands. Prepare to move off.'

They were under orders to wait until the militant convoy was no longer visible. After a few minutes, they noticed all three Shabaab vehicles in the distance turn their headlights on, one after the other, as they headed for their secret camp outside the capital.

The Captain spoke to his team again. 'Let's go!'

Within 25 minutes, the two vehicles were barrelling along Industrial Road, three minutes away from the entrance of their embassy near the K4 roundabout. The Captain changed channel and spoke into his mouthpiece.

'Hello, Zero, this is Callsign Charlie, we are three minutes away.'

The Captain didn't wait for a response; he knew his team would be alert, watching the external security cameras and preparing to open the gates. They headed for the embassy along Jidka Tarabuunka, both SUVs travelling within metres of each other at high speed, their headlights cutting through the twilight created by the street lights. As they approached the embassy, the gates started to open. Within a minute the vehicles were off the street and the gates securely closed behind them. The Captain immediately jumped out of the lead vehicle, cleared his weapon, and walked into the embassy building, turning right and heading for the basement and the temporary operational headquarters for their audacious plan. The radio operator looked up as he barged through the door.

'Send the message now: *Asena is running.*'

Asena, the codename given to Osman during his period as an advisor to the Shabaab militants, was the son of a wolf in Turkish mythology and the connection seemed appropriate to Hassan when he was planning the finer details of the operation. The special forces operator picked up his mobile and tapped in the three words, choosing the recipient carefully and pressing "send".

Across the street the old man, sitting on the upturned barrel, turned away and also tapped in a message, pressing "send" before calling to the barman for another glass of tea.

*

Hassan was cold. Very cold.

Even wearing a fur-lined hat resembling an old fashioned Turkish *bork*, together with a scarf and long woollen overcoat, he could not completely keep the cold out. With his gloved hands buried deep inside his pockets, only his pallid face was exposed to the biting cold that had descended on the city. He looked around him. The day was fading fast and the lights of the capital were imposing themselves on the wintery scene beyond, the leaden clouds hovering menacingly above them, threatening to suffocate those foolish enough to be outside. What few tourists had ventured out to visit Ataturk's Mausoleum had long returned to the warmth of their hotels. He was standing under the colonnade, looking across the empty expanse of the grand square towards the mausoleum, trying to find some shelter from the icy wind spiralling around him, flecks of snow blowing into his face whichever direction he turned, as if punishing him for living in the warmth of Somalia. He took his hands out of his pockets and pulled his sleeve up a couple of inches to look at his watch.

He stamped his feet in frustration.

The head of *Milli Istihbarat Teşkilati*, who was overseeing Hassan's operation, had a sense of humour. Meeting as the sun was setting at one of the highest points in Ankara in the middle of winter within 12 hours of leaving the Horn of Africa was his idea of a joke.

'Why are you stamping your feet, Hassan?' Mehmet, the MIT Director, had approached him from the side of the square but a column had masked his approach. Smiling, he extended his arm and the men shook hands without taking their gloves off.

'It is unseasonably cold at the moment; you chose the wrong week to visit your home city!' Mehmet said.

The men started to walk towards the mausoleum, as if drawn to it by its sense of history, the imposing pillared structure glorifying the life and death of Turkey's founding father, Mustafa Ataturk.

'How is everything going over there, Hassan?' Mehmet stood a good foot taller than Hassan, his face rugged and lined from years of working in the field overseas. He wore a dark woollen hat and a short coat, his breath condensing in the air as they walked together. Mehmet had initially discussed Hassan's plan to destabilise Mogadishu in line with their president's push for more influence amongst forgotten Muslim nations in Africa. He was keen to hear from Hassan himself about how things looked. Reading secret cables only said so much and he had asked Hassan to fly back to the capital at short notice for this reason. He knew when he approved the operation that it was very high risk but, if secrecy could be maintained, there was little chance of it reflecting badly on the Turkish nation, something he held as a red line when authorising all deniable covert operations. Mehmet drew on his cigarette and inhaled before blowing the smoke from between his lips, forcing the air out as if he was beginning to regret his choice of meeting location.

Walking side by side over the decorative paving gave Hassan a moment to organise his thoughts.

'We made contact last month with the al Shabaab faction that operates in Mogadishu. Osman had a lucky escape initially but soon found the right person to speak to. He is about to deploy as the first advisor; the meeting is taking place this evening. I should be told soon what is happening.'

Subconsciously, Hassan again checked his watch. He thought to himself *they are late.*

'Tell me again why they are trusting us to help them.' Mehmet knew the plan, and its origins, but he remained nervous about al Shabaab's motivations for accepting the help which, in his mind, was the biggest risk. He raised his gloved hand again, his cigarette briefly glowing in the half light.

'Firstly, they need more military advice when taking on the AU force. AMISOM has a private military company called Lancing Point, basically a front company financed by the US, which employs dozens of ex-South African and other military freelancers based at the airport in Mogadishu. Our man there says they are doing everything apart from the fighting, but they are at the front line 24/7.' Hassan had forgotten about the weather as he went through the plan again.

'We have a man in Lancing Point?' Mehmet was surprised.

'Well, only a Somali cleaner who listens to anything he can. It's low level, single source and unreliable, but the picture we are seeing through other intelligence makes us believe that Lancing Point are AMISOM's military backbone in Somalia,' Hassan added.

'We have confirmed to Shabaab that we also aim to conduct a campaign in the countries who are contributing troops, similar to what Shabaab did two years ago in Uganda. Al Shabaab think that by weakening support back home and delivering more military success in and around Mogadishu, AMISOM troops will lose heart. We know the West will never deploy troops again to Somalia, leaving the door open for us to step in to secure the capital. Of course ...' Hassan paused for effect, 'Shabaab will not know what has hit them as we withdraw our advisors, who will by then have the locations of the people, arms and ammunition dumps so fundamental to their campaign. We will defeat Shabaab and the Somali people will welcome us with open arms which, in turn, will lead to strong political support from Vila Somalia and preferential access to their onshore and offshore oil and gas reserves.' He finished speaking with a flourish, slapping his gloves together before burying them again deep inside his coat pockets.

Mehmet had been listening patiently.

Both men arrived at the foot of the mausoleum and began to climb the 33 steps to the tomb itself, as if seeking spiritual endorsement for one of the most audacious covert operations in recent years. As they reached the top, Mehmet took a last draw on his cigarette and stubbed it out on a raised ash tray next to them.

Mehmet looked up, coughing into the wind which, if anything, felt even stronger. 'Our founding father created our service 85 years ago, Hassan, did you know that? I doubt there has been a more glorious example of our intelligence capability than your operation in Somalia. You will be making history for our successors to admire and emulate for generations to come.'

Hassan pulled his hat further down over his ears, but even the icy wind could not impact the warmth he felt listening to the Director's words. 'Thank you, Director.'

'How long do you think this will take before we need to commit troops? Six months? A year?' Mehmet was keen to understand the time frame so that he could, eventually, begin to align the other players within the Turkish State apparatus.

'I think we will be able to make some inroads in the first three to six months, assuming the logistics plan runs smoothly.' Hassan left the subject hanging in the freezing air. The delivery of weapons and ammunition, procured by Turkey on the black market, were being shipped via a Middle Eastern country already operating in Somalia under the cover of a religious programme of investment. It was a brilliant plan, but relying on the Arab connection made Hassan uneasy.

Mehmet calmed his compatriot. 'The logistics are working and we have come to a very amenable arrangement. You do not need to be concerned. If things go wrong, we can switch it off in a moment without any traceability back to Ankara. All will be well.'

Hassan remained unconvinced but didn't share his thoughts with the Director. He took his gloved hands out of his pockets and slapped them together to get some blood into them. The men turned their backs to the mausoleum, looking across the square, past the colonnade from where they had just walked, and beyond towards the shimmering lights of the city, nestled underneath the dark clouds above.

At that moment, Hassan's mobile phone buzzed in his pocket. He pulled it out and looked at the screen expectantly: *Asena is running*

Hassan read the message and looked up at Mehmet, his face in shadow from the floor mounted floodlights illuminating the building behind them.

'Osman has deployed. I will prepare the remaining five advisors for their handover next week. The operation has started.'

Hassan pocketed the phone once again and shivered. He needed to get back to Mogadishu and out of the cold.

PART TWO

13

South of Mogadishu, February 2013

Gali closed his eyes and allowed his head to drop onto his chest. He had been up most of the previous 24 hours, trying in vain to prepare his inexperienced Shabaab contingent for battle. He was sitting against a small acacia tree as they waited for sundown, and the attack. He was dressed in a green olive *shalwar kameez* over a pair of loose-fitting, ash coloured trousers, with a black bandana on his head. With the branches reaching out above him providing some respite from the unrelenting sun, he dozed off. The weather in Somalia had been brutal since he had deployed as part of the MIT operation six weeks earlier. There had not been a drop of rain throughout January and the heat during the day made life uncomfortable for Gali, despite being a highly trained special forces soldier.

Part of a unit attached to Turkish intelligence for black ops, those deniable actions so necessary for supporting Turkey's national security objectives, Gali had known Osman for many years. When he had been briefed on the operation, he immediately volunteered to become a mentor for an al Shabaab unit.

As a young soldier, he had often beaten his colleagues in off duty competitions, as well as during route marches while training in the Taurus Mountains, and had earned the nickname Galip, meaning "winner", but Gali had stuck.

He had earned a reputation for being a highly dependable operator within the black ops team. As a result, Osman had given him the more challenging task: to shape up al Shabaab's southern "command": a rag-tag group of disaffected Somalis and foreign nationals who had been tasked with attacking the EU-sponsored training camp south of the airport. Except the last six weeks hadn't been all smooth sailing and his belief in the operation had been shaken by the difficulty in establishing a relationship with the extremists he had been landed with. He had shared his concerns with Osman, who had encouraged him to persevere, but Gali had sensed Osman's confidence in their mission was also dropping.

Despite the challenging conditions, in which his authority was frequently undermined, Gali had spent his time improving the men's weapon handling skills and walking through rudimentary tactics that they would use on the assault. The local al Shabaab commander, known by his men as Teeg, was a hot-headed fundamentalist around 40 years old who had made it clear to Gali that he didn't believe the Turkish deployment was needed, although he always seemed happy to receive logistic resupplies of ammunition and weapons arranged through the Turks. He had led his men for a number of years and their ability to deploy roadside bombs, when they could get hold of the explosives and detonators, as well as carry out rudimentary ambushes of AMISOM vehicles, was well known.

But the scale and complexity of Gali's planned operation against the camp was new to Teeg and his men. In truth, Gali knew they were out of their depth but he believed the Shabaab fighters would still be able to make an impact with a little bit of training. They had chosen to attack the camp in an attempt to introduce doubt into the minds of the young Somali men and women volunteering for the Army and to slow the current numbers putting their names forward. With his eyes closed and sweat running down his face, Gali remembered his last conversation with Osman when he had run through his final plan three days earlier.

'I am going to split the group into two teams of 20. Teeg's running the assault and I will take the fire support team, based close to the settlement next to the camp. I have shared the satellite image with Teeg so he has a good idea of where to direct his men when they breach the camp. I will set the short-term timers with the plastic explosive, but that will be the only time I leave the fire support team. We have plenty of rounds and the night vision should make a big difference, assuming they learn to conserve the battery power.'

Gali was standing up in a small hut, no bigger than ten feet square, the sunlight held at bay by a piece of dark cloth draped across the only open window. The heat inside the room was almost stifling. Osman was sitting on his backpack in front of the ill-fitting wooden door, shafts of sunlight penetrating the room around its sides like laser beams. He was listening intently and making notes.

'Who has the other satellite image now? Osman asked.

'I have everything with me and they will stay in my kit which will be left at the secure base outside the village,' Gali replied.

'OK, what is the extraction plan? How will you get them out? The same way or through the explosive breach in the wall?' Osman was looking down at his notes in his black book, turning the pages in case he had missed anything.

'I will set the explosive charges and they will come out that way. The perimeter will not withstand the force of the blasts. Once the explosions happen, that will be their signal to make their way to the breach so they can exfiltrate the camp. Both teams will meet at the emergency rendezvous; we will then make our way to the vehicle muster point, where we will clear the immediate vicinity in Hilux vehicles supplied by Shabaab's logistics team. I'll give them some credit; they always know how to get away efficiently.'

Osman closed his notebook and slipped it into his inside pocket of his civilian jacket, smiling at that last comment. Gali relaxed, unclipped the makeshift sketch map of the camp from the board leaning against the wall, together with the satellite image, and started to pack everything away in his own kit.

'What are your main concerns, Gali?' Osman stood up and looked him in the eye. At six feet tall, the men stood a few feet apart, both wearing the standard al Shabaab clothing, their own military uniform discarded for the period of this operation.

'Where do I start? Communicating through mobile phones is going to be a challenge, but most of them understand the basic language I have been using. Operational security is always number one; I've told them that they cannot be taken alive and they must bring everyone out with them.' Gali shrugged his shoulders and gave a weary smile. 'Frankly, the risks are massive ...' Gali left that comment in the air, the sound of a dog barking in the distance the only other sound inside the hut.

Osman spoke next. 'I don't need to tell you that Shabaab are expendable, so watch your back and report to me within 48 hours.'

Osman pulled on the battered wooden door, the metal hinges creaking as it swung open, flooding the space with the last remnants of evening sunlight. Osman had signed off the plan.

Osman was now waiting at a safe location ten kilometres away with al Dyihb and his men, fresh from a recently successful complex attack against an AMISOM convoy. The pressure on AMISOM was mounting; Gali had to pull it off.

*

The increasing sophistication of tactics and the rising number of attacks had not gone unnoticed by AMISOM Headquarters and, in particular, by the ex-military contractors working for Lancing Point. Their mission was to provide military support to AMISOM, which included directing troops on the ground during firefights. Those few men who deployed to the front line, alongside troops from Uganda and Burundi, were the most experienced and battle-hardened, and they had the scars to show it. In the years since they had been deployed on the ground, Lancing Point had only ever lost one contractor to enemy fire, although every man had been wounded from stray rounds or flying shrapnel at some point or another. These men, these mercenaries, were unemployable anywhere else; this was their world.

In the last four weeks, Lancing Point's contractors had been surprised by the increase in tempo and sophistication of al Shabaab attacks. In a private bar within their airport camp compound, sitting on plastic chairs, empty beer bottles covering the small wooden tables as each night progressed, the experienced former military men discussed these phenomena and what appeared to be a significant shift in tactics. They knew something was behind it but had been unable to find any evidence on the handful of dead Shabaab fighters they had managed to recover from their recent skirmishes alongside the AMISOM troops.

'How the fuck can they suddenly be so fucking accurate in their firepower, that's what I want to know.' Pete was on his third beer. His large muscular frame, partially gone to fat, made the furniture around him seem too small. Like so many within Lancing Point, he had served in the South African Defence Force, followed by a decade as a "gun for hire", during which time he had been involved in countless tactical engagements across the region, not all of them official. And now he had been assigned to the AMISOM detachment responsible for defending the EU training facility. At any one time there were up to 250 Somali recruits living in tents and receiving basic military training under the watchful eye of EU military mentors, whose job was to prepare them for more intensive training outside Somalia's borders.

By day, there were enough international military troops working as directing staff to deter an attack; by night, when they were bussed back to the safety of the airport camp, the training facility was under the control of AMISOM troops and, therefore, at its most vulnerable. Pete knew it was a high-value target. And he knew Shabaab knew it too.

'I tell you, if those fuckers come anywhere near the base, I will personally lead the counter attack.' Pete, taking a drag on his cigarette, was speaking so loudly the other people in the bar could hear his comments. Pete's suntanned face was lined with experience, and the younger contractors who were sitting with him around the table after dinner hung on to his every word.

'You won't be able to keep up if you down five bottles every night, you fat fuck!'

Andre, a fellow AMISOM mentor responsible for supporting troops in a different sector of Mogadishu, shouted across the bar to Pete, laughing as he did so. He had known Pete for years, both in South Africa and through their contracts with Lancing Point. The camaraderie within the company made the frustrations of working alongside often inexperienced African troops all the more bearable. Along with earning $1000 a day while in country.

'Yeah, piss off, ya fucking townie … at least I'll be with my missus at the weekend,' Pete yelled over his shoulder and took another swig of beer, flicking ash into the tray.

'Keep drinking and you'll not be able to get it up either!' Andre replied to much amusement amongst those in the bar. 'How long will you be away, Pete?'

Pete excused himself and got up from his table, pushing his chair over as he did so, swearing under his breath, and walked across the cement floor towards Andre who was standing at the bar, leaning on his elbows as he listened to the banter around him. The bar was hexagonal, without any walls but a wooden frame held a thatched roof above them. Although not huge, it was big enough to fit the Lancing Point contractors, but not so big that the Wi-Fi struggled to reach every table. Pete joined Andre at the counter, taking one of his cigarettes.

'I haven't seen my missus for two months so I've got a couple of weeks leave. I'm stopping over in Nairobi for a couple of nights before flying to Jo'burg.'

Andre raised his bottle and Pete knocked his own Heineken against it. Pete gave a deep sigh, expelling the air in his lungs through his pursed lips.

'I tell you, if those bastards come to my patch, they won't know what's hit them.' Pete spoke quietly between them. 'Something isn't right. I've never seen them so organised.'

Andre was smaller than Pete, his balding head deeply tanned from years under the sun, his arms covered in tattoos, the legacy of his previous life as a military sniper. His movements were calm and deliberate. He looked up at Pete.

'You need to take it easy, mate. If someone is helping them to be more effective, and I've seen it too, we have to assume that their capability is growing even if we haven't yet seen evidence of it. Just take it easy over the next few days, eh? We may all need to spend more time with our teams so that we can try to gather some evidence. When are you deploying next?'

'I'm out with them for the next 72 hours, then back here for a day, then out of country to Kenya. I can't fucking wait.' Pete finished his beer and put it on the bar, stubbing out his smoke.

'I'm not surprised mate; your missus is bloody gorgeous.' Andre was smiling, their banter the sign of a strong friendship.

'Mate, I'm out first thing so I'm going to hit the sack. I'll see you in a few days, eh?' Pete slapped Andre on the shoulder, who grunted and raised his own beer in response, then walked away from the lights of the bar into the warmth and darkness of the Somali night.

14

South of Mogadishu

Gali's head shot up as his feet were kicked by Mohammed, the leader of the fire support team. Mohammed was laughing, his yellowing teeth prominent whilst chewing khat with his mouth open. Gali had fallen asleep and now the night had set in, the sound of crickets filling the air alongside the hubbub of preparation all around him: the sharp metallic sound of weapons being checked, belt ammunition being slung around the bodies of those carrying machine guns and rounds being fed into magazines.

'Up, up, we go ...' Gesticulating with his hands, Mohammed spoke very little English but had enough to get his point across.

Gali swore. He couldn't believe he'd allowed his tiredness to get the better of him, that they'd allowed him to sleep so close to the op. Pissed off, he immediately began to exert control.

'Get the men together now. I want to speak one more time.' He barked out his orders to Mohammed who disappeared into the moonless night. Back on his feet, Gali looked at his watch. It was one hour before they were due to cross the start line, when they would lay down fire while Teeg's team stormed the camp through the main entrance. He knew it would take 30 minutes to reach their position. He calculated the time remaining and cursed himself for closing his eyes. The image of being in the hut with Osman, his final words, came into his mind.

Everyone was putting their kit onto the vehicles, leaving them with the basics to fight; weapons, ammunition and any other equipment such as wire cutters and grenades. Gali kept a small pack with him, which contained the plastic explosive charges that he was going to use to breach the camp perimeter, along with his phone, a pistol and ammunition in case he needed to join the firefight. He had put the satellite images into a different pack after meeting Osman but had retained the sketch map for reference during the op; he was happy that he was clean from an operational security perspective. As

Mohammed was organising his men out of earshot, Gali took out his phone, selected one of three numbers on speed dial, and made a call.

'All OK?' He spoke clearly, waiting for Teeg to respond.

'OK, we leave now and will be ready for start,' Teeg said.

As Gali closed down the call, Mohammed called out. In his haste to respond, Gali put the phone in his pocket without locking the screen. Within a few seconds he heard a faint ring tone, then a muffled sound and looked down. He put his hand back into his pocket and took the phone out again.

'*Merhaba, bu kim? Gali..?*' *Who is this?* The metallic voice on the phone made Gali's blood freeze.

'What the ...' Gali stared at the Nokia for a moment, reading the words on the screen before turning it off without speaking. He had inadvertently made a call to the ops room in the embassy. He had made a mistake. He instinctively looked around to see who may have watched what had happened but nobody was paying him any attention. 'Fuck!'

Mohammed called out again. 'We are ready, Gali, here, here ...' He could see Mohammed's arms beckoning him. Gali put the phone, now locked, back into his pocket and walked towards Mohammed and his men who were standing in a group waiting for him, their weapons ready, eyes wide with excitement. Gali stood in front of them, his pack slung over one shoulder. Mohammed offered a fully loaded AK47 to Gali, but he refused. The team of advisors had agreed at the outset that they would not directly target AMISOM troops, but they would use weapons for self-defence. It was a condition that had not gone down well with al Dyihb and his men.

Gali started to speak.

'We go in five minutes. We follow the planned route around the village, then take position to cover the entrance from the tree line. Teeg is following a different route. Make your rifles ready now, safety on. Remember, make every round count. And when we set off, no noise!' Mohammed translated Gali's words into Somali, his voice high, a combination of adrenaline and drugs coursing through his veins making his delivery loud and aggressive. Gali's instructions resulted in everyone cocking their weapons, the sharp sound piercing the night's natural ambience. He doubted any of them had applied their safety catches and he wasn't going to check; getting close to these men now carried significant risk.

'OK, let's go.' Gali waited for Mohammed to organise the group and take the lead, and watched as he followed them from the back, the men snaking into the night, his mind thinking about the accidental call he made before setting off. He cursed again and knew he would have to get in touch with the ops room to explain once he got back after the attack.

Gali looked at his watch for a final time. After a relatively uneventful 35 minutes' walk through the open ground beside the nearby village, his team lay up in a tree line, 50 metres away from the camp entrance. They'd used their night-vision goggles during the move in but had now taken them off. From their position he could see the security lights illuminating the entrance's immediate vicinity but effectively preventing the guards from seeing into the darkness beyond. The guards were vulnerable. Gali shook his head at the foolishness of the camp's security. He would never have organised things that way. His fire support team were lined up to his right and left. Mohammed was at the furthest point away to control his men and to have a slightly better view of the assault team waiting at that moment in the darkness behind a row of dilapidated houses which afforded them cover on the far side of the entrance. If they could breach the main gate, they had a chance of causing carnage inside the camp, which would make a strong statement about Shabaab's growing capability.

Gali quietly opened his pack and checked the three explosive devices he had prepared to breach the perimeter close to a track that led away to their right and, according to the satellite imagery, surrounded the camp. Although covered by security lights, he calculated the chaos caused by the initial attack would allow him time to place the devices against the perimeter about 100 metres away without being noticed. He moved back out of the tree line and into the small ditch that ran behind the Shabaab fighters either side of him. He sent a message to Mohammed: *Going to breach perimeter now*

He had agreed what messages he would send, and everyone's phones were on silent, so he was confident they would maintain security throughout. Once the shooting started, it didn't really matter.

Gali moved quietly behind the men who were lying on their fronts, their AK47s held in front of them, waiting for the order to open fire. Gali knew it would be chaotic when it started and was glad to be separated from the fire support team, who were unpredictable. He touched each man's leg as he went, so they knew that he was on his way. When he reached the final man, he paused and looked at his watch again.

One minute to go.

As he pulled down the sleeve of his shirt, he heard the sound of the truck approaching along the coast road. It was on time. He looked towards the entrance where the guards had also begun to hear the approaching vehicle and were looking in the direction of the sound, their weapons raised as their sense of danger increased. Gali slipped away, tapping the end man twice on the leg and disappearing into the night. He initially headed away from the camp but quickly turned left to follow a parallel path about 100 metres away, hidden from view by a row of tents that had been constructed to house the families of those attending the training camp. He moved silently, walking with purpose, waiting for the attack to begin.

The truck's gear-changing was now very close, its headlights approaching fast. In response, the AMISOM guards fired a volley of rounds towards the approaching vehicle. It was as if a switch had been flicked on. The noise suddenly became ear-piercingly loud as the speeding truck came into view of the security lights. With automatic weapons being fired at the driver and an alarm screeching inside the camp, the final approach of the truck, travelling at about 30 mph and fully illuminated by the security lights, took a fraction of a second, colliding with the low cement-blast walls designed to prevent a suicide vehicle attack. The sound of the collision, the sharp report of glass and metal hitting the concrete, filled the air. The truck lifted into the air, hinged at the front, then landed back on the ground with a low thud. For a moment there was silence. Barely a second later, the truck, peppered with bullet holes, exploded into a huge fireball, shooting 50m into the air.

The flash made Gali squint even though he was not in line of sight, followed a fraction of a second later by the enormous crack from the explosion, forcing him to take cover and put his hands over his ears. He crawled up the slope to look at the entrance, which was entirely obscured by flames and thick black smoke, debris falling from the sky in a huge radius in front of the check point. Gali knew they had put far more than the recommended quantity of explosives into the truck.

From where Gali was lying, he could see several uniformed soldiers scattered on the ground, their bodies twisted and contorted into inhuman shapes, some on fire, smoke rising from anything that was flammable. The sound of weapons firing on automatic now cut in, the muzzle flashes easily seen from the tree line where he had been a few minutes earlier. Within seconds, a machine gun opened up from a watch tower inside the camp, its tracer rounds pouring into the trees beyond where Mohammed and his men were positioned. The gunner had not got his range right and was aiming high.

Gali looked again at the seat of the explosion; the truck had been obliterated, a huge crater had appeared, smoking and empty, the remains of the truck spread across the road and embedded in the fence by the entrance, which was now unmanned and vulnerable. He was waiting for the appearance of his assault team and, as hoped, they emerged from behind the houses. Unsteadily at first, they started sprinting towards the entrance, avoiding the burning debris, heading straight for the open camp. The supporting fire from the tree line was incessant, but so was the machine gun inside the camp, which was beginning to find its range.

Gali couldn't wait any longer and sprinted past the remaining tents, the sounds of shouting coming from the other side of the canvas. He darted across the perimeter dirt track in full view of the security lights, but confident that AMISOM's attention would be focused on the attack at the main gate. He slipped down by the sand bags that had been placed on the outside of the wire fencing and brought his pack off his back. He took out the three small devices, all on a timer and activated by a simple switch, and carefully placed them against the wire fence, tucked between the fence and the sandbags. He was sure that the blast radius would achieve two things: it would create a space large enough for the assault team to escape through after they had attacked the camp, and he was certain that the buildings immediately inside housed recruits. He had already rationalised what he was doing, and he believed that his actions were for the greater good of Turkey. The loss of life of a few Somalis at his hands was acceptable collateral damage.

He moved with great speed, placing the devices a few metres apart at what he considered to be structurally weak areas of the fence. He was just placing the third device when he heard voices, sharp but still distant. It sounded like soldiers were heading towards his position along the perimeter track from the rear of the camp, some 100 metres away. He knew that the AMISOM force was likely to have a quick reaction force on standby, but he had miscalculated where they would deploy from. He'd assumed they would aim for the entrance and stay inside the camp, rather than use the rear exit to deploy. With only so many Shabaab fighters limiting his options, he made a call not to cover the rear gate. It proved to be a mistake.

Gali flicked the switch and placed the final device on the ground a further five metres away from the last one, next to a cement post against which the barbed wire was secured. The sound of the fire-fight raged inside the camp; the fighters under Teeg's command must have been encountering some stiff resistance from the African Union troops. The devices had a ten-minute timer and all three were now live. With no decrease in the volume and with the quick reaction force fast approaching, he darted back across the track and dived into the chaotic patchwork of tents, huts and people, some of whom had now come out onto the tracks that criss-crossed the area to see what was happening.

Gali knew they would all be within the blast range of the explosives but he didn't care, he needed to get back to the tree line to take charge of the fire support team. He noticed that the machine gun from the watch tower was now tearing up the ground where the Shabaab fighters had initially laid up, but he hoped Mohammed had followed his instructions to change positions, fire a few rounds, then move again. He had no idea whether they had survived but when he saw flashes of flame emerging from a position close to the tree line, he knew they had listened to him.

Running quickly in a crouch to lower his profile, his pack once again on his back, the darkness was finally giving him the cover he needed. Flashes of gunfire and the occasional explosion from a grenade thrown by AMISOM troops punctuated the night sky, but he was confident he was out of range of those troops who were no doubt getting organised to see off the assault team. Gali knew he would have to instruct Mohammed to withdraw his men soon, especially if they were going to cover the exfiltration of Teeg's team, assuming they could make it through the camp. The sounds of battle were everywhere, the sheer volume of rounds being fired from so many different locations, all within a square kilometre, was a terrifying experience. Gali, although a veteran of many such moments, always felt shocked by the scale and ferocity that a military tactical action could produce. The complex attack he had planned was every bit as terrifying as anything he had experienced before. Only when he was out of range of enemy weapons did he ever feel truly safe.

As he ran, the screams and shouts from the people in the village and those who had been camping nearby were beginning to fill his ears more than the sounds of battle. He looked around and realised he had taken a wrong turn, ending up on a dusty track with no obvious way to get back to where he needed to be. He looked at his watch: four minutes to go. He had to retrace his steps and get back to the tree line as soon as he could. Suddenly, without warning, he felt a blow on the side of his face which momentarily knocked him off his feet. His head was spinning and his right ear was thumping from the pain. He paused and put his hand to his temple, his fingers feeling fresh blood from a wound caused by whatever had hit him. He picked himself up and kept running back the way he had come, the sounds of voices constantly around him.

As he tried to see into the darkness, he dropped onto one knee and took off his pack, digging his hands inside to pull out the night-vision goggles he had stored there earlier. He quickly slipped them onto his head and flicked the switch; hearing the familiar whirr of the electronics, his world suddenly came alive in an alien scene of green hue. He looked around and, for the first time, knew he was in trouble. The crowd of Somalis who had poured out onto the track were shouting at each other and pointing to where they thought he was. He could see them clearly and needed to use the advantage of his goggles to make his escape. He had another trick up his sleeve; he looked at his watch once more.

One minute to go.

He put the pack on his back and started to run. He watched as some men launched themselves towards him but he shoulder-charged them away, able to time his blows more accurately by seeing the attackers through his goggles.

'Any second now,' Gali said out loud as he ran, as much to prove to himself that he was still in control.

The fire-fight seemed to have reduced its intensity, the sound of gunfire less frequent, and he could imagine the assault team moving through the camp more cautiously until they heard the devices explode, which would signal their moment to escape. Gali kept running and was close to the end of the track where he had to turn left when the flash in his face blinded him completely, so much so that he stumbled forward and fell face down onto the ground. He was confused; he knew there would be a flash but he hadn't heard the detonation. His mind was racing, trying to work out what the hell was going on.

The first kick was aimed at his midriff which immediately winded him. He involuntarily curled up into a ball as a second and third kick came in from different sides, and then a metallic blow on his head from the torch that had blinded him, the shouts and screams growing louder and louder coming from all sides. And then everything stopped as the first of his devices exploded less than 50 metres away. The kicking immediately halted as the attackers dived for cover. He knew he only had one chance to escape.

Moving with great speed, he managed to get up and started to sprint away from his attackers, slightly off balance, turning left away from the buildings, huts and tents, and the people, and on towards the original firing position in the tree line. Stumbling because of the speed he was running, he used the goggles to plot his path through the shrub. The second device exploded, both deafening him and knocking him off his feet. He had strayed too close to the perimeter track and had been in direct line of sight of the blast. The sound of the machine gun suddenly entered his consciousness again. The blow to his ear had deprived him of hearing on one side. His sensations were now becoming confused as he again picked himself up and started staggering towards where he thought the Shabaab fighters were located.

He needed to send a message to Mohammed. He reached into his pocket and tried to tap out the number but tripped over a tree root. His face was in the dirt as the third device exploded; the sky lit up with an orange and red glow from the blast. He was still holding his phone as he rolled onto his side, moments later getting up onto his knees. He put one hand down to steady himself and tapped out the message to Mohammed: *I'm on my way back. Stay there until I arrive. 5 minutes*

He pressed "send" and pocketed the phone.

As he did so, an automatic weapon opened up close to his position. He turned his head and could see the muzzle flash about 40 meters away from the edge of the populated area to his right. He ducked down and calmed his breathing, quickly making a few simple calculations: he was probably about 100 metres away from the tree line but the attack was beginning to turn to favour AMISOM and so he knew he had to extract himself as a priority. He had no intention of going back to the tree line; the proximity of the machine gun had made that an easy choice. Instead of meeting Mohammed, he decided at that moment to save himself and head towards the emergency rendezvous point they had agreed earlier, a point on the approach track about 250 meters away from the camp. He knew he would have to go through the shrub but guessed the bearing he needed to follow, and started to move off, staying as low as he could as he went forward cautiously.

Gali's breathing was heavy, his orientation impaired, but his remaining good ear delivered news he feared most. The shouts he heard were in accented English.

'Over there!'

'Open fire!'

Spurred on by the soldiers on his tail, Gali ran with all the energy he could muster, any thoughts of a covert exfiltration gone. Weaving through the shrub, he dodged and ducked as rounds from their automatic rifles flew past his head and splintered the trees around him. On he went, legs pumping, arms swinging to maximise his pace and give him leverage through the increasingly open ground.

'Just another two minutes ...' Gali said to himself, trying to put some distance between him and the pursuing troops.

He fell again, the crash to the ground so violent that he knocked all the wind out of himself. The firing continued but it was less accurate. He was nearly safe. Just a little further to get out of their range. As he lay on the ground trying to get his breath back, he heard voices close by.

'He was here ... everyone, wait; let me listen.' Although distant, the accent was different from the voice he had heard earlier. He could hear the AMISOM soldier's heavy breathing. The patrol that had remained on his trail was getting closer. Gali needed to take the initiative. He rolled onto his side as silently as he could and slipped his pack off once more, this time to remove his pistol that he had kept in there for emergencies.

And this was an emergency.

He still had the advantage, though. He knew the weapon was already cocked with a full magazine, so all he needed to do was slip off the safety and squeeze the trigger. He moved slightly to turn his head in the direction of the voices, even though it was difficult to know precisely where they were as he had lost hearing on his right side.

Gali scanned the ground, turning his head slowly left to right until he eventually spotted them about 25 metres away, heading straight for his position. Without hesitation he got up and, in the same movement, fired his pistol, dropping the first soldier and making the others dive for cover. He could see that those closest to him were not equipped with night vision equipment so he decided to press home the moment. Unsteady on his feet, he quickly fired again while advancing on the AMISOM patrol's position, this time aiming at the second soldier who he could see was lying prone on the ground. The soldier cried out as the two rounds hit him in the shoulder and back. This was Gali's moment to escape. Their heads were down and they could see nothing in the darkness. He immediately turned and set off, his movements now laboured as he struggled for breath, narrowly avoiding a large branch that lay across his path.

Gali had covered about fifteen metres, the shouts in English receding, when the explosion blew him off his feet and onto his back. Still conscious but numbed down his right side from the blast and in deep shock, he tried to get up again. As he was on his knees trying to steady himself, the second grenade exploded in front of him. The blast ripped the goggles off his face and he fell backwards, the sensation of burning growing across his body. The explosion from the third grenade barely registered. Gali felt nothing more than the sensation of being hit by a moving car. By now he felt little pain. His body was in deep shock and shutting down. The sounds of the attack were diminishing rapidly, his grip on life ebbing away as the blood from his injuries flowed out, his carotid artery fatally cut by a piece of shrapnel. As he lay on his back, eyes closed, losing consciousness, his breathing was laboured and he coughed, the blood from his wounds now entering his lungs, drowning him from within.

As he took his last breath, his pocket lit up with a message.

*

Pete had been struggling to keep up. He had decided on a whim to deploy with the quick reaction force for the evening, knowing that it was highly unlikely that they would be called on to do anything apart from conduct a few random perimeter patrols throughout his 12-hour shift.

When he had heard the truck bomb detonate, he had immediately split his team; the first section were sent to the entrance to reinforce the guards there, while the second patrol, under his guidance, would use the rear gate to approach the attack from outside the camp. He had eight men, two machine gunners, and they were all up for a fight.

Pete had grabbed his own night-vision goggles issued by Lancing Point to give him some advantage as the AMISOM troops were, in general, poorly equipped. He had guessed that there would be an assault on the camp at some stage and hoped that the sheer number of AMISOM troops, mostly Ugandans, would pull together and get organised to repel whatever was being thrown at them. The scale of the assault had surprised him; he needed to move fast.

Leaving behind two men to provide security at the rear gate, just in case the attackers made it that far, he quickly got control of his patrol, now six men, and headed out of the camp and onto the perimeter track. The quantity of rounds being fired suggested that this was a premeditated and deliberate complex attack. He knew there was a high chance of being overrun, but he had a hunch that his decision to approach from outside the camp was the right one. It was a long shot but he had a highly motivated team with him.

He steered his diminished patrol off the perimeter track and away from the security lighting towards the buildings and shrub that surrounded the camp. Moving quickly, he slipped his goggles on when they had moved into the dark, giving quiet directions to the infantryman on point in the patrol. Everyone had been calm, but they moved with a determination that gave him confidence. And then he saw him: a bearded man, wearing dirty Somali clothes and carrying a backpack, dashed across the track into the relative safety of the buildings about 50 metres ahead of them. He passed on the message and they picked up the pace. As they approached the more populated area, he noticed that people were everywhere, shouting and screaming, their noise mixing with the sounds of battle, the confusion and chaos magnified as a result. He kept his men calm and focused. At one point he called them to a halt, gathered close by and spoke quietly.

'There's a lot going on over there,' Pete said, pointing in the direction of the growing crowds amongst the buildings, 'but there's a runner. I just saw him cross from the fence and I think he must be somehow involved so we are going to try to capture him. It sounds like the locals have already found him so let's get moving towards the shouting.' Pete was always calm under pressure, his desire to capture one of the attackers his overriding priority.

After following the shouts of the locals, Pete again caught sight of the man running away from the buildings and into open ground. As soon as his patrol reached the edge of the inhabited area, he gave a quick-fire control order and the patrol opened up with their rifles in the general direction of the escapee. They were moving quickly, sensing they had the advantage, when the first explosion happened. Pete was thrown to the ground, and the closest soldier to the explosion on their right flank fell, mortally wounded. Getting back onto his feet was a struggle but Pete knew they could get the man if they kept up the chase. He encouraged the remaining members of the patrol, now down to five, to get up. The fearless soldier on point again led the chase, picking up the pace and covering the ground quickly. The second explosion was less of a shock and they were protected from the blast.

They pressed on.

After the third explosion, he held everyone back to scan the night, the distance covered by the goggles limiting his ability to see too far, but there he was, getting up and running forward, his legs and arms pumping like an Olympic athlete in the 100 metres final. He told his men to close the distance rapidly, firing when they could, but the man was a skilled fighter. After another pause when the man must have fallen, he appeared and, turning to face his pursuers, he fired one round which took out Pete's lead soldier. Then, as the patrol took cover, the man advanced on their position, taking out a second soldier lying on the ground. Pete recognised the tactics of a trained professional. They were in mortal danger and he needed to eliminate the threat. He immediately removed the first of three grenades and threw it towards the man, moving slowly away from the patrol, into the darkness beyond.

With the AMISOM troops tending the injured soldiers under torchlight, the gabble of radio chatter filling the air as they called for back-up and medical support, Pete walked up to the figure lying lifeless on the ground. When he stood over him, he could see that his face was unrecognisable, the skin burned off by the impact of the final grenade, his clothes ripped and scorched from the explosions. Judging by the quantity of blood on the dirt underneath his body, he had bled out. Still wearing his goggles, Pete looked around the body, then crouched down above him, checking for anything that might be of interest. His pockets were empty bar a single Nokia mobile phone, miraculously still on and with an unread message. He picked it up and opened the message: *Xagee joogtaa? Where are you?*

Pete read the message a couple of times before putting it into his own jacket pocket and retracing his steps. He picked up the pistol that was lying close by, making it safe and slipping it into his waist belt. He quickly found the backpack but, after a cursory inspection, there was nothing of interest inside it apart from some rounds of ammunition for the pistol the man had been using and what looked like a sketch of the camp. He slung it over his shoulder and walked off.

The fire-fight had finally stopped. Either the al Shabaab fighters had escaped or they were dead, along with a fair number of his Ugandan soldiers who had left their country to help bring peace to this troubled corner of

Africa. He shook his head and focused on the remaining troops in his patrol.

He pulled the goggles off his face and walked back to the soldiers, who were trying to keep their comrades alive. He knelt down and took over the CPR on the second injured AMISOM soldier. He could tell he would not make it, but he did what he could. The rhythmic action of pressing the young soldier's bare chest twice a second gave him a sense of purpose. After a few minutes of hard effort, and with little chance of medical support arriving at his location, he checked for signs of life. His neck was heavily blooded and his lips were pale. Pete squeezed his fingers against his neck but he felt no pulse.

'He's gone ...' Pete said to no one in particular but one of the soldiers kneeling close to him started saying a prayer under his breath.

Pete got up and walked away, wiping the blood from his hands on his trousers. He would throw them away when he got back to camp. He always did when someone else's blood was involved. He pulled out a packet of cigarettes, his hands shaking from the exertion as he fumbled to get one out, then lit up, uncaring whether Shabaab fighters were still in the vicinity. Either way, the firing had stopped, and all that was left was shouting in the distance and mourning close at hand.

As he pulled on the cigarette, inhaling deeply, his mind started to wander; his flight to Nairobi was in a few days' time and he needed a break from the securitized environment he had been living in for the last eight weeks. And once back in Kenya's capital city, he had already arranged a meeting at the New Muthaiga Shopping Mall to share some of his insights into al Shabaab's increased effectiveness. With the dead man's phone in his pocket, something he would not share with his colleagues at Lancing Point, at least he finally had something interesting to report to Jo.

15

Riyadh, Kingdom of Saudi Arabia

The British diplomat walked out of his apartment building and into the night, crossing the wide pavement and opening the door to the taxi. It was a Saturday evening and, with a three-hour time difference to the UK, he knew it might be another late night.

'Sports Café, Thalia Street,' he instructed the driver, who pulled out into the traffic.

The evening was warm and he was wearing a T-shirt, jeans and a pair of trainers. He opened the window of his taxi to feel the breeze, looking up at the tall, glass-fronted buildings as he passed along the wide boulevard. He had been angling for a posting to the Middle East since starting his training and, after six months in the country, he had established a strong network amongst the expat community, even if the local Arab population had been difficult to penetrate. But it was early days; he had another two and a half years of this life, and he intended to make the most of it, despite its natural climatic challenges. The journey wasn't a long one and he was soon out of the taxi, the relative humidity already making his T-shirt stick to his back.

As he walked towards the bar, he pulled out his phone and sent a brief message to his colleague on her office mobile, knowing she would pick it up first thing: *Just meeting my contact from the port authority at the sports café. J*

The bar was on the roadside, just a stone's throw from the city's international airport. He knew his contact, who lived on the coast, had recently returned to the capital for some in-country rest and recuperation. It was a sports café with bells on: row upon row of large television screens were arranged along each wall, all tuned in to the big match. A mezzanine gave an even better view of the huge screens hung precariously above the long bar. With a key Saturday night football match about to start, he headed inside and took a seat in front of one of the screens covering the match. Any Liverpool game drew an expat crowd, but when it was against Manchester

United it was likely to be extra busy, so he was surprised he found a stool to sit on. He didn't have to wait long to ask for a drink, and, as his tonic arrived, his phone buzzed in his pocket: *Where are you? I'm at the bar. Micky*

Jack looked around and saw his friend Micky about ten metres away, his neck straining to see where Jack was. They caught each other's eye and waved. The man who worked for the Saudi Ports Authority picked up his drink and made his way through the crowd, deeper into the café, to join Jack sitting at the bar.

'Great to see you, Micky! How's your weekend been?' Jack had got up to shake his hand and, after finding a spare stool, they sat together and chinked glasses. Even without alcohol, some habits were hard to drop. 'What do you think the result will be?'

'Yeah, it's been great thanks ... it'll be a home win to Liverpool, no question about it.' The diplomat would have been surprised at any other response considering Micky was a scouser wearing a replica Liverpool shirt, trekking trousers and trainers completing the outfit.

'How about you, how've you been?'

'All good, thanks. I went skydiving yesterday, which was pretty intense. You should try it one day!' Jack said.

'No chance!' Micky replied, laughing at the thought of his large frame jumping out of an airplane. 'They wouldn't have a parachute big enough for me.'

Jack was an athletic man in his late twenties and had quickly established a range of activities for his weekends to help deal with the pressure of work. As a political officer in the British Embassy, he was focused on understanding the interaction between the host nation and its ties with East Africa, in particular the emerging influence of Turkey in Somalia. He had arranged to watch the match because of what Micky had mentioned when they had last shared a few drinks a month earlier, during his previous in-country time off.

They had initially met when they had both been invited along to a meal in a local pizza restaurant by a group of expats early on in Jack's posting. The last time they had met in the sports café, Micky had pulled Jack to one side to report that he was concerned about some irregularities in the loading of ships bound for Somalia's main port, Mogadishu. He knew Jack worked in the British Embassy and had asked him for some advice.

'Jack, I am meant to be overseeing operations but I don't have the final say on anything – that's left to the locals. I noticed something strange about a Panama-flagged ship heading for Mogadishu. Basically, it had a container on board which didn't appear on the manifest. That's abnormal, you know what I mean?' Micky's accent cut through his words. 'What do you think?'

Jack's intuition had immediately kicked in, but he played it all down. He was keen to make a name for himself. 'It's probably just a cock-up, you know what they're like. I would leave it for now, but why don't you have a check through your records to see if it was a one-off?' Jack's advice had seemed reasonable at the time and Micky had accepted it without question. Micky was relatively new to the Gulf and didn't want to jeopardise his tax-free salary. And he liked Jack and trusted his advice.

Jack ordered a second round of tonic and coke for them both and, amid the noise and loud music filling the bar during half-time, he turned around to survey the scene. It was alive with couples having dinner, and groups either watching the sport or socialising together. He knew even then that he would never get used to being in this type of environment without alcohol to accompany the evening. When their drinks arrived a few minutes later, Jack ironically offered to chink glasses with Micky again, before raising the subject of the ghost container. Gently leaning towards his friend, he spoke close to his ear.

'Did you ever establish whether that container issue was a one-off or part of a pattern?' Micky's role in operations within the Saudi Ports Authority in Jeddah had been a revelation for Jack, and he knew his position could be very useful for his own work. Jack had explained that he worked in the embassy on political matters, but Micky's interest was only limited to preserving his job. He didn't ask any other questions, which suited Jack.

'Well actually, yeah, I found some more information out about that. There was an earlier shipment that also had an extra container that didn't appear on the ship's manifest. I checked right up to the last ship to head in that direction and it's happened again. So that's three shipping containers over three months using the same ship.' The man spoke quickly, fully aware that he was sharing valuable information with his friend. 'What do you want me to do about it?'

Jack took a drink from his glass and thought for a moment. The teams were heading back out onto the pitch at Anfield. He wanted to wrap the conversation up.

'Do nothing for now. Can you let me know who else may be aware of the ghost containers and who would have the authority to let something get loaded without it appearing on the manifest? No rush ... next time we meet.' His mind was already making some basic calculations and he needed one last piece of information. 'When did you say the last shipment left port?' Jack asked very casually, as if he really wasn't interested in the answer.

'Er, I think it was last Wednesday, yes, it should have left at 9am but it was delayed and left at midday because there was an issue with the loading ... so about three days ago,' he replied.

Jack took another swig of his tonic and slapped his friend on the arm, 'Thanks Micky, that's good to know. I would just keep an eye on it, no need to rock the boat. Excuse the pun!' They both laughed. 'Just cover your own arse in case.' Jack tried to make his advice pragmatic and as low-key as possible.

'Yes, that's what I plan to do. Thanks mate, hope that was useful.' But the football had restarted and Micky's attention was already drawn to the gloriously green pitch on the TV. Watching the events thousands of miles away, engrossed in the moment through the screen, it was easy to forget that they were surrounded by desert.

Jack finished his drink. 'Micky, I need to finish off a report so I'm going to head off. Great to catch up.' Liverpool were leading so Micky was in good spirits.

'No worries Jack, great to see you, mate. Let's do it again next time I'm in the capital,' Micky replied.

Jack slipped away through the mass of people crammed into the bar and made for the exit. By his calculation, they had about four days before the ship docked in Somalia.

The next morning, Jack was at his desk before anyone else. He had needed to do some online research about the ship and to investigate Saudi Arabia's relationship with Somalia more generally. After a couple of hours, he had found what he needed. When his colleague, whom he had texted the night before, strolled into the office carrying a Starbucks coffee cup, she remarked that he had obviously had an earlier night than expected. He shrugged, said hello, and turned back to his laptop and the report he was preparing. He wanted to keep it short so that there was more chance of it being read quickly.

CLASSIFICATION: RESTRICTED

From: Station, Riyadh;

To: Station, London; Station, Nairobi; Ambassador, Mogadishu;

CC: Ambassador, Riyadh;

Priority: URGENT

Subject: Irregular Shipment; Saudi Ports Authority (SPA), Riyadh

1. *Meeting with contact working in Jeddah for SPA reports several shipments between Jeddah and Mogadishu containing a single container unrecorded on the manifest.*
2. *Shipments appear to be regular – every month – with three examples detected so far, all using the same ship. Last shipment left Jeddah four days ago on seven-day passage (precise arrival Mogadishu tbc).*
3. *Use of open source suggests the name of ship is MV Caldo Porta.*
4. *Background: KSA conducting long-term mosque building programme across Somalia.*
5. *Recommend investigation at Mogadishu Port (if security situation allows) as difficult to establish facts in country.*

Signed: JHG, 3rd Sec Pol

Jack pressed "send" and looked at his watch. It was too early to phone Kenya; he would wait a couple of hours then make the call. He planned to speak to his colleague, whom he had met during a familiarisation visit to Nairobi a few weeks before. She had introduced herself to Jack and asked him to share anything unusual that might be happening between the Gulf region and Somalia. After stumbling across the initial information, he had not paid much attention to it until he had met Imi. When he knew that someone was genuinely interested in what he was working on, his instinct told him that Mickey's information was worth following up, which had led to the hastily arranged meeting the night before. Now he just had to wait and hope the report didn't get lost in someone's in-tray.

*

It was Sunday morning.

Pete loved Sunday mornings when he was away from Mogadishu. He had woken up early; vivid memories from the attack on the camp had been filling his dreams each night since it had happened. He had lost three of his men from the patrol that had pursued the Shabaab fighter. The man's behaviour and his obvious tactical awareness made Pete think that something wasn't right. He had brought the phone with him, along with a photograph of the pack and the rounds inside. He thought it would be useful for his meeting later.

Pete had long enjoyed a relationship with the UK, mainly through his father, who had served with the Light Infantry regiment during the fifties and sixties, but the connection had continued when his younger brother, who had successfully applied for a British passport, had signed up to join the British Army as a logistics expert. Whilst Pete had chosen to remain rooted in Africa, using his South African passport through his mother who was originally from Johannesburg, his brother had travelled the world and experienced the highs and lows of military service in the northern hemisphere. Having a parent with the right birth certificate had made all the difference in life for him.

Nine months earlier, during one of his overnight stays in Nairobi, Pete had visited the British High Commission to apply for a visa to visit his brother in England. Once he had completed his application form, and following an internal call from the consular team, a young woman with a strong accent had appeared in the waiting room and invited Pete to join her for a coffee. After discussing what he did in Mogadishu for half an hour, she asked him whether he would be willing to report back on anything out of the ordinary. The woman knew that Lancing Point was funded by the US and was as close to a CIA front as you could get, but that didn't deter her. She had said that by agreeing to do so would smooth all future requests for visits to the UK; she even offered him money for his trouble, but Pete earned enough from Lancing Point. He wasn't motivated by financial gain, he simply wanted to help a country he felt extremely close to, so he had agreed.

Pete finally got up at 10am after surfing through the news channels for a couple of hours, leaving him an hour to shower, change and take a cab to the New Muthaiga Shopping Mall. After a piece of toast and jam, he walked through the hotel lobby and hailed a taxi from a line waiting to the left of the entrance, their engines idling, adding to the vehicle-induced smog that plagued Nairobi most days.

Pete got in and sat behind the driver. 'Hello, mate. Thigiri Ridge Road, please, the shopping centre up there.'

'OK, Boss.'

The car moved off and within 15 minutes was pulling into the long car park running just behind the main building. Pete had steered the driver to this side rather than the main entrance on advice from Jo, whom he had met a few times after their initial conversation at the High Commission. Since agreeing to share anything interesting from his time on the front line with AMISOM, his meetings with her had been slightly awkward affairs. He had talked about the kind of operations he was involved in and she had politely taken notes, but he knew he wasn't sharing anything of real interest. He had a feeling this meeting would be different.

After lighting a cigarette, he walked to the northern end of the car park as the taxi drove off in the opposite direction. Circling round the front of the shopping centre, he headed to an outdoor café with dozens of chairs and tables arranged haphazardly behind a low wooden picket fence painted dark green, the stone-coloured parasols bearing the name of Kenya's famous brand of beer keeping the sun off the seating area.

Pete looked around and saw a few families nearby watching their children clamber over obstacles in a play area, their shouts of delight the only other sound along with the low rumble of cars driving along Thigiri Ridge Road 50 metres away. He knew why they had always met here. Jo had said that anyone who's anyone always drives past this shopping mall, heading for the more secure and better equipped Village Garden shopping centre located next to the UN compound in Gigiri, further up the road.

He sat down and checked his watch. With a minute to go before their appointment, he looked around again. The waitress was just coming over and behind her he could see Jo, standing in the shade, phone pressed to her ear, waving to say she would be over in a few minutes. He ordered a cappuccino.

'Hello, this is Imi.'

'Imi, it's Jack from Riyadh. Do you remember we met a few weeks ago when I visited Nairobi? How are you?'

'Yes, I remember. Good to hear from you. You do know it's Sunday morning though, right?' Imi wasn't overly happy about taking a work call on a Sunday morning from someone at another embassy, but she didn't let it show in her voice. She barely knew Jack but she had softly recruited him into her network of contacts and colleagues who might be able to help her one day. Her ability to get people to do her bidding was one of her strengths.

'Ah well, you know Sunday's a working day here …' Jack broke off for a moment. 'Listen, Imi, I've sent through a report which I think you need to look at before the end of the day. If you want any further info, give me a shout, but it's all a bit thin on the ground to be honest and it might be nothing.' Jack spoke guardedly.

'OK, no worries Jack, thanks for the heads-up. Have a good one. See ya.' Imi hung up, turned her phone onto silent and walked towards Pete, intercepting the waitress on the way and ordering a green tea.

'Hi Pete, good flight?' They shook hands, Imi's fingers disappearing into Pete's huge grip. 'I keep remembering that we should high-five instead,' Imi laughed.

'Alright, Jo, good to see you. How have you been?' Pete asked.

Imi had chosen the name Jo after reading his visa application and discovering that his mother's name was Joanne.

'Yeah, all good here. The usual chaos that is Kenya's capital, you know …'

For a few minutes they talked about Nairobi's famous traffic problem and the complete lack of order on the roads. As they were talking, a small Bulbul bird hopped momentarily onto a chair between them, optimistically looking for signs of a pastry. They both stopped talking to watch its rapid movements, its fawn-coloured head nervously looking side to side for predators, while at the same time tilting its head to get a better view of the table. It did a final, rapid scan of the area and, realising it would have to find a different table, flew off, its yellow under-feathers the last thing they saw as its tiny wings flapped frantically away.

'Bloody beautiful little things, aren't they?' Pete surprised Imi with the tenderness in his voice.

Imi waited a moment before asking the question they both knew was coming.

'They are … anyway, how have things been up there?' Imi took out her notebook and a pen, carefully unscrewing the lid and placing it on the table in front of her. To any casual observer she was a western journalist interviewing someone in a café. A perfectly innocent thing to do which failed to attract any attention from the few people in the area.

Pete drew in a breath and exhaled slowly, giving himself a moment of calm before speaking.

'It's been a bit shit, if I'm honest. The last couple of months have been pretty busy. The tempo has been higher than anything I can remember, especially in the last few weeks, with attack after attack taking place right across each sector. I've never known anything like it. You've seen some of the reports, I should imagine.' Pete paused when he saw the waitress walk over with his coffee and Imi's tea.

After the young Kenyan girl had walked out of earshot, Imi replied. 'I have noticed a lot of reporting, yes, but without eyes on the ground it's difficult to gauge the reasons behind it.' Imi's military experience was minimal, so she steered clear of offering an opinion, but even to her untrained eye, the reports she was reading, written by Megan in the embassy in Mogadishu, were a worrying development.

'The other boys have all said the same thing, eh, that Shabaab's accuracy has improved and there has been an increase in the complexity of the attacks. It's like they have suddenly found an unlimited supply of weapons, ammunition and explosives, and their planning seems to be better. But we have struggled to figure out what's behind it, y'know. Well, that was until the other night ...' Pete spoke with the same passion as he had done in the Lancing Point bar before the training camp attack, only this time his voice was quiet, measured.

Imi was scribbling notes as he spoke, and by the time she had finished her last sentence and raised her head, Pete was taking something out of his trouser pocket which made her audibly gasp. He placed the blooded Nokia phone, now in a zip-up sandwich bag, on the table between them and pushed it towards her.

Imi quickly grabbed it and slipped it into her bag on her lap. 'Let's keep that out of sight for now, Pete, shall we? So, what's the story?' Her heart was racing as she picked up her pen again.

'Well, the other night we had a bit of a catastrophe to be honest. I won't go into too much detail but there was a huge attack on the EU training facility south of the city, loads of AMISOM and Somalis killed and injured, Shabaab deaths, too, it was awful. You probably heard about it.' He stopped speaking, waiting for Imi to respond. When she looked up, she nodded.

'I was with the QRF that evening, ready for a normal 12 hour shift ...' Pete explained.

'Hold on – *QRF?*' Imi had never heard the term.

'Quick reaction force. It's a bit of a misnomer for AMISOM because they are so poorly equipped but, basically, it's a bunch of soldiers who can deploy anywhere within the tactical environment to reinforce other troops, or to conduct independent actions against the enemy. After the truck exploded at the entrance, which I found out later immediately killed six Ugandan troops, I split my team and took one half out of the camp to sweep round to a tree line where I thought the Shabaab fighters were likely to be based, and I was right.'

Pete took a sip of his coffee, taking his time to explain the story as clearly as he could. The act of doing so was also giving him sense of release. 'So, as we were heading round, I saw a figure dart across the perimeter track and disappear into the makeshift village that has sprung up close to the camp. I don't know if you know it ...' Pete asked.

Imi shook her head.

'Well, to me, there was something about him that didn't seem right. He had obviously placed some explosive devices against the perimeter because when they went off, they took out one of my guys. Anyway, we pursued him for about ten minutes into a semi-forested area and then he did something I have never seen Shabaab do. He stood up and advanced on the patrol from about 30 meters away, and started firing at the men, on his own, with a pistol, wearing night-vision goggles. Shabaab don't do that, they use AK47s and, more often than not, they run. And their shooting is normally pretty shit too, eh. They're cowards, apart from the suicide bombers, of course, but they're brainwashed. Anyway, he took two of my guys out straight away and when I thought he was going to finish us off, I took out a couple of grenades. At that moment he turned and ran; our heads were down, you see, the young soldiers I was with were, by then, shitting themselves. The guy with the pistol was dominating the situation ...' Pete paused again, his voice low as he took a sip of his coffee and carried on. 'So, I threw the grenades, three in total, and killed him as he tried to escape.'

After a moment, Imi stopped writing. She looked up, shocked at what she was hearing. 'And this phone belonged to him I take it? Is it still working?'

She tapped her bag.

'Yeah, it was when I picked it up, but it's since run out of battery.'

She kept her voice calm as she spoke again. 'Did you look at it at all, open any messages, look at its call history?' Imi's pen was poised over the page.

'When I got to him, he was a mess. There was nothing left of his face or the front of his torso, and the phone was the only thing he had in his pockets which survived. There was one message that was unread, which I looked at, but it didn't mean anything to me. That was all. The strange thing was he had been wearing night-vision goggles when he advanced on my patrol, which is very unusual, and when I went through his pockets he didn't have any khat anywhere. None at all. Most Shabaab fighters have some to hand. Granted, his clothing was pretty ripped up so I can't be sure about that. I also found the pistol he had used and a backpack with some ammunition in it nearby.' Pete had been focused on Imi's face as he was speaking, with an intensity that unnerved her.

'There's one more thing, Jo,' Pete said. 'The guy was not a Somali. He was definitely a foreign fighter. He was well built, well nourished, and in good condition, as much as any dead body can look after what he went through,' Pete chuckled to himself, the soldier's black humour cutting through his words. 'But it didn't seem right to me. I don't have any explanation for it.'

'Does anyone else in Lancing Point know about the phone?' Imi asked.

'No, they don't. They know about the body but I think it's already been cremated to be honest. I didn't care too much what happened to it.'

'OK well, it's probably best they don't know, I'll get it checked out.' Imi paused. She knew he had been through a traumatic experience and even though dangerous situations had clearly gone hand in hand with his life, it still must have been a very difficult event to witness.

'How are you feeling?'

'Honestly, I'll be fine once I get back to Jo'burg and the missus ...' Pete grinned and winked at Imi, who looked down at her notebook, momentarily embarrassed by the insinuation.

While Pete had been speaking, a few more families had arrived and were heading for the play park. He looked up, took a mouthful of his coffee, and turned away towards the hedgerow and the road beyond. At that moment, a couple crossed his vision and took a table about ten feet away from where they were sitting. He could hear them choosing what to drink, which meant their privacy was now compromised.

'Do you want to move, Jo?'

'No, it's fine, I think we are done here anyway.' Imi closed her notebook and slipped it into her bag next to the phone.

'Shall we pay?' Imi took out her wallet and turned around to call for the bill. She didn't really know what more to ask. What Pete had described, albeit very light on detail, had terrified her. She had no idea how someone could go through that one minute, then calmly sit at a café and talk about a few days later. But the phone was dynamite and she was keen to get it forensically examined.

When Imi had left some money on the tray containing the bill, they got up and walked towards the main entrance together. They had never done that before and Imi guessed there was something else that needed to be said. She turned into a shadowed alcove, close to the main entrance.

'If you ever find out who that guy was, will you let me know?' Pete asked.

Imi looked at him. 'I don't know, Pete. Honestly? I doubt it. But leave it with me, I'm sure it will produce something of interest. Look, I've got to go … thank you for arranging the meeting. It's been good to see you. You have my email address if you want to meet on your way back, in case you remember anything else. But usual drills: don't include any detail other than a time and place to meet, OK?' Imi looked up at his deeply suntanned, slightly jowly face, his greying hair cut short, his clothes neatly pressed and clean. He looked remarkably well, but his eyes were somewhere else, even though he was looking right at her. 'Have a great leave. I think you've deserved it!'

'Thanks for the coffee, Jo. I will. Take care of yourself, eh.' Pete waved to avoid a handshake, and walked off towards the entrance of the shopping mall. During every meeting with Imi, or Jo as he knew her, Pete had always believed that she was a mainstream diplomat, piecing together information about a country that the UK was deeply interested in. The thought that he was an asset, working for the UK's Secret Intelligence Service, had never occurred to him.

Sometimes ignorance is bliss.

16

Vila Somalia, Mogadishu

'Good morning, Bashiir,' Christian said, announcing his arrival at the Chief of Staff's office by knocking on the thick wooden door as he stepped over the threshold. The office had an old oak desk to his left in front of the windows, covered with an array of papers, two comfortable armchairs in front and an occasional table between them. Behind Bashir's desk, Christian had previously noticed a bookshelf full of titles as diverse as *One Flew Over The Cuckoo's Nest* and *Somalia: the definitive guide for visitors*, both in English. On his right, against the wall, sat a three-seater leather sofa. The double doors to the President's suite of rooms were directly opposite where he was standing. The strip lights hanging from the ceiling were permanently on as the thick curtains were always drawn, as much to keep out the heat of the day as to reduce flying glass in the event of an explosion outside. The international community hadn't invested in protective glass for the President's office complex, an oversight in Christian's mind now that he was living there pretty much full time.

For a room that was only the President's outer office, it was certainly imposing. Christian made a beeline for the desk, his arm outstretched to greet the President's most trusted aide.

'Hello, Christian, how are you today?' Bashiir got up and shook his hand as he had done pretty much every day since Christian had started working as an advisor for the Defence Minister two weeks before.

Bashiir, younger and slightly shorter than Christian, looked every bit like the Somali civil servants seen criss-crossing Vila Somalia every day: very slightly overweight, dark suit slightly too big, faded white shirt with the top button permanently undone, and a lifeless tie pulled down from the neck as if it had been strangling him on the way to work. Bashiir's looks were deceiving, though. He had one of the brightest minds Christian had come across in Mogadishu's political nerve centre and he was able to make judgements about what was right and what was wrong with an intellectual ease Christian hadn't been expecting. Educated overseas, Bashiir was a political appointee from the right clan who could be trusted to watch the President's back when it came to the often deadly game of politics that had plagued Somalia for over two decades. As his Chief of Staff, Bashiir held sway over the President like no other aide, and his word could end political careers as easily as initiate them. The longer the President stayed in power, the longer Bashiir kept his job. The logic was perverse, and open to corruption, as the country had witnessed for many years.

As a result, Christian treated Bashiir with a great deal of respect. If anything, although they had known each other from his previous role, his respect for him had risen as each day passed in his new appointment within Vila Somalia. Fortunately for Christian, Bashiir liked him and could see the benefits of having a British security advisor inside Vila Somalia, mapping out how the international community should be supporting Somalia's fledgling security forces. So far, Christian's pragmatic approach to the role had resulted in very positive comments from those he was working alongside, and Bashiir had passed these on to him. Christian had responded by saying that the Somali cohort was not his main concern, however challenging that may be; the real battle was aligning the security representatives from the international community. Bringing their collective resources together for the benefit of Somalia, rather than for the benefit of their own foreign policy objectives, would be a huge step forward, but in the last few years it had been an impossible task. Both men understood the challenge Christian faced and, for now at least, he knew he could rely on Bashiir's support.

'I'm very well, thanks,' Christian said. 'I was wondering whether the President will be in later on today. I have put together a summary slide deck which describes the current levels of support being offered by the key donors, and how we may want to begin to influence some of your partners over the next few months. I would only need about 20 minutes, and Minister Hassan is keen to discuss it. We don't need a decision; we just want to share the thinking.'

He looked to his right and the suite of rooms that made up the President's private office. He had only entered the main reception room on one occasion, when he was initially introduced to the President in his first week. Since then, he had not crossed the threshold.

Christian knew that his approach to the role was new and likely to induce a scratching of heads. This kind of detailed analysis and long-term planning appeared to be missing from the small staff that supported the Defence Minister, Abdulla Hassan. But this is what Christian had signed up to do, and he was making progress, albeit slowly.

'Let me check.' Bashiir guarded the President's diary like the crown jewels; nobody knew exactly what the daily schedule was apart from him. He opened the side drawer on his left and took out a black, A4-sized leather diary. He opened it by pulling on a thin red ribbon, then turned a page before scanning down the detailed entries with his forefinger. At the bottom of the page, he looked up.

'I'm not sure it's going to work, Christian; he has several international visitors today and I don't think he will be finished in time to see you. Perhaps you could come back next week.' Bashiir closed the diary with a snap and replaced it in the drawer. Christian smiled. It wasn't the first time he had experienced this absence of forward planning. The most sensible thing would have been to suggest a time and date for the following week, so that other appointments could be fitted in around it. But that wasn't going to work with the President, who was more often than not reacting to events and at the beck and call of international representatives demanding short-notice meetings. Christian reminded himself that it was Thursday, the last day of the week, after all, and he was meant to be leaving Vila Somalia mid-afternoon to meet Megan at the B&B. Perhaps it was a good idea to delay the appointment.

'Thanks for trying, Bashiir. I can brief him anytime, and I am sure Minister Hassan will see him before I do anyway. I'll leave it for now. See you later.' Christian smiled and raised his hand as a goodbye.

'Christian! Wait a second.' Bashiir had got up again from behind his huge desk and was walking around it towards him. 'Where are you living when you are not in the guest room at Vila Somalia? Are you in a hotel in the city or do you escape to Airport Camp?' He was smiling as he asked the question.

Christian was sure he knew the answer but he told him anyway.

'If I stay in Mogadishu, I hole up at the B&B near Airport Camp, otherwise I head back to Nairobi where I have an apartment.' He was looking at Bashiir who had raised his eyebrows, a blank expression across his face. 'Do you know the B&B? They keep a pretty low profile as they've been operating for years, keeping the peace with both sides, you know?' Christian thought anyone who was connected to the international scene would have heard about the B&B, but it seemed he was wrong.

'No, I've never heard of it. Sounds extraordinary. Who runs it?' Bashiir asked.

'Well, it's a Norwegian couple who came over here a couple of decades ago working for an NGO and decided to stay.' Christian replied.

'Of all the places to live, huh? Well, perhaps we should take tea there one of these days.' Bashiir patted him on the arm as he turned away and returned to his desk. Christian's audience was over. It was time for Bashiir to focus on matters of state.

As Christian walked out of the office and turned left, several Somalis dressed in suits walked past him, nodding their recognition before going into the Chief of Staff's office. He followed a long corridor which kinked around some stairs that led up to the first floor before eventually opening up into a large entrance hall containing airport-style security scanners and a posse of guards, where all foreign visitors were met. Christian showed his pass and was waved through.

He was now so used to the access that he didn't really think about how hard it had been in his previous role to speak to certain ministers when he had been trying to arrange media visits. Now, all he had to do was make a call, follow up with an unannounced visit to an outer office, speak to an aide and, within hours, the meeting was arranged. The only person who bucked that trend was the President. But Christian could live with that.

He stopped at the entrance to check his watch before opening the door and walking outside; it was 10 o'clock and he had three hours before his inaugural international security working group meeting inside the conference room at MIA, or Airport Camp as it was known in Vila Somalia.

This would be the first time in his new role that he would meet the security representatives from the international community face to face. Also invited would be the various transnational organisations that had a big stake in what was going on in Somalia, such as the United Nations, the African Union and the European Union. The recent upturn in al Shabaab attacks was likely to dominate the meeting and he had decided not to seek any sort of decision on any subject during this first outing; he was more interested in meeting each rep to gauge their response to his appointment. He had access to officials in Vila Somalia that many of those in the conference room could only dream of. He needed to manage his position carefully; making enemies within this group of predominantly alpha males would not be helpful to his cause. Fortunately, he had received positive comments from all but a handful of players, probably because they knew that with Christian on the inside, they needed him as much as he needed them. He consoled himself with the thought that he could make the whole arrangement work as long as there was some give and take. The one positive was that his friend, Mac, had flown up to Mogadishu and would be at the meeting.

He stepped off the curb and approached another check point just in front of the building. Manned by Somali Army guards, it provided an additional layer of security between the Office of the President and the main Vila Somalia complex, which housed every government department. After showing his pass again to the men, whose faces he was beginning to recognise, he walked over the faded white cobble stones and into the administration block's large entrance hall. He turned left and entered the café at precisely the same moment that Muna was getting up to leave. They instantly walked towards each other.

'Christian! Hello, stranger! Am I no longer of interest to you now you are mixing in such exalted company?!' Muna smiled and gave Christian a warm embrace, her mint green *garbasaar* enveloping him as they hugged. They hadn't seen each other since before Christmas and the way she greeted Christian inside Vila Somalia would never have been permitted on the street outside. But nobody seemed to mind.

'Very funny, Muna, great to see you too. Are you leaving?'

'Yes, I have to chair the Returns Committee, for what it's worth,' Muna replied.

'What's that?' Christian asked.

'Ugh. Remember I told you about the restaurant manager from Minneapolis? We list all the roles where there are vacancies in government online, set out the minimum requirements for each one, a bit like a job description but much more basic, then look at the list of applications that have been emailed in by Somalis from across the world over the last month. Except they hardly ever match, so we just accept the lot and do what we can ... it's *so* depressing.' Muna had turned into Christian's body, lowering her voice theatrically as she over-emphasised the word "so", her American accent giving it added bite. Christian laughed and at the same time shook his head. He turned to the boy at the counter and asked for a tea, his hand signals now well-tuned for the task.

'Keep smiling, Muna. Your time will come,' Christian said.

'Yeah, yeah, I know. Next time tell me about your holidays. Have a good day, Chris, gotta go.' And with that she was out the door with a flourish and heading for the stairs. He liked Muna and had decided that one day he would visit her in the US without the constraints she faced living in Mogadishu, assuming she survived her time in Somalia and went back home. The murder rate amongst journalists and returning politicians in Mogadishu was high. She just needed to remember the security advice he had given her a few months earlier.

His tea arrived quickly and he thanked the boy for bringing it in a paper cup, something he had made arrangements for early on in his time in Vila Somalia. He walked out of the café and back into the heat of the morning, the warm wind blowing across the car park, causing his cream linen jacket, which he wore most days, to flap wildly in the breeze. Vila Somalia was one of the highest points in the capital and the air was never still. He walked around the corner, back through the outer check point in front of the entrance to the Office of the President and, instead of retracing his steps, he turned left and headed along the side of the building until he reached his single-story accommodation, partially hidden by some tall acacia trees and mercifully sheltered from the full force of the wind. The downside was that he was next to the perimeter wall which, when he had first moved in, had given him sleepless nights.

His apartment was surprisingly comfortable. There was a bathroom, a small kitchen, a sitting room and a bedroom, all containing the basic furniture and items that you would expect to find in a standard hotel suite. His experience of living on operations around the world had prepared him for the worst, so he had been pleasantly surprised by the comfort afforded him. He had brought the minimum quantity of clothing and, in a utility room beyond the kitchen, he had access to a basic washing machine. With such a high ambient temperature outside, together with the constant warm breeze, drying clothes was very quick and he could be hanging his shirts back in the wardrobe in a couple of hours. He had access to a fast internet connection and his mobile coverage was also good. All in all, he had become quite used to the conditions.

What he didn't enjoy so much were the occasional bursts of gunfire, often quite close to the compound, although he was yet to experience a mortar attack, which had happened all too often in the past. His plan to work for four weeks in the city, but to escape to the B&B for an occasional overnight stay every couple of weeks, was designed to keep him sane. Christian was looking forward to getting out of Vila Somalia later on. And he had two weeks left before his first leave back in his apartment in Nairobi where he would be able to get a proper rest.

He sat down on an old two-seater leather sofa which had seen better days and sipped his tea. Almost as soon as he has put his cup down on the side table and closed his eyes, his phone buzzed in his pocket: *Hey Chris, can't wait to see you later. M x*

He and Megan hadn't seen each other since flying back to the UK together before Christmas, so they had arranged to meet up at the B&B for the weekend. Although Megan was officially not meant to be off camp when on duty in Mogadishu, she had decided to stretch the rules since the B&B was only a few hundred metres from the back gate. She had lined up transport to get her back in case there was a crisis, and her logistics manager, Krishna, was on hand to cover the arrangements. All Christian had to do was navigate the meeting in Airport Camp, then jump into his transport for the short trip round to the B&B. It was the first time in two weeks that he would be stepping outside the secure perimeter of the huge Vila Somalia complex.

Should be there around 4 if all goes well. C x

He had spent much of the Christmas and New Year period in the UK thinking about his feelings for Megan, their time together on the flight home as precious as anything he had experienced so far with her. Their mutual family commitments had resulted in lots of Skype calls so, now that they were more able to be with each other, they wanted to take every opportunity to meet up.

Christian finished his tea and grabbed his daysack, along with his laptop, slipping it inside next to his weekend gear. He checked to see the windows were closed, turned off the air conditioning, and stepped out of his accommodation, locking the door behind him and putting the key in the top pocket of his pack. He knew that his privacy was unlikely to be respected as he was sure that his room had already been entered during his absence, but he still went through the motions of securing his personal space all the same. He had nothing to hide.

He walked back through the check point and into the main government building, taking the stairs up to his third-floor office to prepare some notes for the meeting later. Miko was coming to collect him at midday, so he only had an hour or so to get everything done.

At five minutes to midday, Christian popped his head into the Defence Minister's outer office and said goodbye to Said, his Chief of Staff, who had organised an office for Christian next door to his own and very close to Minister Hassan's. Christian was very happy with the arrangements and had thanked Said for helping him to settle in. They had struck up a very good working relationship.

'The Defence Minister will be leaving in half an hour, Christian. He said he will see you there.' Said was very formal and respected positions of authority without hesitation. And that extended to Christian, who had quickly learned to maintain the appropriate professional distance from Said.

'Thank you, Said, I will see you on Sunday, have a good weekend.' Christian touched his chest with his right hand and slipped away down the stairs and out into the carpark where he was hoping Miko would be waiting. And he was there, engine running, door ajar so that he could listen for Christian's arrival.

'Miko!' Christian shouted his friend's name amicably. Miko pushed the door open and got out.

'Ah, here I am again, driving a Christian in the heart of a Muslim city!' Miko reached out and they gripped hands, touching their right shoulders together in friendship. They had experienced a lot together in the last few months. Christian got in behind the driver while Miko closed the doors, which took more effort than normal.

'What do you think of new wheels?' Miko asked.

'Impressive! When did it arrive?' Christian had known that the B&B security business was going to invest in a B6 armoured Land Cruiser but thought it wasn't due to arrive for a few more months.

'Well, the contract to move you around the city brought with it some benefits and I think your embassy has given us one of their vehicles that arrived two weeks ago, so basically it's a loan until we get our own in a few months.' Miko was clearly happy about the arrangement. 'Where are we going, Boss?'

'Oh, Airport Camp, then, once I text later on, I will need a lift from the front gate to the B&B, probably around 4pm.' They had already left Somalia's political centre of gravity, navigating the security measures on their way out. Christian looked behind, out of habit, noticing the pick-up truck with eight Somali guards carrying AK47s falling in behind their vehicle. As they passed the scene of the bomb attack all those months ago and headed away from the main check point, Christian experienced a very strong flashback from that day. He needed to change the subject in his head.

'So, how do you feel about driving in this, then?' The new car smell was still evident.

'Well, you know, Shabaab just see Casspir armoured vehicles and so this looks like any Land Cruiser, so I am happy.' It was white, pretty much like every other unarmoured Land Cruiser in hot spots the world over, including Mogadishu, so in a sense it was inconspicuous. Certainly, a lot more inconspicuous than a Casspir.

'How is the new job?' Miko asked.

'I'll tell you after this meeting!' Christian laughed as he took out his phone to read a message that had just come in: *We will also have some company over the weekend, but only for an hour or so. M x*

He read the message twice and replied with a furrowed brow: *Not sure I understand*

He pressed "send" and continued to answer Miko's question. 'I have to work with a bunch of security experts who all want to help Somalia, in line with their own foreign policy objectives, rather than actually sitting down with the Somalis and asking what they need. So, they may see me as a help, or more than likely, a hindrance.'

Christian watched the city pass by through the armoured side window in relative silence, the noise from the street completely removed by the armoured protection.

'Hindrance? What is this fancy word?' Miko said, turning his head slightly. He then spoke into his walkie talkie and continued to scan the road. The pick-up truck with the guards overtook them and now led the two car convoy.

'A pain in the arse,' he replied.

'Yes, that is phrase I understand.' Miko laughed again. They were making good time. As they drove round the K4 roundabout, Christian's phone buzzed once more. 'You're a popular man now in new job!'

I'll explain later

'Very good, Miko.' Christian said. He quickly read the message and put it out of his mind. He had more pressing things to focus on right now.

Christian got out at the entrance to Airport Camp, which was just beyond the main drop-off area for the airport terminal building. The wide, solid metal gates were manned by AMISOM guards, who were casually standing in front of them, waiting to check identity documents of pedestrians and vehicle drivers. Once Miko had driven off, following the one-way system, Christian stopped and took a moment to take everything in. It was an odd place; the security check points leading up to the airport ensured only *bona fide* vehicles and pedestrians, all unarmed, could get through. Between those check points and the Airport Camp main entrance in front of him was an area that was probably the safest place in the city. It had the terminal building along one side and, on the other side of a small roundabout, about 30 metres away, a row of shops and down-at-heel cafés, providing all the basics needed if one had time to kill ahead of a flight or, presumably, before being collected on arrival. Except rumours were rife that some of the men who seemed to sit around in those same cafés all day were spotters for al Shabaab, keeping tabs on life at the airport and calling in anything out of the ordinary. In his previous role, Christian had met the President's Chief of Staff in one of them to discuss some visit arrangements after Bashiir had just landed back in Mogadishu. Christian had known he was being observed that day, and he had the same sensation again now.

Once he had navigated the AMISOM guards who opened the front gate enough for him to walk through he only had to cover 100 metres to the newly built conference room, sheltered by trees, just beyond the main car park. He walked past the blast walls that overlapped the pedestrian entrance and headed towards the meeting. It was the first time he had been back in the camp since leaving his previous role and collecting his stuff from the office. On a whim, he pulled out his phone and dropped a message to Fred to let him know he was around, in case he had time to meet up.

The sky was full of fluffy white clouds, gently floating across the azure sky above him, conspiring to block out the sun's rays at least for the time being. The humidity had not let up, though, and he was already looking forward to getting into the conference centre's air conditioning. As he made his way across the tarmac, his shirt beginning to stick to his back, he looked around him. There were a few dusty vehicles parked up haphazardly around him.

The main emergency gate, which opened onto the city's only runway, was on his left. To his right, nestled amongst a row of trees close to the perimeter of the camp on the side of the car park, stood the two-storey white-washed airport headquarters building where he had spent many hours in his previous role. He was surprised by his sense of nostalgia.

It was surprisingly quiet. There were no aircraft engines running and all he could hear was the wind blowing across the open space, embedding fine sand into anything that stood in its path and dragging with it items of litter that danced across the ground. The distant sound of tin cans rattling around the car park in random, wind-induced patterns reminded him how unrelenting the environment was in Airport Camp. Although there were other hazards to contend with living in Vila Somalia, he was glad to be away from it all.

He presumed that most people had already arrived and so traffic was at a minimum. Beyond the security fencing to his left, he could see a row of small, unmarked white turboprop planes lined up on the pan close to the terminal building. Christian smiled to himself and realised that most of the international attendees had chartered private planes to carry them in relative comfort from Nairobi's Wilson Airport, the smaller of Nairobi's two air hubs, which serviced light aircraft and private jets. He didn't blame the delegates for opting to use them; flying into Mogadishu from Nairobi on the regular African Airways jet was not for those with a nervous disposition, and it was notoriously unreliable, even if it was the quickest route.

After briefly following the main road that dissected the camp, he turned right towards the entrance, along a path that was hemmed in by six-foot-high concrete blast walls on either side. He could see some people milling around, dressed in a variety of clothing styles and immediately spotted Mac; he was wearing a very creased mocha-coloured linen suit, an untucked white linen shirt, brown military boots and a Panama hat to cover his bald head. He looked every bit a caricature of an army officer from colonial times. Christian knew that, as dishevelled as he appeared to be, Mac had curated the look to perfection.

'Christian, my dear chap, great to see you.' They shook hands warmly, Mac's Scottish accent sounded out of place after two weeks engaging with people whose first language wasn't English. 'Ready for the vipers' nest?' Mac had obviously been waiting outside for Christian to show up. 'Get here OK from the new digs? How is it in VS then?'

'Hi Mac, really good to see you too. So many questions! Yeah, everything is fine at the Somali end, I'm just interested to know what's waiting for me in there.' Christian pointed with his thumb as he spoke, the humour in his voice deliberate to reassure Mac. 'Vipers' nest? Well, that depends ... come on tell me, who do I need to look out for?' They had exchanged emails about the participants, but a face-to-face briefing was always going to be more useful.

'I doubt he will come, but if the Turkish rep is here – he's a senior naval officer from the embassy in Nairobi – he may well be reticent to join in the conversation. They seem to be doing everything they can to ignore our collective pleas to work collaboratively. Last I heard, they are making moves with the President to set up a training academy in addition to the EU training camp which got hit the other week.'

Mac had led Christian to a quiet spot around the side of the conference building, out of earshot of the other delegates. 'And you'll need to give Bob Swartz, the US rep, some of your time. They are pretty key because, as you well know, they have the money. He's an interesting character, a contractor who has worked for the US in Somalia for about 25 years, if you believe everything he says, so there's not much history he doesn't know ... but that doesn't mean he has all the answers. Don't roll over for him.'

'Cheers, Mac. The Defence Minister will be here so I am not expecting to do much apart from networking around the group,' Christian said.

'Yeah, just check everyone out. You're not going have to say much today apart from when you get introduced.' Mac gently took Christian's arm. 'Come on, I'll introduce you to a few of the guys.'

*

'And, finally, we would like to welcome Christian Travers from the UK who has recently been appointed as a strategic advisor to Defence Minister Hassan. Welcome Christian.'

Someone around the large conference table started to clap, and suddenly the ripple effect resulted in an unexpected round of applause, mainly because people didn't want to be seen not to be clapping. Slightly embarrassed, Christian acknowledged the words and nodded towards various points around the large conference room. The Chairman, currently a Brigadier General from the Ugandan Peoples' Defence Force, had run through the agenda, lingering on the recent spate of attacks across all sectors, before finally introducing Christian.

'Thank you, sir. As you all know by now, I have been in post in Vila Somalia for about two weeks. I would like to see myself as someone who can better connect what our hosts, the Somali Government, need for their security to increase capability and effectiveness, and what the international community is able to contribute. The more we collaborate, the more effective we will be working with Defence Minister Hassan and his team. I know there are many strong relationships that already exist, and I hope to enhance these if I can.'

Christian spoke with clarity and purpose, finishing by looking across at the Minister, who nodded his approval. He surprised himself – inside he was a bag of nerves. As he mentioned the comment about working together, he looked at the Turkish naval officer, who had arrived at the last minute and was sitting quietly to his left making notes, avoiding eye contact with anyone. Perhaps Mac was right about them.

'Thank you, Christian. I think we should see this as a positive step forward in our work with Minister Hassan's team. I know Christian is keen to understand what we are trying to achieve and to get to know everyone on a personal level going forward.'

Introduced by Mac before the meeting, Christian had only briefly spoken to the Brigadier and hadn't said any of those things, but he wasn't wrong, and by saying them, he was also creating the right environment. From what Mac had said, agreements made in these meetings were often completely ignored once they stepped back on board their private aircraft and headed south to the bright lights of Nairobi. He knew that most business would not be done in this forum.

'If I may just say something.' Bob Swartz had turned on his microphone and was leaning forward towards it, scanning the room as he spoke. 'For the US, the key issue here is coordination. We are all keen to ensure that the Somalis are able to take over the security role from AMISOM at some point in the near future, and to achieve that we need their men and women to be trained to a standard that is compatible with Somalia's requirements.' Swartz paused, long enough to take a swig of his black coffee before resuming. 'And I would like to think that everyone around this table agrees with that sentiment.' He then stared directly at the Turkish officer, who was still writing in his notebook. 'And we need to know that our friend here will do all he can to align his country's interest to that goal.' He finished speaking, turned off his microphone, and sat back.

There was an uncomfortable silence for a few moments while everyone waited for the Turkish representative to respond. He eventually looked up, having decided that Swartz's dig was directed at him. He calmly pressed his microphone button.

'Thank you. We in Turkey recognise the long-suffering Somali people as our brothers and allies. Our goal is to support Muslim communities wherever they are being oppressed or are in need of assistance. This is not new; it has been central to our foreign policy for many years.' He paused, turned a page in his notebook, and continued. 'As a responsible member of the international community, we will always act in line with the wishes of the host nation, in this case Somalia.' He turned to the Defence Minister and nodded to him, receiving a response in kind. 'Our military forces are some of the best equipped and efficient in the world and we intend to ensure that our brothers receive the most effective support that we can offer.' He finished his short speech, turned off his microphone and sat back, closing his notebook and putting it in his briefcase.

The sound of a microphone going live momentarily preceded Bob Swartz's immediate response, 'Yes, but are you working alone with the Somalis or are you working with the international community?' His question, delivered tactlessly, led to murmurs around the table. The collegiate atmosphere was evaporating and everyone knew it.

The Turkish naval officer leant forward once more, turned on his microphone and spoke without emotion. 'Thank you, Mr Swartz. It is for the Somalis to decide how they want to shape international support, and we all know they need greater capacity in many areas of their security forces. The most important thing is to support Minister Hassan and his team, no?' He posed the question to the US representative, but it was Minister Hassan who spoke next, pressing the button in front of him and tapping the microphone to make sure it was working.

'Thank you for explaining your position. I will make sure we discuss this in greater detail when we are back in Vila Somalia, and I look forward to welcoming you and your colleagues to our offices soon.' He nodded at the Turkish officer. 'As a nation we are very grateful for everyone's support and I am certain that with Christian coordinating our engagement with you all going forward we will reach a position that suits everyone. And now, I am sorry, but I have another appointment that I must attend to.'

The Defence Minister stood up and shook hands with the Chairman to his left, before walking around the back of the attendees towards the exit. Unsure what to do, Christian also got up from where he was sitting further down the table and accompanied him to the door.

Once outside, Christian spoke first. Although he was very cautious of being drawn into bilateral arrangements between the Somali government and Turkey, he really needed to know what was going on if he was to manage the overall levels of support.

'What did you make of that intervention from our Turkish colleague, sir?' Christian was beginning to stray off reservation with the question, and both men knew it.

'Christian, let me explain something to you.'

They had stopped on the path between the blast walls. The Defence Minister looked around to make sure they were not going to be overheard. 'We need a lot of support from everyone. I need you to organise this support and to help me make the decisions to harness it. Bilateral support is inevitable and we are open to anyone who wants to commit themselves to supporting us in that way. Whether that's Turkey, the US, or in your case, the UK.' Minister Hassan was facing Christian and gave him his full attention, his hands in his suit trouser pockets, using his shoulders to emphasise some of his words. Christian could tell he was uncomfortable and was trying to work out whether it was because of his question.

'I completely understand, sir. All I ask is to be briefed on what your plans are with them so that I can maintain an overview, which will obviously help Somalia's security forces in the medium to long term. That's all I am trying to do.' The two men were standing close to each other; Christian had never had such a tense conversation with the Minister. He felt like he was on thin ice; secrecy and bilateral agreements went hand in hand, so what he was asking was likely to ruffle feathers, potentially including the Defence Minister's.

'I understand, Christian. I will share what I can with you. In the meantime, I think you had better get back in there as it seems to me there is a lack of coordination amongst our most valuable partners!' Minister Hassan laughed at the same time as slapping Christian on the arm and turning to leave.

'Thank you, sir, I will do my best.'

'I know you will, Christian, I know you will.' Minister Hassan waved one hand as he spoke over his shoulder and hurried away.

Christian stood there for a moment and took a deep breath. The gravity of his position suddenly hit him hard. He was at the mercy of the international community's squabbling security representatives, an ally seemingly heading off in a different direction with the tacit support of his hosts, who, in turn, were providing him protection in Vila Somalia. He knew he had to maintain relationships in all directions but, until this moment, he hadn't quite appreciated how hard it was going to be. He looked at his watch; it was nearly four o'clock. He wanted to wrap the meeting up as soon as he could. Taking a deep breath, he walked back into the building and turned left towards the main conference room.

'Does anyone have any other comments they wish to make before we end the meeting?' The Uganda Brigadier General looked around the room, his metaphorical gavel about to come down on the afternoon's session. It was ten past four and the need for the attendees' charter aircraft to take off before darkness set in, mentioned to the Chairman during an earlier break, had brought the meeting to premature end.

'Just one last thing from me.' Christian had switched on his mike. 'If anyone wants my card, I have left a pile of them by the door. I would be more than happy to meet up either here or when I am back in Nairobi. Just get in touch.' He looked across at the Chair to indicate he had finished.

'OK, good, thank you all for coming and see you in a month's time. The meeting is closed.' The Chairman's final words led to a scraping of chairs as the attendees got up, gathering their laptops, notebooks and other papers, the sound of several hushed conversations beginning to take place around the room. Mac made his way across to Christian, who was watching the desk by the entrance to see who might take one of his business cards. The Turkish officer picked one up as he walked out of the conference room.

'Blimey, that was one of the most ill-tempered meetings I have been to yet,' Mac said. 'You've got your work cut out there. Anything I can do, just give me a shout. I'm friendly forces, remember! Just let me know.'

'Cheers, Mac, I appreciate that. I'd forgotten how parochial people can be. I do think the UN has got a big role to play here, though, so perhaps we should sit down and discuss the best way to corral everyone.' Christian had always believed that the pre-eminent international organisation, the UN, needed to show some leadership, but he also knew that Mac was often frustrated by its world-famous bureaucracy.

'Sure, that's fine. I could do with a good night out in Nairobi to be honest. Next time you're back, let me know, and we can go out for dinner.' With that, Mac shook hands with Christian and made his way out of the conference room, making a detour to say goodbye to some of the stragglers who were still in the room. Christian also did a tour of the room, shaking hands with those who were left, including the Brigadier General who was in discussion with a junior colleague.

'Excuse me a moment.' The Chairman turned away from his conversation and smiled at Christian.

'Christian, thank you for speaking today and for taking on this role. It is going to be a very difficult challenge for you. We know the weaknesses within the Somali security forces and we need a collective effort to make improvements. We do not want to be in Somalia for ever! I am here to support you. You gained our respect for your actions last year so, if there is anything you need, just let me know, you have my number.'

'Thank you, General, I appreciate that.' By the time they had finished speaking, the room was almost empty. They shook hands and Christian walked away towards the exit. As he left the room, having picked up the remaining cards, he walked out of the building headed for the main entrance to the camp where he was due to meet Miko. On the path he received a message on his phone: *Boss! Yes, I am here, fancy a lift to the rear gate?*

It was Fred, who had finally responded to Christian's initial text, and just in time. Christian replied: *Yes, where are you?*

No sooner had he sent the text than Fred's 4x4 pulled up at the end of the path. As he approached the car, Christian heard his name called out from behind him. He turned to see the Turkish officer taking a cigarette out of his mouth and grinding it onto the sandy footpath, just to the left of the entrance. He must have been waiting for him to come out. Christian stood still, turned back to Fred to indicate he would be a moment, then watched as the Turkish officer approached him, briefcase in hand, a determined look on his face.

'Christian, my name is Murat.' They shook hands very formally; there was no hint of warmth in the action or in his demeanour.

'Good to meet you. Have you been waiting for me?' Christian asked, knowing the answer but wanting to give him the chance to explain himself.

'Yes, of course. Look, I have a plane to catch so I will be brief.' He produced another cigarette, offered one to Christian who declined, then put it in his mouth and lit it with a Zippo lighter which had an ornate figure painted on its body. 'We are not going to fall into the trap that has existed here for many years: donors eventually finding agreement and then waiting for months for financing to be put in place only for the actual delivery to take even longer to realise. Do you know how long it took the EU to agree to, then build, and finally supply manpower for the camp that was discussed in there?'

He jabbed his forefinger towards the conference centre. As he did so, the Brigadier General and the junior officer walked past the two men. A flurry of apologies for blocking the path and some side-shuffling followed.

'Four years! Four years! That is not how Turkey works. We do not shy away from a bad security situation. We will support the Somali military how we want and they will be grateful for our support. And there is nothing you can do to change that.' He took another drag of his cigarette and waited for a response from Christian, who was making a rapid calculation on how to reply to such a provocative statement.

'OK, well, thanks for sharing that with me, Murat. My goal is to find the best solution for the many problems facing Somalia's military, and one of those is uncoordinated bilateral arrangements that undermine and devalue the overall effort being made by the whole international community. If you are not willing to work with us, then I will have to do my best to ensure the Somali Government understands the implications of such an approach. If I didn't, I wouldn't be doing my job.' Christian had opted for a direct answer that made it clear he would use his influence over Defence Minister Hassan to get all international donors to work together.

'Well, we shall see. I have your card; I will see you around.' At that, Murat dropped his cigarette on the ground and walked past Christian without any further acknowledgement. Christian stood there, watching him walk towards Fred's car then turn left out of sight.

'What the fuck?' Christian said under his breath, then started walking towards Fred's car. Fred leaned over and opened the passenger door. He quickly shook off the brief meeting with Murat and looked at his old friend.

'Fred! How's it going?' They clasped hands as Christian closed the door.

'Ah well, you know, Boss, we are surviving. All good here,' Fred replied.

'Just give me a second, I need to tell Miko where to meet me.' Christian pulled his phone out to send the text to Miko, allowing him 20 minutes to catch up with Fred before meeting his security team at the rear gate.

'It's just like old times, Chris. How's the new job?' Fred asked as he drove away.

'How's the job? That's a very good question! I thought it was going well until today, and now it seems that to do my job, I will have to bring in line the entire Turkish nation!' Christian was speaking light-heartedly, but there was an element of truth in his words that Fred recognised.

'Is that what that was all about? I have seen that guy before, at a military event we were covering in Nairobi last year – is he the Turkish Defence Attaché?' Fred had an encyclopaedic memory for faces.

'Bingo. He's Turkish navy and obviously has a role up here, even though there is an embassy in the city. I guess he must cover this patch as well.' Christian's brain was buzzing, trying to figure out what he could do about the situation. He had the Defence Minister's support but now Murat had effectively said he was going to do what he wanted regardless. He had no idea how he was going to manage the issue.

'Anyway, how's the team, how's the new management?' Christian asked.

'The UN team has stepped in for now, but I gather whatever was behind their initial decision to take the management in-house, they seem to have reversed it already. But you know the guys – they are happy when they are out and about, finding stories or covering AMISOM deployments. As long as we are meeting our monthly targets, the UN is happy,' Fred said, smiling.

Fred had already pulled up just short of the rear gate and they were stationary, engine running, watching the guard sitting in his small hut, the air conditioning blowing quietly inside the vehicle.

'I can't believe they have already changed their minds. Why would they do that?' Christian was looking out of the window and staring blankly into the trees, the wind pulling their branches into irregular patterns just outside the car. 'Unbelievable.'

'Honestly, Boss, even though I know you briefed them constantly on what we were doing, and they saw all of the output from the team, I just think they felt they could do it better. I think that feeling stemmed from before you arrived. You know they're control freaks. They over-estimated the task and as soon as they saw productivity dropping under their watch, they panicked and reverted to how it was. I don't think there was a conspiracy, I think they are all just incompetent.'

Fred's logic made sense, but Christian couldn't quite believe that it was as simple as that. For the sake of the team, though, Fred's version of events was likely to be more popular than any other conclusion he might draw. 'Yeah, that makes sense, Fred. You always have your finger on the pulse, don't you!'

'Ah well, that's what you employed me for, Chris; remember what you called me at the beginning?'

'One-step-ahead-Fred!' Both men spoke at the same time and laughed at their in-joke.

They allowed their laughter to recede before noticing the arrival of Miko's armoured white Land Cruiser beyond the gate.

'OK, that's me,' Christian said.

Fred drove a little closer and waved at the guard who by now was looking nervously between Miko's vehicle outside the camp and their own 4x4 inside on the service road.

'Take it easy, Boss, and stay in touch.' Fred turned the car so that he could walk directly towards the pedestrian entrance. They slapped hands again and Christian got out.

'Great to see you, Fred, and say hi to the guys. Stay safe.'

With that, he closed the vehicle door and walked through the open pedestrian gate, waved at the AMISOM guard who had sat back down again, watching the action with little interest.

'No escort today, Miko?' Christian said as they shook hands and he got in behind him.

'No. Short trip, no need. I have my weapon in case.' Miko tapped the bag on his lap.

'Let's hope it's oiled and ready then, huh?' Christian laughed at his quip.

'Very good, very good, ha-ha.' Miko acknowledged the joke and told the driver to head off.

Within a couple of minutes, they had weaved through the chicane at the entrance to the street, overlapping concrete blocks to prevent a truck bomb approaching the building, and had driven through the security gate which led to the B&B's parking area behind the house. For Christian, this was as close to feeling at home as he could get for now.

17

The B&B, Mogadishu

Christian picked up his bag from the vehicle and walked into the high-ceilinged entrance hall in the B&B, a large house in a quiet suburb of Mogadishu that had, up until then, been spared the worst of the violence that had touched most areas of the city over the previous two decades. Set over three floors, surrounded by mature gardens and enclosed by high, white-washed walls on all sides, it was one of many similar sized properties along the street and across the district. The owners had explained to Christian that the neighbours in this area had looked out for each other over the years and made strategic alliances with all parties in the various conflicts to ensure their survival during the worst of times.

He put his bag down and walked into the dining room to the left. The long, beautifully polished wooden dining table, surrounded by a dozen chairs, was bare except for a small floral arrangement in the centre. On an adjacent side table there were the plates, cutlery and crockery stacked ready to be set for tea. A ticking clock on the far wall was the only sound he heard.

'Hello, you!' Megan had walked in without Christian hearing her.

'Megs!'

They immediately hugged, their arms holding each other tightly, their bodies together, relief mixing with happiness. Christian kissed Megan on the cheek, then their lips met with a desperation that neither of them could control. They kissed deeply, their feelings for each other overpowering their natural sense of restraint.

'Oh Chris, not here ...' Megan was breathless, but knew they had to control themselves. Christian knew it too as they kissed again.

'I know ...' Christian broke off gently, savouring the taste of Megan's lips, his eyes closed, breathing hard. They paused long enough to listen for approaching footsteps, but all they heard was the *tick, tick, tick* from the clock.

'Let's find our room,' Megan whispered. They moved apart for a moment, Megan running her fingers through her hair, Christian looking around to see whether they had been observed. 'Where are the owners?' Megan asked.

'I'm not sure, but I have a feeling we'll need to be downstairs for tea pretty soon,' he said, looking across at the side table.

As they were both regaining their composure after the intensity of those few minutes on their own, the sound of someone walking down the wooden stairs brought them back to the present. Arne, the Norwegian co-owner of the business, walked into the dining room, smiling broadly and with his arms outstretched. Arne and Suzie had lived in Mogadishu for nearly 20 years, running a successful B&B and security business from this grand old house. He primarily ran the security side, while Suzie looked after the front-of-house, managed the kitchen and oversaw the guest experience. They even had a professional chef from Italy living and working in the house on a 12-month contract; his cakes were becoming well known by a growing number of international regulars in Mogadishu.

'Christian and Megan, I'm so pleased to welcome you both to our house again!' Arne was an unusual mix of entrepreneur, extreme explorer, security guru, political influencer and, when they had guests staying, hotel manager. He was about six-feet tall with thick, blond hair, turning white in places, worn long and without much care. He dressed in expedition type clothing most of the time, including his infamous checked shirt, which complimented his lean frame, strong features and stubbled chin. Christian always imagined he'd just left his cross-country skis outside in the snow but looks could be deceiving. He hadn't survived in Mogadishu for all this time without being very well connected to some of the most influential people in and around the city.

They shook hands, Arne giving Megan a kiss on each cheek.

'It's almost tea time and Marco has made some delicious banana cake for the occasion! I'm going to set the table; why don't you both take your things to your room and someone will call you in about half an hour's time.' Arne handed over their key and explained where their room was located.

Christian led the way followed by Megan, who was carrying a small day sack over her shoulder. She was dressed in a beige linen shirt over a knee-length, brown cotton skirt, her cream flat shoes completing her look. They had been given a room on the second floor, facing away from the front of the house. It was simply furnished, with a large wooden bed, two side tables and a chest of drawers beneath a tiltable mirror. On the chest of drawers was a lit candle in a large ceramic bowl, its aroma filling the room. The windows on two sides of the room were open, their carved, wooden shutters closed across them letting in some sunlight but slowing the progress of the breeze that was gently blowing through the room. A rug on the tiled floor between the end of the bed and the drawers added the finishing touch. A door in the corner led to a small bathroom.

'What a beautiful room, Chris!' Megan had walked over to one of the windows, opened the shutter, and was looking out across the rooftops, just visible through the canopy of trees that seemed to surround them as far as the eye could see. They were not at all overlooked.

'I could get used to this.' Christian approached Megan, the heal of his suede brogues marking his progress across the tiles. He slowly wrapped his arms around her waist and kissed her neck, easing them both towards the bed. 'How long do we have?'

They had both briefly fallen asleep. Christian woke first and slowly opened his eyes to take in his surroundings. He had been imagining being with Megan for a long time, and the thought of spending two nights together had kept him going over the last two weeks. Megan stirred, then rolled over into his chest.

'Hi there,' Christian said.

'What time is it?' Megan asked, her voice sleepy.

'I expect we're about to get a call for afternoon tea!'

'Do we have to get up?' Megan pulled the sheet over her head in a show of defiance.

'I'm so glad we're here,' Christian said, leaning on one side, looking at the outline of Megan's body. She pulled the sheet down so she could see his face in the twilight.

'Me too. You know it's a bit of a risk for me but as long as nothing happens at work, we should be fine.' Megan had already mentioned her fragile situation at the embassy, and how she was taking a chance by being there with him. But it wasn't what she was really thinking. Since her failed relationship, she had actively avoided trying to meet anyone, but she knew that Christian was different, and, for the first time in years, she felt like she could trust a man again. Breaking a few rules was worth it.

He stroked her cheek gently. 'I'm sure it will be fine but if you have to go back and stay in the embassy, that's cool. We have time, you know?' Christian didn't want Megan to compromise herself with her leaders in Nairobi or London, but he longed to be with her.

'I am really happy when I'm with you, Chris. You know that, don't you?' She didn't really know what to say, her words were not exactly what she had intended, but she felt compelled to let him know her feelings. She wanted reassurance; *needed* reassurance. After being so focused on herself and on achieving success in her career, her strong feelings for Christian were beginning to create a conflict.

'I'm happy too. I haven't felt like this for a long time.' He couldn't quite bring himself to say Jessica's name, but they both knew what he was saying.

The sound of a car horn from a nearby street entered the room, the fading light bringing with it the growing chatter of crickets from the garden to signal the end of the day.

'I guess we ought to go downstairs; I think we're a little late!' Christian didn't want to embarrass their hosts, although he suspected Arne knew they wouldn't be on time for tea.

'I guess we should!' Megan replied, putting her feet on the floor and walking round the bed to find her clothes. Christian also got up, closed the windows and then the shutters before turning on a low-wattage side light, illuminating their naked bodies.

They looked at each other and smiled. The sound of someone climbing the stairs made them both dress more quickly; they exchanged a look that wouldn't have been out of place between two teenagers caught by a parent.

'Christian, Megan, tea is ready downstairs!' It was Suzie's voice, her Norwegian accent making the words sing through the wooden door.

'Thanks, Suzie, we'll be there in a minute, we just fell asleep,' Christian replied as he put his shoes on.

'Ready?' Megan asked a moment later. They both checked themselves in the mirror before opening the door and stepping into the wood-panelled corridor, now lit by a decorative ceiling light. They closed the door and set off for the dining room.

'Did you say we were getting some company this weekend?' Christian asked.

'Yes, Imi is going to pop in on Saturday. She wants to see you,' Megan replied.

'Imi? It's a long way for her to come just to see me,' Christian said, as much to himself as to Megan. They had arranged to have a catch-up when his initial four-week stint in Vila Somalia was up.

'Come on, I'm starving!' Megan wanted to change the subject. She briefly looped her arm through Christian's as they descended the final flight of steps, the sound of conversation filling the entrance hall. They walked into the dining room to find Arne, Suzie, Marco and Miko sitting around the table, engrossed in a discussion about the health benefits of Marco's banana cake.

After a very relaxing day on the Friday, listening to the call to prayer at the nearby mosque while sitting together under the shade of a large umbrella in the garden, talking for hours, Saturday came round far too quickly.

Just after lunch, Megan and Christian were sitting in the garden again, drinking a cup of tea and talking about when they would next be in the UK. They had both decided they needed some normal time together, away from East Africa.

Their attention was caught by the opening of the main security gate and the arrival of a white B6 armoured Land Cruiser, similar to the one Christian now used when he navigated Mogadishu. They watched as it pulled up. Miko got out, opened the rear door, then stood aside as Imi stepped onto the gravel. Her sunglasses were pushed onto her head to keep her blond hair from her face, and she was wearing her customary skinny jeans and white shirt, a satchel over her left shoulder.

'Hi guys,' Imi waved as she walked towards them, smiling as she hugged Megan and kissed Christian once on the cheek.

'Hey, Imi, you've come a long way. How was your flight?' Christian asked.

'For once it was on time. I landed about an hour ago. You know what a scrum it can be to get through passport control,' Imi replied as she dropped her satchel onto the grass next to their table. 'Chris, I hope you don't mind me barging into your weekend, but do you have some time to talk through a few things while I am here? I know that once you get back to VS I'll not be able to see you.' She looked at both of them and smiled. Megan got up, saying she would find someone to make another pot of tea.

'Yes, that's fine. Has anything happened?' Christian was still sure there had been some sort of change of plan and he was a little on edge as a result. 'Do you want to talk somewhere privately or are you OK out here?'

'It would be better if we could go elsewhere. Is there a room we could use?' Imi asked, showing her ignorance of the B&B. 'I've never been here before – it's amazing, isn't it?'

'Yes, it is. I think there is somewhere although we run the chance of being overheard, if that's a concern. Let me check.' Christian got up and walked towards the front door to find Arne or Suzie, just to clear it with them. Imi picked up her satchel and followed him.

After walking through the entire house, his hosts were nowhere to be seen; even the kitchen was empty. He eventually found Miko in the garage watching a movie online. He confirmed that he had dropped them all off in town to buy some provisions and that they would be back in about 90 minutes.

'It looks like everyone's gone out,' Christian said when he returned to Imi in the entrance hall. 'Why don't we sit in the dining room?' As they went in, Megan appeared carrying a teapot and some fresh milk. They found some mats, a couple of cups and set everything down. Megan squeezed Christian's hand and moved towards the door.

'I'll leave you to it; I'll be either in the garden or in our room, Chris.' With that, Megan left the room and shut the door, catching Imi's eye as she went.

Imi and Christian sat down next to each other, their backs to the shuttered windows. She took out her laptop, plugged it in and fired it up. 'Just give me a minute.'

While Imi was logging in, Christian got up and poured the tea for them both. 'Milk?'

'Yes please.'

By the time he sat back down again, her screen had come alive with the landing page just waiting for her to fill in her credentials. She had a USB stick plugged into one of the ports that she had taken from around her neck. Christian stared at the laptop screen, momentarily confused. Imi logged in and turned to face him. Christian looked down before raising his head and looking at Imi. She had set the meeting up to be this way. He sighed and imperceptibly nodded his head.

'Chris, let me explain ... I hope you understand that we needed to know that you would take the role and that you were committed to it ...' Imi paused, but only momentarily before continuing, watching his expression closely as she explained what was happening. 'Once I knew you were going to sign the contract, I needed to reach you as soon as possible to give you the full picture. Obviously, you have worked out that the role is funded by station Nairobi.' Her use of the term "station" to mean MI6 was in common usage within government and military circles, and she knew it would be familiar to him.

Imi continued to watch him as she picked up her cup and took a sip. 'Mmm, nice tea.'

Christian didn't say anything for a few moments. 'OK, well, thanks for finally telling me the truth. That I am not being funded out of the defence department. I don't really know why you couldn't have explained this to me earlier, but I guess you had your reasons.' He got up from the table and walked around the room, rolling his shoulders and shaking his arms, as if the sharing of the secret had anesthetised his muscles while he'd been sitting down.

'I take it you want me to do a bit more than resolve the security dilemma in Vila Somalia,' he added before sitting down again.

'Yes, in a word. Look, we don't have long and, although we know there is nobody in the house, I need to run through a few things with you quickly. Are you OK with that?' She took out her notebook and ripped out a couple of pages, handing them to Christian along with a pencil. 'Make some notes, but nothing too explicit, just to remind you if needs be. Then, once you have recalled everything, burn the notes.'

As Imi started talking, Christian felt like he had suddenly returned to his military days, sitting in secure rooms listening to complex briefings about impending operations. Except this was unexpected and he was not ready for the implications of what was being said to him. It was meant to be a relaxing weekend, but Imi's visit had changed it into something quite different.

'Chris, we need you to be reporting back on what you see, what you hear and who is coming to VS, obviously while doing your current role. In particular, we are keen to pick up on anything you may manage to uncover about Turkish influence around the Government and, obviously, anyone who has access to the President. For us to be able to shape our own strategy in country, we need to be able to understand what our rivals are doing, or planning. Do you think you can do that?' Imi asked.

Christian's mind was in a spin. He hadn't written a single note and was trying to visualise what he was being asked to do. 'But I have no access to the President or his diary, it's guarded by his Chief of Staff, and I can't just hang around his outer officer watching and waiting. Apart from defence related matters, I get to hear next to nothing from elsewhere in government, apart from tit bits from the Minister for Returns, who is a friend. I don't see how I can help.'

Christian's logic had kicked in, perhaps as much in response to the risk he was being asked to take as to the reality of what he could achieve in the role. He instinctively wanted to downplay expectations. His mouth had gone dry, a combination of fear and excitement.

'Chris, we are paying you a lot of money to do this. I know you may not think that you can gather intelligence as I have described, but you will find a way, subtly, to put yourself in a position to be more informed. Have a think about how to do it, think about your daily routines, think about how they can change, offer to do things for people, hang around a bit more, talk to more officials. Personal assistants are a great source if they trust you, and your familiarity and recognition in Vila Somalia will improve, especially after your performance at the security meeting on Thursday.'

Imi was flattering Christian in the hope that he would begin to see the potential of what he was being asked to do. 'It's not going to happen overnight, though; you'll have to build up to it gradually.'

The reference to the security meeting went over Christian's head. 'OK, I will have to think about how I do that; leave it with me for now. But how will we communicate?' Christian had now accepted that his role was going to change profoundly, even if those around him in Vila Somalia would, hopefully, know nothing about it.

'Thanks for bringing that up. This is the encryption software we normally use. It's very secure. Let me show you the principle.' Imi was clearly technically competent. She opened her notebook and drew some lines to demonstrate how the process flowed until Christian understood what he would be expected to do. 'We'll run a few test exchanges to make sure you get the hang of the encryption then, once you're happy, we will use that method to communicate going forward.'

Imi demonstrated the technique on her laptop after downloading the software; 'Open a text file, write a simple message, then encrypt it before attaching it to an email.' She also ran through the method Christian would need to employ to decrypt messages sent from her. Christian soon got the hang of it. 'The last thing is to make sure you delete unencrypted messages.' Imi was moving the mouse of her office laptop and opened Yahoo! on her browser.

'Yahoo!?' Christian asked, sounding slightly dismissive.

'Yes, extremely secure if hiding in plain sight is the chosen approach, which it is. People check their Yahoo! accounts all the time, but there's no record on basic network scans exactly which account people check, so even if you use their internet, which you will, you'll be fine. As long as you don't give your laptop to anyone investigating your online behaviour, we should be OK.' Imi wasn't smiling when she spoke. 'So, we just need a couple of email addresses, then we should be good to go. How about I set one up as nairobigirl941@yahoo.com?' Imi smiled at Christian, catching his eye, trying to lighten the mood.

She had hoped that this part of the briefing was going to be a little less intense compared to what she had been saying beforehand. She was already very happy that Christian was fully compliant with her proposal and it was clear he was beginning to relax.

'What about you? Just make sure you add three numbers.'

'Well, I guess it has to be mogadishuboy265@yahoo.com,' Christian replied, a lightness in his voice.

'Perfect!' Imi started the process of setting up her address first, then passed the laptop to Christian to complete his own. A few moments later, she sent a test message to him, with the subject *Happy Days*.

Christian suggested he get his laptop from his room so that they could run through the procedure while they were together, to which Imi agreed. He got up and headed for the door. As he opened it, he was surprised to find Megan sitting on the bottom step of the stairs.

'Hi Megs, what are you doing here?' Christian spoke before his mind had fully engaged, quickly answering his own question, 'To make sure nobody interrupts us. Got it. I'm just going to get my laptop.' He stepped past her and climbed the stairs.

Half an hour later, after running through the procedure a few times, and confirming that both emails worked, Imi started to pack things away. She had one last thing to say.

'Christian, it goes without saying that you don't want to get caught doing anything that will draw attention to yourself. Just send me regular reports, keep them brief, and let's see how things go. If you feel at any stage that you have been compromised, or you feel as if you are in impending danger, send me a message on your phone with the word "Toro". Once you send that codeword, we will get you out of Mogadishu for good from wherever you are. Is that clear?'

'Yes, that's clear … Toro. OK.' As a former member of the British Army, he knew the implications of what Imi had just said. As soon as he realised that the UK special forces team in Airport Camp were on standby to extract him if things went wrong, the gravity of his role finally sank in.

Imi walked out of the room first, initially to see Megan, but then to find Miko who was going to take her back to the camp. Within a few minutes, Imi had left. Christian and Megan were again alone in the house. He walked upstairs to leave his laptop in their room, then wandered into the garden to join Megan where they had been sitting before Imi's arrival. They retook their seats as if the last hour hadn't happened at all.

They sat together without talking for a long time, both deeply immersed in their own thoughts. Finally Christian spoke, his voice barely a whisper.

'You knew all along, didn't you?'

Megan had known from the first meeting about Christian's role in Op Trinket in Nairobi that this moment would come, and she had rehearsed her response a thousand times.

'What do you want me to say, Chris? If it makes it any easier, I wasn't very happy about it either, but I couldn't tell you, we had to wait. And it's Imi's op.' Her mind had tried to find the right words but they came out in an order that only added to her anxiousness. 'I didn't want you to be involved, but you are and I couldn't stop it.' Megan looked away, her eyes filling up unexpectedly. She felt wretched and deeply upset now that the whole situation had come out. Used to being in control, she felt helpless to influence what came next. A veil of uncertainty seemed to have descended over their relationship.

Christian was sitting to her left, a round, slightly rusting metal table in front of them both. He finally spoke.

'I saw Fred today. Did I ever tell you about Fred?' Megan nodded silently;

her eyes now dry as she turned to look at him. 'He said that the UN has done a U-turn over my role; they are already recruiting someone else for it after only a few weeks of saying they were taking it in-house.' Christian's voice was firm and clear, the whole situation beginning to clarify in his mind. 'I don't suppose you knew about that as well, did you?' His voice wasn't harsh, but he wanted answers, and Megan knew she needed to be as honest as she could be.

'Chris, I don't know anything about that, please believe me.' The atmosphere between them was hurting her so much. She bit her lip before adding, 'But it wouldn't surprise me if it had been part of Imi's plan.' She had already said too much, but her feelings for Christian were getting the better of her. She was petrified that he would react badly to her knowledge of his recruitment. She had known that she was complicit from the moment Matt and Imi had briefed her; it had been a secret she wished she had never known.

'Megs, if we are going to be together going forward, we have to be honest with each other.' He delivered the line without any hesitation but with enough tenderness to let her know that he wanted to make this work.

'No, we have to trust each other, Chris. There's a difference. Sometimes I am not going to be able to be honest with you while we are out here. I'm sorry, it would be the end of my career if I was.' Megan was now crying, tears slowly rolling down her cheeks and dripping onto her shirt. Christian reached out to hold her hand and wiped the tears away with his other hand. They looked at each other properly for the first time since starting to talk. They tried to smile, but their faces were too conflicted to manage it. He was coming to terms with the situation. He knew that she would be aware of everything that he was going to be doing and realised, in that split second, that she wouldn't be able to intervene, whatever the situation. It struck him that Megan must have been feeling powerless.

'I think I understand, Megs. I'm sorry, it's just a shock. I wish someone had just talked to me about this at the start. I want to help, you know me, you know the kind of person I am. But seeing Imi like that and then realising that all of this had been planned for a long time. And that you'd known all along. Well ...' He let the words drift away on the breeze.

'Thanks, Chris. I hope you understand that it's not in my hands. I have to keep out of it, but we can still see each other when you come out of Vila Somalia. I want to see you, of course I do, but we cannot talk about this again.' She was regaining her composure as they walked slowly into the house and up the stairs.

They reached their room and, while Christian searched for the key in his pocket, Megan kissed him tenderly on his cheek. He opened the door and they walked in, closing it behind them.

'Shall we lie down?' As they stood together by the bed, Christian hugged Megan who lay her head on his shoulder. The shutters were loosely closed, allowing the sunlight to infiltrate the room, leaving a trail of abstract shapes flickering across the floor.

'Yes.' He barely heard her reply.

They kicked off their shoes and lay together on the bed, wrapped in each other's arms, lost in their own thoughts.

'Megs, I understand and I'm not cross with you. And I will do whatever it takes to protect you. It's going to be OK,' Christian said quietly, close to her ear.

'We have to make this work. And then we have to figure out what comes next,' Megan replied.

They lay together, falling in and out of sleep until they were both awoken by the sound of the returning shoppers in the entrance hall, the commotion filling the house with conversation and laughter below them.

'I guess it's time for tea.' Megan's voice was light.

'I guess so.' They had scarcely moved since lying down. It was as if they had been fused together, unwilling, or unable, to face whatever came next.

Megan raised herself up onto her elbow and put her hand on Christian's chest, slipping her fingers under his shirt and touching his warm skin. He held her face softly in his hands as they looked at each other.

'Listen, army boy, please stay safe for me and for our future,' Megan said gently, her face close to his. They leant towards each other, kissing deeply. She relaxed into his body and they held each other again. The sounds from downstairs continued to filter up to the second floor but they didn't care about preparations for afternoon tea. They felt as if their stars had finally aligned. They needed each other more than either of them could express physically. The last couple of hours had changed their relationship in a way they both understood intuitively, their closeness in the room sealing an unwritten contract of their commitment to each other.

'I will, I promise.' He smiled. 'Now, whether we like it or not, we are expected downstairs to try Marco's latest delicacy from the kitchen!' He tried to lighten the moment. Her words had taken him by surprise and with everything that Imi had said to him, he needed some time to process all that had happened.

As they walked down the stairs, Megan said, 'I'm leaving this evening, Chris. I have a team meeting first thing, and I have to be back to check my inbox.' Megan's professional side had resurfaced, which Christian acknowledged.

'Is Miko taking you back or is Krish coming out to get you?'

'Miko is dropping me at the rear gate before sundown and Krish will get me from there. How about you?'

They hadn't even thought to discuss their travel arrangements over the weekend but had assumed they would both be returning that evening.

'Yeah, I'm heading back this evening as well, so I'll be in the car with you before Miko drops me back at VS. We're leaving around five o'clock I think.'

They reached the dining room to find Arne laying the table for afternoon tea.

'Hi guys!'

'Hi Arne, can we help?'

*

Mohammed sat with his feet in the water. Despite the recent dry weather, there was still a flow to the river and he watched as a small stick he had thrown into the current gently drifted off to his left, making its way across the surface of the river, xylem-like, twisting and turning, until it flowed into the vast Indian Ocean. He stared for a while into the distance, looking east, wondering what lay beyond the horizon. He had started to think about these things of late. He didn't know why, but he seemed to be more attuned to what was happening around him. He threw another piece of wood onto the surface and watched it meander away out of sight.

He wasn't far from where he had been attacked by the man all those months before. The scars on his face had healed, more or less, but the mental impact of that day, and the events of the following weeks, had caused him great distress. He had stopped sleeping through the night, something his mother said that he had always done from being a small baby. He had lost his appetite and only ate because he didn't want to disappoint his mother who somehow managed to produce some food for him each day. And he had lost his friend, Ali, to the terrorists in Mogadishu.

He felt sad and lonely most of the time, but couldn't tell anyone, and didn't know how to describe his feelings. Even if he had managed to find the right words, he knew his father would have little time for him; his mother would smother him in love but without understanding the emotions he felt every day. And now he didn't have a best friend; at least, his best friend wasn't the same person that he remembered growing up with.

He reflected on his first meeting with Rasuul, and the promise of carrying out revenge against the soldiers who had killed his friend, *their* friend. Except he had felt scared ever since he had been beaten by the farmer. When he finally understood what had happened to him, once his own wounds had become less painful a few days later, without anyone ever finding out, he cried quietly every night, soaking his thin pillow with tears. His relationship with his best friend had also changed that day. His mother had banned him from seeing Ali after she heard their agreed story about having a fight. It was over two weeks before they met again and Ali, fired up by the loss of his explosive devices, had press-ganged Mohammed to go with him to Mogadishu to steal some more. It was a trip Mohammed did not want to take but felt unable to prevent all the same. And it had changed his life.

Everything from that moment and the weeks afterwards was a blur. Ali saw him every day, telling him that they would be able to finally avenge their friend's death. But as each day ended and Mohammed walked back to his family, he became increasingly scared about what was going to happen; as scared as he had been when they had been caught red-handed by the farmer.

He picked up another small stick, shaped like a dowsing rod, and held it for a moment, its Y-shape shaking in his hand, before he lobbed it into the centre of the river.

Rasuul's promise of actually blowing up an AMISOM vehicle had consumed Ali's life, but Mohammed knew he wanted nothing to do with it. If only he could have said something then. Instead, he had gone back to Mogadishu with Ali to meet Rasuul again; they were told where to be the following week so they could meet a man, who Rasuul had said would be in charge, collect the explosive device and take it to where the attack would happen. They were going to help the man to set up the ambush. They had driven to the location and carefully lowered a heavy metal box onto the dirt road. The man had said that it was packed with nails and ball bearings from the market. Once it was beneath the surface, the man had driven the vehicle away out of sight. When he had returned, they each covered their tracks as they trailed the wires away from the road and across some grassland until they found a small depression about 150 metres away. The man had connected everything for them and then said that they now needed to wait. Each evening they covered the controller with plastic sheeting, and the following morning they returned to the same spot with the man, who said that a convoy would be passing through soon.

Eventually, on the third day, after lying in the grass out of sight for a couple of hours, they heard the sound of a large truck changing gear, then another, and when they crept up to the top of the small ridge they spotted three AMISOM vehicles driving along the road towards the ambush site, about 30 metres apart. The bomb was at the apex of a bend in the road as it curved away from them. The man had quickly connected the final wire and they both watched the lights blink on the controller that he held in his hands. That day, a second man had come with them and while they were hunched over the controller watching the vehicles through the tufts of grass in front of them, he was behind them, set back, filming everything on a mobile phone.

As the first truck drove past them, the man had encouraged them both to press the button together, but Mohammed couldn't do it and had held his hands between his legs in childlike defiance. The man's language changed quickly, threatening Mohammed, but there was no time to argue. As the second vehicle approached the spot, Ali felt no such hesitation and moved his hand to rest his finger on the black button, then he pressed it.

They brought their heads up to peer towards the smoke pouring from what was left of the vehicle, dust filling the entire area. After the deafening explosion, all Mohammed could hear were the screams of the men staggering from the vehicles, their bodies on fire. He could make out two men, their uniforms burning, aimlessly walking into the grassland next to the road then collapsing forward, lifeless, their bodies smoking, their screams extinguished.

The man with them had initially whistled then grabbed them both, telling them to get up and run, but Mohammed had pushed the man's hand away and stayed for a few moments more. By the time he turned round to leave, he could see Ali and the man in the distance, running away, shouting at each other excitedly. The second man was still filming the scene behind him, but he also put his camera away and started to run. Mohammed scrambled down the bank and followed them. The sound of ammunition exploding in the distance accompanied their escape as they made their way to the man's vehicle, already pointing in the direction of a narrow track that would lead them to safety.

Mohammed had refused to go out after that. He told his mother that he felt unwell, day after day. When Ali came round, he told her that he didn't want to see his friend. Only after a week did he finally walk out of the house and start to face people in his village. They were far enough away from the attack not to be implicated, but the responsibility he felt for the men he saw dying in front him had resulted in sleepless nights. He couldn't get their faces out of his mind, however hard he tried.

And when Mohammed finally decided to see Ali, he knew then that he could no longer be his friend. Ali had been excited about the attack, but Mohammed felt sick. When Ali told Mohammed that Rasuul wanted them both to go to Mogadishu, Ali had told him he couldn't wait to get out of his village for good. He had been promised some new trainers, like Rasuul's, and was told he'd be able to earn money working in the market. But Mohammed had refused to go. He wanted nothing to do with his friend, who he now struggled to recognise. It was as if he had become a different person, intent on violence, on hurting people. Mohammed shook his friend's hands off his arms and ran away from him. And he didn't stop running until he had no energy to run any further. Ali had followed him at first but had soon given up, calling him names, shouting that he would make new friends in Mogadishu.

Mohammed had run to the spot he was sitting at now and stayed there for a whole night, cowering under the bushes close to the river, hoping that he would not be taken by any of the cheetahs he had been told inhabited the region. At one point, in the dead of night, he had been woken by the breaking of a twig close behind him. He had held his breath, his heart pounding in his chest, but after a few minutes the sound had moved away. It had probably only been a small antelope but for a brief moment he had actually wanted to be killed. Anything to end the constant dreams he had been having about the attack.

Mohammed lifted his feet out of the water, pulled his legs up against his body and wrapped his arms around them.

Resting his chin on his knees, he started to cry again, his body gently rocking forwards and backwards. Tears poured down his face, his sobs quietly drifting across the water, as he tried to forget the images inside his head.

18

Turkish Embassy, Mogadishu

Corporal Hakan Kiliç took his headphones off and hung them next to the radio equipment in front of him. He pulled his pen out of his sleeve pocket and filled in the log, signing off after another 12-hour shift, this time overnight. Hakan had two more to go in the current cycle of three nights, three days, and one day off. It was a punishing schedule over such a long period of time.

He was exhausted and was looking forward to his bed in the accommodation building on the far side of the car park. Spending 12 hours in the basement as the ops room radio operator, with only a few minutes to use the toilets in the main embassy building, was starting to get to him, especially as morale was so low following the incident at the training camp.

Hakan had been on duty that night. He'd just received his briefing from the day shift and had taken his seat; he'd been feeling fresh and had made himself a cup of coffee. He was often on his own in the basement but that night he was surprised nobody else had been with him, considering Gali's involvement in the attack. Hakan looked up to Gali. As someone who had grown up in the same town in the west of the country, albeit several years later, Gali had showed a lot of interest in Hakan's military career, taking him under his wing, which led to his eventual recruitment into the team with responsibility for communications.

So, when Hakan had received a call from Gali just after he started his shift, he was confused. Protocols dictated that the deployed personnel should never use their mobile phones to call the ops room. They shouldn't even have had numbers saved in their phones. They had GPS beacons in case there was an emergency, so his call was highly unusual, and he knew that he would be in deep shit for having made it. Except Gali hadn't spoken. In fact, after asking whether it was Gali at all, the phone went dead. He had immediately logged in online to check Gali's GPS tracker, but it had been in his other gear stored away from the fighting and hadn't moved. Hakan didn't understand why Gali hadn't had it with him, or why he hadn't spoken. It was only later that he had learned that Gali had never made it back to the Shabaab location. To this day, nobody knew what happened.

Ever since that moment, he had been torn; should he have mentioned the call or kept it quiet to protect Gali's reputation? Gali was probably dead anyway; what more could anyone do to him but rubbish his good name? So Hakan had decided to keep it quiet and not mention it. Nobody would ever know anyway; he was in charge of communications and had eventually wiped the call from the ops room mobile soon after the news had filtered through that Gali was missing, presumed dead. He had made a promise to himself that when he was next on leave back home, he would visit Gali's family – his parents, brothers and sisters – to tell them what a hero he had been, how he had died defending their great nation and that he had not lost his life in vain.

Hakan walked up the steps after briefing his colleague, who had taken over on the day shift. He needed to grab some food from the kitchen and get his head down.

'Morning, Hakan.' Hassan, the senior intelligence officer in the embassy, spoke automatically as he brushed past him and hurried into the basement. Hakan knew Hassan's weekly Monday video call with Ankara was about to start. He reached the top of the stairs and breathed in the air from the main corridor, then turned right and walked slowly towards the kitchen in the hope that he would be able to grab some *kaşar peyniri* and *yumurta*. He didn't need much more than eggs and cheese, not before sleeping.

'OK, sir, we are connecting now.' The day shift operator moved out of the chair facing the screen and took a seat out of shot, towards the back of the room.

'Hello, Mehmet.' Hassan was wearing a freshly laundered white shirt, its top button undone and, as usual, his grey tie was pulled down from his neck. He opened his notebook and held his pen, placing his briefing notes on top to give the update to Mehmet, his boss in Turkey.

'Hassan, tell me, what's happening?' Mehmet was sitting at the head of a long oval table, accompanied by several other officials on either side of him, in one of MIT's fully equipped video conference suites. A small Turkish tea was steaming away in front of him. The video quality was excellent, and

Hassan could see and hear everything that was going on 4,300 kilometres away in his country's capital city.

It had been more than ten days since the attack on the EU training camp and nothing had been heard of Gali. They reluctantly concluded that he had been killed and were now making arrangements for his kit to be returned to Turkey, and for his next of kin to be informed.

'I received a message from Osman at the end of last week. Firstly, he has Gali's kit, so the satellite images are secure. He also said that, according to his Shabaab contacts, Gali never made it to the ERV but the remaining Shabaab fighters ...'

Mehmet interrupted him. 'ERV? We have some non-security people here, Hassan, please keep language clear,' Mehmet said.

'Of course – emergency rendezvous. The place where they would meet in case of a problem or as planned after the attack, so that they could re-group and move to their vehicle muster point.' Hassan cleared his throat. 'As I was saying, Shabaab were focused on their own escape rather than looking for missing Turkish soldiers. Nobody saw Gali after he left to set the explosives.'

Hassan spoke without emotion and looked at his notes quickly.

'We know from what they have reported through Osman that they lost 15 men in the attack but managed to bring all their injured out with them.' Hassan let that last comment sink in. 'As you know, we also have an asset in the private military company Lancing Point based at Airport Camp. We finally managed to speak to him yesterday. He reported that the contractors working with AMISOM that evening had recovered a body but he understands that it has already been cremated, along with all the dead Shabaab fighters from the attack. He said it's completely normal for that to happen. The key thing is, he heard them say they were dealing with 16 bodies, not 15.'

Mehmet was making a few notes. 'OK, that's fine, so it looks like he is dead.' He paused for a moment, out of respect, but soon carried on. 'Please make the arrangements, Hassan. The operation continues, we have come too far now for this to be pulled. What else do you have for me?'

Hassan fidgeted in his seat for a moment, giving himself a few moments to read through his notes. 'Osman has said that they cannot launch any more attacks until the latest shipment of ammunition is delivered, so he has said that our guys will use their time to take stock and begin to identify future targets for when the military deployment is authorised. This background intelligence work will be vital in achieving the swift defeat of Shabaab.'

'OK, next?' Mehmet was obviously in a hurry.

'Just a couple of points: firstly, Osman has met a member of Shabaab's recruitment team, and he has been told that there are some suicide bombers who can be lined up for a specific attack in the city, teenagers apparently, so we have that up our sleeve when we need to bring this operation to a climax.' Hassan was so engrossed in the details of his operation that the mention of young people being involved in his plan, albeit indirectly, was business as usual. Around the table in Ankara, the reaction was different, although he didn't pick up the whispered comments between the attendees.

'OK.' Mehmet knew they had embarked on a mission that could have collateral damage, but he was a ruthless professional and a veteran of many such operations. Addressing his colleagues around the table, he said, 'Please remember that the success of our country's foreign policy relies on this operation, and other operations like it, being conducted with precision and without emotion. You are all here because you are also committed to that mission. Now, let's keep focused on the job at hand; go on, Hassan.' Mehmet knew that members of his team had little or no experience of overseas operations and, occasionally, when the details came out, it was inevitable that some would find it hard to process what was being done in the name of the Turkish state. Mehmet had handpicked them for that reason.

'Finally, my last point: I received a report from our Defence Attaché in Nairobi last night. I forwarded it to you first thing, along with an image. There was a regular monthly security meeting at the end of last week in Airport Camp, which we are members of, but for reasons you are aware, we are maintaining a distance so that we can pursue alternative approaches to supporting the Somalis – outside of this operation, of course.'

'Of course, so why do I need to look at it?' Mehmet was getting a little impatient, he looked at his watch.

'The Somali Defence Minister has agreed to the appointment of a British officer as a strategic advisor in Vila Somalia. The image is his business card. From what Commander Murat said, the man could become an obstacle to his efforts to establish a strong bilateral agreement with the Somali Government for increasing our presence through normal military channels. It's one to watch, that's all.' Hassan had debated whether to mention Murat's report at all but, since the loss of Gali, together with a lack of other positive news, he felt he had needed another item to brief the MIT Director.

'OK, Hassan, let's tie up the loose ends with Gali's belongings and I will make sure we do everything here.' Off microphone, Mehmet spoke to one of the people around the table, then re-joined the call. 'Good. Let's speak again in a week. Thank you, Hassan.'

'Thank you, Mehmet, I'll be in touch.' The operator emerged from the corner of the room and stepped in front of Hassan, grabbed the mouse, and closed the link with a click.

'It's gone,' he said as the screen turned blue.

Hassan sat back and sighed deeply. The operation was still on track to be a success. There had been no other problems with the guys in the field. Osman's comms had been consistent and his briefings were positive about the impact the team of five was having on the extremists. His ambitious plan was still running and nothing had gone wrong from an operational security perspective. Notwithstanding the loss of Gali, a man he had hardly known, he was content. The logistics trail seemed to be working well and was completely deniable. He made a note to check later on where the shipping container was, but first he needed a cup of tea.

'Thank you,' he said briefly to the operator as he got up, grabbed his things and ascended the steps.

*

Imi was sitting at her desk in Nairobi, her head in her hands, staring at the mass of papers on her desk. Still exhausted from her flight back from Mogadishu via Wajir, she had brought coffee in a takeaway cup to the office and had been on the 4th floor for about an hour. She pulled out a file marked 'ME – Restricted' from a pile in front of her and rummaged through to find what she was looking for.

After meeting Pete at the shopping mall the previous weekend, she had alerted Megan to Jack's report from Riyadh, asking whether she had any sources who worked in Somalia's port. Megan said that she did know someone who worked there and had previously lived in the UK, but it would take a while to fix up a meet.

Imi knew the window to investigate that particular shipment had closed, and the container had probably been moved out of the port by now, but she figured the regularity of each passage gave her hope that there would be a fourth and that this time she would get someone to report back. Like Jack, she too had an inkling this was a significant issue; she just had no idea how or why at this stage. She closed the file and sat back, taking a sip of her coffee and looking around the empty floorplate. It was still only 7.30am.

Her mind also drifted to what Pete had given her. As soon as she had got back to the office following her meeting with him, Imi had packaged up the phone and sent it, via a diplomatic bag, to the UK's Government Communications Headquarters in Cheltenham. She had been thinking through the implications of what it may hold pretty much every day since it had gone to the post room. Pete's opinion that the man was not a Somali was interesting, although any chance of trying to conduct any post mortem tests were impossible. However, the phone was likely to hold one or two nuggets of information, even if the man turned out to be a foreign fighter, essentially a gun for hire, siding with Shabaab's cause rather than the many other extremist groups conducting campaigns across the continent. She knew it would be a couple of weeks before there was any news.

Being patient was part of the game she played.

19

British High Commission, Nairobi

Three weeks later, Imi's first two hours in the office had been spent initially reading the report, then speaking to Megan on the secure line to confirm some of the details. As predicted, by tracking the MV Caldo Porta, they had learned that it was again heading to Mogadishu. It had docked two days earlier, exactly four weeks after the previous shipment. Within three hours, its cargo had been disembarked using the ship's own cranes. Once again, the cargo included a container that did not appear on the manifest, a fact confirmed to Megan by text message from her contact inside the port operation room. The final sentence from Megan's report had made Imi stop in her tracks: *The ghost shipping container was picked up and transported to a facility on the outskirts of the city just off Industrial Road, a site known to be linked to the Turkish Embassy.*

Megan had pulled a blinder; she had asked her contact to look into the discrepancy, but not to investigate it, by promising to divert some of her overseas development aid budget to install new security fencing around the port, which was regularly penetrated by thieves stealing cargo from the dockside. The contact had not only identified the container but, as instructed, he had also marked it with black spray paint.

Imi smiled at her own foresight. She had proposed an intelligence exchange between the UK and the Somali National Security Advisor's team when Abdulkadir Aden had arrived back in Mogadishu from his time as a councillor in West London. She seized the opportunity and he had agreed to the arrangement. During her discussions with Aden, Imi had learned that Somalia's top security official was being fed information on an almost daily basis from a network of assets across the city who watched certain locations. Imi had requested authority from Aden for Megan to tap into that network via the NSA's office when the need arose, to which he had agreed. The confirmation of the Turkish connection had come from a credible source who was assigned to watch their embassy. Her foundation work had finally delivered something actionable.

In her report, Megan explained that the container had received an escort from two black vehicles which had exited the embassy compound just as the lorry carrying it had driven past. Once the container had been identified by the black paint mark, the asset sent one of his people to follow the small convoy on a motorbike; his initiative had proved to be decisive. The container had been driven to the facility and then into an open warehouse which closed immediately. Imi blew out her cheeks and pushed her hair from her face. She needed to take this to Matt. She sent him a short email: *Matt, We need to discuss a development re Somalia/Turkey. Are you free today? Should also be getting something from GCHQ later (you may get a call from them – I've been a bit pushy). Imi*

She then started to draw out everything she knew about Turkey's influence in Somalia and the wider region onto a mind map; it was how she worked, seeing the bigger picture and connecting seemingly unrelated events. Like so many people in the intelligence business, she didn't believe in coincidences.

Imi's desktop chimed to let her know she had received a reply from Matt. Even though he was only sitting 25 metres away, putting everything down on paper, in emails, was how he wanted things to be done: *Today might be a stretch, Imi. I've got a couple of video calls then I'm out from 4. Back in again first thing. I'll block out an hour at 8am tomorrow. Matt*

Imi closed the email and created an entry in her online calendar. She then went back to her mind map. She had "Turkey in Somalia" circled twice in the centre of her sheet of A3. Lines drawn out from the central bubble covered the classic analysis tool headings: political, economic, social/cultural, technological, legal and environmental. She added a seventh heading: security.

Imi initially wrote some known information against each subheading, ending with the international security meeting forum. She knew Turkey was unwilling to be collaborative with the wider international community; as a result, everyone assumed they were working bilaterally with the Somali Government. She hadn't written much under economic apart from "foreign direct investment". She also added a single sentence against the legal subheading "UN Arms Embargo on Somalia". She revisited the map and added more thoughts. After repeating this process for a couple of hours, researching specific areas of interest to fill out the picture a little more, she had made progress, but it still felt as if something was missing. The shipping container had its own line drawn directly to the centre, with two branch lines drawn to economy and social/cultural. What on earth was Turkey doing with four shipping containers coming from Saudi Arabia which had been deliberately excluded from the manifest? Imi's head was beginning to ache. She did have one outstanding question and wrote a quick email to Jack in Saudi: *Jack, just a quick one on the shipments. Tell me again, what is KSA doing in Somalia? Best, Imi*

She could see he was online so she waited for a few moments in case he was sitting at his desk. She needed a break; the report from GCHQ had been promised several times and they had said it would be sent before lunch UK time. It couldn't come soon enough. Imi knew she had to get as much info together as possible before seeing Matt the following morning. While she waited, she wrote a short message for Christian and encrypted it, sending it to mogadishuboy265@yahoo.com. His two reports so far had been as expected: light on anything of immediate interest.

Jack's reply finally arrived: *Hi Imi, how are you? Great to hear from you. KSA has been delivering a mosque building programme across Somalia for a number of years. J*

An idea struck Imi and she replied quickly: *Thanks Jack, good to hear from you too. Where else is KSA running similar programmes? Do you know? I*

Imi was staring at her screen, willing Jack's reply to appear quickly. It dropped into her inbox.

They've been at it for decades, building schools, colleges, mosques, you name it. It's basically one huge propaganda campaign. Worth $Bns. They're either active, or have been active, in places like Sudan, Somalia, the Western Balkans, especially Kosovo and Albania, Pakistan and Turkey. Does that help? J

By 4.30pm, Imi was sitting downstairs in the café hoping for inspiration, watching Edith closing up. Located on the ground floor and partially open to the elements, the atrium was at the centre of the building, decked out with classic easy-on-the-eye wooden furniture surrounded by huge tropical plants, their broad leaves reaching high into the air and bearing down on the tables as if eavesdropping on every conversation. Imi was sitting alone, deeply preoccupied, drumming her fingers on the table top and periodically flicking the nearest cheese plant away from her head. When at last her mobile pinged, she pulled it out of her jeans' pocket and read the message. It was from Ralph in GCHQ: *Imi, I've sent through a report about the package you sent over. Sorry for taking so long, we've been inundated recently. Let me know if you need any follow up.*

'Finally,' Imi muttered under her breath as she took her last swig of coffee and dropped her cup in the recycling. 'How can the coffee here be so crap when we are living in bloody Kenya?' She said it loud enough for Edith to hear.

'It's because we export the best stuff!' Edith laughed loudly from behind the counter, her Kenyan-accented English echoing around them.

'Touché, Edith, see ya tomorrow.' Imi headed for the door, her face unmoved by their exchange. Her mind was elsewhere.

What should have been a two-week turnaround for the information about the phone had become three weeks, then four. She had been desperate for some news, any news, that would help her understand what was going on in Somalia. The shipping container had been the first solid piece of intelligence; she hoped the report from GCHQ would fill in a few more blanks. Her heart started beating just a little bit quicker as she raced up to the 4th floor and she was back at her desk within a couple of minutes. Pulling up her chair, she quickly shook the mouse awake so that she could log in to her desktop computer. The unread email was sitting at the top of her inbox in bold, entitled: "Analysis of Somali Mobile ending 588".

Dear Imi,

I wanted to accompany the formal results with a personal note as I know you asked for a thorough investigation of the phone found on the Shabaab fighter.

First off, there are partial finger prints but they don't match any databases that the Serious and Organised Crime Agency have access to. You'll be able share them as you see fit; the digital images are in the file. There was some blood on the handset which may be of value at some point.

The phone itself is a Hormuud Telecom mobile registered at the end of last year. We managed to extract some numbers and text messages, all of them on Somali mobile networks, and did an investigation of where those mobiles are currently paging (where they are!). We found that all of them bar one are moving frequently in and around Mogadishu, as well as further away. However, we couldn't cross-match any of the numbers with our database. They're new to us. I have entered them onto our log, but I'll leave any additional action to you.

One number though was static, like it's an office mobile, so we focused on that one. It's still up and running, and the location has been narrowed down to a small area in Mogadishu, close to the K4 roundabout. Looking at the map, and discounting businesses that are unlikely to have been in comms with our friend, we are left with two likely outcomes: first, someone who is senior within Shabaab is living in that area and uses it to communicate with various teams, which could be an important break for us. Or, second, the phone is based in the Turkish Embassy.

Do you want to initiate a tap on it?

All Best,

Ralph

Imi sat back, an instinctive reaction after reading the email for the first time. After a moment, she read his note again, then opened the attachment to scan the report. She would look at it later on. Ralph's covering email had summarised the key points. She got up and walked to the wall where her map of Mogadishu was pinned. She cross-checked the report and drew a rough triangle onto the map with a blunt red crayon. Along with countless private residences and small businesses, including a hostel, the projected location of the mobile phone was sitting plum in the middle of the cell map she had drawn and directly on top of the Turkish Embassy. She circled it and stood back to take it all in.

The office was beginning to quieten down as people left for the day. Imi walked to the coffee machine, so deep in thought she could have been sleepwalking. She untied her hair band and, after pulling her hair tighter than before, replaced it. She needed to wake up so she pressed the machine for her second coffee of the hour.

It was going to be a long evening.

20

Vila Somalia, Mogadishu

fter spending two weeks in Nairobi, which included a long weekend in Mombasa by the coast with Megan, Christian had arrived back in the capital of Somalia with renewed energy and a determination to increase his usefulness to Imi. Until now, she had only received pretty routine information from him. While on his R&R, he had spent a long time thinking about what his role should be now that Imi had briefed him on the real purpose of his contract.

He had taken to pen and paper to forensically analyse his role and how he could make himself more aware of what was going on, trying to find opportunities to dig a little deeper into what the Turkish in particular were doing. He had also concluded that if he got caught, it didn't really matter whether British special forces were on standby or not. In Vila Somalia, he would be thrown into the nearest jail cell with little due process. He had rationalised that he would be released before anything went too far down the judicial route, but it would be an uncomfortable period of incarceration which he was keen to avoid.

At first, whenever he thought about what he had been asked to do for Imi, particularly when he allowed his imagination to consider more risky endeavours beyond simple observation, his mouth had gone dry and he had quickly started to feel a mild panic rising up inside his chest. Being with Megan during their long weekend away had helped take his mind off things. However, they had both adhered to Megan's request not to discuss his role and therefore, as a result, he had felt unable to share the feelings he was experiencing, which made everything worse. He had been involved in risky activity in the military, but this was of a different order of magnitude.

Christian sat at his desk in the office next to Said and continued to work on a PowerPoint presentation covering his initial analysis about optimising international security assistance, which he planned to present to Minister

Hassan and, if he was content, to the President. In the corner of his screen an icon appeared, telling him that he had received a new email. He looked up and checked the room – a habit whenever he received an email now, even though most of them were unrelated to his mission. He clicked the icon and waited a moment.

From: nairobigirl941@yahoo.com

To: mogadishuboy265@yahoo.com

Subject: Ideas for summer holidays

Once the email was open, he clicked on the encrypted attachment. Imi had said not to open her emails in the office, but Christian was too keen and felt confident that he was in a secure place. The process of decrypting the text file took a few moments to reveal the original message: *Chris, something has come up. Would be good to know when the next inbound visit from TU reps is scheduled. Let me know asap (need reply by close of play today). Imi*

Christian read the message again and pressed delete, then opened his 'Recycle Bin' and deleted it from there as well. If his laptop was forensically examined, he had been told by Imi that they were likely to find all the messages, but by then he would be out of the country. That was part of the emergency extraction plan, anyway.

The message had fired him up and he started trying to figure out the best way to get the information. Anything arranged with the Defence Minister was straightforward as he had read-only access to his online diary and he checked Hassan's schedule frequently. He had identified a couple of options when it came to understanding who was visiting the President, but he was yet to test his theories out. He needed to act today. He also needed to get his current project in a place where he could actually deliver it to his ministerial boss. Putting aside his growing nervous excitement, he focused on the final few slides of his presentation before lunch.

After an hour and a half, Christian got up and stepped into Said's office to check whether the Minister was in.

'Hello, Said, could I have a word with the Minister?' Christian had got used to the ease of access and realised that informality was the key, as long as he had the right relationship in place.

'Hi, yes, he is going out in five minutes, but just go through.' Said raised his hand inviting him to enter the Minister's office.

'Minister, good morning.' Christian waited for the Defence Minster to look up from something he was reading.

'Yes, Christian, go ahead.'

'Sir, I have finished the draft presentation on the optimisation of international security assistance and, as we discussed, I would like to share it with you before taking it to the President. Shall I put something in your diary for the next couple of days?'

'Yes, that's fine, thank you, Christian. While you are here, the President has just asked me, along with the NSA, to meet the Turkish Ambassador when he visits next week. I am going to suggest that you join us for a part of the visit as the Defence Attaché from Nairobi will also be there. I will have to ask you to leave at some point, though, as we will be having bilateral discussions. I hope you understand.'

Minister Hassan was a tall, well-built man. His hair was thinning and he possessed an air of supreme self-confidence, a trait that was rare amongst his fellow public servants. He had spent a lot of time outside Somalia during the worst years of the civil war but had returned to Mogadishu around the time that al Shabaab had emerged as the primary threat to peace in Somalia. He was dressed in a tailored navy jacket, white shirt and, unusually, was without a tie. And he was an unashamed Anglophile.

He smiled warmly at Christian then looked down again to finish what he had been reading. 'Speak to Said and make sure it's in the diary for you as well. And speak to Bashiir; try to get half an hour to brief the President before they arrive,' he added in his almost accent-less English as Christian was walking out of the door.

Christian looked at Said, who sat with his back straight, reading glasses perched on the end of his nose, studying his desktop screen, his right hand moving the mouse with deliberate precision. A couple of clicks later, he looked at Christian above his glasses.

'All done. Wednesday. Midday.'

'Thank you so much, Said,' Christian said, and he meant it.

He walked along the corridor to the stairs and descended to the ground floor, hastily crossing the entrance hall to the café where he waited for a moment in line before ordering his usual lunch of spicy vegetable samosas and a can of coke. He could have gone to his accommodation to eat his lunch, which he had done in his first couple of weeks, but now he took a seat and made it easier for people to speak to him and for him to broaden his network. He took his linen jacket off and hung it over the back of the chair.

He couldn't believe his luck. He hadn't had to lift a finger and he was already lined up to join a senior visit to Vila Somalia by a Turkish delegation. Although he had enough to write back to Imi already, he wanted to do some more digging. Disappointed not to see Muna, who normally made an appearance in the café at some stage over lunch, Christian finished his food and walked back to his office. He wanted to crack on with his presentation before seeing Bashiir later in the afternoon.

By four o'clock, Christian was happy with the work he had done and told Said that he would be finishing things off in his accommodation. He closed down his laptop, put it in his bag and headed for the stairs. Once out in the sunshine, the breeze warming his face, he walked across the cobblestones towards the Office of the President, putting his sunglasses on his head while he held his security pass for inspection by the Somali guards, who by now simply waved him through. He stepped into the entrance hall and stopped by the security machine, taking out his phone and his keys, then placing them on his bag. The metal detector went off each time he walked through, regardless of what was in his pockets, its sensitivity shot to pieces. It always made him smile and it was something he'd mentioned in one of his messages to Imi.

Christian walked along the corridor towards Bashiir's office. He hoped that the Defence Minister had already made a call to him, but he needed to set something up just in case they hadn't spoken.

He met Bashiir outside.

'Ah Christian, how are you?' Bashiir was walking quickly towards him, having just left his office. 'How was your leave? Are you coming to see me?' Bashiir was smiling and pointing to his own chest.

'Hi, Bashiir, yes, I'm well thanks. Leave was good, really good,' Christian replied. 'Er, yes, I am, or I was ... I just wanted to talk to you about briefing the President on some defence matters. Minster Hassan asked me to arrange something.' They had both paused, facing each other in the quiet corridor.

'Give me a minute, OK? I'm just going to get a tea and I'll check when I'm back.' Bashiir obviously wanted more than a tea because he immediately walked into the bathroom. Christian continued to his office and took a seat on the sofa, the first visit in a couple of weeks. He looked around the room for any obvious changes to the room's overt security.

The room was silent. He knew the President was out of the building and none of the usual flunkies were hanging around. They only ever seemed to appear when the President was in his office. In the two weeks after his weekend at the B&B, Christian had paid a lot more attention to the routines in both Bashiir's office and the Defence Minister's. He had watched carefully, listened intently, and hung around a lot more than he normally would have done. In those two weeks, he had written two encrypted reports to Imi, both of which he felt were light on detail. Even though she had reassured him that these things took time, and to continue to get under the skin of Vila Somalia, he wanted to do something that would yield some useful intelligence after his R&R.

He had already scanned the room on previous visits, looking for hidden cameras. He had even managed to manufacture a conversation with the military head of security at the building's entrance, who had confirmed there were no devices installed in either the Chief of Staff's office or the President's suite of rooms saying, 'They don't want people to know what they do in there.' Christian's military past had helped him broker these conversations.

Whether what he had been told was true or not, he didn't know. He had to assume that there would be some sort of passive security somewhere. In the same conversation, he had also managed to uncover a significant piece of information: both rooms were scanned for devices every month by two members of the National Security Advisor's team. These titbits of information were also sent to Imi.

He pulled out his notebook and pencil, placing them on the arm of the leather sofa. He heard footsteps emerge into the corridor, then turn away and walk off towards the entrance hall. He looked at his watch and set the stop watch running.

When he heard Bashiir's footsteps echoing down the corridor towards him, Christian stopped the timer: 4 minutes, 35 seconds. He made a mental note of the time, opened his notebook and started writing a 'to do' list for the next few days.

'Christian! You're still here. Have you been sitting there the whole time?' Bashiir was already heading for his desk holding a paper cup. He sat down and immediately opened his side drawer to take out the President's diary.

'Yes, just making some notes for my briefing to Minister Hassan tomorrow.'

'OK, so he has very little time next week, but there is a chance on Tuesday afternoon but only for 15 minutes. Does that work?' Bashiir had obviously not been contacted by the Defence Minister.

'Minister Hassan had suggested the following day, just before the Turkish delegation visits. He also mentioned that he wants me to be present for part of that meeting.' Bashiir looked up and stared across his office at Christian, he face inscrutable, as if he was thinking through the implications of Christian being there.

'Did he? OK, well, I'll take a look.' He turned a page and started to write something onto it. 'OK, all done, you come in 30 minutes before, at 11.30am, and then you can stay in the room with everyone. How does that sound?' Bashiir closed the diary and put it away. He opened his laptop and tapped a few keys.

'Thanks, Bashiir, that's really helpful. See you later.' Christian got up and walked out as Bashiir's attention had already moved to his screen. Christian left the presidential building and turned right for his accommodation. Once inside, he took out his laptop, put it on the kitchen table and sat down. He started to write the text file to Imi.

Hi Imi, I am briefing the President in his office a week on Wednesday at 11.30am, alongside the Defence Minister, then staying for a visit by a Turkish delegation at midday. No idea who will be coming from either side but probably Defence Minister and NSA will be with Pres. Is there anything you need me to do? C

He encrypted the file, opened Yahoo! and clicked on "new message". He attached the message and pressed "send", then deleted the original text file before closing his laptop again.

It was warm in his kitchen and he sat still, leaning back in his chair. He listened to what was around him; without the air conditioning running there was near silence inside his accommodation, bar the hum of city life creeping in through the poorly fitting windows. And the voice in his head saying: *Can you really do this, Christian?*

He got up and tried to put it out of his mind. He made a coffee and sat back down to finish his work, half expecting a reply from Imi, trying not to keep checking his email account.

*

Across town, about four kilometres as the crow flies from where Christian was sitting, Hassan was hovering in the first-floor corridor outside the Ambassador's office holding a sheet of paper. He could hear the Ambassador on the phone, his words inaudible through the thick wooden door. He was pacing the carpet, unable to stand still, repeatedly running his hand across his thinning hair, nervously pressing it against his scalp. He looked again at the printed note he held in his hand, which had just arrived from Nairobi on their secure IT Network.

Attention: Hassan Güler, Mogadishu

From: Commander Murat Keskin, Defence Attaché Kenya

Subject: Visit to Somali President

Hassan,

I have just been informed by the Somali Defence Minister's office (by email) of the attendees for meeting a week on Wednesday;

- *The President*
- *Defence Minister Abdulla Hassan*
- *Abdulkadir Aden (National Security Advisor)*
- *Christian Travers (Strategic Advisor to Defence Minister)*

You may want to join the visit. Let me know.
I'm looking forward to your reply,
Murat

Hassan had immediately requested a short-notice meeting with the Ambassador to make sure he was added to the invitation list. Although he didn't need to break cover, he wanted to get the measure of this man who seemed to be so trusted within Vila Somalia. Having a Brit potentially getting in the way of his covert operation was a problem, particularly in the latter stages when unfettered access to both the President and the Defence Minister was going to be vital. They needed their own man inside Vila Somalia by the time the operation was concluding, something the Ambassador had planned to propose before they discovered that the British advisor was already in post. There couldn't be two of them, which meant the Brit had to go. He knocked on the door when he heard the conversation end.

'Come in, Hassan, come in.'

21

British High Commission, Nairobi

'Long night, Imi?' Matt was already on the floorplate and shouted across the room when Imi stepped out of the lift at 7.30am, heading for her desk. Hearing Matt's voice, she stopped and turned round.

'Yep. Got home at midnight. I'll be with you in a few minutes, we might need longer than an hour.'

Matt walked towards her. 'OK, I'm inviting Becky to join us. She is unconnected and will be able to offer some thoughts.'

'Great, the more brains on this the better.' Imi managed a smile but turned away to prepare her things and print off another copy of her briefing note that she'd already sent to Matt the evening before.

Five minutes later, a coffee in her hand, she was standing outside the 'box', waiting for Matt and Becky to join her. Becky, Matt's deputy, was focused on China's influence in Kenya, so her knowledge of what was going on in Somalia was thin at best; she would be ideal to bounce ideas off. And Imi liked Becky. Older than Imi by about ten years, she admired her success and, if she was completely honest with herself, she was modelling her own progress against Becky's record, which was impressive.

Becky arrived first – black jeans, grey cashmere rollneck jumper and brown leather ankle boots. She always managed to look both smart enough for work but completely comfortable in her own skin. To Imi, she was every bit the seasoned intelligence professional. Not much got past her and Imi felt reassured that she was joining the meeting.

'Come on. Matt will be over in a minute.' Becky punched in the code and opened the door, stepping in first, followed by Imi. They both rearranged the chairs around the table and pushed the others to the side. Matt joined them and closed the door.

After a few moments getting themselves sorted out, Matt spoke. 'So, Imi, what do you have? Let's focus on what we know, what we can do, and what the risks are, OK? Becky, jump in any time.'

Imi was suddenly and unexpectedly nervous, her confidence tested by their combined experience as intelligence officers. It was a strange and unwelcome feeling. She ran through everything that they knew, pausing only to answer questions from Becky and to clarify points for Matt. After 20 minutes of intense three-way discussion, Imi brought her initial briefing to a conclusion: 'So basically, we have a foreigner – we can't prove this – who was setting explosives as part of the deadly attack on the EU training camp. This person was wearing equipment that Shabaab have never been known to use, he was an expert shot with a pistol and he was carrying a phone that had potentially called the Turkish Embassy just before the attack.'

She had pinned the map on the wall by this stage and was pointing at the embassy in the heart of the red crayon triangle. Imi drew breath and took a sip of coffee.

'We also have a credible report that four shipping containers sailed from Jeddah in Saudi Arabia to Mogadishu, entirely off manifest, and the rogue containers – at least the last one – was driven, and escorted, to a warehouse near Industrial Road which is used by the Turkish Embassy. What's in it, we don't know. What we do know is that some of the other containers on the ship are connected to Saudi Arabia's long-standing, and ongoing, programme of exporting their version of Islam through building mosques, colleges and schools – amongst other activities – in fellow Muslim nations; perhaps of interest, that list includes Turkey. Also, the recent upturn in complexity and frequency of Shabaab attacks against the AU mission is unprecedented.'

Imi looked at both Matt and Becky, searching their faces for any questions.

'Finally, we know that Turkey is dragging its feet through the conventional international security assistance mechanism that is run by the UN and the AU force.' Imi hesitated for a moment. 'And I'm aware this is a bit of a leap, but we know Turkey is doing all it can to support Muslim nations that are struggling, particularly those in Africa. The increase in military aid elsewhere could well be the template they're using in Somalia. That in itself isn't a problem, but what we have here doesn't make sense if all they are going to do is be a bit of unilateral military support when it comes to training Somali soldiers.'

Imi drank more coffee as she finished. Her nerves were on edge; she sensed that this was her time. She wanted to do it right. Both Matt and Becky looked at the briefing notes Imi had supplied, just to check some details. Becky then looked at Imi's mind map again.

She spoke first. 'Imi, thanks, this is quite comprehensive. And not far off shocking if I am honest. I agree that we can't make too many assumptions, but it's worth playing some of these scenarios out. Shall I?' She looked at Matt, who nodded, concern etched across his face.

'Let's first of all say the fighter was Turkish. What does that mean? And why would he be communicating with the embassy just before a devasting, well-resourced attack? To me, in this scenario, the two events are linked through him. And, of course, the container must be involved. It's too much of a coincidence for it not to be. Alternatively, the person was just a foreign fighter who had managed to buy night-vision goggles on the black market and the phone call was to a senior Shabaab leader, holed up in the area covered by the map, letting him know that they were about to cross the start line. This option could lead us to assume we have killed a senior tactical commander on the ground. Have we picked up any reports online of any related chatter on the subject, Imi?' Imi made a note on her pad to follow that up. 'We'll need to look into that too. So, which one is most credible?' She looked at Matt.

'I think it's too early for us to jump to any conclusions about a fellow NATO member working alongside al Shabaab for reasons we cannot possibly know at this stage. And, although I am sure the shipping container is important, we can't connect the two activities right now. We would obviously need more evidence to do so. So, I'm not going to discount it, I am just going to park it for now. What I think we need to do, as a matter of urgency, is tap the phone, get the boys in Airport Camp to get eyes on that warehouse over the next few days – leave those activities to me – and get your man in Vila Somalia to find out what he can. He is our only source close to the action.' He hesitated for a moment. 'Imi, we are going to have to share this with Megan.'

Becky looked slightly confused but said nothing.

'Leave it with me.' Imi replied.

'Becky, any more from you?' Matt was starting to gather what little he had brought into the 'box'. The meeting was wrapping up.

'Thanks, Matt. I do think we need to proceed with a great deal of caution here, though. If there is some sort of covert military assistance taking place by an element of the Turkish state, we would need to be absolutely rock solid before taking this to anyone in Ankara.'

Becky's advice brought simultaneous nods from Matt and Imi.

'OK, good work, Imi, thanks. Let me know about the arrangements for both the activities we discussed and keep Becky and me informed of any developments.'

'Will do, thanks for your time.' Imi moved to take the map off the wall and gathered her things together while Becky undid the door, the whoosh of air exiting the room before they stepped out.

Matt walked over to his desk and asked Becky to join him for a moment.

'Becks, look, what Imi has just said worries me a great deal. I'm going to brief Tom in London, in person. I'll get the overnight flight booked for this evening. I'll be away for a couple of days. Keep close to Imi, she's on to something, but I don't want this to spiral unnecessarily, OK?' Matt had opened his side drawer to extract his passport while he was talking.

'No problem, Matt. Safe flight.' Becky walked away to her own desk and logged in to her desktop.

Matt then sent two emails: the first to his PA asking her to book his flight, and the second to Tom Burbridge, the Africa Director in the Foreign Office.

Hi Tom, excuse the brevity, we need to meet tomorrow morning. There is an urgent matter we have to discuss. I am flying in overnight. Should be in Central London by 10am tomorrow. Travellers? Matt

He knew he wouldn't receive a reply for a couple of hours, taking into account the time difference with London. He made his plans regardless; this matter couldn't wait and Tom needed to be brought into the decision-making process.

*

When Matt pulled up in the taxi, Tom was already waiting inside the entrance of The Travellers Club, the favoured London haunt for senior members of the foreign service. The non-descript façade was ignored by most passers-by, but 106 Pall Mall held many secrets about Britain's foreign policy. Matt paid off the cabbie and wearily walked up the steps, carrying a small bag. Although he'd flown business class and enjoyed the luxury of a bed, his mind had been too active to sleep very much. The two whiskies he'd consumed hadn't provided the desired effect. After a shower in the terminal at Heathrow and a change of clothes, he'd managed to make good time through the morning traffic. He was only 15 minutes late.

He stepped onto the pavement, shivered, then walked up the steps to the entrance. His suit offered no defence against the English winter.

'Matt, how very good to see you.' Tom walked towards his guest. He had replied to Matt as soon as he'd got in the previous day, then spent the next hour with his PA unpicking his schedule to accommodate the short-notice meeting. 'I take it this can't wait,' he chuckled as they shook hands.

The two men walked through the entrance hall, up a couple of carpeted steps, and along the corridor to the library's swing doors. Books lined the oak-panelled walls, each volume a silent witness to the countless secretive conversations that had been conducted in their midst over the years. A sense of discretion wrapped around them both like a protective coat. At the far end of the long room, they sunk into deep leather armchairs, battered from decades of use, separated by a side table, and facing the French doors which opened onto the club's outdoor space in Waterloo Gardens on warmer days. This was always where the two men ended up.

'Have you eaten?' Tom asked Matt as Alejandro, a long-serving steward, walked in and approached them silently.

'I have, but you know what airline food is like, and it was hours ago. If there is anything going, that would be great, thanks.'

Tom ordered a club special sandwich and a pot of coffee. He also asked Alejandro to close the library doors once he had brought everything.

'Yes, sir.'

Alejandro knew what that request meant.

After ten minutes, during which time they talked about their families, Alejandro reappeared with Matt's brunch and the drinks, which included a bottle of water. He left everything on the small table between the men and left, closing the doors behind him. Tom knew he would also place a sign in front of the door, asking members not to disturb for the next half an hour. It was a tradition respected by everyone at the club.

The room was silent, save the distant ticking of the ancient wall clock, imperial booty from the nineteenth century. Matt excused himself and tucked in to the sandwich, not realising until that moment quite how hungry he was.

'I take it this is serious,' Tom said to Matt, who was mid-bite, his voice still low enough not to be heard beyond their chairs. He poured them both some coffee.

'Do you remember an operation in Syria last year, involving the Turks and the Kurds, the one where the US ended up losing one of their special forces guys in a bombing?' Matt took another bite; his hunger needed to be satisfied before he could fully commit to the conversation.

'Vaguely. I wasn't looking in that direction from my desk, but I do remember something about it. Tell me, why is that important?' Tom replied.

Matt wiped his mouth with the napkin, took a sip of his coffee and finally felt a bit more like himself.

'When the CIA investigated the bombing near a border town called Jarabulus, on the Euphrates River, they uncovered a plot by the Turkish MIT to destabilise the region by attempting to draw other actors – basically the US – into the civil war on their side, by bombing them and blaming the Kurds. The Turks don't care about what is happening in Syria, all they want to do is wipe out the Kurds and they see the Syrian civil war as their opportunity. Last year, when various special forces teams were scoping out who was who and where the lines were being drawn, several explosions occurred in the area which eventually took out a team of Green Berets. They were pissed off and the CIA waded in, as only they can.'

'So, what happened?' Tom knew nothing about the detail and still wondered why Matt had flown back to the UK to tell him the story.

'The CIA had a conversation with their Turkish counterparts and let them know in no uncertain terms that, unless they backed off, paid compensation and shared their future operational plans in Syria with the US, they would be the recipient of a black op themselves. It was an empty threat, of course, but they have complied until now.' Matt took another sip of coffee, then poured some more from the pot. 'You're probably wondering why I've come all this way just to tell you that. Well, I have a hunch the Turks are doing it again, in Somalia this time. And with significant collateral damage to our African allies in Uganda and Burundi. I need to discuss what we can do.'

Tom's interest was piqued. 'I read your note, thanks for sending it through.' Matt had fired off a very brief summary of what Imi had shared in her briefing.

'Tom, we are going to tap the embassy phone and put the special forces guys on standby to conduct a raid on the warehouse; I need clearance to do that. I am also going to need to brief your counterpart in Turkey as I have a feeling that we may need to have a similar discussion in Ankara with our Turkish opposite numbers if anything emerges that suggests the Jarabulus operation is being repeated. I am already talking to my opposite number in Turkey; she's been there so long she's pretty much embedded with the MIT, so if anyone can dig around, she can. There's one more thing.' Matt was in full flow now. 'Until I get proof, if there is any, this is just a hunch. It is also possible, just possible, that the Turks are breaking the UN arms embargo under the cover of the Saudi Islamisation programme, bringing arms and presumably ammunition into the country to supply Shabaab. To what end, we do not know, but presumably it's all about increasing Turkey's influence.'

Matt rubbed his eyes for a moment.

'And there's a lot of untapped oil and gas onshore and offshore that everyone's trying to get their hands on the rights too,' Tom interjected.

Matt looked up, and groaned audibly, looking away in apparent disgust.

'I hadn't considered the fossil fuel angle at all. Shit. Every time I run through these possibilities, I tell myself I'm overreacting, but I cannot find another reason for the shipments. And we have clarified with Riyadh that the Turks are not involved in the Somalia programme. I can't believe that they would go to this trouble just to get ahead economically. The stakes are way too high if they became exposed.'

Matt stood up and stretched, staring out of the window, glad he was inside in the warmth.

'What do you want me to do, Matt?' Tom's voice jolted him back to the conversation. Tom knew that he would need to authorise any action that was likely to have any sort of diplomatic fall-out.

'Well, firstly, I could do with your support getting the military onside. I need all the phones to be tracked and for a UAV to overfly the target areas to try to identify any linkage between the operations on the ground and the Turks in Mog. I will also need to authorise the special forces to take a look inside the warehouse, and I will need GCHQ's resources to monitor the static phone that we have identified. Something tells me it's key. I can fight my way through the Whitehall bureaucracy to achieve all of that, but it has to happen yesterday, Tom, and I need you to speak to your contacts in Main Building. The MoD are normally pretty good, but I need you to call in some favours for this one. Can you help?'

Tom had so many priorities waiting on his desk, all relating to the Arab Spring unfolding across the Muslim countries in the north of the continent, that this request for support in Somalia was going to be a challenge for him.

'Matt, I'll be honest, I can't promise anything. I have enough requests for support to exhaust our resources three times over.' He left the comment out there for Matt to digest. 'I thought we had someone inside Vila Somalia. Can you not get him to do your dirty work?'

Tom knew that Christian, although willing, was entirely unsuited to complex espionage work, but the pressure he was feeling to support emerging flashpoints across North Africa was a factor he couldn't ignore.

Matt noted Tom's use of the word "your"; Tom was an excellent foreign service director but he was also a political animal who would not want to be drawn into any ensuing enquiry if the operation went belly up.

'I've got one of my officers holding his hand, and he will have to do more, but he can't do it alone; we would be reckless to put him at risk.'

Both men simultaneously looked away from the conversation, taking a break before the next round of discussion.

'Matt, leave it with me. Use what you have. Make sure that Megan in Mogadishu is aware of what steps you're taking and get your asset in Vila Somalia to earn his keep. Even if you plant something in there to potentially discredit the Turks, it will buy you some time. I'll speak to someone over in the MoD about the UAV but don't hold your breath. If I were you, I'd focus on tapping the static phone. It strikes me that's important. And for God's sake don't wake the neighbours when you go into the warehouse. That's all I can do.'

Tom finished his second cup of coffee and started to get up. Matt followed his cue and dusted the crumbs from his sandwich off the front of his jacket as he stood up, grabbing his bag and turning for the door.

'I appreciate it, Tom. I'll keep you in the loop of course. Becky is also now read-in, so she will handle things with our officer.'

'Who is the officer?' Tom asked as they approached the library door.

'Her name is Imogen Standforth, known to everyone as Imi. She's bloody ambitious and very effective. But she sees this as her big chance, hence why I have assigned Becky to keep close to her.'

'Imi, yes, I remember her. She walked into my office without an appointment when she had been assigned the role in Nairobi, just to let me know that she was going out there. Nobody had ever done that from your place before.' Tom laughed to himself at the memory. Matt rolled his eyes, knowing that was exactly the sort of things Imi would do.

'Thanks, Tom, really appreciate the help – and brunch!'

'How long are you staying?' Tom asked, pulling the door open and moving the sign to one side.

'I have a meeting with our west country colleagues in town, then I'm on the return flight this evening.'

'Oh my God, Matt, you're mad!' Tom led Matt back through the entrance hall and opened the main door, politely waving away the doorman. They stepped onto the street, the cold wind making short work of their clothing again; Matt shivered involuntarily. 'But if this is as serious as you suggest, which I think it is, then you're better off there.'

'Cheers, Tom, let me know how you get on.'

After they shook hands, Matt took the steps down to the pavement slowly, his legs stiff from sitting down, his circulation not quite what it should have been. It was a combination of international air travel, freezing weather and a familiar tension he always felt when he knew decisive action was required to uncover another country's nefarious activities. He sighed, pulled his jacket tighter, regretting turning down the offer of a coat from his wife before he took the taxi to Nairobi Airport the night before. He headed off towards Waterloo Place to catch a cab. His mind turned to Christian in Vila Somalia. He knew he had to get him to do more but, with no time to provide him any specific training, they were going to have to improvise and hope he was as resourceful as everyone said he was.

International conspiracies were dangerous environments for seasoned professionals; they were no place for gifted amateurs.

22

British High Commission, Nairobi

The next morning, Matt called Imi over to his desk as soon as he walked into the office after his overnight flight from London. He looked shocking; he was sleep-deprived, hungry and in need of a shower. But he had to speak to her before he went home to freshen up.

'Imi, you are authorised to use whatever means necessary to gather HUMINT via Christian. That includes covert activity in the key offices and setting up the monitoring equipment via the special forces team in Airport Camp. I'm hoping we will get clearance via the MoD and their HQ in Regent's Park Barracks today for the boys to do a recce of that warehouse; proceed on the basis that they will support. I have arranged the mobile to be monitored with GCHQ, and it should be live now. We will get transcripts every 12 hours starting tonight at 2000hrs. Becky is here for you to discuss your approach. Please use her. Otherwise, I'll leave it to you, OK?'

Imi was taken aback by Matt's list of instructions. His response to her briefing had been non-committal, but she knew his trip to London had been unplanned, so something must have hit a nerve. Her heart rate increased as she contemplated what she had to do.

'Thanks, Matt, that's all fine.' The calmness in her voice belied the nerves she felt.

'One last thing. We are going to be asking a lot of your man inside Vila Somalia. But he cannot fail. And he cannot get caught at any cost. There is a lot riding on this. Whatever you decide to do, he has to be able to execute it. Is that clear?' Matt was staring at Imi; the seriousness of the instruction and the authority with which he delivered the words, painted across his normally genial and optimistic face, shocked her. For the first time in her career, Imi felt the weight of responsibility for a man's life bearing down on her.

'I understand, Matt. He'll be fine, he won't fail. I'll bet my life on it.'

23

Vila Somalia, Mogadishu

Christian woke up with a start, as if someone had not only walked over his grave but trampled on it repeatedly. It unnerved him, forcing him to get up and look around the room, the feeling almost visceral. He looked at his phone to see the time and walked into the kitchen in his boxer shorts. The air conditioning was grumbling away in the living room, the cool air barely making it across the apartment, but it was OK, he was able to sleep most of the time. He turned on the kettle and stared out of the grimy window at the perimeter wall beyond. Not for the first time, he wondered who and what was on the other side.

Nine times out of ten, if he walked out of the main gate and took a coffee in one of the many cafés surrounding Vila Somalia, he would be fine. But he didn't want to find out what might happen on the tenth occasion. And that fear drove everyone's behaviour from within the international community. Conquer the fear, manage the threat, and Somalia would be a better place for everyone. He shook his head. He was convinced the international community had got it wrong.

The absence of risk appetite amongst most western nations, following the United States' notorious expedition to Mogadishu, depicted with deadly accuracy in the film *Black Hawk Down*, was at the heart of the problem. That fiasco had framed every policy decision by international donors ever since.

He poured the boiling water into the teapot and dropped in a Yorkshire teabag from a supply he had brought back to Africa after Christmas. Philosophising over, he turned his mind to Imi's request to meet later on at the B&B. It was obviously something important for her to fly out, but her message was low-key, routine even: *I just need to give you something. Should be quick meeting. I've booked a room.* He wasn't due to be staying there for another week, but he had no complaints: the food at the B&B was excellent.

Miko picked him up from the main car park at 4.30pm and they drove straight there. It was the last day of the working week so he was able to slip away slightly early. He was in jeans, shirt and a cream linen jacket and had brought overnight gear because driving at night was generally avoided, but he was still confused by Imi's request to meet. He had even asked Miko if they could take a detour, just for a change of scene. 'No bullshit, Christian, we go straight there,' had been his reply. He was clearly under strict orders to get him there as soon as possible.

When he got out of the white Land Cruiser, Imi was sitting in the garden drinking tea, reading a magazine that she must have brought with her. She looked over and waved an arm, beckoning him to join her.

'Welcome back to paradise!' she said.

'Hi, Imi.' He put his bag down and took his sunglasses off. 'What's going on?'

'Hello, Chris, you OK? Thanks for coming.' Imi closed her magazine and offered him some tea. 'It's warmish.' She was acting as if they were sitting in the garden of a Nairobi Club rather than in the middle of one of the most dangerous cities in the world.

'No thanks, Imi, I'll grab a beer later. When did you get in?'

'I took a flight from Wilson Airport at lunchtime. I've been here about an hour. I'm heading back tomorrow.'

'Are you staying here?'

'Yep. I've booked us both rooms. I presumed you didn't want to go back tonight.'

'No, travelling at night in Mog isn't advisable unless you're armed and well protected.'

He took a seat next to her. Nobody was near them in the garden as Imi made small talk for a few minutes. Eventually, she came to the point.

'Chris, I need you to do something for us, which is why I'm up here. We need to talk it through inside my room. Shall we go up there now?'

'Sure.' They got up, collected their things and walked towards the house. On the way through, they bumped into Arne, who welcomed Christian like a long-lost friend, and pointed him in the direction of his room on the first floor. Imi kept going up the stairs to the second floor, heading for the same room Christian had stayed in with Megan four weeks before. It was the only guest room on that landing and offered a degree of privacy.

'Come up once you're sorted, Chris.'

He dropped his bag, threw some water on his face and went up to Imi's room, carrying his laptop in case he needed it. He knocked gently on the door.

'Come in.'

He opened the door and was invited to take a chair at the end of the bed facing Imi, who was already sitting down and had laid out on the bedclothes a number of items in front of them both. He studied each one in turn. Imi searched his eyes and said, 'Chris, I need you to do more than simply watch and report. What I am going to ask you to do is going to carry more risk than simply asking a few questions and writing an encrypted email or two. I am going to need you to become active, rather than passive. However, I cannot make you do any of this. So, if you do not feel comfortable making that step, I will fully understand. I'll put all of this away and leave.'

'Nobody else can do this but you,' Imi continued. 'You have proved yourself to be more than competent at thinking on your feet and using your initiative. There are not many people in my profession who would have acted with such decisiveness as you did when you saved Megs, and I have no doubt that you can deal with similarly stressful situations.' Her eyes had never left his as she spoke quietly. 'Which is why I have complete confidence that you will come through for me.' Imi's northern accent added gravity to her words.

The intensity between them was unlike anything he had experienced before. The surge of adrenaline pumping through his body was almost overwhelming. After a moment, Christian stood up and turned away, walking around Imi to the window, blowing air out of his lungs, trying to calm his body, that sense of panic rising up in his chest again.

The room was silent. Imi didn't say anything as he brushed past her and leant against the open window frame, blankly scanning the rooftops in the distance. After some time, he turned round, his arms crossed, still leaning against the frame of the window and trying to look calm.

'OK, Imi, what do you want me to do?' Talking to her back, his voice was flat, unemotional, as if he was already entering the same frame of mind as when he was faced with a difficult mission in the Army. He retook his seat opposite her.

'Thanks, Chris. Firstly, the reason I am here is because I need you to place something in the President's office when you go in to brief him. Can you remember when it was last scanned?'

Chris was sitting down again and looked away. 'It should be due in the next couple of days.'

'OK, that would be ideal; we expect them to find it eventually, anyway.' She leaned forward and picked up the mobile phone and handed it to Christian. 'This needs to be placed in the main reception room of the Presidential suite. Once you turn it on you don't need to touch it, and it will not emit any audible sounds. It's sourced from the international market and we have placed a Turkish sim card inside it, so when they find it, and turn it on, they will figure it was left by someone in the delegation. It's completely untraceable to the UK. Except, it's not a normal mobile phone; it's a highly sensitive, voice-activated listening device that transmits audio files using burst transmission rather than constantly polling for a signal like a normal phone. The files are received using another piece of equipment that will be based in our secure compound in Airport Camp, which is where I am going to be spending a lot of my time over the next few weeks. There's a long-life battery – again untraceable – so it should last a good month.' Imi handed the phone to Christian.

He already knew that when she referred to the secure compound, she wasn't discussing the embassy that was newly built close to the lagoon on the other side of the runway. She was talking about the UK special forces base elsewhere in the camp, used by the resident detachment and MI6.

'All you need to do is place it down the side of the seat that you are sitting on, make sure it's out of sight, then carry on. Obviously, turn it on first. We know you will be able to do this from Megan's initial meeting with the President. In terms of getting it into the President's suite, from your report the X-ray machine always triggers the alarm, so do exactly what you normally do when you go through the machines. Go to the toilet before you go in to turn it on. Have it with you as if it's your normal phone, but make sure your actual personal phone is in a pocket so you can easily bring it out. Nobody will suspect anything once you've placed the device. OK?'

'Yep, that's clear.' He put the phone in his bag for now. 'You said you expect them to find it.'

'Yes, any half decent search of the room will pick it up, more than likely by the cleaners. It will be handed in and there'll be a bit of a panic. There are a number of permutations depending on what the Somalis do; best case scenario they conclude it's a covert monitoring device and drag the Turks in, which will discredit them and buy us some time, or they'll think it's a mobile that's been left behind and arrange to hand it over to them.'

'And worst case? Christian asked.

'Do I need to answer that?' Imi replied, dead pan.

'And what did you mean, "buy us some time"?' Christian had picked up the throw-away comment from Imi. His suspicions that something was in play were confirmed by her comment.

'Honestly, Chris you don't need to know. Shall we move on? The next thing is this.'

She picked up a small metallic object no bigger than a 50p piece. It was highly malleable, one side of it a dull matt grey finish, the other side black. She passed it to him.

'It's highly magnetic and also a powerful transmitter. It needs to go on the Turkish delegation's car.'

She looked at Christian again, searching his face for any signs of doubt. 'The tech guys say it can adhere to pretty much anything with metallic content, and it's specifically designed for vehicles, most of which are armoured over here, so wherever you put it, it's likely to stick. If you can, the place that is washed least is the exhaust pipe, and yes, before you ask, it is designed to withstand the heat.'

Christian flipped it around in his fingers before putting it in his bag with the phone.

'How do I activate it?'

'It's already live, so we'll know exactly where your bag is going to be over the next few days!' Imi smiled at Christian.

'And this is a last resort.'

She picked up the last item on the bed, handing it to Christian, who immediately cleared the weapon to check it was unloaded, let the working parts slide forward and squeezed the trigger, the dull click sounding out of place in the bedroom. He put the safety catch back on and placed it in his bag. She also gave him two full magazines.

'If you need more rounds than this, you're in the shit.' Imi winked at Christian, who returned a wry grin.

'That's reassuring.' Christian hadn't hesitated in taking the 9mm pistol, a Browning, a weapon he was familiar with from his military service and the same type of weapon he had used in the café to take out the Shabaab fighter. It was the first time he had received a weapon without signing for it.

'Obviously don't take it into the Office of the President; there's no need for you to have it there. I want you to have it with you when you travel. I know Miko is armed, but it will do no harm for you to be similarly equipped.'

Her logic was sound, but he couldn't help thinking that there was another purpose for the side arm.

'What if I'm caught with it?' Christian didn't have any diplomatic cover and there was no reason why he would have the weapon if stopped by the Somalis.

'Don't get caught. It's completely deniable, I'm afraid.'

He loaded one of the magazines into the weapon, placed it in the bag and put the other magazine in a separate compartment to avoid everything rattling together.

'Does Megan know about any of this?' He had to ask. It was the first thing that had entered his mind when he first looked at the items on the bed.

'Yes, she does.'

'Is there anything else?' Christian wanted to get out of the room and be on his own.

'No, see you downstairs for dinner later.'

Imi smiled again as he picked up his bag and left the room without looking back, the last rays of the sun pouring through the open window and filling the room with a bright yellow and orange glow. Imi got up and moved the two chairs back to their place. She knew Christian and Megan had slept in this room. She first sat on the edge of the bed, then lay down, pulling the throw over her as she rolled onto her side. Her arms held the pillow close to her face and she spoke so quietly she could barely hear her own words.

'I'm really sorry, Megs.'

*

Megan was still at her desk in the embassy when she got Christian's text message: *Darling Megs, really wish you could be here tonight, but understand why you can't. C x*

Megan had been back in Mogadishu long enough to be missing Christian already. She couldn't quite believe the effect one man could have on her. She had never felt like this, it was different to anything she'd experienced before. The way he made her feel was intoxicating; she longed for his touch, having him lie with her as they had done in Mombasa. Away from the securitised environment in Mogadishu, she had worried that their relationship would be somehow different but everything had been fine; it had been perfect, in fact. She desperately hoped it would be the same when they eventually got back to the UK together. She suddenly felt like she had to make up for lost time.

After her engagement had fallen through, she deliberately shielded herself from any new emotional attachment to the point where people had made jokes about her being married to her job. She had become used to going home after a working day in the Foreign Office, even when her colleagues were going to The Clarence on Whitehall for drinks, something she had always enjoyed doing in the past. After she had been selected as the Ambassador in Somalia, some of her colleagues had unkindly suggested it was the best place for her.

As it turned out, they were right.

Megan had fallen hard for Christian but knew she had to maintain her professional distance; something she found difficult to endure. They both had plans to meet again at the B&B the following weekend, so Christian's text had confused her. A profound sense of foreboding washed over her and she immediately walked out of her office and along the corridor to the small room housing the Top-Secret terminal; she would only normally check her messages once a day in the morning for anything of interest. She quickly logged in and opened her inbox. There was a message from Imi.

CLASSIFICATION: TOP SECRET

From: Station, Nairobi;

To: FCO, Head of Africa; Station, Nairobi Chief; Station, Nairobi Deputy Chief; Ambassador, Mogadishu;

CC: London Centre, File;

Priority: URGENT

Subject: Op TRINKET – latest update

1. *Turkish Delegation visiting VS next Wednesday.*
2. *Our source – codename HUSSAR – will join meeting and will be briefed later today; authorised to conduct covert ops and for personal protection to be issued.*
3. *Communications monitoring in place and ACTIVE.*
4. *Mobile phone: transcripts every 12 hours commencing 2000hrs tonight.*
5. *Shipping container: planning underway to investigate storage facility over next 96 hours.*
6. *Extraction plan updated.*
7. *More to follow in 24 hours.*

Signed: IS, IO3, Nairobi Station

Megan shut down the screen and logged off. She got up and walked out of the secure room, pulling her phone out of her pocket as she did. *Yeah, sorry, bit snowed under. Will see you next weekend. M x*

It was a lie. She imagined that Christian had asked about her and Imi had said that she was busy, hence the text. To know that they were both together in the B&B, drawing Christian deeper into Imi's operation, made her feel as if she was going to explode. She headed towards the entrance of the small embassy building and spoke to Krishna, her logistics manager, who was sitting in his office, glued to his screen.

'Krish, I'm just heading out for some fresh air. I'll probably see you tomorrow morning. Night.'

'Good night, Ma'am.' Krishna was an ex-Gurkha, a skilled driver, master of logistics and an indispensable member of Megan's team. Standing at just over five foot five inches tall, his black hair was greying a little, but his physique showed no signs of ageing. Even at 46, he was probably one of the fittest people Megan knew. He had served a full career in the Army and after retiring he had decided not to stay in the UK with his family. Instead, he moved back to Nepal to run a charity for children who had suffered bereavement. He had set it up with his wife and eldest daughter, using money donated via the Nepali government, but it had only been seed corn funding and, without other sources of income, they had soon run out of money. Rather than wind it up, they had decided to focus on the most difficult cases using his pension income. After a few months, though, it was clear he needed to return to work to ensure the survival of the charity. Following a call to a retired British Officer with whom he had worked in the past, Krishna was advised to apply for his current role and had been successful. The money was good, even if he didn't get home very often.

Megan stepped outside and walked out of the main pedestrian gate, taking the path around the side of the building towards the ocean. Situated well away from the airport complex on the other side of the runway, the embassy had been built about 40 metres back from the shoreline and elevated about four metres above sea level. Its location offered near private access to the Indian Ocean behind the embassy's barbed wire fencing. However, one decent sized wave and the entire building would be engulfed. It was her first diplomatic mission that regularly practised tsunami drills.

She didn't have to go far to feel the freedom of the sea. The warm wind was blowing in her face as she walked through the dunes and over a low rise which gave way to the most magnificent view of the Indian Ocean. She stopped and sat down between two tufts of grass, listening to the tide lapping against the beach a few feet in front of her. She kicked off her shoes, the sand soft on her skin, then unfolded a grey pashmina that Krishna had brought back from Nepal and wrapped it around her shoulders.

The sun was already out of sight behind her, the evening's warmth its gift. The fading light was transitioning the eastern sky into a most glorious, reflected sunset. The darkening clouds streaked across the yellowing sky, as if someone had grabbed hold of them and pulled them one by one, from right to left, their edges tinged with crimson by the sun's final rays. Megan stared at the scene unfolding before her eyes, comforted by the rhythm of the waves under what felt like an endless sky. Further out to sea, as darkness descended, the lights were getting brighter on the ships moored up, all facing the same direction, waiting their turn to enter the port.

Megan sat there and took it all in, memories flooding back of her childhood at her grandmother's house in Italy where she would watch the sunset sitting by the lake. The feeling of dread that she had in her stomach brought tears to her eyes. She wiped them away with her sleeve, but still they came. She felt helpless, unable to influence events.

Imi had taken advantage of Christian's natural desire to serve his country. But she didn't blame her, it's what she did. But she couldn't lose Christian in the chaos of Mogadishu; she promised herself that she would not let that happen. She knew she had to trust his instinct; after all, it was what had saved her life when they had met.

Pulling herself together, she took out her phone as she sat in the growing darkness: *Stay safe, Chris. I love you. Megs x*

Her phone lit up almost immediately: *I love you too. Chris x*

She could barely read the words. Christian's message was the tipping point for her emotions. She sobbed uncontrollably. Tears streamed down her cheeks, her cries lost in the wind and the relentless, lapping surf.

24

Tuesday Evening – Industrial Road, Mogadishu

Five days after Christian had been briefed by Imi at the B&B, the two battered Somali pick-ups left Airport Camp just after midnight. Driving together in close proximity, there were four men in each. They accelerated past the almost deserted security check point on the road leading to the airport terminal and made their way at high speed towards the K4 roundabout. The vehicles looked shabby, but the engines were highly tuned and in peak condition. The shortest route to their target location was left up Jidka Tarabuunka, through Hodan District, but they headed straight on towards the port, keeping Bakhara Market on their left. With little traffic to impede their progress and an almost full moon to provide twilight conditions, they made their way indirectly to the warehouse complex. About one kilometre short of the target, they pulled off the main road and parked up close to the disused football stadium, once the proud home of Somalia's national team, but more recently the site of macabre killings at the hands of al Shabaab. They had reached their designated final rendezvous before their short journey to the warehouse facility.

The teams checked their weapons and equipment, then confirmed that they were ready to move. The first vehicle set off, the roads around the industrial zone quiet, the second vehicle following 100 meters behind. Both vehicles were now travelling at slow speed. As they approached the compound, gated and secured by a high razor-wire fence, they both turned off into a small side road that ran adjacent to the facility. They could see that it was quiet; there were very few people around at this time of night. Both vehicles spun round and pulled up, their engines idling, while the teams got to work.

Three soldiers exited the first vehicle to patrol around the rear of the facility, their weapons held ready, fingers poised over their trigger guards.

'Starting the perimeter patrol now.'

Everyone was miked up on a secure radio channel.

'Roger,' the operational commander responded from the front seat of the first vehicle.

Men from the second vehicle also slipped out from their pick-up, carrying specialist equipment, their weapons slung behind their backs. Within a minute they had cut their way through the fencing and were inside the compound, checking the area for anything unforeseen. Their balaclavas would protect their identities and their clothing was native, designed to confuse any witnesses to the raid. They didn't plan to make any noise unless they were ambushed.

As they crouched inside the fence, a third man slipped through the gap and sprinted for the corner of the building. The team had conducted a dry run the night before, as well as several drive-bys over the previous few days, and they had concluded that their best hope lay in picking the lock at the rear of the building, out of sight of the main road. The men patrolling behind the warehouse complex radioed in that all was well.

'Just on the lock now.'

'Roger.'

There was a distant click and then silence. The hum of the city could be heard in the background, the occasional crackle of automatic gunfire punctuating the relative silence, but the immediate vicinity of the warehouse was quiet. As the designated lock expert opened the outer door, he called two team members forward. They went in quickly, checking the corridor using narrow beam torches for security cameras and sensors.

The teams' pre-op assessment was that the facility was not professionally secured, bar standard locks, so that it didn't draw attention to its actual use. From first glance, it looked like they had been right. As the two men walked carefully along a corridor, rubbish littering the floor, they could see offices through glass windows on either side of them, all in darkness and showing signs of neglect. The corridor led to a faded cream-coloured door, the plywood chipped and rotten on the bottom. The first man slowly turned the handle and pushed it gently.

The door swung open to reveal a large storage area, big enough to park a dozen coaches. Around the side there were abandoned wooden crates, dozens of cardboard boxes and rusting, formerly blue or black, barrels. The floor was marked by vehicle tracks and the walls were lined with signs, ropes, broken shelving and, along one side, about 20 metal wardrobes, side by side, their locks smashed, doors wide open and spewing their contents onto the floor.

They used their torches to scan the space as quickly as they could. The sky lights, some cracked and dirty, permitted the moonlight to illuminate patches of floor. Otherwise, the warehouse was in darkness. They carefully scoured the walls for any threats and, when they were satisfied there were no security systems operating, they walked more confidently towards the centre of the space, which was occupied by a large blue shipping container. They walked around it, looking for two black spray-painted marks; they soon found them to the rear.

'OK, we're in and the container is still here.'

'Roger.' The operational commander was listening to their progress from inside the vehicle, keeping tabs on the external patrol, his eyes and ears on the immediate vicinity. Both engines were still running, ready for a quick exit, but everything was going to plan.

He checked his watch: 0055hrs.

'We need to be clear within ten minutes.'

'Roger.'

The two men who had entered the main warehouse were now moving with greater purpose, confident that there were no booby traps or nasty surprises. They pulled open the container with gloved hands, their torches revealing a completely empty space. They looked on the floor but found nothing of interest apart from a couple of cigarette butts. One of the men picked one up and put it in his pocket.

'Smell familiar to you?'

The other man sniffed and said, 'Gun oil.'

'Yep. Look, I'm going to have a quick look through those crates in the corner.'

'OK.'

Walking away from the container, the man started to look at the stack of empty crates, checking for anything that could prove the presence of weapons shipments or other related equipment. Crate lids were strewn across the floor at its base, all showing signs of having been removed with force, their hinges splintered and irretrievably damaged. The man walked a little closer for a better look. As he slightly twisted one of the crates to look inside, he managed to cause a mini avalanche. The sound of the wooden crates hitting the floor could be heard outside. He had to step back quickly to avoid getting hit from above.

'Bollocks.' The first man cursed under his breath, heard by everyone.

The second man looked across. 'Nice one – blame the rats!'

'Big fucking rats.' The comment came from outside the warehouse. There was always time for humour.

'All OK?' The man by the rear door said into the radio.

'All good.' The second man inside answered as he walked across to join his oppo who, by now, was looking at what he had disturbed.

'What's that?' The first man was shining his torch on a crate that was now leaning at 45 degrees facing them at waist height. He leaned forward for a better look.

'Bingo!' He reached into the crate carefully and removed a pair of night-vision goggles which had clearly been left behind when the remainder of the equipment had been offloaded from the container. He checked to see if there were any more inside but it was empty.

'OK, we have a pair of NVGs, so I think we have evidence,' the first man said as he turned to leave. They both immediately headed for the door leading to the exit, the second man speaking on the radio as they went.

'We are heading out now, one minute.'

They were soon at the rear door. After leaving the building, the man who had secured their entry reset the lock and ran to catch up with them as they waited at the fence. They went through one at a time, the last man quickly reconnecting the strands of wire with small clips designed to remove any evidence of their entry to the casual observer. Within 30 seconds, everyone was back in their vehicles and accounted for.

'Let's go.' The operational commander spoke calmly as both vehicles accelerated away into the Mogadishu night.

25

Wednesday – Vila Somalia, Mogadishu

The morning after the special forces raid, Christian was at his desk earlier than usual.

He had hardly slept. Not because he knew anything about the raid, but because the reality of what he was being asked to do had hit him as soon as he lay down. His plans and preparations had been going round and round in his head until he started to see the grey light of dawn creeping through the poorly covered windows. Unable to go for a run, he had put on a pair of shorts and exercised on his living room floor, doing whatever he could to get the tension out of his body. After countless press-ups, star jumps, burpees and yoga-like stretching, he had eventually collapsed, exhausted, leaning against his sofa. After half an hour, he had managed to get up and make a cup of tea. By 7am, he was walking across to the ministerial building, exhausted.

Opening his laptop, he ran through the presentation one last time, hardly taking it in. He then checked his Yahoo! account, but there was nothing from Imi. Then, as he had done throughout the night, he scrolled back to look at Megan's message from the previous week. Since that exchange, they had only spoken on the phone twice, and on both occasions there was a tension which had made the conversation disjointed. It was as if they were tiptoeing around the one subject that they both wanted to discuss but, for professional reasons, they couldn't. He hoped that they would soon be able to spend some normal time together away from the constraints of Somalia.

Christian walked down to the café when Said had arrived, offering to bring him something on his return but Said had declined. Sitting at one of the far tables in the café, Somalia's civil servants popping in to pick something up before heading for their offices, he searched for Muna; he needed to talk to someone with whom he felt comfortable. By ten o'clock, having been sitting in the café for nearly an hour, notebook open, writing thoughts and thinking through his strategy for hiding the device and fixing the tracker on the car, he reluctantly walked out and back up the stairs, butterflies in his stomach. After his unexpected meeting with Imi the week before, he had quickly decided that he wasn't going to contemplate getting caught doing what she had asked and had tried to banish negative thoughts from his mind. The prospect of being detained in a Somali jail was unthinkable.

At 11.15am, he got up from his desk, the tiredness he felt balanced by the surge of adrenaline he was experiencing – the fight or flight emotions taking over his body. Despite what he was feeling, he walked calmly with the Minister out of the building and through the outer security cordon to enter the Office of the President. As expected, the scanner alarm sounded as he walked through, even though he had put his personal phone and his keys on the top of his bag, which trundled its way through the X-ray machine. The covert device was in his inside pocket, and they never asked anyone to remove their jackets. Even the Minister had remarked on how ineffective the system was. A little way down the corridor, Christian excused himself from the Minister and entered the men's toilets, where thankfully he was alone. Once inside a cubicle, he took out the device from his jacket pocket and silently turned it on.

After spending a few minutes in Bashiir's office, they were asked to go through into the President's suite. They walked along a short corridor and then turned right into the magnificent reception room that he remembered from his first visit. It contained three large ornate sofas on three sides of a square, with the President's own throne-like seat filling the gap. He had been shown to the sofa on the left. Minister Hassan sat next to him but closer to the President. Bashiir then walked in and sat on the sofa opposite Minister Hassan. All Christian could think about was how the hell he was going to achieve what Imi had asked him to do.

'Christian, would you like to start?' The President was talking to him.

'Christian?' Bashiir's voice broke into Christian's thoughts.

'Oh, I'm sorry, sir. Yes, on the table in front of you is a handout giving an outline of the …'

Christian was talking but wasn't really concentrating. His mind was elsewhere; he was on autopilot. He had rehearsed what he was going to say and delivered the briefing as planned, with Minister Hassan chipping in when he felt his opinion was needed. Even his answer to the question about how to blend support from the international community as well as working bilaterally with individual nations didn't cause a stir. After what felt like only a few minutes, his time was up and Minister Hassan closed down their discussion. The President seemed very happy with what he had heard and stood up to shake Christian's hand, who had quickly moved from his chair.

'Thank you, Christian, I can see bringing you in to help us is going to be a huge benefit for Somalia.'

'Thank you, sir.' If Christian had been more alert, he might have recognised the compliment for what it was but, throughout the entire time he was in the room, he could hardly think of anything other than finding the opportunity to hide the device.

His heart was racing. He walked back to where he had been sitting and busied himself pulling all the briefing notes together. As he was doing so, Bashiir led both the President and Minister Hassan out of the room to meet the Turkish delegation.

'Christian, come through when you have collected your things, please.' Bashiir's command was clear: *Don't stay in here alone.*

'Just one sec.' As he spoke, he dropped his papers deliberately. 'Bollocks; sorry, I'll be there in a sec, Bashiir.'

'OK,' Bashiir said, then left the room.

He had bought himself a few precious seconds. But which sofa would the Turks sit on? Where would he sit? He had to make a decision and quickly. He moved across to the sofa where Bashiir had just been sitting and, after briefly looking towards the double-door entrance, hearing the talking beyond, he slipped the phone down the side of the seat cushion furthest from the President's chair. He checked that it was out of sight and grabbed the rest of the papers and walked hurriedly out of the room, his hands clammy, sweat on his brow, his heart rate pounding.

As he emerged in the Chief of Staff's office, he had a moment when he was alone, as he knew that they would meet the delegation at the entrance of the building and walk them back to where he was. He put the papers away in his bag, told himself to get a grip and drank some water that was on the side, not caring whether it was his or not. He wiped his hands on his trousers, took a deep breath and waited, hearing the drumming of his heart in his ears. He was panicked but knew he had to go with it. He tried to concentrate on who he was going to be meeting. He had managed to get the list of the delegation from Said and had shared it with Imi a few days after they had met in the B&B.

A moment later, the Turkish Ambassador walked in, led by the President and flanked by Abdulkadir Aden and the Defence Minister. Trailing behind with Bashiir was Commander Murat and Hassan Güler, who he assumed was one of the Ambassador's more senior diplomats. He shook hands with the Turkish delegation, exchanging a slight nod of recognition with the Defence Attaché, then warmly shook hands with the Abdulkadir Aden. They all walked into the Presidential suite, Christian at the rear.

By now Christian's mind was almost numb with anxiety. As the last person walking into the reception room, he was at least relieved to note that the Ambassador, the Defence Attaché and Hassan Güler were all sitting on the sofa to the right of the President where he had placed the device. The National Security Advisor and Minister Hassan were on the left. He breathed slightly more easily as he was asked to take a seat facing the President.

As expected, the President replayed some of what Christian had said to him a few minutes earlier, stressing the need for a coordinated response from the international community to support the Somali security forces. After about ten minutes, it was clear that the Turkish delegation was becoming increasingly uncomfortable with Christian's presence, an observation also picked up by the Defence Minister, who nodded to the President.

'OK, well, thank you for joining us, Christian. I gather you have another appointment.'

On cue, Christian got up, nodded to those sitting around the room and walked out, accompanied by Bashiir, who had been sitting at the side of the room.

Once in his office Bashiir said, 'Are you OK, Christian? You don't look very well. Why don't you get some rest?' He looked concerned and patted Christian on the arm as he turned to go back into the meeting.

Christian was drenched despite the air conditioning. He slung his bag on his shoulder and walked outside. He knew he had no more than an hour to do the second task, but first he needed to calm his nerves. He decided to head back to his accommodation to change his shirt and to try to think things through. The stress of what he had done in the President's suite had taken a lot out of him.

After throwing some water on his face, and now in a fresh shirt, he went back outside into the burning sun. Leaving his bag behind, he put his sunglasses on and walked towards the car park where several vehicles were lined up, including two armoured Casspirs. He walked over to the group of AMISOM soldiers hanging around at the back of one of them and struck up a conversation. He glanced at his watch; he was in time.

'Hi, lads, how are you?' Christian was back in army mode.

'Hello, sir, all good thank you.'

Some of the men, who numbered seven in total, were smoking. They were relaxed, some with helmets on, chin straps undone, some without. All of them were wearing sunglasses.

'Can I crash someone for a ciggie? I've run out and I'm not heading back to Airport Camp for another week.'

'Here you go, Boss.' One of the Ugandan private soldiers stepped forward and offered him a local cigarette, then pulled out a Zippo to light it.

'Cheers.'

Christian hadn't smoked for a long time. He knew he had to take a drag without coughing, otherwise his credibility would be shot. After inhaling deeply, he blew the smoke out with only the slightest of coughs.

'Bloody hell, what do you put in your cigarettes in Uganda?' They all laughed together.

For a few minutes they stood, talking about the weather and the heat. Then one of them said, 'Sir, are you the ex-army contractor who shot the Shabaab fighter last year?' Christian had noticed from the first minute he had walked up to them that he was looking at him with a little more intent than the others.

'Yes, I am.' A murmur of appreciation filled the space between them.

'Hey, lads, I don't suppose any of you spotted which car drove the Turkish Ambassador who arrived about 20 minutes ago, did you? There would have been three men get out and walk to that building over there.' The idea to somehow use the soldiers to help him had only formed in his mind when he saw them hanging around.

'It was that one, Boss, the black SUV over there.' He leant round the back of the truck and pointed.

"Over there" was about four cars away on the same side of the car park, reversed in as the Casspirs were, a row of tall palm trees beside the pavement providing shade across the backs of most of the vehicles.

'Could one of you do me a favour?' It was now or never.

'Sure, Boss, what do you need?' The private who'd asked him the question about the Shabaab fighter spoke first.

'Thanks. OK, so, could you walk up to the front of the vehicle and tell the driver how lucky he is to be driving such a bloody smart car? Just cause a bit of a distraction.'

Christian was taking a huge risk, but he needn't have worried. His actions the previous year, by shooting the Shabaab fighter, and then for having demonstrated such compassion by visiting Private Masika in hospital, was known to most of the AU troops in Airport Camp. He was on safe ground; they would do anything for him.

'No problem, Boss, I'll go now.' And almost immediately the soldier ambled away around the front of the Casspir towards the Turkish SUV.

Chris dropped his cigarette, winked at the soldiers, disappeared round the back of the truck and slowly made his way along the path behind the vehicles, choreographing his pace to be in step with the soldier who was in front of the vehicles. As he approached the SUV, one car away, he paused and bent down to tie his shoelace. He needed the driver to get out of his car before he could move, otherwise he would be spotted in the driver's wing mirrors. He put his hand in his pocket and removed the transmitter. The seconds felt like hours. He tied and untied his laces twice, listening to the soldier making the most extraordinary noises of appreciation about the vehicle until the car door finally opened. Christian glanced up to see that the driver was getting out. He reckoned he had about ten seconds before both the driver and the soldier would turn and look at the car together. He moved forward in the crouch position, obscured from the main buildings in Vila Somalia by the line of palm trees and a hedge. As he reached the SUV, he took one last look at the driver who was about three feet away from the soldier and reached forward to place the transmitter underneath the exhaust pipe, well away from prying eyes. As he did so, he suppressed a scream as the red-hot metal burnt his fingers while he was pressing it into place.

It stuck, as Imi had said it would. But he had burned his hand.

He quickly got up, turned round and out of the corner of his eye saw the driver turn to face his car without paying him any attention at all. Christian kept walking towards the soldiers. He didn't look back or change direction until he was behind the cover of the Casspir and amongst the men again. His heart was beating hard once more, his adrenaline, not for the first time today, surging.

'Thanks, lads, just needed to check the tyre pressures.' He winked again and moved off, the men laughing with him as he left. He turned to look back after a few moments to see the decoy soldier also walking back to the group. He put his hand up as a thank you, the soldier replying in kind. Within a minute, he was approaching his accommodation.

When he reached his front door, he realised that his hands were shaking uncontrollably as he tried to dig his key out of his pocket. That feeling of panic that he'd experienced in Mombasa was back, but ten times worse than he remembered. He was breathing too fast, struggling to take in air, his heart rate too high. His left hand was fumbling in his pocket; he could feel the key but was struggling to grip it between his fingers.

Finally, after a few seconds, he got hold of it, pulling his hand out of his pocket with exaggerated motion as if it didn't belong to him. Then he battled with the lock, unable to find the grooves to push the key in. For what felt like an eternity, cursing under his breath, his breathing rapid, his head feeling light as he leant against the door, he eventually slid the key in and opened it, all the time trying not to use his right hand which was causing him unimaginable pain. He stepped inside the room, his hands shaking uncontrollably, and just managed to close the door with his elbow before he collapsed to the floor, his legs giving way, sliding down the doorframe, completely out of control, afraid, his mind starting to blank out.

His hold on reality was fading fast as he sat slumped against the door, his feet straight out in front of him, rigid with shock, his breathing even faster now, his hands gripping the air with a tension he couldn't control. The pain in his right hand was finally numbing, but so was his grip on the present.

He tried to see where he was but his vision was fading, his sense of the present disappearing. He tried to look around, to recognise *something*, his hands in front of him, claw-like, screaming with pain. Why were they both hurting? Christian's sense of the present was fading fast into unfamiliar territory. He heart was pounding in his ears, his breathing failing to draw sufficient oxygen into his bloodstream.

He closed his eyes. He was scared; he didn't know what was happening and he didn't understand where he was. It was as if he was observing his own body from somewhere else in the room. His breathing was too fast, he was hyperventilating, his eyes closing. He was hallucinating, the soldiers crowding around him, prodding him with their weapons, laughing at him, kicking him with their boots, feeling every dream-like blow. The Turkish Ambassador thrusting the phone into his face, shouting unintelligible words at him; were they English? He wanted to speak to himself, to calm down, to tell them to go away, to take back control, to stop breathing so quickly, but he couldn't move. And then, slowly, as he fell sideways onto the lino floor, his head breaking the fall, he finally passed out, the pain leaving him at last.

He began to wake from the nightmare. Lying sideways on the floor, his eyes closed for now, he felt the lino, smelt the dirt and the dust, the sensation of his shoulder on the ground, his face inches from the floor. His lack of understanding as to why he was there filled his mind. His breaths came more slowly now, but the feeling of discomfort in his hands was still acute. He heard a siren but couldn't place it. He began to connect sensations in his body again. His hands were painful and made him cry out in anguish when he tried to move them, but instinct told him that he had to work through the pain. He tried to open his eyes but all he saw were blurred images from somewhere he recognised but couldn't place.

His mouth was dry and he slowly, awkwardly, licked his lips, trying to moisten them, to let him speak. Time seemed to have stalled; he was on the floor by the front door. *Why?* The sound of the siren had stopped then started again. No, it wasn't a siren, it was another sound. His left hand was beginning to feel normal again, the painful tingling sensation in his fingers finally subsiding, but his right hand was screaming with pain as if acid was dripping onto his skin.

One by one, he flexed the fingers on his left hand. He was regaining control. He managed to open his eyes and this time he could see his room, the sense of relief audible. His breathing was now more measured. He lifted both hands in front of his face and turned their palms towards his eyes. He managed to sit up. He first looked at his left hand, which was beginning to get some colour back, then looked at his right. Two of his fingers were raw, the skin in places having been burned away. But he couldn't work out why. He wiped his face with his sleeve, rubbed his eyes with his left hand and took some deep breaths as he finally began to fully return to the present. He was desperate for something to drink.

Finally, Christian pushed himself up from the floor with only his left hand, using the door as a crutch and grabbing whatever he could to leverage himself back onto his feet. He looked at his watch but he had lost all track of time. He made it to the kitchen, poured himself some water and gulped it down. He walked carefully back into the living room and slumped in the single chair. He suddenly remembered why his right hand was hurting so much. He got up to find his first aid kit in the bathroom. He wasn't thinking straight but he knew he needed to apply cream and to bandage up his hand. When he was done, he walked back to the living room to sit down again. His phone rang almost immediately. He picked it up without looking at the screen.

'Hello.' His voice was weak.

'Hi Chris, it's Megs. I've been trying to call you, is everything OK?' Megan's voice was so sharp and clear he held the phone away from his ear for a moment.

'Sorry, I don't know what just happened. I think I blacked out. I'm OK, but I'm really tired.' Megan had to listen hard to even hear him.

'Oh my God, Chris. Where are you? Is anyone with you?' Megan's concern was evident in the tone of her voice.

'It's OK, really, I'm fine. I'm in my room so I'll just hole up here for a while.' Christian barely had the energy to hold his phone, let alone talk.

'OK Chris. God, I wish I was there. Look, try to keep drinking water, it's probably dehydration. Call me when you wake up, OK? Speak later then, bye.'

Megan sensed something had happened but knew there was nothing she could do to help.

'OK, bye Megs.'

Christian ended the call and dropped the phone, falling into a deep sleep, slumped in the chair.

It was the middle of night when he eventually woke up. He had been sitting awkwardly on his single chair and needed to get up to stretch and move to his bed. The events of the previous day flooded his mind as soon as he had worked out where he was and why he had ended up there. The panic started to well again, his hand throbbed, and he remembered what happened at the front door. Holding whatever surface he could find to balance, he walked slowly into the kitchen for some water, then into the bathroom. He removed the bandage from his hand before he undressed and stepped into the shower, holding on to the tiled wall as the cool water washed over him, keeping his injured hand away from the spray. Refreshing his skin made him feel human again. After standing under the water for ten minutes, he turned off the flow and stepped out, drying carefully before reapplying the dressing. His hand was very painful; he just hoped he wouldn't have to seek any medical help. That would make things tricky. He opened the bathroom cabinet and swallowed two codeine tablets. He also realised he was starving, so he walked back to the kitchen for a bowl of cereal, albeit he had to use long-life milk. After putting his bowl in the sink, he eventually found his bed and, within minutes, he was sound asleep.

The next day, Christian woke with a start. He looked around and realised that his phone was ringing. He reached across to it and pressed the button.

'Hello?' Christian tried to sound awake.

'Christian, its Bashiir. Where are you?'

'I'm in my room – how can I help?'

'Come to my office as soon as you can.' Bashiir didn't wait for an answer and hung up.

Christian started to speak but soon stopped. He looked at his watch; ten o'clock. 'Shit!'

He grabbed some clothes and dressed quickly. He picked up his phone and keys, threw his jacket on, then left. The codeine had killed the pain but had also made him sleep in. He was still trying to clear his head when he walked through security and into the long corridor leading to the Chief of Staff's office. He had a sickening feeling in the pit of his stomach. He knocked on the door and stood there, waiting for an invitation to enter.

'Come in, Christian, come in.' Bashiir was standing next to his desk. 'What's happened to your hand?'

'Oh, I burnt it on the kettle – stupid thing to do. It should be fine in a day or two.'

'OK, well, are you feeling any better than yesterday? You looked terrible and, if I am honest, you don't look that much better now.' Bashiir was staring intently at Christian.

'I'm not sure what it is – a bug or something. I'll be fine. Anyway, you wanted to see me.' He was calm but he was steeling himself for a question about yesterday's events.

'Yes, a couple of things.' Bashiir moved back behind his desk and sat down. 'After you left yesterday there was a discussion about bringing one or two additional advisors to support Minister Hassan in defence. The President was a little unenthusiastic to be honest and asked me to speak to you, to ask your opinion. The Defence Minister thought it might work, but I wanted to check with you first.'

Christian almost laughed out loud to release the tension he had been feeling in his body since getting the call from Bashiir.

'Well, if the advisors have clearly defined roles and responsibilities and, if they get on well, for example, if they were from the same country or shared a similar military doctrine, then there's no reason why it couldn't work out. If those criteria aren't met, there's every chance advice will be confused and the overall effectiveness will be harmed by the lack of coordination. It's what's happening amongst the international community and what I'm trying to tackle. Does that help?' Bashiir was making notes and nodding.

'Yes, that's what I think too. OK, the next thing: the cleaners found this last night.' He opened his right-hand drawer and picked up a mobile phone, holding it in the air to show Christian. 'Do you know anything about it?'

Christian had been expecting the question and despite his mental preparations to answer it confidently, he was momentarily struck dumb.

'Er, no, no, it doesn't belong to me; I have mine here.' He took his phone out of his pocket to show Bashiir.

'Yes I know that, Christian, because I called you 15 minutes ago.' Bashiir laughed to himself, then studied Christian's face closely. 'I just wondered whether you'd seen it before.'

The initial shock over, Christian responded more confidently. 'No, never.' He was shaking his head, feigning interest in what Bashiir was holding. 'Where was it found? Could it have been dropped by one of the Turkish delegation?' He sounded assured to himself; a good sign.

'Yes, that's what I was thinking. It was dropped down the side of one of the cushions in the Presidential suite.'

'Have you tried turning it on?' Christian asked the question before his brain had caught up; he needed to move the conversation on, not keep the focus on the device.

'No, it's dead, probably run out of battery.' Bashiir dropped it back in the drawer and looked up. 'Take the day off, Christian, it's Thursday today anyway, give yourself a chance to rest.'

'Thanks, Bashiir, I will. See you next week.' He gave Bashiir a mock salute with his bandaged hand and walked out. Whatever energy he had left was draining out of him fast as he took each step towards the entrance hall and relative safety. He pulled out his phone and texted Miko: *Come and get me as soon as you can, thanks.*

He needed to rest, Bashiir was right, and the best place to do that was at the B&B for his fortnightly weekend away. He got back to his room and, after packing some things, he sat down waiting for Miko's response. He pulled out his laptop and drafted a message to Imi, letting her know what had happened. He then sent a message to Megan: *Hi Megs, I'll be going over to the B&B a little earlier than normal. See you later. C x*

*

As soon as Christian had walked out of his office, Bashiir wrote an email to the Turkish Ambassador, explaining that one of his team may have dropped a mobile phone and if he wanted to collect it, he could come over before the end of the day or next week.

26

Monday – Turkish Embassy, Mogadishu

The Ambassador was sitting at his desk under the artificial glare of a single strip light hanging from the ceiling, his curtains drawn across the windows keeping out the morning sunlight, his air conditioning churning away in the corner of the room.

He hated being in Somalia and he hated his office even more. He had applied for the job in Malta, a post he had been courting for the previous 18 months, but a female colleague had managed to land his dream diplomatic appointment. Instead, he had ended up sitting in a grand old villa in Mogadishu; somebody, somewhere was telling him something.

It had been five days since his meeting with the President of Somalia in which he had proposed offering a defence advisor to work alongside the British contractor. He had been rebuffed by the President, but the Defence Minister had been more open to the idea. He had asked the question on behalf of Commander Murat, but in the car on the way back to the embassy, Hassan had been very outspoken about the need for the "British guy" to be replaced sooner rather than later. Both he and Commander Murat had explained that they had time to wait, but Hassan was adamant. He had not said anything at the time, choosing instead to wait until his weekly meeting with Hassan to bring the subject up again. He looked at the clock on the wall to check whether he was on time. He heard footsteps stop outside his door, then a knock.

'Come in, Hassan, come in.'

Hassan was wearing a blue suit and a white shirt, his tie pulled loose below the open top button. He looked pallid, as if he had been living in a cave all his life. The Ambassador commented on his appearance.

'Hassan, come in and take a chair. My goodness, you look terrible! Are you OK?'

'I'm perfectly well, thank you.' Hassan sat down.

'We'll need to instal some sort of ultraviolet machine in that basement of yours, you look positively unhealthy!' The Ambassador didn't like Hassan or how the MIT operated from his embassy without ever sharing any details of their activities. 'OK, well, thank you for coming. I wanted to ask you about last week's meeting in Vila Somalia and, in particular, your insistence that the British advisor be replaced. What did you mean by that?'

The Ambassador, sitting behind his desk, placed his elbows on the edge, his hands touching together at the fingers as if he was about to say grace.

'Sir, you know I cannot go into operational details. We cannot wait for the end of his contract for reasons I am not at liberty to share. We need to replace him as soon as possible and that's all there is to it.' Hassan spoke clearly, without the emotion of previous conversations with Commander Murat on the same subject.

'Well, I do not know what you intend to do but I want no part in it. We have a long-term strategy in this country and we have time on our side through the work Commander Murat is coordinating in Nairobi. Our role here is to ensure we maintain and enhance our relations with the Somali political leadership. I do not want that to be impacted by some ill-thought-through plot by MIT to replace someone who clearly has the trust of the leaders of this country. Do you hear what I am saying?'

The Ambassador was sailing close to the wind. Even though he ran diplomatic affairs in Somalia, he had no influence over MIT operations, and Hassan could easily make life difficult for him if he felt he was being prevented from carrying out his mission.

'Sir, I simply ask you to leave it to me. What we are doing here will bring glory to Turkey and will enhance your reputation within the diplomatic service. I will say no more on the subject.'

'OK, Hassan, I will leave things to you as you ask.' The Ambassador was deeply concerned and personally humiliated by this wretch of an intelligence officer, but there was little he could do apart from report it back to Ankara.

'The last thing I wanted to ask is about Osman. When is he likely to be back here? I haven't seen him for a long time and I want to organise a spring get-together of all our people in the region, including those in Nairobi, of course.' The Ambassador had moved his diary in front of him and was leafing through some pages.

'A spring event?!' Hassan was incredulous and the tone of his voice had risen in response. 'A *spring* event? This is an operational environment, Ambassador! This isn't some cushy posting in the Mediterranean where we spend our time attending cocktail parties!' Hassan started to get up, anticipating the end of the meeting.

'I'm sorry, Hassan, but diplomatic life must go on. I don't expect it's something you would enjoy, anyway.' If Hassan heard the Ambassador's snide remark, he didn't acknowledge it. He was turning the door handle when the Ambassador spoke again.

'There's just one more thing, Hassan. I received an email from the Chief of Staff last Thursday asking whether we had left a mobile phone in the President's office during our meeting the day before. I had it collected yesterday. I've asked Commander Murat but it's not his, so I guess it must be yours.'

The Ambassador lifted it off his desk and was holding it out to Hassan to take.

'I know you often carry two phones so ...' Hassan glared at the Ambassador, his eyes wide, and put his finger to his mouth, urging him to stop talking. He walked over to the desk and took the device from him, studying it briefly. He immediately found some paper, leant on the desk to write something, then turned the paper round for him to read: *This is a covert listening device, you fool!*

Hassan looked at the Ambassador who had gone white as he read the words again. Hassan turned on his heel and walked out of the office, slamming the door behind him. He stormed down the stairs to the main corridor then descended to the basement ops room. The duty operator was there.

'Hello, Sir!' Corporal Hakan Kiliç said.

Hassan held his finger up to his mouth as he pulled out the listening device and carefully prised it open using a screwdriver on the desk. He removed the battery and the sim card. Satisfied that it no longer had the power or the ability to transmit, he handed it to Kiliç.

'Send this back to the lab in Ankara in a diplomatic bag. It needs to be forensically analysed and I need the results yesterday. When is the next flight out?' Hassan was looking at a calendar on the wall to check the flight schedule.

'There's a flight on Wednesday; that's the first chance to get it back home.'

'OK, that's fine. Where is the operational phone?'

Kiliç opened a drawer and handed it to him; 'It's charged up but there's been no traffic on it.'

'Of course there hasn't because they are not meant to be calling in. This is an emergency line!' Hassan was angry as he walked away from Kiliç's desk. Corporal Kiliç followed him with his eyes, his disgust at the way he was treated by Hassan evident on his face.

Hassan dialled a number and waited for the ring tone. Instead, it went straight to voicemail. 'Osman, it's me. Get in touch urgently via the normal channel. We have a target in the city.'

Hassan immediately walked up to his office on the first floor to prepare the message that would be placed at the dead letter drop in the city for Osman to collect later that evening. He had no time to lose. He was certain the British advisor had placed the device in the room. And the only explanation was that he was working undercover for MI6. And if that was the case, he was now a legitimate target.

Memories from Syria came flooding back, the moment his plans had been exposed, challenged by the Americans, supported by the British, the humiliation from inside MIT when he had to return to Ankara, his tail between his legs. But this time would be different. He would be not thwarted again.

He was seething as he typed the note. He assumed that the British had listened to his conversation with the Ambassador and they would know he wanted to remove the man from the advisory role. But they didn't know anything else. Why would they?

He reassured himself his plan was still on track.

27

Monday – MI6 Compound, Airport Camp

I mi had pretty much moved full time to Mogadishu after briefing Christian on what she wanted him to do. And the risks he had taken so far had paid off. They were getting detailed tracking data on the vehicle, although there was nothing out of the ordinary so far, and they had received some valuable reporting from the listening device Christian had placed in the Presidential suite.

She had taken over one of the bunks in the modularised accommodation complex hidden behind a 10-foot-high blast wall that surrounded the compound inside Airport Camp. Her bunk, which was on the ground floor, measured about three metres by four and consisted of a single metal bed with mattress, a side table, a lamp, a chair and a small wooden desk. It also had a sink, a mirror and a wardrobe for storing her limited clothes. Along with her faithful sleeping bag, she had internet access and privacy. She didn't need much else, although it wasn't somewhere she would choose to spend more than a few weeks.

She had a good working relationship with the special forces troops and their support staff, who were deployed to Somalia, but she had never lived side by side with them like this before. A few minor adjustments had been made to cater for her while she stayed. Whenever a female was living in the compound, which happened from time to time and was normally a member of MI6, the second ablution block was out of bounds to men. Even though the soldiers were deployed for four-month rotations, everyone seemed happy to accommodate the change.

Imi was sitting in the operations room, a hot coffee steaming away on her desk, her laptop open. Behind her was the duty operator from the military team who was monitoring communications, including the Turkish Embassy phone and the vehicle tracker. She looked at her watch. There was an hour to go before her secure video teleconference with Matt and Becky in Nairobi.

It was a routine meeting but at least she had an important update to deliver.

'What time's your VTC, Imi?' Tommo, the duty operator, asked over his shoulder. 'Will you want me to leave or do you want to take it in the secure room next door?'

'It's at 3pm, so not long. I'll be next door, thanks Tommo.'

She picked up the night-vision goggles the team had recovered from the warehouse and toyed with them in her hands, thinking through why the Turks would be giving this kind of equipment to al Shabaab and, if they were, what else they were providing. The two men who had stood inside the container had also smelt gun oil, but that was inconclusive as there had been no evidence of weapons or ammunition. She pondered for a moment or two longer, then printed off the transcripts from the monitoring device and the map of the vehicle's movements. She picked everything up and walked into the empty secure room which contained the video conference suite. After retrieving her coffee and water bottle, she spoke briefly to Tommo and went back in. She wanted to type out a few notes before the call started.

After about 20 minutes there was a knock at the door. She got up to open it.

'Another transcript has come through from this morning.' Tommo handed Imi a sheet of paper that had been roughly torn off a printer next door. She sat down and read its content.

'Jesus Christ.' She spoke under her breath and reread the transcript, returning to the sentence: *What we are doing here will bring glory to Turkey and will enhance your reputation within the diplomatic service. I will say no more on the subject.*

She immediately started to make a few additional notes until it was time for the VTC to start. She opened the link and waited for the connection.

'Hello, Imi. How are the boys treating you in Airport Camp?' Matt was upbeat and smiling as he asked the question.

'Hi Matt, hi Becky, very well, thanks. They keep themselves to themselves, you know. I have an update, which is literally hot off the press.' Imi found her notes and the latest transcript. 'I've just emailed these over to you, but here's the summary. As you know, HUSSAR managed to place the device in the Presidential suite and, as hoped, the Chief of Staff believed that the phone had been left by the Turkish delegation and got them to collect on Sunday.' Imi paused in case either Matt or Becky wanted to add anything but they were both heads down writing.

'Go on, Imi,' said Becky.

'OK, so, we have the transcript from the Presidential suite where the Ambassador proposed placing a second advisor in Vila Somalia alongside HUSSAR – you have that with you. We also have several transcripts from inside the Ambassador's office, much of which looks to be interesting background but nothing immediately relevant. You have those as well but they are not a focus.' To emphasise what she was saying, Imi held up a couple of sheets of paper to Matt and Becky. 'However, the last recorded conversation, which they must have had today, is critical.'

She found the print-out and summarised the exchange.

'I think we can assume that Hassan is Hassan Güler, a senior MIT officer in the embassy. He attended the meeting in Vila Somalia and met HUSSAR. Judging by the conversation in the Presidential suite and this conversation today, it looks like there are two schools of thought on the timing to replace HUSSAR as a strategic advisor. Certainly, Hassan's language is a concern. The Ambassador and the Defence Attaché seem content to bide their time, but Hassan is keen for a change much sooner. I am not clear what that means yet. Leaving that for discussion, the reference to Osman is interesting; if he is not at the embassy but is still in Somalia, where is he? And who is he? Can we try to find anything out about him through Ankara? I know it's a long shot.'

Imi took a sip of water and continued.

'There is also the final line on the transcript when someone says to Hassan, "Hello, sir". That's not the language of an MIT junior; not even the Turks are that formal within their service. No, my guess is that the person who said that is military. So probably part of the team who provide their close protection. But why would he take the listening device into that environment? I have no answers on those questions at the moment. Finally, I think it's safe to assume that the Ambassador knows nothing about what MIT does inside Somalia – we have guessed that for some time but it's reasonable to make that assumption now. And the Ambassador obviously did not suspect anything about the device and only when he mentioned it did the room go quiet. We can presume Hassan quickly realised what it was and sent it away to be analysed.'

'Yes, back to Ankara ...' Matt mused.

Imi looked up at the screen and saw both Matt and Becky talking off microphone. While she waited she drank some water.

'Imi, sorry, I just wanted to clarify a couple of things with Becky. Firstly, I want to thank you for getting us this far. We have already achieved some extraordinary access considering the pieces we were playing with, so well done.' Matt's round face, his unkempt curly hair and brown eyes seemed to fill her screen for a moment as he was speaking. 'I think we are beginning to get sufficient evidence to point towards an MIT plot to replace HUSSAR, but I suspect this is a small part of a wider operation. How they plan to do that is anyone's guess. Discredit him in the eyes of the Somalis? That would be my approach. Leave that with us, Imi, we'll try to run up a few scenarios here.'

Matt's mind was in overdrive.

'It's this wider operation that is the issue; we are still lacking any tangible evidence to call it out. We have the night-vision goggles recovered from the warehouse, the transcripts suggest they want to force HUSSAR out of his post, so it's worth bringing Megan in to see what she can do to shore up support for him in VS.'

He looked up to make sure Imi had noted the task.

'And God only knows what Hassan was referring to when he talked about bringing glory to Turkey. We also have a missing member of staff in the Turkish Embassy, somebody who is senior enough to be known to the Ambassador but who must be MIT from the fact that the Ambassador doesn't know where he is or what he's doing. And they are soon going to be casting their suspicions about where the monitoring device originated, even if it is technically deniable.' He took a breath. 'Have I missed anything?'

Matt turned off the microphone again for a moment to speak briefly with Becky beside him. There was lots of mutual nodding.

'OK, so I will reach across to our station in Ankara to see if they can shed any light on it for now. Imi, Becky and I agree that we continue to monitor the phone tap in the embassy. We can assume the listening device is now inoperable and shortly on its way to Ankara. And track where the vehicle goes, although it may also be a red herring.'

Imi watched Matt stroking his beard as he spoke, a sure sign that he was worried about the entire situation.

'Let's see if more comes out from those two sources over the next few days. I think our best option is to wait for additional evidence before taking it to Ankara. We will also keep the option open of briefing the National Security Advisor on their activities. We will use that as our leverage against the Turks if and when the time comes. We may need to do both anyway. Are you happy with that, Imi?'

Imi put her thumb up. 'Yes, that's fine, thanks.'

'OK, good. So, for now, the risk to HUSSAR hasn't increased as there remains no specific targeting against him. If you want to head back here for a face to face, I'm comfortable with that. Is there anything else, Imi?' Matt was picking up his things.

'No, Matt, I'll stay up here for a few more days then perhaps head back after the weekend. Thanks.'

'No probs, see you soon, Imi. Cheers.' Matt and Becky both waved as the connection closed down.

Imi got up with her things and went outside to send a text to Megan, who was in the British Embassy on the other side of Airport Camp: *Megs, can I come over to see you this evening? Say 7pm.*

She put her phone in her pocket and went to her room for a rest. As she closed her door, she turned the side light on and pulled the blinds down, even though her window was a matter of inches from the blast wall. She untied her hair, undid her jeans, slid them off and got into her sleeping bag. She had quickly learned that lying in bed was the only place she could actually think in Mogadishu.

There was nothing to do but wait. She presumed that Christian was oblivious to the Turkish proposal, and although it wasn't a life or death situation, the fact that a member of the Turkish MIT, a similar organisation to MI6, was talking about removing Christian early had set alarm bells off in her mind. She was surprised Matt hadn't said something similar. But she trusted Matt and respected him for his long experience operating overseas. She would take her cues from him and Becky. She knew she had to explain what was happening to Megan, but she couldn't say too much. Megan knew that Christian had already been taking some risk and had been injured while doing so. He and Megan had spent another weekend together at the B&B, and Imi knew they were getting very close. If Megan was aware of the veiled threat that had been made by Hassan Güler, she might begin to take matters into her own hands. She didn't want to give her any opportunity to do that.

Imi's phone buzzed in her jeans on the floor. She leaned half out of bed to retrieve it and read the reply from Megs: *Sure, why don't you come over for some supper? The chef has made shepherd's pie! M*

Imi replied immediately: *Great, I'll get one of the guys to drop me off. I*

She looked at her watch. It was 4.12pm. After a busy few days, she was tired and decided to have a nap. She turned her light off. The room was suddenly filled with monochrome light through the closed blinds, the few rays of sun reflecting off the light grey coloured floor, walls and ceiling. She closed her eyes and rolled over, quickly falling into a deep sleep.

*

Imi was standing outside the accommodation block, close to the entrance to the compound, waiting for her vehicle to be driven round. It was a warm night. She wore a pale-yellow cotton dress and a pair of leather sandals. She had a small bag with her and a light grey cotton cardigan. She had washed her hair – she wanted to look as if she had made an effort for Megan.

Tommo had come off shift and volunteered to drive Imi across the airport to the British Embassy. As the vehicle swung round, she hopped in and they set off, the security guards closing the gate behind them.

'Alright, Imi?' Tommo was in his early twenties and a Lance Corporal in the special forces. He was doing well in his career and had never worked with anyone quite like Imi. The special forces routinely work alongside MI6 in far-flung places around the world, but it's the hot spots, the countries that have fallen into conflict and which threaten the stability of the UK, where a deployment of special forces troops work hand-in-hand with the Secret Intelligence Service.

'I'm alright, Tommo, thanks. You OK? How long you been out here so far?' Imi was amused by Tommo's obvious desire to spend some time outside the operations room with her.

'It's our second month now. It's been busy, yeah, it's been OK.' He was making good time as they skirted the airport terminal and took the internal road rather than going straight on towards the security checkpoint and, beyond that, the city.

'How long will you be with us, Imi?' They were passing an old passenger aircraft, abandoned close to the main runway, a large hole in the fuselage close to the wing, the result of an RPG rocket grenade attack during the civil war.

'I'm not sure, to be honest, maybe a week or so. Why do you ask?' Imi introduced a lightness into her voice.

'It's great having you in the compound. It's such a change to have a female living and working with us.' Tommo spoke with complete honesty.

Imi laughed and said, 'Well, I'll take that as a compliment!'

The journey continued in silence.

'We're nearly there now. Shall I wait? How long will you be? I'll come over any time, just let me know.'

'Oh thanks, Tommo, no, don't wait, I'm having supper. Can I text you a bit later?'

'Sure. Here we are, see you later, Imi.'

The vehicle pulled up at the entrance and Imi jumped out. 'Thanks, Tommo.'

The main gate to the embassy compound was opened by a guard. Megan had come out to meet Imi and, after a hug, the two of them walked into the building together.

'You look great, Imi!'

'Thanks Megs, you look great too.' Megan in jeans and a shirt, her sleeves rolled up to her elbows.

They walked through the corridors towards the rear of the compound and crossed an outdoor garden before entering a smaller building, which was Megan's accommodation. They went inside and sat down on the sofa in her living room. Imi brought her bag onto her knees and pulled out a half bottle of semi-chilled Pino Grigio.

'Ah, thank God for diplomatic bags!' Both women laughed as they opened the wine and poured themselves a glass each.

After they had eaten on a small dining table behind the main sofa, they moved their plates into the kitchenette and sat down again, looking at each other.

'How was last weekend at the B&B with Christian?' Imi wanted to move the conversation onto business.

Megan had also been waiting for the opportunity to speak to Imi since coming back to the embassy from the B&B.

'Christian injured himself doing something the day before we met up. His right hand was a bit of a mess but it will heal. What worried me most was that he said he blacked out in his room after the injury. He didn't want to talk about it, of course, but something was different in him. What are you asking him to do, Imi?'

'Megan, you know I can't go into details. We wanted him to help us covertly monitor a conversation and he did a brilliant job. The day he was doing those tasks was especially hot; he was probably dehydrated.'

'Yeah, that's what I said to him as well.' Megan knew there was no point in pushing it but she tried once more. 'Please don't ask him to do anything that is going to risk his life, Imi; I don't want to lose him.'

'It's nothing like that, Megs, honestly. He has signed up to helping us out, and you have seen most of what has been happening from the Top Secret reporting. The Turks are doing something that seems very odd. We are just trying to understand what that is and to nip it in the bud. Somalia is no place for lone rangers riding to the rescue of the Somalis; there's an entire army of international donor countries out there who are trying to work together to help them. We cannot let the Somalis be distracted and reeled in by a country that is probably only interested in one thing – their bloody oil and gas reserves.' Megan nodded and accepted Imi's statement at face value, but she wasn't happy.

Imi sat there for a moment, staring into space, the silence between them lengthening.

Eventually Megan said. 'Are you alright Imi?'

'Am I alright? Yeah, yeah, I'm fine.' Imi had just realised what she had said. That must be it. The Turks are making a strategic play for influence in return for a large slice of Somalia's untapped oil and gas fields. It made perfect sense to Imi who was wondering why she hadn't thought of it before. She slowly, imperceptibly, shook her head from side to side before returning to the conversation.

When she spoke, Imi's voice was soft, her northern-accented words rolling together.

'There is something we would like to ask. There is a chance that the Turks are going to try to discredit Christian in the eyes of the Somalis. It would be good if you could set up a meeting with the NSA, and possibly the Defence

Minister, just to reinforce the good work he is doing and to get a sense if there is any change in attitude towards him. Obviously we can't share anything we know at the moment, but that time might come.'

'Sure, I'll get on to them both and arrange a couple of meetings.'

'Thanks.' Imi stretched slightly, relaxing once again. 'Bloody hell, Megs, that was a lovely meal! Can you send your cook over to our place? Our food is rubbish!'

'No chance, he's all ours.' They laughed together, but it was strained. They both knew that they were dealing with a serious issue to which both women desperately wanted very different outcomes. Megs looked at her watch, as did Imi.

'Time to go?' Megan raised her eyebrows and looked at Imi, who nodded and started to get up.

Imi texted Tommo, who replied almost immediately, saying that he would be ten minutes.

'Got yourself a driver, Imi?' Megan admired Imi's ability to get people on her side.

'My very own special forces trooper!' They both laughed again, this time more naturally, as they walked through the embassy to the entrance.

Megan stopped by the gate and held Imi's arm gently, the sound of the approaching vehicle bringing an urgency to her actions.

'Imi, I can't lose Christian. Don't make him do anything that is going to put his life at risk. Promise me.' Megan was emotional, she knew it, but she didn't care. She had realised that Christian was the single most important thing in her life, but her ability to influence the course of events was limited.

The moment was interrupted by Tommo's arrival.

'Night Megs, thanks for supper, it was a lovely evening.' Imi squeezed Megan's hand as they briefly embraced, then slipped out of the gate and walked quickly towards the vehicle.

28

Tuesday – Vila Somalia, Mogadishu

The morning after Imi's meeting with Megs, Christian was downstairs in the café, where he was meeting Muna. She had sent him an email asking him to join her. While he was waiting, a text came in from an unknown Kenyan number: *Christian, can we meet away from Vila Somalia? I am coming to Mogadishu this weekend and would like to talk about your role. Murat (TU-Navy)*

The noise in the café was rising as civil servants came in waves to buy a morning tea and to have a gossip. All the tables were taken and it was standing room only. After reading the message again, Christian thought about the reason behind Murat asking for a meeting. Perhaps he wanted to align his activities to the rest of the international community after all, or perhaps he wanted to discuss the idea of having another advisor work alongside him, to try to persuade him it would be a good idea. Either way, it seemed sensible to make the effort. Before replying, he sent another message: *Arne, would I be able to stay this weekend? Possibly two nights – Friday to Sunday – not sure yet. C*

Christian was also beginning to understand the rhythm of work in Vila Somalia and had by now realised that his weekends were his own. So, as long as he managed to negotiate a good rate from Arne and Suzie, he would stay there as often as he could afford to. And being so close to Airport Camp would make everything more convenient if he met up with the Defence Attaché. At least if he was away from Vila Somalia he could get around a little easier. And Imi didn't need to know everything he did.

Hi Murat, sure, why not? How about this Friday? I need to make some arrangements and will confirm timings and location later. Christian

That gave him three days – plenty of time. He pressed "send" and took a sip of tea just as Muna walked in, bobbing around the people packed into the café, trying to catch Christian's eye. She eventually made her way over to him and sat in the chair that he had saved for her with his jacket and bag.

'Christian, how are you? You got my message then?' They hugged briefly and sat down together. 'It's been a while. What've you been up to?' Muna was in Somali blue, which along with her headscarf made her look like she was wrapped in her country's flag.

'All you need is the star!' Christian smiled as he joked about her appearance. 'You look stunning, Muna, seriously.'

'Ha ha, Christian! Oh, we all like the British sense of humour, right?' She laughed too but, unusually for her, she didn't look towards the counter to order herself a drink. 'By the way, what happened to your hand?'

'I burnt it on a kettle.' Christian held his right hand up, which now only had two smaller bandages on the individual fingers.

Muna looked nonplussed. 'Look, what are you doing for the next hour or so?'

'Er, nothing in particular. I have some work to do up in the office but that can wait. I need to sort out some admin for this weekend, but apart from that I'm free. What's on your mind?' Christian was enjoying the levity and relaxed atmosphere.

'OK, well, I have my car here and I wondered whether you wanted to come with me for a drink? It's a little place I know not far from here and there's an outdoor terrace. I'd have you back here in no time.' Muna was looking around, barely focused on the conversation or what she was saying. 'That is if you're allowed out!'

Christian had never been out of Vila Somalia unless protected by Miko and his security team. His contract was pretty clear that he had to use the assigned security for all movement around the city. However, after the events of the last week, he had begun to feel cooped up inside Vila Somalia. Even spending two days with Megan at the B&B hadn't shaken off the way he felt. Since he had collapsed in his room, he had become increasingly self-conscious about his covert activities within Vila Somalia. He had begun to feel conflicted; he felt sure it would only be a matter of time before something happened that exposed him to his hosts, who would take a dim view of his actions, but at the same time, he felt emboldened to take risks. It was what Imi wanted him to do, after all. He knew he needed to accept the offer.

'Of course I'm allowed out! Are you kidding?!' Christian said, balancing the consequences.

'Great, come on then, let's go!'

They squeezed their way out of the café and went towards Muna's car which was parked in the shade of the palm trees. Christian was going to stand out in his western clothing and his white, albeit, suntanned face. As they got in, Muna threw a bag at him. 'Here, wear this.'

Inside the bag was a purple niqab and a shawl. He put the niqab on as soon as Muna had driven through the main security gate, the shawl doing a good job of covering his jacket.

'You look great.' She glanced sideways as she spoke, working through the gears with ease as she cut through the traffic. Christian was feeling extremely self-conscious and hoped they wouldn't get stuck in any traffic queues, allowing passers-by to notice him in the front seat. Fortunately, apart from the natural rhythm of the city's roads, they kept moving.

'I have a sense I'm being kidnapped, Muna. Where are we really going?'

Muna was concentrating as she drove further away from Vila Somalia, travelling along busy streets heading what seemed to be north. 'It's just a small place not far up here, just another couple of minutes.' After turning down a series of quieter streets, they soon pulled up outside large, anonymous-looking dark green metal gates. The journey had taken no more than 15 minutes. Within a few seconds, one of the gates opened and Muna drove into the courtyard, the gate squeaking as it closed behind them, the metallic crash resonating across the open space. 'You can take that off now,' Muna said.

Christian removed the niqab and got out. There was silence, apart from the sound of traffic in the distance. Muna was already walking through a door into the building. He followed, intrigued by her behaviour as much as anything else. The house, if that is what it was, resembled a colonial-style villa, with shuttered windows and balconies on the first floor. Clematis plants were flowering against the walls, softening the faded white stucco and giving a Mediterranean air to the place. The main entrance had several steps leading up to the impressively large wooden doors that opened into a high-ceilinged entrance hall, the tiled floor making his steps echo loudly. Ahead of him, Muna walked past a reception desk, through some French doors and back outside again, where she stopped next to a couple of chairs gathered around a metal table on the edge of a neglected garden, the perimeter wall thirty feet in front of them overgrown with rambling roses and sorry-looking climbers.

Over the wall he couldn't see anything but a deep blue sky, the sun hidden by a parasol.

'What is this place, Muna?'

'Sit, Christian, please. You are my guest. This is a hotel that very few people know about, but it's one of the most secure places in the city if you want to have a private chat.'

'And we are going to have a private chat, I presume,' Christian replied, not sure what to make of the cloak and dagger behaviour from Muna.

A girl arrived wearing traditional Somali dress, carrying a tray containing two glasses of tea, a small silver pot with sugar lumps piled high and two spoons. As soon as she had set it down, she disappeared back inside and closed the door. They were entirely alone.

'Christian, thank you for coming. I don't want you to be away for long in case someone wonders where you are, and I have something I need to say to you.'

Christian dropped a sugar cube into his tea, his body suddenly feeling the need for some glucose. He stirred it slowly as he listened.

'Christian, I have to come clean with you. You are British, I am American Somali, your country and my country, my new country, share everything and we have a special relationship, right?' Muna was scrutinising his face. 'Truth is, I have known a lot of Brits in my time. I have always been looked after by you guys. It's time I repaid the favour.'

Christian nodded, murmuring agreement. 'OK.'

'I am not *only* the Minister for Returns; I also work with Abdulkadir Aden, our National Security Advisor, as part of his executive team. If you like, I keep an eye on what people are doing and saying around Vila Somalia, something you know I am quite good at.' Muna was watching Christian closely, her expression conveying a deep sense of concern.

'Well, you're just full of surprises, aren't you?' Christian hadn't expected her to say this.

Muna forced a smile. 'So, as part of my role I have access to intelligence that is shared from our network of informers. We have informers watching buildings of interest, we have informers watching people of interest, and then we have informers who are covertly gathering intelligence on our sworn enemy, Shabaab.' Muna dropped three sugar cubes into her tea, stirred it vigorously and took a loud sip before carrying on. 'Obviously what I am saying stays between us. I am trusting you with this information because it's important. Not many people know what I really do and that includes people you work alongside on a daily basis, OK?'

Muna clearly wanted some confirmation that he understood what she was saying.

'Absolutely, Muna, you can trust me.'

'OK, thanks, I knew I would be able to. Anyway, I was in a meeting first thing this morning and we were shown some intelligence from someone who is currently in deep cover within a Shabaab unit outside Mogadishu. He can only send texts occasionally, but when he does, they are normally actionable and high value, OK?' Muna's voice had become serious as she was talking. 'And when he hears things, they usually end up being right.'

Christian had finished his tea by now and was listening intently. He still didn't know what Muna was going to say and found the situation he was in utterly bizarre.

'Christian, the message he sent through overnight was that his Shabaab unit has been tasked to prepare a suicide bomber for a target in the city.' She looked at him. 'The target is a white male and he works in Vila Somalia.' She paused to look at his face. 'Christian, there is only one white male who works in Vila Somalia.'

Christian heard what Muna said but couldn't process it. It didn't seem real; why would that happen? He had so many questions. 'Muna, what are you saying? None of what you have told me makes sense. Why would I be the target for a suicide bomber? You must be wrong; your source must be wrong.' Christian didn't believe it.

'Well, firstly I am sorry that you have been dragged into our internal civil war and yes, he could be wrong. We agree that it is very odd for you to be put on a list, but I'm sorry to say that when people are on those lists, they generally stay there until they are killed.' Christian's response was to shake his head, incredulous at what Muna was saying to him. 'We have asked our source to monitor this information and to try to find out some context but we are not expecting anything. Asking the wrong questions will guarantee he ends up lying dead in a ditch on the Afgoye Road.'

'Yes, but Muna, nobody in al Shabaab knows me; it's mad to think that I have done anything for them to even know who I am. There's no way they could know I had anything to do with the bomb attack last year. No, it has got to be wrong.' Christian wasn't so much worried, more confused by the whole surreal experience of being driven out to this discreet villa to be told something that made no sense.

'Give me a minute, Christian.' Muna got up and walked inside the house, leaving Christian alone, looking across the garden, the once green grass now faded to brown and bare in patches, the sprinkler system a distant memory. He scratched his face with both sets of fingers and told himself to keep calm; he would discuss this with Imi when he got back to VS. He was secure inside the compound and when he travelled to the B&B he was in an armoured vehicle and well protected from that particular threat. There must be some mistake, he told himself again.

Muna reappeared with the car keys and said, 'We have to go now. Are you ready?'

He followed her back through the building and into the car. A man walked out to open the gate just as Christian put the niqab and shawl on again. The drive back to Vila Somalia was incident-free and in virtual silence, but Muna's message had put him on a high state of alert. As they swept into the final few hundred metres before reaching the outer security cordon, Christian looked across the road at The Blue Café. It was the place where he had first met Megan and it held a poignant place in his memory. But it also signified the start of a life he had never expected to experience.

He finally broke the silence between them. 'Thanks for the tea, Muna. It's always good to have a change of scene.' He smiled as Muna parked the car.

'I like you, Christian, and I trust you. I do not want to see you get hurt, that's why I have taken some risk to share this with you. What I said couldn't be said here. Look, before you go, give me your mobile number, just in case anything changes.' Muna reached for her handbag to retrieve her phone.

They exchanged numbers and he opened his door to get out. 'I guess I'll see you around.'

Muna looked across at Christian who was now standing, holding the door and leaning down to look inside.

'Christian, this is serious, whether you believe it or not. Just take care;

speak to your security team and ask them to vary your normal routes.' Muna pronounced it the American way, as *rowts*. 'Take all the usual precautions and I'll be back in touch if and when I know some more, OK?'

'OK, thanks Muna.' He closed the door and she drove back out of the complex.

Christian walked through the security cordon to his accommodation. Once in his room, he made himself another black tea and sat down to try to take in what had just happened. Considering he had just been told that he was on an al Shabaab hit list, he was feeling surprisingly calm. It felt surreal, as if he was part of some elaborate joke. He just couldn't see why he would be a target. Sitting in the relative silence of his living room, the air conditioning unit chugging away in the background, his legs crossed while he cupped his tea with both hands, he concluded that the warning from Muna had to be a mistake.

He let out an exaggerated, audible sigh. He knew he was in the thick of something, he just didn't know what, and even if he mentioned it to Imi, she was unlikely to share anything with him. She would just brush his questions away. He wasn't so naïve as to believe that his actions weren't connected to the Turkish efforts to force a military advisor onto him. But how could that warrant the risks he had taken? And now this. No, he began to suspect that a game was being played around him that he was not a party to. Christian put his empty glass down, the teabag still inside, and rubbed his face in his trademark way, trying to bring some clarity to his thinking. In that moment, he reminded himself what Mac had once said to him: *Only worry about the things you can control, Christian.*

He reached across to the side table and switched on his laptop, quickly bringing up the Yahoo! Home page. He also opened a new text file and starting typing out a message to Imi:

Imi, several things to report. Firstly, I have been approached by the Turkish DA to meet him this weekend away from Vila Somalia. Planning to see him in one of the cafés opposite the airport terminal, or maybe the B&B. Also, just had rather bizarre experience. The Minister for Returns, Muna Abdulahi, whom I know and trust, asked me if I would accompany her into the city for a drink. I agreed (I know what my contract says but I needed a change of scene). She drove and we ended up in a very discreet hotel where we sat in the garden. She explained that in addition to her ministerial role, she was also senior in the

NSA's internal security team. She said that one of their sources within an al Shabaab unit close to the capital has reported that a white male who works in Vila Somalia has been listed as the target of a suicide bomber. It would appear I am the only white male who works in VS. There are no further details. I protested that this cannot be true. I plan to carry on as normal. Let me know your thoughts. Christian

He typed out a message and, after the encryption process, sent it off.

Checking his inbox, he saw that Arne had replied, saying it was fine to stay at the weekend. His next message was to Megan: *Fancy another illicit weekend in the B&B? C x*

He needed to see Megan again, even after Muna's warning. He didn't believe that the intelligence could be true. And it felt like something had changed for the better between Christian and Megan. They were starting to make plans for a visit to the UK during her next leave, although they both knew that a more permanent arrangement in England together would have to wait. Megan's tour as Ambassador still had another five months left to run. By then Christian's contract would be over and he would already be back in the UK. He hoped that by the time she returned to the UK, he would finally have his own place. The money he was saving from this contract was building a decent deposit for a small house close to where his parents lived. After the pain of losing Jessica, he was finally feeling like life had dealt him a positive hand. At least, that was his plan.

Lovely! I can only stay on Friday night. Got lots to do and early meetings on Sunday. M x

*

Imi was sitting on her bed reading the message from Christian when there was a knock on her door. She put her laptop down on the side table and got up.

'Who is it?' she asked.

'It's Tommo.'

She opened the door and saw Tommo standing in his uniform, brown boots, combat trousers and a camouflaged T-shirt, his dark hair surprisingly long. He had a sheet of paper in his hand. 'You need to read this. That phone in the Turkish Embassy has finally been used.'

'Thanks, Tommo.' She looked him in the eye and forced a smiled, then took the paper and closed the door. Her heart beat had already risen from reading Christian's message. The time stamp on the sheet, used to identify when the call was made, showed that it had taken place the morning before.

Osman, it's me. Get in touch urgently via the normal channel. We have a target in the city.

She sat down, this time on the edge of the bed, and read it a second time. There was that name again – *Osman*. The call must have been shortly after the listening device had gone offline.

She thought about a time when someone had left a similar message to Imi during her training to become an Intelligence Officer in MI6. On that occasion she was living in the field, under cover, only communicating via dead letter drops. If Osman was living in the field, perhaps alongside an al Shabaab unit, that would explain an awful lot.

'Fuck!' Imi muttered under her breath as the realisation hit her that Muna's informer could be in the same Shabaab unit as Osman.

Looking at her watch, she suddenly thought that he could have already visited the drop, probably the evening before, and received whatever details had been passed to him. This report all but confirmed that there was a covert operation taking place in and around Mogadishu, in all likelihood funded and directed by the Turks. And with Christian's message, the situation was clearly becoming serious.

The individual lines that she had been pursuing were finally beginning to take some form. The non-Somali fighter found dead following the attack on the training camp had intrigued her. Without testing the body for DNA, it offered no clues, apart from the phone recovered from the body. That phone technically linked him directly to the Turkish Embassy. And now a message had been translated from Turkish, ordering someone who was referenced by the Ambassador, to get in touch about a 'new target'.

The night-vision goggles were also important, and the discovery of the shipping container in a warehouse known to be used covertly by the Turkish Embassy added another layer of evidence, but it remained circumstantial at best. Why was the shipping container coming to Mogadishu from Jeddah, a major port in Saudi Arabia? Were they delivering military equipment to the Turks in Somalia? Imi had so many questions running around her head.

She thought back to the recent uplift in al Shabaab attacks on AMISOM troops. Many of them had taken place at night. But why would Turkey be trying to undermine AMISOM by illegally supporting a proscribed terrorist organisation, the sworn enemy of every western nation supporting Somalia's fledgling democratic institutions? Her mind was trying to connect the dots, but hesitating to do so, the implications too horrendous to contemplate. If the Turks were somehow implicated in the rise of al Shabaab attacks against AMISOM, for whatever reason, this must be another operation in the making. But why would they be doing that and how was it linked to Christian? She conceded that if he was removed from the Defence Minister's office and replaced with a Turkish advisor, their ability to influence decisions would be significantly enhanced. Just as she had planned with Christian's appointment. And, if they intended to make a strategic play to gain influence in Vila Somalia, they could be in pole position to exploit the vast mineral wealth sitting below the surface, onshore and offshore. Removing Christian would be a sensible move. But why plan to kill him? The sudden realisation that Ankara could be trying to jump to the front of the international queue for access to their natural resources had only dawned on her the night before. She closed her eyes and swore quietly again under her breath.

Imi let the paper drop onto the bed beside her. She breathed deeply and closed her eyes, her back straight as she filled her lungs and let the air out slowly, like a whisper. The enormity of the conspiracy, if that's what it was, had shocked her. She wracked her brain to find another reason for all of the interconnected pieces of evidence, but she couldn't find one. The warning issued to Christian by Muna clearly fitted into her theory but she struggled to believe that Turkey would authorise an attack on a British citizen on Somali soil.

She needed to send an urgent report to Matt but first she needed to answer Christian's message. Still perched on the edge of her bed, she opened a new text file on her laptop.

Christian, DO NOT meet DA in B&B or opposite terminal. Meet inside airport terminal. Re the meeting with Muna, don't do anything different, normal precautions, but obviously do not go out of VS without Miko and the team from now on. I'll be in touch. Imi

Imi encrypted the message and sent it off.

She then picked up her laptop, got up from the bed and opened the door to her room, grabbing her bag on the way. In five minutes, she was back in the ops room and connected to the Top Secret network. Her heart was pounding as she laid her fingers on the keyboard.

She had to get this message right; her reputation and Christian's life depended on it.

29

Sitting in his office the following day, the sun at its zenith, Murat was looking out of his window across the treetops of Sigiria-Karura Forest that backed onto the Turkish Embassy compound on Gigiri Road. He had received confirmation from Christian to meet in the terminal café on the Friday morning at 11am. He had then written a standard briefing note to the embassy staff in Mogadishu, setting out his plans, requesting accommodation and letting them know his flight times so that he could be picked up from the airport. Almost immediately, Hassan had called him to clarify the details of the meeting, and to ask Murat to make a note of the vehicle Christian was driving. This, he said, was just in case he ever needed to be booked in for a visit to the Turkish Embassy in the capital. Deeply sceptical, Murat had agreed to do so.

Murat put the phone down and sat back. He recalled a conversation with a member of his own MIT detachment in Kenya soon after arriving in his new post, when he was told that Hassan had been unexpectedly transferred from a role in south east Turkey, close to the Syrian border, to Somalia the previous year. Nobody had a good word to say about Hassan in Nairobi. Murat knew nothing about him, or what specific role he played in Somalia, beyond the activities that he imagined a senior member of MIT to be engaged in. Something wasn't right, though. The way he thought he could simply reverse a decision taken at the highest level in Vila Somalia about ending the British advisor's contract didn't stack up. And now he wanted to know about his vehicle details. However loyal Murat was to his country and its objectives in East Africa, he despised behaviour that clashed with his own military ethos of fair play. He was so concerned, he picked up the phone to the Ambassador in Mogadishu.

The call was answered on the third ring.

'Ambassador speaking.'

'Sir, it's Commander Murat, good to see you last week, and thank you for taking my call. Do you have a moment?'

'Of course, Commander Murat, how can I help?'

'Let me cut to the chase. The subject is the British advisor and Hassan's enthusiasm for replacing him as soon as he can, rather than waiting for the right time as we discussed. It really doesn't make any sense to me. It was evident from the meeting last week that we had to wait until the Somalis were ready for either a second advisor, a request which is currently being considered, or for the current advisor to be replaced when his tenure comes to an end. Is that how you saw it? The President and Defence Minister were quite clear about that.'

Murat was treading carefully, but as the senior military man in the region, he had some influence in both MIT and his country's diplomatic circles.

'Yes, that's what I understood too.'

'Good. Well, that's all I wanted to check. I am a little concerned about Hassan's behaviour; he seems to be talking about replacing the British advisor imminently. Do you know anything about that?' Murat asked the question cautiously.

The Ambassador took a moment to answer. 'Well, I spoke to him yesterday and he wasn't very happy about the situation, that is true. But otherwise, I had no reason to be concerned.'

The Ambassador was embarrassed that he had potentially brought a covert listening device into the embassy and wanted to forget about it as soon as he could. He knew his career was at the mercy of Hassan, so he chose not to mention anything else he had said, or the incident with the device. 'Was there anything else?'

'Yes, just one more thing. He seems to think the Brit may be invited over to the embassy in the near future because he was asking me to take a note of the vehicle details. It's just very strange. If we want his vehicle details, we ask him for them, surely.' Murat sensed he was going to get nowhere.

'Well, I did tell Hassan about a social event in the spring, so perhaps he was thinking we could invite him to that.'

'A *social* event?' Murat's surprise was evident in his voice and was as non-plussed at Hassan had been. 'OK, well thank you for your time. Goodbye, Ambassador.' Murat hung up, no less worried.

He looked across his office, seeking some sort of inspiration, when his eyes settled on a bookshelf in the far corner of the room. He picked out his copy of *Snow*, written by the great Turkish author Orhan Pamuk. It had been a number of years since he had read the book, but his memories of the story reverberated with the claustrophobia he felt every time he flew into Mogadishu. He had managed some fairly difficult situations with his military counterparts across the international community over his country's role in Somalia, but he had a foreboding about the current situation. Although Hassan was on his patch, he wasn't his problem. As long as Hassan didn't screw up Murat's plans, or in other ways tarnish his reputation in Ankara, he could do whatever he liked. He simply didn't want the fallout from some botched MIT operation to implicate him. He needed to protect his career ambitions if he feared Hassan's actions were likely to compromise him. He had heard enough stories about MIT to know how easily that could happen.

Opening his laptop, he began to write a confidential message to his desk officer in the Ministry of Defence Headquarters in Ankara.

Attention: Vadit Bürsin, MOD Ankara

From: Commander Murat Keskin, Defence Attaché Kenya

Subject: URGENT – Damage Limitation

Vadit,

I am writing about a highly confidential matter. I will dispense with the formalities. I believe that Turkey is about to commit a grave error of judgement in Somalia, and I need your help to prevent it from happening. As soon as you can, please find an hour to establish a secure video feed with our Embassy's conference room so that we may discuss the matter.

I'm looking forward to your urgent reply,

Murat

On his way back from lunch on the ground floor of the embassy building, walking alone along the corridor leading to his office, his phone pinged in his jacket pocket. He stopped and took it out, hoping to see Vadit's name on the screen. He was disappointed. Instead, it was from Hassan in Mogadishu, inviting Murat to call him when he had some time in the afternoon. He took out his key and opened his office door, closing it behind him as he walked to a large leather armchair, one of two in the corner of the room, facing his desk but set back from it. By sitting there, he felt he could generate some perspective on a situation. He used it when talking to visitors. He felt able to think matters through more clearly from the chair, looking as it did out of the window and across to the forest's canopy.

He dialled Hassan's number.

'Hello, is that Murat?' Hassan had clearly been expecting an imminent call from the moment he sent the text.

'Yes, you know it's me, Hassan. What do you want to talk about over an insecure line?' Murat thought it very odd that Hassan was being so carefree about speaking over their embassy-issued mobile phones.

'It's nothing serious, Murat, I just wanted to clarify the request I made earlier. There's no need to note the vehicle detail, the event I mentioned will not be taking place. Is that clear?' Hassan was talking to Murat in code, or at least he was trying to. Murat still couldn't work out why he hadn't just written a secure message to him.

Murat hesitated slightly. 'Yes, I think so.'

'Good, OK, well, the team will meet you as planned.' Hassan ended the call without waiting for a reply.

Murat pulled the phone from his ear and looked at the screen, shaking his head. He got up from the armchair and rounded his desk, pulling out his seat as he did so. He opened his laptop to check for a response from Vadit.

I can dial in at 2, does that work? V

Murat looked at his watch. He had ten minutes. He starting typing his reply, confirming that he would be there and pressed "send". He immediately walked into an adjoining room to ask his secretary to arrange for the conference room to be free and then walked to the defence section kitchen to make a coffee to take down with him. As he stood in front of the machine, the sound of beans being ground and highly pressured water being pumped through its pipes, Murat took a moment to think about his imminent video call with his desk officer.

Both times Hassan had spoken to him today they had been on an insecure mobile. The only reason he would do that is to introduce some deniability to whatever he was discussing. Murat thought the request to note the vehicle details was strange this morning; the counter order this afternoon made the whole thing highly suspicious. And if MIT were going to conduct some sort of deniable action in Somalia, where car bombs happen every day, Murat wanted nothing to do with it. And the fact that he had set up a meeting with the British contractor in two days' time linked him to whatever Hassan was planning in Somalia's capital. He was very uncomfortable with the whole situation. He needed to make sure that he and the defence section were as far removed from whatever MIT were planning in Mogadishu as possible. For the first time as a defence diplomat, he needed some top cover. He picked up his black coffee and walked towards the conference room.

*

Across the city, close to downtown Nairobi on the 4th floor of the British High Commission, Matt sat at his desk, barely taking in the movement and low-level conversations on the floorplate around him. He was in a world of his own, leaning back in his chair, holding the report Imi had sent through the previous afternoon. He had replied before he left for the evening, copying it to Becky, as well as to Tom in London and Megan In Mogadıshu. After back-to-back VTCs all morning with London, discussing corporate governance, Matt had returned to his desk to reflect on what he had written in his reply.

Imi had asked permission to pull Christian out of Vila Somalia based on what she had been told in his secure message about being a target for an al Shabaab suicide attack. Together with the other threads of intelligence, it was clear, she had said, that Christian was in mortal danger. Imi felt the risk to his personal safety was now too serious for him to continue in the role. He had done a brilliant job, but he was untrained and the risks no longer justified his involvement. His contribution should be brought to an end. Imi insisted that they had enough evidence – the night-vision goggles, the spike in attacks against AMISOM, the transcript from the listening device, the explicit warning from Muna, the intercept from the Turkish Embassy – of a plot to destabilise Somalia. She was sure their intent was to steer the Somalis into their arms, to give the Turks preferential access to the most lucrative oil and gas blocks across their extensive on- and off-shore deposits. At the very least, they had uncovered a plot to harm a UK national.

Matt had not agreed.

In his reply, Matt had stated that firstly, before accepting what HUSSAR had been told by his contact, Muna, Imi would need to verify the intelligence with Abdulkadir Aden, the Somali National Security Advisor. However credible Muna's warning was, she was undeclared as an intelligence officer and had admitted as much. The gravity of the warning needed formal confirmation, something Imi would need to do the following week. However, he knew that she would not be able to refer to any specific tip-off about the plot to attack Christian and would have to try to elicit the information from the Somali National Security Advisor in a face-to-face meeting, which would take some time to arrange. He had emphasised to Imi that this was to be prioritised. If Aden confirmed the intelligence, they would consider acting on it, but not before. He had also explained to Imi that they were not yet ready to present their evidence to a Turkish representative in either Ankara or London.

Matt simply knew too little to connect all the dots, to be able to make a move that was likely to seriously affect relations between two NATO nations.

He then turned to the Nairobi team's analysis. They had concluded that there probably was a plot to destabilise Somalia, perhaps with the intention of stepping up Turkey's support for Somalia's military forces, potentially with the long-term aim of getting closer to Somalia's carbon deposits, but it was only conjecture. They had all agreed with the analysis that Western donor nations were extremely unlikely to deploy military forces into Somalia to tackle the threat from al Shabaab, thereby leaving a hole for Turkey to fill if they chose to do so, but they couldn't prove any of it. It was one thing putting together a hypothesis; it was quite another to take it to a friendly sovereign nation, effectively accusing them of an international conspiracy to destabilise another sovereign nation. There was absolutely no evidence of either activity. Matt knew it was completely deniable by the Turks.

If they could get some more evidence, he mused, such as another transcript from the phone in the Turkish Embassy, or if the vehicle tracker started to visit places frequented by HUSSAR, they could probably move. For now, though, they simply didn't have enough on which to act.

Out of the corner of Matt's eye, he saw Becky approach his desk. She gestured to pull up a chair, Matt turned to her and smiled, stretching his arm out by way of invitation.

'Penny for them ...' Becky said as she crossed her legs and let her hands gently rest on her faded denim jeans. 'I've read the reply to Imi; I think you are right to wait.'

'This is the challenge of intelligence work; we have to operate on solid facts, not just hunches, however enticing they may be. I know there is a lot of very strong corroborating evidence, but if we take something to the Turks that is half-baked, we will be the standing joke in Whitehall. And the DG would never sign it off anyway.' The stress in Matt's voice was clear to Becky; she knew Matt well.

Matt leant forward and took a sip of coffee, knowing how the game worked. He ran through his thinking with Becky, who listened intently. Once they had enough to put together a credible case, his preferred method of raising the issue in order to seek some answers was through diplomatic channels in Ankara, or possibly through the Turkish Ambassador in London. He also had the option of sharing what they had with the Somalis, but that remained a card up their sleeve, to be used as leverage as required. Both he and Becky had also explained to Imi that while HUSSAR was in Vila Somalia, he was relatively safe from any attack. The only fly in the ointment was his meeting with the Turkish Defence Attaché at the airport on Friday morning. Although he absolutely rejected any notion that the Defence Attaché was somehow luring him out of Vila Somalia to set up an attack, he would ask Imi to deploy the special forces team, covertly, to keep an eye on him. Christian would be oblivious to it, but they would have his back.

The meeting with the Defence Attaché aside, Christian was not due to be outside Vila Somalia until the weekend after next, therefore they had at least seven or eight days to begin to turn the diplomatic wheels into motion in London and Ankara.

For now, he said, everyone just needs to sit tight and hold their collective nerve.

30

Thursday – Bakhara Market, Mogadishu

Ali was excited. The last few weeks had been like no other he had ever experienced. He felt valued, like he was a key member of the team, Rasuul's team, and he had been rewarded for his loyalty.

He had been taken out of the city one evening, a couple of weeks earlier, where he had met some Shabaab fighters. He stared in awe when they jumped down from their Hilux vehicle and was tongue-tied when they spoke to him directly, as an equal. So in awe of the respect they gave him, he barely remembered what they had said to him. Ali was taken into a small concrete building close to the parked vehicles, where Rasuul and another man, whom he did not recognise, sat him down on a chair in the middle of the room and gave him a cigarette. A Turkish cigarette. They were very hard to come by in the city. He felt like he had made it. Life didn't get much better.

When they had walked in and closed the door, a small overhead light had been turned on by Rasuul, but the room was still quite dark, the windows blocked with wooden planks to prevent light seeping out. The fighter sat opposite Ali on a single plastic chair. Rasuul spat noisily on the dusty ground and crossed his arms, leaning casually against the wall. He was not going to be leading this conversation.

'Ali, I have heard some very good reports about your progress, about your courage and how committed you are to joining the fight.' The Shabaab fighter tapped Ali's knee to get his attention as he spoke to him, his voice cutting through the smoke filling the small space between the three of them. 'We have decided that your time has come.'

Ali inhaled the cigarette like a pro; he had been practising whenever he managed to get hold of some in Mogadishu. He had made his throat sore from coughing so much when he first started, but now he was proficient. He knew it was important to act like the Shabaab fighters to be considered one of them.

'Inshallah the time will soon come when you will be martyred, Ali.' The fighter paused to take a drag on his cigarette and wait for any reaction. 'We have selected you to join our fight, as an equal, so you will have the opportunity to become famous. People will speak of you for many years to come.' The men continued to draw on their cigarettes although Ali had stopped, his hands frozen by his lap, the cigarette burning down without meeting his lips. He was staring at the man in front of him but he could no longer see him. His mind was trying to take in what this fighter, this Shabaab fighter, was actually saying to him.

'Very soon you will also be given a gift from us, something new for you to learn while we prepare for your martyrdom. Do you know how to ride a motorbike, Ali?' The fighter took a final drag on his cigarette and dropped it on the floor, the butt smouldering in the dirt. Rasuul remained silent a few feet away.

'Er, yes, I mean no, just small mopeds, that's all. But I learn fast, I will be a good rider.' Ali's voice was cracking but he was telling himself to be strong, not to be like Mohammed, who was weak. He had been chosen to be a martyr, someone who was going to experience something his old friend Mohammed would never experience. He had never felt prouder.

Back in the capital the following day, Ali had been given a battered old Japanese motorbike and told to learn to ride it. He spent hours getting used to the machine's controls and power, weaving his way through the flow of human traffic in the market, tentatively at first, then faster, learning how to handle himself on the streets. He felt invincible when he was riding it and hardly fell off at all now. He soon became confident and saw Rasuul often, telling him how much progress he was making.

Then one day, when he was getting some money from Rasuul for fuel, he had been given a heavy rucksack to wear while riding the bike. He was told it would help his balance. Ali didn't mind, he just wanted to be as good a rider as possible before his martyrdom. And although it had been a couple of weeks since he had met the fighter in the building outside Mogadishu, he was no nearer to knowing when it was going to happen.

It had been a normal day when Ali parked up the bike and walked into a garage to leave the keys by the front door. He had done this every day after practising. The garage had always been empty, but in front of him were several men surrounding an old blue minibus, its doors wide open, the seats and footwells filled with heavy plastic bags. He had learned not to stare so he quickly turned away, stepping back out into the yard and squatting by the bike. He picked up a cloth and started buffing the red paintwork, as he did every day. What he had seen had sent his heart rate racing.

'Ali?' Rasuul had appeared at the door of the garage behind him and was looking across at Ali, a cigarette in the corner of his mouth. Rasuul was wearing designer jeans, white trainers and a royal-blue polo short with an emblem of a horse on the chest that Ali thought he recognised.

'Yes, Rasuul. I have left the keys in the usual place. I am just going to clean the bike before I finish.' Ali was suddenly nervous. He knew something was about to be said that was important. He was looking at the ground, fearful of looking at Rasuul's face.

'OK, Ali, thank you. I have some news for you. We have a date and a time. But not yet a location. So tomorrow we will meet here but there will be no more riding. Tomorrow we go through what you will be wearing on the day, so that you can get used to it. You are good at learning, yes?' Ali was hanging on his every word.

'Yes ... I am ...' Ali words stuck in his throat momentarily. He looked up at Rasuul; his eyes were moist from the emotion.

'I will not let you down, not like Mohammed did. I will show everyone that I will die as a martyr should.' Ali's words were spoken with a determination that pleased Rasuul; he knew Ali was ready. He had done well in recruiting him and turning him into a foot soldier.

Rasuul walked back into the garage and closed the door behind him without saying another word.

31

Friday – Medina District, Mogadishu

C hristian had woken early, even though it was his day off. He had done a work-out in the vicinity of his room. For once he was grateful for the breeze as he walked back inside and started stretching, thinking through his meeting with the Defence Attaché later that morning. He sipped some cool water out of a bottle from the fridge. He had decided that he was going to do a lot of listening; he was interested to know what Murat was going to say but definitely wasn't going to compromise his position or give the DA any opportunity to put a wedge between him and the other international donors. He really had nothing to lose and he had a bonus night at the B&B with Megan to follow. He knew he couldn't keep it quiet from Imi, who would be rightly furious at the risk he was taking, but his desire to be with Megs was overwhelming.

After taking a cool shower, he changed into a navy linen shirt straight off the line, cream chinos and leather deck shoes. He packed some clothes and his wash kit into a bag and made himself a cup of black tea, his nervous energy rising. The work-out was supposed to have taken the edge off, but it clearly hadn't worked. He sat down again.

Hey, Megs, what time are you planning to arrive today? C x

He leaned his head back and closed his eyes, waiting for his phone to buzz with a reply. He didn't have to wait long.

Hey, Chris, I am just finishing some things off for my meetings on Sunday morning then I'll head over. Around lunchtime if I'm lucky M x

Chris smiled as he thought about seeing Megs later on. He looked again at his watch and texted Miko.

Miko, can you get here a little earlier than planned. Say 10.30am?

The reply was almost instant: *Sure, Boss, be there soon*

Just before 10.30am, Christian walked down to the car park. He had found some shade under one of the palm trees when he saw his white armoured Toyota Land Cruiser drive through the main security gate towards him. Miko got out of the car and, as Christian approached, he held the passenger door open for him.

'Hello, Christian, how are you this day?' Miko's use of English, though rarely grammatically accurate, had become strangely comforting to Christian.

'What? No *and once again I take a Christian into the city of Muslims*?' Christian tried his best to mimic Miko but it didn't work and, while both men laughed as they closed their heavy armoured doors, it was subdued.

'Not today, Christian, today we have to be serious, and tomorrow, and maybe Sunday as well.' Miko's tone was different to usual and Christian didn't need to ask why. 'We have heard some intel about another car bomb in the city, so we watch and drive with caution.'

Christian instinctively looked through the back of the vehicle at the trailing pick-up filled with his AK47-armed support team.

'What have you heard?' Subconsciously his heart rate increased. The fact that Miko's intelligence had effectively confirmed what Muna had told him sent shivers down his spine.

'The usual, no specific intel, just that there is something planned, but no other details. I don't know where the police get their intelligence but you know they are right 50% of time here.' Miko was very alert, looking at everything on the street, his head moving from side to side, giving the driver instructions to pass some vehicles more quickly than normal. The atmosphere in the car was tense.

Within minutes, he had rounded the K4 roundabout and was slowing down for the road humps and the security check point outside the airport.

'What is plan, please?' Miko turned around to look at Christian, who had been staring out of the window towards the airport buildings.

'I have a meeting at 11, which I think will probably last no longer than half an hour, but I will text you. If you can stay close to the terminal building, I will come straight out to meet you.' As soon as they pulled up at the drop-off zone, Christian tapped Miko on the shoulder and opened his door. 'And Miko, keep an eye out for anyone hanging around.'

'OK, Boss.'

Christian walked through the main entrance and was briefly held up by a small queue to pass through security. As he collected his watch and phone, he realised that he hadn't checked if there was a specific room where they were meeting. He decided to hang around in the middle of the airconditioned check-in zone, aiming to be as visible as possible both for Murat to spot him and for security cameras to register his presence. He acknowledged several armed guards who were surveying the passengers, on the look-out for a threat. Reading between the lines of Imi's last message, he figured she didn't want him to be hidden away in a dark corner of some shady café, which was sympathetic to al Shabaab and where someone could administer a fatal injection without anyone seeing him slump to the ground, suffering from 'heart failure'. He sighed, telling himself to get a grip; he had been watching too many films.

Lost in thought, he didn't see Murat approach him.

'Hello, Christian, thank you for coming to see me.' Murat was in an open-neck shirt and a jacket, his hand outstretched.

Momentarily thrown by Murat's stealthy approach, Christian grabbed Murat's hand and shook it before suggesting they head towards the café area, which was located at the end of the terminal building.

'No, Christian, there is a VIP room here which we can access – let's walk over there instead.' His manner was confident, his demeanour much more accommodating than the last time they had met after the security conference. Christian agreed and followed Murat to the same room where he had spotted Megan talking to the National Security Advisor many weeks before. Inside the room, they sat down opposite each other on the lavishly decorated, ornate single chairs. Murat ordered some tea for them both from the waiter who had led them to their seats. It didn't take long for him to return with their drinks.

'Thank you for seeing me, Christian.' Murat made small talk while the teas were poured. 'I know you are busy and getting around the city isn't the safest enterprise these days.' He gave a resigned look at Christian.

'Thank you for reaching out. I think it's very important for us to know each other a little better.'

Christian noticed that Murat had a bag with him and concluded that he must have arrived on the early morning flight and was probably on his way to his accommodation.

'Do you stay in your embassy when you are here?' Christian asked.

Murat looked at his tea, which he had picked up. 'Yes, it is functional and safe. How about you?'

Christian had anticipated the question. 'I live in Vila Somalia and only leave to fly out to Nairobi, unless there are meetings at the airport, like this one.' Christian picked up his tea to use as a prop. 'So, Murat, I was intrigued to receive your text message. I thought you had made your position pretty clear on Turkey's approach to delivering security sector reform in Somalia. Has anything changed?' Christian hadn't planned to be so direct but had decided to dive straight in.

Murat took a moment to reply. 'I wanted to talk to you about the possibility of a Turkish military officer joining you to advise the defence minister.' There was no circuitous route to the subject of the meeting and Murat had also taken the most direct path. 'I would like to explore whether this could work.'

Christian was sipping his tea, watching the man opposite him. The VIP suite was typically ostentatious in manner, with large, elaboratively carved wooden furniture, overly decorative standard lamps and highly colourful paintings in heavy frames lining the walls. Large tasselled rugs lay across the tiled floor joining the huddles of chairs and sofas that filled the space. They were not alone but their conversation was unlikely to be overheard, with Somali pop playing over the tinny speakers behind them. Somewhere, out of sight, an incense stick was burning, filling the room with a sweet, intoxicating aroma.

'I was asked the same question by the President's Chief of Staff after your meeting last week. And my response then will be the same now. The best way to give clear, unambiguous advice to Somalia's leaders is to reduce the opportunity for mixed messages based on cultural and conceptual differences. I believe having a second advisor from a completely different military environment would be a mistake.' Christian genuinely believed that it would be a complete mess if he let it happen and he would most likely lose all support from the wider international community's security representatives.

The conversation went back and forth several times until Murat eventually gave up trying to explore ways of working together. He explained that he needed to get into the city for another meeting and started to gather his things, indicating the meeting was over. It had lasted 23 minutes. As they were walking out of the VIP room, Murat spoke casually, without looking at Christian.

'So how do you protect yourself around the city, Christian? You must be the only westerner who lives in Mogadishu on a regular basis.'

The question, the way it was worded, immediately put Christian on edge. 'I have excellent security provided by the UK,' Christian lied. He wanted to give the impression that he was protected by the full resources made available from the British Government, not just a private military company charging $1000 a day.

As they opened the terminal door and stepped outside into the growing heat, they briefly shook hands again.

Murat spoke first. 'I am sorry we were unable to find a solution. I have done all I can. It is out of my hands now. See you around.'

At that, Murat turned and walked away from the entrance, stepping off the pavement towards the opposite side of the road to a waiting black SUV. Christian watched him go, noting the registration number of the vehicle as it drove past him and away from the airport. At that same moment, Miko pulled up by the curb. He got out to open Christian's door. The sense that Christian was an important individual was hard to miss from Miko's actions. That's how he wanted it. As they quickly pulled away and headed for the exit and the B&B, Murat's words echoed in Christian's head: *It is out of my hands now.*

The vehicle was idling on the side of the road facing towards the city when the black SUV roared past, kicking up dust in the swirling wind. Moments later, the white Toyota drove past them, almost immediately turning left towards the Medina District that lies alongside the airport perimeter. The Toyota accelerated away quickly.

'Follow them.' Hassan's voice was high-pitched, the stress of the moment and his unfamiliarity of being in the field evident in his increasingly erratic behaviour. 'And keep up with it!' he shouted at Corporal Kiliç, who was driving, even though he should have been asleep after his night shift. Corporal Kiliç's hatred for this MIT superior officer was reaching new depths.

'Sir, if I get any closer, they will see us as we are not in a covert vehicle.' The Corporal kept his voice level, despite his growing anger at this pointless driving task. Any one of the others could have done this for Hassan.

'Yes, yes, OK, slow down, slow down, but don't lose it ...'

Corporal Kiliç slowed the black SUV down and soon lost sight of Christian's vehicle which had navigated a bend in the road ahead.

As the black SUV rounded the same bend, Hassan spotted Christian's vehicle turning right into a side street, about 100m ahead of them. Hassan told Corporal Kiliç to slow down again, passing an old white Hilux 4x4 close to the junction, its bonnet up, a man leaning into the engine compartment.

'Of course, there are no plates on these cars,' Hassan said under his breath.

When they arrived at the end of the junction, Hassan looked down the side road and saw a series of security barriers acting as a chicane. Beyond, 100m metres away, turning into a compound, was the white Land Cruiser.

'OK, let's head back. I have seen enough.'

As they drove back to the embassy via K4 roundabout, Hassan was lost in thought. After what he had seen, he knew he had to call Osman urgently. He stared straight ahead, trying to think, mumbling to himself unintelligibly, his fingers tapping repeatedly on his knees. When they slowed down for some traffic, Corporal Kiliç glanced sideways to look at his passenger. In all the months he had been working in Somalia, he had never seen Hassan like this.

They soon pulled into the embassy compound as the gates were opened by the security team and parked close to the main building's entrance. Corporal Kiliç turned the key to kill the engine and, stifling a yawn, broke the silence. 'Sir, I am going to get my head down. I need to rest.'

Hassan turned his head for the first time on the journey and looked at his driver. 'If you must.' Hassan got out and crossed the parking area to the main entrance without another word. He quickly walked downstairs to the secure MIT office and pushed the duty operator to one side as he pulled open the drawer and retrieved the emergency phone.

'Go and get some tea!' Hassan ordered.

The soldier immediately pushed his chair back and stepped out of the room, closing the door carefully behind him.

Now alone, accompanied only by the background hum of communications equipment, Hassan sat down at the table, a single bulb hanging by a wire from the low ceiling creating a pool of light around him. He paused for a moment, his left hand flat on the table and his other holding the phone, his thumb poised over the keys. The plan for this weekend needed to be confirmed. He needed to leave a message at the dead letter drop for Osman as a matter of urgency. He opened the Nokia phone and punched in Osman's number, waiting for the answerphone to kick in to leave a message.

The phone was answered almost immediately.

'Hello?' It was Osman.

'What are you doing answering the phone? It's breaking all protocol. Hang up!' Hassan was instantly furious with Osman.

'Look, Hassan, I'm tired, save me the effort, just tell me what I need to know now.'

'No! I will leave the message in the usual place. It is imperative that you pick it up tonight!' Hassan immediately hung up.

*

The black SUV had been observed, undetected, at close range by the special forces team which was on the ground on Imi's orders to provide overwatch for Christian. Two vehicles at different locations, four special forces soldiers in each, all perfectly at one with the environment through their disguised appearance and behaviour on the road. They were professionals at blending in.

In their outwardly battered 4x4 Hilux pick-ups, all driven expertly and discreetly by the team from Airport Camp, one vehicle had watched Hassan's vehicle pick up the tail of Christian's Toyota as it sped away from the airport terminal, while the other had been further along the route.

Between the two SF vehicles, one of which was parked up close to the B&B, their secure radio chatter was succinct.

'The guy's speed is all over the place so we're hanging back.' It was Tommo.

'Roger,' came the reply from the second vehicle.

The black SUV was driving at erratic speeds, suggesting they were trying to check for a tail. Tommo's vehicle had remained at a safe distance while in pursuit, meandering along the road, knowing they could afford to lose sight of it.

'It should be coming past you shortly.'

'Roger.'

As the front seat passenger, Tommo was commanding the operation, his weapon, grenades and spare magazines stowed in the footwell, ready for any eventuality.

'The B6 has turned into the B&B street and the target vehicle has just passed us. Heading off now.'

'Roger.' It was Tommo's turn to acknowledge the update.

By the time they had line of sight of the black SUV, it was already a few hundred metres away at the top of the road, turning right towards the city, the second special forces vehicle following at a discreet distance having closed the bonnet and set off in pursuit.

As Tommo's vehicle approached the junction, about to join the other Hilux, he noticed a white Toyota Land Cruiser appear in his side mirror, driving up the road then turning right into the side street towards the B&B.

Both special forces vehicles followed the SUV to the Turkish Embassy, providing cover for each other, then returned to Airport Camp via the back gate.

When he finally returned to the ops room, Tommo wrote up the report for Imi and emailed it on the internal secure network. He picked up his weapon and daysack before heading to his room for some sleep. He knew it was going to be a long couple of days.

CLASSIFICATION: TOP SECRET

From: Airport Camp Det;

To: IO3, Nairobi Station;

CC: Ambassador, Mogadishu;

Priority: URGENT

Subject: HUSSAR Overwatch – report

1. *HUSSAR left with assigned security after meeting with TU Defence Attaché (DA).*
2. *TU DA exited in first black SUV in direction of city centre.*
3. *HUSSAR did <u>not</u> return to VS; instead drove to B&B followed by second black SUV (likely TU intelligence officer and team conducting surveillance).*
4. *HUSSAR entered B&B location without incident.*

5. *Whilst following the second black SUV back to the TU Embassy, a second B6 Armoured Toyota Land Cruiser (white) was observed heading towards the B&B.*

6. *Second black SUV made its way back to TU Embassy.*

7. *Both callsigns returned to Airport Camp without incident.*

8. *Nothing further to report.*

Signed: AT, Op Commander, Airport Camp Det

32

Saturday – B&B, Mogadishu

Christian was sitting opposite Megan in the main dining room. The sun was already high in the sky after they had spent most of the morning in bed. The house was empty, Arne and Marco having gone into the city for some provisions, supported by Miko and the security team. Suzie had flown out of the city for a few days R&R in Nairobi with a friend from Norway. Only the gate guard was left.

'What time is Krishna coming to pick you up today?' Christian was tucking into a freshly baked croissant with Somali honey, and spoke with his mouth full. 'Sorry!'

Marco's ability to produce western staples with such limited resources was legendary.

'He's coming at two. I have to get back because I am meeting the NSA at 8.30am in VS and I need to do some prep.' Megan looked at her watch to see how long they had left together.

'Oh, that's great. Maybe we can meet for a cup of tea in the café when I get in. I'll be travelling back around the same time,' Christian replied. He had never seen Megan in Vila Somalia during one of her formal visits and he was beginning to wonder whether anyone really cared that they were in a relationship.

'Ooh, that'd be a first! Maybe, but I don't want to start rumours around the capital.' Megan was smiling, giving Christian a look that said the total opposite. She added a little more jam to her toast and bit into it, the crunch echoing around the dining room.

Christian finished a mouthful and wiped some honey from his plate using the last of the croissant and forced a smile. So much was unsaid between them. Megan had read Imi's report and wasn't surprised that Matt had said the operation remained on track. Matt was very unlikely to act without enough evidence to support his decisions. It didn't make Megan feel any better about anything and she knew how much Christian was at risk. But she had signed up to the operation and given Matt her word that she would support Imi, who was pulling it all together.

When Imi had sent a text the previous afternoon, asking where she was and when she would be returning to the embassy, Megan knew that her movements had been tracked. Information that would, in all likelihood, be passed back to Matt via Imi. After specifically asking her not to go off piste by Matt, not to make any rash decisions that would put her at risk, she had been caught out. Why, against all advice and her professional instinct, had she made the decision to spend the weekend at the B&B?

Because she had fallen in love.

An already complicated situation was getting more so by the minute. All she could do was trust Imi. And Christian's strong sense of self-preservation.

Christian looked across the table at Megan and smiled. 'Penny for them?'

He had been on edge since his meeting with Murat the day before but had tried his best to shield his feelings from Megan, who looked like she had enough on her mind anyway. The parting words by Murat, *It is out of my hands now*, came to him again. What did he mean by that? He had mentioned it in his report to Imi, which he had sent as soon as he had arrived at the B&B. He also wanted to tell Megan about it, he wanted to share with her what Muna had said about being on al Shabaab's hit list, but he couldn't. He felt so conflicted. He knew she probably knew more than she was letting on. It was a potent cocktail of real-world events that were combining to put unmanageable strain on him.

The burden was almost too much to bear.

Christian felt his body tensing so he got up and walked towards the coffee pot that was on a side table behind Megan. He even shook his arms out a little, without making it obvious, to lose some of the anxiety he was feeling. As he walked past Megan, he reached out and touched her shoulder, her hand instinctively reaching up to momentarily touch his. The silence in the dining room was punctuated by the ticking of the clock on the far wall; he poured two cups from the pot and slightly awkwardly placed them on the table next to Megan, adding the milk jug. He still had a couple of small bandages on his hand but the wounds were healing well.

He pulled up a chair next to Megan and faced her, taking her hands in his. 'I can't wait to be with you away from this country. I love you, Megan, so much.' He stared into her eyes, the fear he felt, the frustration at not being able to share everything with her, showing itself as the tears started to run down his cheeks.

'Oh, darling Chris, I love you so much too. It will be alright, I promise.' She held him now, his head on her shoulder as he quietly sobbed. His emotions were hitting hard; everything that had been going round in his mind for months came out at that moment. The fear he felt but couldn't share with Megan. The realisation that he was in the middle of a storm and didn't know which way to turn to seek shelter. In that moment, in that dining room, he knew beyond doubt he wanted to spend the rest of his life with Megan.

'Chris, we will get through this. Let's take some time off and piece everything together so we can move forward. I'll ask my grandmother whether we can stay at the farm in Italy.' Her voice was light, she was controlling her emotions, too, but it was difficult. She stayed strong for Chris but her own feelings were also at breaking point. She lifted his head and held his face in her hands, a steeliness in her eyes that belied her feelings. They kissed so tenderly they both wanted the moment to last forever.

'We'll do this together, right, army boy?' Megan's words broke the moment and they both smiled. Christian wiped his eyes with his sleeve and sniffed, then looked up and saw Megan's expression of surprise.

'Very romantic, I know, sorry.'

They laughed. He kissed her on the lips and the cheek, holding her face in his hands, touching her soft skin before running his fingers through her hair, seeking comfort in her smell and touch.

'It's OK, I'm sorry, I don't know what happened there. I guess … it's the pressure of living here, it has to come out.' The moment was over.

He turned to take a sip of his tepid coffee.

'Hey, fancy some fresh air?' Megan said, getting up from her chair. She needed to lighten the atmosphere or she too would crumble.

They tidied away their breakfast things and carried them into the kitchen before walking out through the main entrance and into the garden. Once outside, they found a shaded spot with two chairs and a table; they had picked up a couple of month-old magazines to read as a distraction. The voices of children chattering drifted across the garden from the surrounding houses, along with the occasional car horn. It was a soundtrack they were used to at the B&B and nothing seemed out of the ordinary. If anything could be considered ordinary in Mogadishu.

After several minutes, lost in their own thoughts, Megan reached across to hold Christian's hand as they sat in silence, listening to the afternoon drift away. It was precious downtime they both needed. Breaking the spell, they both looked up when they heard the familiar sound of the B&B's vehicle returning through the gates.

Shortly afterwards Krishna also arrived, earlier than expected.

'OK, that's me.' Megan had already packed her overnight bag and was ready to leave. There were more people milling around the house now but they still managed to find a moment to speak in private before she left.

'It was so good to see you, Chris.' They were holding each other tightly, the need for reassurance a shared emotion

'It was so good to see you too, Megs.'

'I definitely needed a little Christian time ...' Megan pulled her head back and smiled, her hands stroking his cheeks, the tears in her eyes belying her fears for his safety.

'See you for that tea in the café tomorrow morning! And don't be late.' She kissed him on the cheek and turned away, walking across the garden to Krishna who had the vehicle running, waiting to take her to Airport Camp.

*

The Somali teenager was on his haunches, leaning against a tree on the opposite side of the junction for the B&B. He was far enough away not to attract any interest from the locals, who probably kept an eye out for strangers. A stray dog was sniffing around the bags of rubbish that had been abandoned near the road, close to the teenager.

'Shoo.' He threw a stone at the dog.

Unless someone was really looking for him, he was invisible. He knew how to blend in and be unnoticed. This is why Rasuul used him around the city. He had arrived in the morning and had been told that he was not to leave until he saw a white Toyota come past. As soon as it was out of sight, he took out his phone and tapped out a short message: *The white Toyota just left.*

He knew he had to wait until another message came in before he could leave and get paid. It took several minutes but eventually it arrived: *Which direction?*

The teenager stared at the phone. He started tapping out a reply: *It went towards the airport.*

There was nothing more he could do but wait for his next instruction. It was very unusual to get into dialogue like this. He watched the dog absentmindedly. He hated dogs and threw another stone at it. A few minutes later, his phone buzzed again: *It hasn't passed K4. Are you sure?*

A network of watchers had deployed to track the Land Cruiser but something had gone wrong. Although he didn't know this side of the city as well as his own patch, he knew enough already to suggest one possible reason for it.

Perhaps it has gone into the UN camp.

He waited. Ten minutes went past before he received his final text: *OK, come back. Be in the same place tomorrow morning from 6.*

33

Saturday afternoon – Airport Camp, Mogadishu

Imi had spent a restless night in her room, working through the implications of Christian's meeting with the Turkish DA, the words, *It is out of my hands now* going round her head, preventing sleep. In the end, she got up and walked into the ops room to map out everything that she had gathered so far. She must have missed something, but what? And now she knew that the vehicle with the tracker had been seen close to the B&B she probably had enough to go to Matt. But when she looked hard, there was still something missing.

The vehicle tracker had given some useful intelligence on its movements, but without any other corroborating evidence, the driver could have been going out for an ice cream for all Imi knew. It was so frustrating. And on top of that, her attempts to set up a meeting with the National Security Advisor in Vila Somalia had fallen on deaf ears; it would be a couple of weeks because he was leaving the country for an overseas conference on Tuesday. Quite how Megan had managed to secure his time was something of a miracle.

When Imi had discovered through Tommo's report that both Christian and Megan had met at the B&B, when neither of them were supposed to be there, she once again felt hugely conflicted. On the one hand, at least she knew where Christian was, but on the other so did the MIT officer from the embassy. Getting the text from Megan, confirming what she had already guessed, was no comfort to Imi, who knew that now was not the time for setting off any alarm bells. Imi needed Megan on side, especially as she had access to Abdulkadir Aden the following morning. And because she didn't want Matt to think that she wasn't in control.

Imi looked blankly across the ops room and realised she had absolutely no influence over events at all. Everything she was doing was reactive or, at the very least, contingency planning.

Returning to her room, she got up and paced around the small area,

276

leaning against the wall opposite her bed, tilting her head up, looking for inspiration from somewhere. She had been biding her time before calling Megan, but it was time to speak to her. She took her phone from her jeans pocket and dialled her number.

'Hi Imi.' Megan answered almost immediately.

'Hi Megs, how was your mini break?'

Megan sighed before answering. 'What can I say? I shouldn't have gone over there but I had to. I just have a premonition that I'm going to lose him, and I needed to see him again. It's no excuse but that's the truth.' She felt uncomfortable explaining her feelings to Imi like that but she had decided that she wanted to be honest. They could remove her from post, pull her back to London again for another dressing-down, but at least this time it was for what she felt was a legitimate reason.

'It's OK, Megs, I'm not going to mention anything to Matt. As far as he is concerned, Christian decided to take a city break after his meeting yesterday and chose not to share his travel plans. If anyone is in the shit, it's me for allowing him the freedom to think he could make that kind of decision. He knows his own mind, I'll give him that.' Imi's tone was conciliatory; she didn't want to pick a fight with Megan. She needed her as much as Megan needed Imi. They were going to have to work together to keep Christian safe. 'At least I know where he is.'

'So, what can I do to help?' Megan's voice had lost some of the emotion and she was falling back into ambassadorial mode again. There was another pause before she added: 'Do you need me to repurpose my meeting with Aden in the morning?'

'I do, yes. Look, I'll send some instructions via email. We can then clarify anything you need to know then, OK? Oh yes, how are you getting in? Your security detail is away this week, isn't it?'

'Yes, terrible timing. I'm taking the AU convoy first thing, assuming it's on time. OK, bye, Imi.'

'Hold on, Megs, one more thing – when is Christian planning to return to VS?'

'He's going to be there for about 8.30am. He has a meeting first thing. Why?' Megan's voice gave away her concern at the question.

'No reason. I'm just trying to piece together his travel plans. OK, thanks, bye Megs.' She hung up.

Imi was running on fumes and she knew it. After ending the call and before going in search of some food, she grabbed her notebook to set out her instructions for Megan in an email. She also needed to send another update to Matt, reflecting her change of plan about approaching Abdulkadir Aden via Megan's meeting in the morning, to seek confirmation about the intelligence on Christian. Imi had decided to share Aden's family situation back in the UK with Megan, leverage she had been holding back until that point. If Megan felt that the NSA wasn't cooperating, she had Imi's authority to use it. The whole approach was likely to make life difficult for Christian for a while, especially with Muna, but that was a price worth paying to expose the Turkish conspiracy.

Tommo heard the printer kick in and walked across to it from his desk in the ops room. He knew it would be an intercept from the tapped phone in the Turkish Embassy. And he knew Imi had been waiting for something all day, and that whatever operation Imi was leading, it was reaching a crucial stage.

When he had received orders from his commander to deploy on a daytime overwatch mission in support of Imi's operation the day before, he knew things were getting serious. They rarely went out during the day, to minimise their exposure around the city.

And he was on standby again, with the same team, to deploy at immediate notice into the city in support of HUSSAR. The vehicles were prepped and ready, the team resting in the crew room waiting for the order to go. A preliminary contextual briefing was scheduled for later. Tommo had a feeling it was going to be a full-on 24-hours.

He tore the sheet off the printer and walked round to Imi's accommodation. When there was no answer, he headed round to the kitchen, and then the dining room next; there were very few places she could be and he knew she was still in camp.

Imi was sitting alone in the corner, absentmindedly eating a banana.

'Hi, Tommo, what have you got for me?' Imi's voice sounded weary.

He walked across the empty room.

'I have another report for you. Let me know if there's anything else you need.' Tommo turned away and headed for the door without waiting for a reply. He knew she was dog-tired and needed time to think. Everything else could wait.

'Shit!' Imi stood up. She re-read the few lines on the transcript, trying to figure out what she was looking at, processing the exchange, focusing on the final line:

No [voice raised] I will leave the message in the usual place. It is imperative that you pick it up tonight.

Imi immediately set off back to the ops room, Tommo in her wake. Once there, she started typing an urgent message to Matt in Nairobi.

CLASSIFICATION: TOP SECRET

From: Station, Mogadishu;

To: Station, Nairobi;

CC: Station, Nairobi Deputy Chief; Ambassador, Mogadishu;

Priority: IMMEDIATE

Subject: Op TRINKET – urgent update

1. *Latest transcript from TU Embassy mobile phone attached.*
2. *Confirmed between Hassan and Osman.*
3. *Assessment: further evidence linking senior MIT intelligence official to possible Turkish military covert operation with al Shabaab, implying use of dead letter drops for sharing urgent operational details. Corroborating evidence now essential re HUSSAR / al Shabaab target list. Meeting planned between NSA and UK Ambassador in morning to verify this intelligence. Also recommend SF detachment provides overwatch in city for next 24 hours to cover all essential travel. I will send through details later.*

Signed: IS, IO3, Nairobi Station

Imi immediately briefed Tommo on her plan.

*

Commander Murat felt the buzz in his pocket and pulled out his phone. He was sitting on the veranda of a lodge close to Lake Naivasha, miles from Nairobi, surrounded by his family and friends, watching the sun go down. It was a message from Vadit in the Turkish MoD:

Sorry to disturb at the weekend. I have an answer for you, but you are not going to like it. This line is insecure but thought you would want to know straight away. I have a contact in the organisation we discussed. He has just told me that a large team is being readied to deploy to your patch. They have been preparing for months with pathfinders already in country. Did you know anything about that?

Murat read the message twice then muted his phone. He didn't want to spoil precious family time. Not with a message like that.

34

Sunday morning – Mogadishu

The sun's rays marched westwards, enveloping the city, street by street, with a pale orange light. It was still early but he was in position. He returned to where he had been the day before. Even the dog was still around. His phone was charged and he knew to wait. He picked up a stone and threw it at the dog, which flinched then carried on examining the latest rubbish bags dumped next to the others. The smell was getting worse as more bags were piled up. He couldn't wait to finish the task and get back to his side of the city. He was so focused on looking for the white Toyota that he didn't see the battered Hilux 4x4 parked 50 metres away, facing in his direction, seemingly empty.

At the K4 roundabout, just down from the Turkish Embassy, the second teenager crouched down close to a café serving people waiting to catch buses into the city centre. He really needed some tea after such an early start but knew he couldn't risk taking his eyes off the traffic and missing the white Toyota. The smells and sounds from the café were torturing his senses. He was good at noticing things that stood out too. As he had arrived and hidden his bike behind a pile of discarded tyres set back from the road, he saw the SUV parked to one side of the roundabout, its glass blacked out like the colour of the car. The vehicle said power and guns; he turned away, unwilling to risk getting caught looking in its direction.

Rasuul handed Ali the rucksack and helped him put it on. He carefully secured it around his waist and made sure that the chest straps were also clipped in. Ali was sitting astride his cherished motorbike, legs firmly planted on the ground, self-confidence and pride oozing from his every action and movement. Rasuul stepped back and glanced at his watch.

'Today is the day, my friend. Insha'Allah it will bring you glory and everlasting gratitude and respect from your brothers in Shabaab.' He took another drag of his cigarette and passed it to Ali, indicating that he should finish it. 'Remember, Ali, I will be close to you, you do not need to fear, nothing will go wrong. I will be watching.'

Ali took a couple of drags of the cigarette and threw the butt away from the bike into the dust. He turned the key and pressed the ignition. The engine kicked into life and he revved it several times, something he had done every time he had mounted the beautiful machine, the gift from his brothers.

'I will make you proud of me. I will be a martyr in my village, unlike Mohammed, who will never be as important as me.' Ali was shouting over the sound of the engine. He had been dreaming of the chance for martyrdom, to be remembered as someone who fought the infidels, who did not run away from them like his old friend. 'When do I leave?'

'Now, my brave friend! Drive to the corner where I showed you, close to the Parliament building, and wait there with your engine running. Do not get off the bike, do not take your pack off, do not talk to anyone. And do not park too close. It is very important that you do as I have said. Now, go. I will follow.'

Ali didn't speak; he was concentrating on pulling away without jolting forward. He engaged the first gear and slowly let out the clutch to start his journey. In a moment he was gone, out of sight, the sounds of his engine slowly being replaced by the sounds of market traders setting up their stalls. Rasuul walked away and grabbed the other teenager who was hanging around, half in and half out of the garage. He needed a replacement in case Ali made a mistake.

'Come on, I need you to be with me this morning.' Rasuul roughly pushed the startled teenager in front of him down a narrow path between two concrete buildings, pockmarked with old bullet holes, until they came to the pick-up truck, its engine idling, waiting for Rasuul to get in. The teenager tried to speak but was slapped across the face by Rasuul.

'Be quiet, no talking. OK, let's go.'

In Medina District, the look-out checked his phone for the time. Quarter to eight. Driving towards him, navigating the chicane, was a white Toyota. He turned away immediately and held his phone in front of his face, tapping out the message: *It has gone past.*

He stood up and put the phone in his pocket, beginning to walk down the road in the same direction as the Toyota. He didn't see the old Hilux pull up alongside him until it was too late. The occupants were out of the vehicle before he had a chance to say a word. The first man held him up by his neck, throttling him, the man's other hand forcing his eyes closed with his fingers, while the second man searched his pockets, pulling out the phone and making sure there wasn't another one. Before the teenager could make sense of what had happened, he was thrown down onto the floor, landing in the rubbish bags and scaring the dog which yelped as it darted off. A few seconds later, the vehicle accelerated away. The teenager hadn't seen its colour, or anything about the men who had stolen his phone. And not a single word had been spoken.

Probably just some thieves trying to make a fast buck. But with an old Nokia phone?

Rasuul saw the text and waited for the second message to confirm that the target vehicle was on its way through the city. They had pulled up 50m away from where Ali was sitting on the motorbike, on the same side of the road, but short of where the minibus was parked. Rasuul was fidgeting and lit up another cigarette, the morning heat beginning to fill the car. He opened a window slightly to let some smoke out, the teenager sitting behind him coughing slightly from the fumes. He slipped his hand into an inside pocket of his designer jacket and pulled out the remote detonator, still in neutral mode, ready to be armed. After ten minutes, his phone lit up again: *It's gone past me.*

Rasuul looked at the phone and took a final drag of his cigarette, then threw it out of the window. The vehicle was idling, parked just off the main road but with a good view of the scene. He changed position in his seat and waited, his foot tapping unconsciously in the footwell. He knew they had about ten more minutes before they would be here.

*

Christian was sorting out his bag when his phone pinged. He checked a couple of pockets before pulling it out to see who it was, hoping it was going to be Megan wishing him a good morning.

Christian, I have just been told, it's today. If you're out, CHANGE YOUR ROUTE, we can talk when you get in. Muna

He could hear Muna's American accent pronouncing it *rowt* even as he read the text, but there was nothing remotely funny about the message. Its content immediately put him on alert and he instinctively started looking out of both side windows as he spoke.

'Miko, change of plan, we need to go into VS a different way today. I can't say where the int has come from but I've been told there is likely to be an incident waiting for us if we don't.'

'OK, Boss, no problem, we'll go via Industrial Road.' Miko spoke calmly and gently, prodding the driver who understood enough to find a turn-off before the K4 roundabout, taking the back streets around the city. Miko had heard similar rumours via his own source in the police over the last few days.

'Any clue where this is? K4? VS?' Miko turned his head and half-looked at Christian as he asked the question.

'No, I have nothing else.'

Christian looked down quickly, half-distracted, closed the message from Muna and then texted Imi: *I have just received a text from Muna, it's going to be today. I'm about to let Megs know so she can inform the AU convoy commander. C*

As the vehicle turned off the main drag, he tried to call Megs but it didn't connect. He pulled the phone from his ear and looked at his signal strength. He had four bars, it should have been fine. Perhaps she was driving through a dead spot; Casspirs were notoriously bad for mobile comms when sitting in the back.

He tried again. As he did so, his phone pinged. He took the phone from his ear and put the loudspeaker on, waiting for a connection, then opened the message: *Megan is in the B6 with Krishna, the AU convoy was going in too late. I've just found out. I am trying to call her but I can't get through.*

When Christian read the message his blood froze; he was momentarily lost, unsure what to do. His call still wasn't getting through to Megs. 'Oh no, please no!'

Miko immediately turned again, this time fully looking at Christian. 'What's up?'

'Miko, forget what I just said, the British Ambassador is driving into the city in an identical car, we have to turn around and get back on the most obvious route to warn her! Now please!' Christian shouted the orders to Miko, his mind racing at the turn of events.

'Come on, come on ...' Christian had dialled Megan's number again. This time it connected.

'Hello, Chris?' Megan spoke with some hesitation. 'What's going on? I have had like ten missed calls from you and Imi ...'

'Megs, darling, there's no time to explain, you have to turn around, do not go into VS! Where are you?' Christian was trying to be restrained but the stress of the situation was evident in his voice.

'Chris, what's happened, why are you talking to me like that?'

'Megan, there's a bomb out there, in a vehicle we think, they know what I'm driving, you have to turn around, I'll explain later, please just do it.' Christian spoke quickly, the gravity of the situation creating a profound sickness in the pit of his stomach.

For a moment, there was silence, just the sound from the inside of a moving vehicle. 'OK, Chris, hold on ...' Megan must have put her hand over the phone because suddenly all Christian could hear was a muffled conversation.

'Miko, we have to catch them up, please drive as fast as you can ...' Christian had the phone glued to his ear while half-shouting to Miko in the front.

'It's OK, Boss, we will drive like wind,' Miko replied calmly, catching the driver's eye and waving him forward energetically until he sped up. Miko then spoke on the radio to tell the second protection vehicle that they needed to keep up. 'This is not a good situation, Christian, not good,' Miko added.

After what felt to Christian like minutes but was only seconds, the muffled discussion ended and the line became clear again. 'OK, Krishna is going to turn around just ...'

The explosion could be heard right across the city.

*

Arne was drying the breakfast dishes when he heard the blast. He stepped out into the garden and looked up, traces of black smoke beginning to drift skywards in the distance.

Imi had run out into the compound's parking area after the message from Christian, in the hope that she could somehow make things OK from there. Unable to reach Megs, she just stood and stared. Then she heard it, booming across Airport Camp. Unable to hold herself any longer, she crumpled into the dirt, her head in her hands.

In Vila Somalia, the explosion was loud enough to make everybody go quiet. Muna immediately got up and ran through the café, heading to the building's entrance, knocking over a table and sending tea crashing to the floor, the shouts from the people at the table following her out.

'Oh Christian!'

The two British special forces teams, with different tactical missions, deployed in separate Hilux vehicles, heard the blast from their separate locations. The second team had already left their vehicle and were closing on the target when the Land Cruiser came into view, too late to prevent what happened next but with enough warning to take cover from the blast. Inside the second vehicle, riding behind Christian's Toyota, they all exchanged looks and immediately sped up to get to the scene of the bomb.

Christian's vehicle was by now travelling as fast as the traffic would allow, weaving in and out of cars and lorries but, inside the vehicle, time had stopped for Christian. They had cleared the K4 roundabout and were well on the way to the Parliament building when they saw the smoke rising from the road. As every other vehicle slowed down and pulled over, Miko directed the driver to press on, to get to the scene as soon as possible. Christian, who had been holding the phone next to his ear, lowered his hand, the line dead and put it in his pocket. He knew what had happened. 'Not again,' he said under his breath, so Miko didn't hear him.

They soon arrived, greeted by a scene of carnage. On the side of the road there was a small crater where a vehicle had once been, and next to it was a delivery lorry that was on fire but still recognisable, and on the other side of that vehicle, shielded slightly from the blast, was Megan's B6, upside down and badly damaged. He hoped the armoured plating had done its job to protect her.

Miko took charge and barked out orders, 'Christian, our security isn't here so stick close to me.'

Christian opened his door and took the pistol from his bag, cocking the weapon as he got out and placing it in his waistband.

He tried to take in the scene.

Shop alarms were going off and there was moaning from injured civilians who had been in blast range of the bomb. The smell of cordite and burning material, acrid and choking, filled his nostrils.

It was a sensation he had experienced before in Mogadishu.

'Not again, Jesus Christ, not again ...!' Christian shouted to himself as he and Miko ran towards Megan's Land Cruiser, the broken glass crunching under their feet. He couldn't even begin to take in the wider scene of devastation; he was focused on one thing only, saving Megan. When he reached the car, he bent down to look inside. The driver, Krishna looked like he was asleep, his head leaning against the window, blood pouring down the side of his face and from his ear, crumpled in a heap. In the back, he could see Megan, hanging by her seat belt, doubled over, her head and arms extended downwards. She was moving slightly. Christian noticed the door was miraculously unlocked and yelled to nobody in particular as he tried to use all his strength to pull it open, but it was jammed shut. He pulled on it again then realised that there was a large lump of metal stopping it from opening fully.

'Shit!' he shouted out loud. 'Megan, can you hear me? It's Christian! Megan, can you hear me?' Christian was on his hands and knees shouting at her, banging on the window, trying to rouse her, desperately trying to move the chunk of metal while Miko, who had moved away, was giving orders to the Somali guards who had just arrived. The situation was extremely grave.

In what seemed like seconds, there was suddenly another person standing next to Christian, then another, both of them speaking English.

'Get hold of that piece there, yeah, take that side and shove it, that'll free it. Come on.' Christian followed orders but didn't comprehend who was giving them. It didn't matter, though; the three of them were instantly working as a team.

After a couple of minutes of hard effort, the metal block had been dislodged sufficiently for the door to open enough to get inside. Breathing heavily, Christian wiped his hands on his trousers and stepped carefully into the rear of the vehicle, trying to take Megan's weight, needing to check that she was alive.

'Megs, it's me, Christian, can you hear me?' Her hair was across her face, the blood from the gash on her head already beginning to mat together, blood trickling down her cheek, which was a good sign.

'She's alive but she's bleeding, we need to get her out,' he called out over his shoulder to the two men outside the vehicle. Christian stroked Megan's face carefully and spoke so quietly that only she would have heard. 'Please, stay with me, darling.'

'Uh ...' Megan groaned quietly. He kissed her head, undid the seatbelt and gingerly lowered her down onto the roof, then backed out of the vehicle and repeated what he had said inside to the two men standing highly alert next to the vehicle.

'It's alright, mate, we'll take over from here. We'll get her into our wagon – we have our med kit here so we'll take her to the hospital pronto.'

One of the men was taking control of the situation, speaking calmly to Christian, who was still trying to come to terms with what had happened. 'Mate, my name's Tommo. We are from the det at Airport Camp, it's all good.' Christian at last had a chance to take in the two men, both of whom carried weapons slung over their shoulders.

The area was becoming noisier as people arrived on the scene, shouting, calling for medical support, and throwing their arms in the air in anguish at the loss of life. In the distance, he could hear sirens: ambulances starting their journey from the nearby hospital.

Christian stared blankly around him. He was in the middle of the road, debris and people beginning to mill around him, when he first heard the engine from a motorbike. Miko was on the other side of the road, talking to his security team. Christian was in a state of deep shock but his instincts were highly tuned and he knew that the sound wasn't what he was expecting. He turned round to get a better look at its source.

It all happened so fast.

Squinting his eyes through the smoke that was drifting across the road, he saw the rider heading towards him out of a side street about 50 m away and immediately drew his pistol, holding it to his side. At the same time, he heard two shots off to the right somewhere, further down the street, which made everyone flinch and turn the other way. But Christian stayed firmly fixed on the motorbike, which was continuing its unsteady journey towards the crash site.

When the motorbike was less than 20m away, it suddenly stopped. The rider, a young Somali boy, carrying what looked like a rucksack, got off and carefully kicked the stand back to balance the bike, its engine still running. He stood next to the motorbike, staring at Christian, mumbling something that Christian didn't understand, before starting to walk towards him. In a second, Christian dropped down onto one knee, pulled up his weapon and took aim, firing two shots at his body. At the exact moment he fired, several more shots were fired from somewhere else on the street. Ali was thrown sideways onto the ground from the force of the rounds cutting into his torso, his arms flailing above his head.

For the second time that morning, time seemed to stop for Christian. And for the second time since arriving in Somalia, he had been called on to use deadly force. He shook his head, trying to make sense of it all. He got to his feet slowly, looking around for the source of the other shots. Confused. Numb.

'Mate, he's dead. The detonator was neutralised and the area looks to be clear. There's more of us on the ground, so we should be OK now. Let's get the ambo out of that vehicle and patch her up, eh?' The taller of the two special forces soldiers had stepped behind Christian without him realising it and put a hand on his shoulder. 'She'll be OK, leave it to us.'

'I need to go to the hospital with her,' Christian said but without much conviction; he was falling into a state of shock.

'There's no room in the wagon, mate, but don't worry, why don't you call in to the field hospital later on, see how she is?' The reply by the special forces soldier was matter of fact, but the decision wasn't open for discussion. Christian's military training, his respect for authority and for following orders, ended the matter.

The next hour was a blur.

Miko, who had not seen the motorbike until it was too dangerous for him to intervene without hitting Christian or the other soldiers, was determined to get him back into their armoured vehicle. But Christian refused to leave until he knew Megan had been carried to the waiting Hilux vehicle and driven to the field hospital inside Airport Camp by the special forces det. When she had eventually been stabilised, lying on a combat stretcher on the road, surrounded by the remnants of an ordinary city street, she was carried to the vehicle and driven off by Tommo. The second Hilux then carefully extracted Krishna from the damaged B6 and did their best to stabilise him before also driving straight to the AU field hospital.

The scene had by now become chaotic. TV news crews had arrived, Somali police were directing traffic, fire trucks were dousing the flames and countless ambulances had filled the road, ferrying the injured and the dead away for treatment or identification. In the midst of everything happening around them, Miko led Christian to their vehicle, carefully navigating their way from the scene, acknowledging the police who were clearing a route through the chaos for them. They drove slowly back towards the B&B, leaving behind the post-explosion chaos.

'Miko, where are we going? I have to go to the hospital.' Christian was barely audible, his head on his chest, defeated.

'My friend, we go to safe place then we decide what to do next. We need cup of tea,' he replied, his voice flat.

Christian hadn't touched his phone in over an hour and when he pulled it out to look, he found numerous missed calls and messages. He looked out of the window as he watched the city pass him by. The further they travelled from the bombing, the more normal life became. That was the thing with living in a city so used to extreme violence. He looked at the phone again; he couldn't deal with Imi and Muna right now.

But there was one message he knew he had to send: *Nurse Mary, please keep the Ambassador alive, for me. Christian*

He put the phone away, laid his head back and closed his eyes, desperate for something to drink.

*

After calling Nurse Mary several times while at the B&B to ask if he could visit, she had finally answered her phone and immediately told him to *get his arse over to the hospital*. He took it as a bad sign.

Making the arrangements for Fred to meet him at the rear gate at short notice and drive him across camp, minutes had felt like hours.

On autopilot, barely taking anything in, the journey through the camp with Fred passed in silence. He met Nurse Mary at the entrance of the single-storey building.

'Hello Mary, thank you. How ... how is she?' He just about got his words out as she hugged him.

'Hello, Christian, come on, follow me. She is in ICU, this way.'

They turned left into the dark corridor.

'She is being stabilised before flying out to Nairobi later on. She needs emergency care and we don't have all the equipment we need to check her over. And we can't risk putting her on a long flight to the UK.'

Christian stood in the ICU's small viewing area, leaning his grazed arms against the glass to keep him upright. Looking at Megan's bed, second on the left, surrounded by medical staff who were quietly coming and going between her and Krishna, who was opposite, he could hardly hear anything except for the regular beeps from the medical equipment that was hooked up to her.

The bright lights above him made him blink, his eyes, sensitive and sore, affected by the smoke in the air from the blast and fire earlier that morning. His head dropped as he tried to contain his emotions, tried to stay strong for Megs.

Nurse Mary came back into the room and slipped her arm into Christian's before slowly ushering him out, sensing that he too could become a casualty if he stayed too long.

As he looked across for the final time, Christian saw her arm on the top of the bedsheet, dried blood still on her hand, her fingers splayed out, unmoving.

PART THREE

35

Tuscany, Northern Italy – One Month Later

The morning light was beginning to creep over the distant hills behind him, the sky's hue changing from a greying twilight through pinky-orange to a pale yellow that seemed to grow in strength the further he drove from the city. The sun caught in his side mirrors as he navigated the winding road, heading towards Megan's grandmother's *cascina*, her farmhouse, that Christian had heard so much about.

Cutting through the majestic Tuscany hills west of Florence, he felt as if he had the world to himself; too early for much local traffic, the morning light was coaxing the countryside awake, the gentle breeze sowing the seeds of daily life as it blew from village to village. His journey from the hotel had been without incident, bar a refuse truck on his side of the road in a small village, its orange warning lights reflecting on the pastel-coloured houses in the half-light of the morning forcing him to swerve across the road as he rounded a tight bend. He had arrived late the evening before and stayed in the city, ready for the early morning drive.

He checked his satnav and could see that he was close to the farm. He looked on the passenger seat at the flowers that he had bought in the airport the evening before. They looked inadequate considering the circumstances, especially compared to the beautiful surroundings, but he wanted to show that he had made an effort. It was the least he could do. The satnav piped up and told him to turn right, not that he understood Italian, but the map was clear; he had arrived.

He remembered from his conversations with Megan that the farmhouse had a long drive down to the house but, in reality, it was more like a rough track that cut through several fields of olive trees. The land was anything but uniform, though, with row upon row of trees leading the eye out to distant hills, the sense of freedom almost tangible. He now knew what Megan had meant when she had said the farm was the only place in the world where she felt completely free.

The driveway turned sharply downhill and there, on a promontory overlooking a small lake, was the *cascina*, the sunlight just beginning to reflect off its tiled roof and illuminating the surrounding lush garden. It was exactly as he had imagined.

He parked in the shade alongside a small lean-to opposite the front door, the only other vehicle visible an old tractor that wouldn't have looked out of place in a museum. He gathered the flowers and got out of the car, stretching a little as he did so. It had been a long drive. The front door to the farmhouse opened at that moment.

'*Buongiorno,* Christian!' Megan's grandmother was standing in the doorway, dressed in simple farm clothes, a kitchen cloth hanging out of her apron.

He smiled and walked over to her, his hands outstretched, nodding whilst at the same time giving her the flowers.

'*Buongiorno, Nonna.*' He had remembered how he should greet her from his conversation with Megan when they were by the lake in Kenya.

'*Grazie mille, Christian, non c'era bisogno di comprare fiori quando qui ne abbiamo i campi. Mi segua, per favore.*'

She turned and led him into the farmhouse where the morning light had not reached the inner corridor, which remained stubbornly dark. In a moment, though, they were soon walking into what looked to Christian like a living room, filled with morning sunlight, and then, to his left, she led him through a pair of French doors onto a patio area with four wooden chairs arranged around a small table, the canopy not yet opened.

'*Per favore, siediti.*' Christian sat down, her hand gestures the perfect accompaniment to her impenetrable Italian. '*Vorresti un tè?*'

'*Si, si, grazie.*' By now he was going to say yes to anything.

The patio had been designed with one purpose in mind: to overlook the lake. The sun, now high enough over the hilltops to illuminate the outside area, was also beginning to dance playfully on the ripples on the water's surface. It was mesmerising. He found himself completely enthralled with the view and the quietness of the scene. He didn't want to be anywhere else in the world at that moment.

'Did someone order tea?' Megan stepped onto the patio, cups in hand, a bag over her shoulder, smiling so broadly she almost dropped the drinks as she walked slowly towards Chris, who had jumped out of his seat and walked across to her, taking the cups and placing them on the table before gently taking her in his arms.

'Darling, Megs, it's so good to see you. I've missed you so much.'

They kissed for the first time since they'd parted at the B&B, which felt like a lifetime ago. They were both overcome with emotion, the joy at being together again bringing tears to them both.

'Oh Chris, I've missed you too!' They held their embrace for a long time, both willing the moment to last forever. 'You made it OK then?'

'Yeah, the drive was perfect, the trickiest thing has been navigating your grandmother's Italian!' Chris took her very gently by the shoulders, then helped her towards the chairs. 'Come on, let's sit.'

'Thanks, Chris. Yes, I heard what she said from upstairs actually; she admonished you for bringing flowers when the farm has plenty of them already!' They both laughed again as Chris pulled up a chair next to her, the sunlight casting a warm glow over them both.

After a few moments, during which they both sipped their tea and caught their breath, Christian spoke first. 'I never thought I would see you again. When you were loaded into the special forces vehicle I just accepted that your injuries would be too bad. I had seen Krishna too and he was in a terrible state. And when I was at the hospital, there were so many people round you I could barely make you out.'

He paused, the emotion of the memory almost too much to bear.

'Sorry, I have been wanting to say so much to you, I know we have to take it steady,' Christian apologised, looking away towards the lake.

After emergency care in Mogadishu to stabilise her, Megan had been evacuated the same evening to Nairobi and then, a few days later, back to the UK. Her recovery had required a lot of time in hospital at first, then when it was safe to do so, she had flown out to the farm where she knew she would recover more quickly, looked after by *Nonna*. Due to the seriousness of her injuries, the only communications between Christian and Megan had been via email and text, but then only irregularly.

Christian had struggled to understand what had happened that day as he had barely even seen Imi after the incident and had then been paid off to finish his contract early. Imi had sent him a message, apologising for not being able to meet him in person, explaining that she was needed in Nairobi and the purpose of his role had come to a natural end. He didn't know whether the Somalis had been told something or not, but when he finally left, they seemed genuinely sad to see him go, telling him they hoped there would be a replacement soon.

And while Megan was undergoing surgery, spending time in intensive care in the UK, Christian had been busy in the last couple of weeks of his contract, putting in place arrangements to improve collaboration between the Turkish DA and the other international donors – the 'vipers' nest' as Mac has once described them. At least he felt like he had achieved something, even if his mind has been elsewhere.

The one and only time he had seen Imi after the incident had been at Nairobi's international airport before his flight home. After checking in his bags, they had sat down for a final coffee together. She had said little about the op but was glad to know he was OK and that the latest news from Megan was encouraging. She seemed to be in two minds about opening up but, in the end, she didn't. He had asked some questions about the day of the bombing and what she knew, but they weren't in the right place for that kind of conversation.

As he got up to leave, Imi had hugged Christian and said that she thought he had done more for peace and security in Somalia than the majority of people who had ever deployed to the region, armed with good intentions but little influence. Between them, they had prevented a catastrophe. She said he should be very proud of that fact, not that he could ever tell anyone of course. The last thing she said was "see you soon".

After flying back to the UK to stay with his parents in Oxfordshire, Chris still had plenty of blanks to fill in about what happened in Mogadishu and, after taking a few days to reacclimatise, he had explained to his mum and dad that he needed to fly out to Italy at the first opportunity.

Now he turned to look at Megan.

'It's OK, Chris. Being here, but in touch with everyone back in Somalia and Kenya, has given me the chance to reflect on everything that happened. I have come to terms with events, even though I wish they had been different.' She touched her shoulder involuntarily; the break had healed, but the plates were still sore when she sat still for too long.

'Your scar has healed well,' Chris said as he looked at Megan's face, suddenly lost for what to say next.

'Just another hockey scar, right?' Megan smiled at him, remembering their very first conversation. The deep gash from being thrown around inside the vehicle, which ran from her right temple to her ear, had healed remarkably well, aided by a small skin graft.

Christian knew they both needed to take it easy, to rebuild a life together, one step at a time. But he also wanted to know so much. He turned to see *Nonna* walk onto the patio with a plate of eggs and smoked meats.

'*Colazione!*' Megan didn't acknowledge her until she was standing in front of her, putting the plate of food on the table along with some cutlery and two side plates for them both.

Nonna stroked Megan's hair lovingly and left them to it, smiling at Christian who nodded again, thanking her with his pidgin Italian. '*Grazie, Nonna.*'

As Chris was serving them both some breakfast, Megan reached into a bag that she had hung on the back of the chair when she sat down. She took out an envelope and handed it to Christian.

'Open it after breakfast.'

*

Chris had walked down to the lakeside while Megan went inside for a rest. Her hearing was still damaged, which gave her headaches and made her very tired. Add to that the internal injuries she had sustained in the bombing, he knew it would take a while for her to regain her full strength. Megan had told him to read the letter while she was inside. They could discuss it together later, she had said.

He walked down the small track, the sun bearing down on him, giving him a sense of warmth and comfort, until he found an old bench.

'The secrets you can tell us eh?' He patted the ancient wood, gnarled and broken from years of use.

He took out the envelope, carefully retrieving the papers from inside. As soon as he opened the first sheet of handwritten text, he instinctively looked around to check he was alone. You could take a man out of the military, but you can never take the military out of the man.

TOP SECRET

Station Nairobi

Cascina Nonna, Italy

Dear Megan,

You will no doubt be wondering whether I have completely lost the plot sending this letter to you via Queen's Messenger from Nairobi to a remote farmhouse in the Tuscany Hills, literally miles from anywhere in northern Italy. Needless to say, what I am about to write is highly classified and could end my career, but I felt you (and Christian, when he arrives) needed some closure.

I know we have been in regular contact about your recovery and I am so happy that you are getting better every day. Please let me know if there is anything we can do to help going forward. And that's not an empty offer; whatever we can do, from here in Nairobi or from colleagues in Rome or London, we will. We want you back fighting-fit just as soon as you are able to stand the heat once again! That is assuming you want to come back. Let's leave that for another day but know you are greatly missed and your brand of diplomacy is much needed across the globe's hotspots. There are many junior colleagues who are in need of your leadership, mentorship and wisdom (even if they don't know it yet).

What we haven't talked about yet is what actually happened up in Mog over the last six months or so, and the role your close friend, Christian, played in uncovering a spectacularly dangerous plot by a renegade element of a sovereign nation's intelligence apparatus. My head is still spinning at the audacity and arrogance behind the plot, but there are bad apples everywhere. Unfortunately, in some intelligence services, those apples reach the very top. We are yet to see it, but I predict there will soon be changes to the leadership of the MIT in Ankara. It's a long tale, so let me start by piecing together the background and the story as we believe it to be.

Even before Hassan Güler arrived in Somalia, he had been involved in an ill-conceived plot in Syria to draw the US into the fight, by blaming the Kurds for a series of bombings so the US would side with the Turks. Of course, it was never going to happen that way – which is what I mean by ill-conceived – and after a US Green Beret was killed in one of these Turkish-inspired bombings, well, suffice to say it had quite an impact on Washington's future strategy, as you can imagine. Basically, the person who was behind that plot was, you've guessed it, Hassan Güler.

So, when there was a spike in incidents against AMISOM, mostly at night, with a level of coordination unseen in previous al Shabaab attacks, our brilliant colleague Imi knew something wasn't right. She also pieced together through her extensive network the fact that there were ghost shipping containers being delivered into Mogadishu from Jeddah, their contents no doubt originating in Turkey, to logistically support the astonishing fact that the MIT, under Güler, had deployed Turkish special forces as advisors, no doubt from the military force that supports MIT, onto the ground to work alongside al Shabaab. How they achieved that level of cooperation, using Shabaab as their proxy, nobody is ever likely to know in our circles, but it was very bold, I'll give them that. I suppose when you are promising to boost their effectiveness to such a degree, who would say no?

And why did we think this was the case? When al Shabaab attacked the training base south of the airport, someone working in the private military company that provides mentors for AMISOM, managed to kill one of these Turkish 'advisors'. We did a genetic test from some blood found on a phone he was carrying and it came back as a strong match for someone of Turkish origin. Even Imi didn't know that at the time.

Obviously you know how Christian ended up on Imi's radar and what we needed to do to ensure he was left with little alternative to work for us. To be honest, I think Christian would have worked for us for nothing, such is his love of country. In all my years working in this job, I have never come across someone so uniquely suited to this kind of intelligence work. He was an absolute find and Imi did a brilliant job of recruiting him.

'Yep, she certainly did,' Christian said out loud, and momentarily looked up, drawn to the sky by the high-pitched calls from a falcon. But he couldn't see it and soon turned over the page to read on.

Of course, what he didn't know was why we were asking him to do what he did. There was one particular day when we wanted him to leave behind a bugging device in the president's reception room in order to listen to what was being said during an important meeting, but also to try to discredit the Turks in the eyes of the Somalis. And immediately after we asked him to do that, we then expected him to attach a very clever gadget to the Turkish diplomatic vehicle that had delivered the Ambassador, Defence Attaché and Head of MIT into Vila Somalia. Each time relying on his initiative and nerve to get him through. On both occasions, he did a great job, even though he badly burned his hand when attaching the tracking device.

Christian lowered the letter again, remembering back to that day when he experienced what he now knows was a panic attack. He had done all those things described by Matt, that's true, but he had also felt a visceral fear, greater than anything he had experienced in his military career. The danger was different. Less physical, far more psychological. And he had improvised pretty well on both occasions. The adrenaline started to surge in his body again as he recalled the events.

He sighed. Perhaps he should be a little easier on himself.

I am sorry you didn't know any of that, Megan, but, as you can see now with the benefit of hindsight, it was for the best. What those two acts of heroism achieved was to give us extraordinary access to the inner sanctum of the Turkish Embassy, albeit for a limited time, but it also gave us a very good idea where Mr Hassan Güler was spending his time in the city.

What has upset me most about this plot was the collateral damage. Many AMISOM troops were killed along the way, essentially at the hands of our NATO partners in Turkey. It's shocking, which is why it will never come out.

And, of course, we lost Krishna in the attack. He fought extremely hard for over two weeks, but his heart, which nobody knew had a weakness, eventually gave out. The shock and trauma he experienced from being so close to the bomb was what did him in. Like you, he was eventually flown back to the Queen Elizabeth Hospital in Birmingham, specifically the critical care ward where we send all military casualties, but he didn't make it. We have already made arrangements for his family to be looked after and we have made a bit of a donation to his charity, to kick-start it again. His wife could not have been more thankful for what we have done so far, but I will keep an eye on her and the family via colleagues in Kathmandu.

Quite how you survived is one of those miraculous stories. Our consultations with military explosive experts suggest the lorry, which took most of the force of the blast when the minibus exploded, hadn't quite covered the front of your vehicle. It basically came down to inches. No comfort for Krishna's family, but I am so thankful you're still with us.

And what exactly happened on the day itself? This is what I know you want to hear and I am sure Christian will find this enlightening. Imi had been growing concerned that Christian was going to be taken out by Mr Güler's increasingly flammable language towards him. Even the Turkish Defence Attaché had heard enough to quietly start an internal investigation through his own network, which we think must have contributed to Güler's permanent recall to Ankara. Ironically, it was the DA's meeting with Christian that I think prompted him to reach out to his MoD desk officer who, in turn, got in touch with his contacts in MIT to ask a few pointed questions. This is all supposition, of course. And before you ask, yes, we have people in many places but sometimes good old phone intercepts do the job, and Commander Murat's colleague in Ankara was less than discreet when providing Murat with his initial response. Anyway, that's by the by. More on that in a moment.

So, on that Saturday evening Imi wrote to me with her plan, which I approved. She deliberately didn't copy you in. What spooked Imi was the fact that after Christian's meeting with Murat, Hassan Güler had decided to follow Christian and discovered the B&B. And then quite unexpectedly, you also went there, Megan. So, we think Güler had a dilemma, which is why we know he then contacted his man in the field, who we are sure was coordinating the Turkish support to Shabaab, to tell him that there were two white Toyota Land Cruisers roaming around the city, not one. It was a moment for the application of bold initiative and Imi stepped up brilliantly. By Sunday morning, she had already deployed the special forces teams onto the ground. I think they went out at around five in the morning.

She had a hunch that there would be a bunch of dickers – forgive me, it's a term from Northern Island describing informants who reported what they saw to give advance warning of British patrol activity etc – out on the streets, calling in the movement of any white Toyota Land Cruisers. But what was key for me – and thank God for our special forces det – we also needed evidence to present to Ankara on what had been happening. So, team one picked up the first dicker and took his phone, which left the second team to try to locate any others AND the likely place where Shabaab were going to try and take out Christian, if indeed that was the plan.

Of course, that's not quite what happened. When Imi was told that Muna had sent Christian a warning text saying an attack was planned for that day, Imi reached out to warn you, only to find out that you had not taken the AMISOM armoured vehicle transport as expected. Imi was utterly powerless to intervene.

While all this was going on, the second team had been out on the ground, cruising up and down the street from the K4 roundabout to Vila Somalia to identify a possible vehicle bomb when they came across the empty minibus parked on the road, nowhere near a bus stop and suspiciously full of large bags. By the time they had done a second walk-by and confirmed that it was likely to be the VBIED, it was 8am. And they still needed to find who was carrying the detonator, as that is Shabaab's tactic. Thanks to their instinct for this kind of thing, working totally exposed amongst the population (don't ask me how they did it), they then found what they believed to be the command vehicle.

Unfortunately, it was all too late. So, when the first blast occurred, they were watching the right vehicle and immediately deployed to eliminate the threat, which they did with a couple of close-quarter shots. In the post-blast confusion, nobody noticed. The benefit for us was twofold: first, we managed to get the mobile phones from their vehicle which had plenty of forensic evidence, and second, what we weren't aware of was that there was another suicide bomber on a motorbike, armed and ready to detonate in the chaos of the aftermath. As we know, he was taken out of the game by Christian and the special forces team from further up the street that had, only seconds before, neutralised the Shabaab commander with his finger on the button. Once it was made safe, we sent the rucksack to the specialist agencies who looked at it. There was enough plastic explosive in there to wipe out the entire block of buildings. Everyone was very lucky.

As far as the press were concerned, westerners got caught up in a VBIED and the follow-up attack was thwarted by a security team certified to carry firearms in country. The truth will never come out; the conspiracy, as that is precisely what it amounted to, is completely deniable.

As a post script, we managed to link the mobile phones from the Shabaab commander on the ground to the Turkish military advisor, who we think was called Osman, who in turn was linked to the Turkish operative killed by our friend in Lancing Point. And because we managed to retrieve the plastic explosive that was not used, we did some chemical analysis on it and found that it is identical to the plastic explosive that I asked a military friend in NATO to 'borrow' from the Turks during a recent coalition live fire exercise.

So, by the time I knocked on the door of my counterpart in Ankara, we had quite a compelling story to tell. They denied it, of course. As did the Saudis, who were implicated in our file. In fact, there was one other 'casualty', although thankfully not fatal. The source of the information about the shipments, a Brit earning his tax-free dollar, found himself persona non grata and had to leave the kingdom within 24 hours. I'm not sure how they found out he was behind it, but it's immaterial now. I treated that news as an admission of guilt.

And what about the Somalis? What did we tell them? Well, actually not much. We explained to our Turkish friends that it wouldn't look good for them *if the story came out and we settled on a more collaborative way forward, ironically through the work that Christian had been endeavouring to do in the preceding weeks and months. What neither of you know is that the 'advisors' who had been deployed into the field to work alongside al Shabaab units were immediately recalled to Ankara, but not before destroying the stocks of ammunition and explosives that had been shipped into country by the Saudis. As you can imagine, the locals weren't very happy about it and I think the Turks lost two men, but the majority got out. We actually provided some drone cover on one occasion, just to give them eyes on. That kind of cooperation, even when every instinct is to do the opposite, is what our job is all about.*

So Megan (and Christian), that's the story. And I hope I never have to tell something similar again. What's clear to me though is this: Christian has a talent and I know one up-and-coming intelligence officer in Nairobi who is itching to find another role for him once he has had time to decompress. I imagine the final bonus payment on his contract should enable him to find the house he needs and to feel secure enough not to have to seek employment straight away. But the money won't last forever and we would be very happy to hear from him, if that is a course he wishes to pursue.

And as you for you Megan. Get better! Take your time. The FCO will still be here when you are fit and ready to return. The bills will be covered during your R&R and I am sure that with Christian's care, you will soon be back on your feet again. If you need psychological support, I am happy to send someone out to work with you in Italy, if you think that would be better for your recovery. Let's chat about that when the time comes.

So, let's finish in the spirit of how I started. I would not only be sacked for having written this letter, but I would probably do jail time as well. So please, once you have digested the contents and discussed it together, do me the honour of using this letter as kindling for the barbeque and we shall never speak about it again. I will of course deny any knowledge of having ever written it and will claim it to be a forgery if ever it ends up on the front page of The Daily Mail!

Have a great few days together, you deserve it, and thanks for everything you have done for our country.

Best,

Matt

TOP SECRET

Christian sat for a long time, staring at the lake, watching dozens of swifts swooping in great circles above him, then flying low over its surface to scoop up water in their tiny beaks, coming again and again to quench their thirst. He was fixated by their playful flying as well as their perfect aerobatics.

Eventually, having put the letter into the envelope, he got up to walk back to the house, looking up to remind himself where the path was, when he saw Megs coming down to him, walking slowly but with purpose. He started to walk towards her but she indicated that he should stay where he was, that she was going to do this by herself. As soon as she was close, Christian stepped forward as she half-collapsed into his arms. He helped her to the bench and they sat down in silence, Megan getting her breath back, Christian holding her tightly, her head on his shoulder, trying to process the letter and everything it contained. After a moment, they both sat up to look at the water, their hands together, fingers intertwined.

'Looks like we need to organise a barbeque then,' Christian said, deadpan. They both briefly looked at each other and laughed, astonished that MI6's Head of Station in Nairobi had taken such a risk to let them know what had really happened and give them context behind what they had gone through. In many ways, it was a masterstroke of leadership and they were both incredibly grateful to Matt for having had the chance to understand the why, as much as the what. Megan spoke next, both of them lost in their own thoughts.

'So, do you think you will take up his offer?' As soon as Christian had read what Matt had written, the idea had set his mind spinning at the possibilities. And Megan knew it.

'Maybe I will, but ...' He paused, turning to look at Megan. 'I think it's more about whether you want to get back into the saddle.'

They leaned forward and briefly kissed, the breeze blowing Megan's hair across both their faces, the shrieks from the falcon above them filling the sky as if in celebration.

Megan broke off and put her mouth close to Christian's ear.

'Let's talk about that later, army boy.'

ACKNOWLEDGMENTS

The seed for the story behind *A Deniable Conspiracy* was planted many years before I sat down in front of my laptop to write it. Like so many seminal moments in our lives, it is only afterwards that one fully understands their significance.

My memories of living in Nairobi and travelling around that beautiful country remain so vivid in my mind that that they could have been yesterday. Venturing into Mogadishu while based in Airport Camp was, on the other hand, a profoundly dangerous activity. However, the risks I took over that period enabled me to understand Mogadishu at street level. The places I visited, always accompanied by a close protection team, and the people I met, often in very clandestine meetings, helped me create the Mogadishu you read about in these pages. And whilst the story is entirely fictitious, it is inspired by what I experienced and the people I met during my time living and working in London, Kenya and Somalia.

Therefore, I must thank several people for their contributions and support, during the creation of this, my debut novel. To all those individuals with whom I interacted during my time working on Somalia; both in the Foreign Office in London, the High Commission in Nairobi and from across the international community. Diplomats, contractors, journalists, spies, politicians, members of civil society and the international development community. Everyone has, in a small way, contributed to the creation of the characters in this book.

I am deeply grateful to Abukar Albadri, a seasoned journalist who has risked his life over many years to tell stories from Somalia, for his invaluable advice on language and tone. To those who agreed to read early drafts of the manuscript, especially Louise Davies, who gave some fantastic feedback, although I apologise for hijacking your entire weekend at an Airbnb in Kent! You have no idea how important it was for me to hear your comment; "Don't read it at night, you'll never get to sleep." I also want to thank Nick Pyle, a former diplomat with deep experience navigating the corridors of power at home and abroad, whose professional opinion was so important to ensure the details were spot on; always important when discussing matters of state. The red pen corrections from Chris Paterson were extremely valuable and timely, but so too was his validation over the book's readability. I want to thank Andrew Harding, long standing and hugely respected BBC News Correspondent, for agreeing to take a look at the manuscript and endorse it; even though we hadn't met, our shared experiences of Mogadishu and Nairobi made the connection a natural one and I am tremendously grateful to him for his support.

Finally, there are many people who appear in the pages of this book who will forever be unnamed. Their influence and contribution, even if they don't realise it, exist in these pages. I would like to end by thanking my friend and talented publisher, Artin Ahmeti, for his original idea for the inspiring cover image and, of course, Yanina and her team, for their stewardship of the editing and publishing process.

Writing this book has been an incredible personal experience. In many ways, it has changed my life. And, like all major projects, it has not been without its challenges. One thing it has taught me; life can change in an instant, just as it did for Christian and Megan on the streets of Mogadishu. I hope you have enjoyed reading *A Deniable Conspiracy* as much as I have enjoyed creating it for you.

ABOUT THE AUTHOR

Ade Clewlow MBE served in the British Army for over 25 years. His last two years saw him shape the UK's security policy and plans for the Horn of Africa, which included Somalia, a country at the centre of a bloody insurgency and host to a growing piracy crisis. After two years travelling around the region, as well as launching a groundbreaking military operation in Somalia, Ade left the military and took up a role as a contractor in a United Nations-funded strategic communications team, based in Nairobi and Mogadishu, supporting the African Union Mission in Somalia, AMISOM. With unique access inside the heavily defended Vila Somalia, Mogadishu's seat of power, Ade began building relationships and delivering advice to senior political figures inside the Western-backed government. His experiences from that period have inspired this book. Ade lives in the UK and works in the security industry.

A Deniable Conspiracy is his debut novel.